MOONGLOW

Moonglow

A Novel

Michael Chabon

HARPER

An Imprint of HarperCollins*Publishers*

MOONGLOW. Copyright © 2016 by Michael Chabon. All rights reserved. Printed in the United States of America. No part of this book may be used or reproduced in any manner whatsoever without written permission except in the case of brief quotations embodied in critical articles and reviews. For information, address HarperCollins Publishers, 195 Broadway, New York, NY 10007.

HarperCollins books may be purchased for educational, business, or sales promotional use. For information, please email the Special Markets Department at SPsales@harpercollins.com.

FIRST EDITION

Designed by Leah Carlson-Stanisic

Illustrations by Adalis Martinez

Endpaper photograph © Sergio34/Shutterstock, Inc.

Library of Congress Cataloging-in-Publication Data has been applied for.

ISBN: 978-0-06222555-9 (Hardcover)
ISBN: 978-0-06-257213-4 (B&N Signed Edition)
ISBN: 978-0-06-257214-1 (BAM Signed Edition)
ISBN: 978-0-06-246139-1 (International Edition)

16 17 18 19 20   RRD   10 9 8 7 6 5 4 3 2 1

To them, seriously

MOONGLOW

To them

There is no dark side of the moon, really. Matter of fact, it's all dark.

—WERNHER VON BRAUN

AUTHOR'S NOTE

In preparing this memoir, I have stuck to facts except when facts refused to conform with memory, narrative purpose, or the truth as I prefer to understand it. Wherever liberties have been taken with names, dates, places, events, and conversations, or with the identities, motivations, and interrelationships of family members and historical personages, the reader is assured that they have been taken with due abandon.

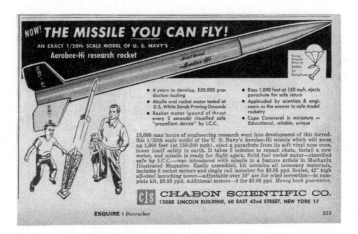

Advertisement, Esquire, October 1958

This is how I heard the story. When Alger Hiss got out of prison, he had a hard time finding a job. He was a graduate of Harvard Law School, had clerked for Oliver Wendell Holmes and helped charter the United Nations, yet he was also a convicted perjurer and notorious as a tool of international communism. He had published a memoir, but it was dull stuff and no one wanted to read it. His wife had left him. He was broke and hopeless. In the end one of his remaining friends took pity on the bastard and pulled a string. Hiss was hired by a New York firm that manufactured and sold a kind of fancy barrette made from loops of piano wire. Feathercombs, Inc., had gotten off to a good start but had come under attack from a bigger competitor that copied its designs, infringed on its trademarks, and undercut its pricing. Sales had dwindled. Payroll was tight. In order to make room for Hiss, somebody had to be let go.

In an account of my grandfather's arrest, in the *Daily News* for May 25, 1957, he is described by an unnamed coworker as "the quiet type." To his fellow salesmen at Feathercombs, he was a homburg on the coat rack in the corner. He was the hardest-working but least effective member of the Feathercombs sales force. On his lunch breaks he holed up with a sandwich and the latest issue of *Sky and Telescope* or *Aviation Week*. It was known that he drove a Crosley, had a foreign-born wife and a teenage daughter and lived with them somewhere in deepest Bergen County. Before the day of his arrest, my grandfather had distinguished himself to his coworkers only twice. During Game 5 of the 1956 World Series, when the office radio failed, my grandfather had repaired it with a vacuum tube prized from the interior of the telephone switchboard. And a Feathercombs copywriter reported once bumping into my grandfather at the Paper Mill Playhouse in Millburn, where the foreign wife was, of all things, starring as Serafina in *The Rose Tattoo*. Beyond this nobody knew much about my grandfather, and that seemed to be the way he preferred it. People had long since given up trying to engage him in conversation. He had been known to smile but not to laugh. If he held political opinions—if he held opinions of any kind—they remained a mystery around the offices of Feathercombs, Inc. It was felt he could be fired without damage to morale.

Shortly after nine o'clock on the morning of the twenty-fourth, the president of Feathercombs heard a disturbance outside his office, where a quick-witted girl had been positioned to filter out creditors and tax inspectors. A male voice spoke with urgency that scaled rapidly to anger. The intercom on the president's desk buzzed and buzzed again. He heard a chime of glass breaking. It sounded like a telephone when you slammed down the receiver. Before the president could rise from his chair to see what the matter was, my grandfather muscled into the room. He brandished a black handset (in those days a blunt instrument) that trailed three feet of frayed cord.

Back in the late 1930s, when he wasn't hustling pool, my grandfather had put himself through four years at Drexel Tech by delivering pianos for Wanamaker's department store. His shoulders spanned the doorway. His kinky hair, escaped from its daily paste-down of Brylcreem, wobbled atop his head. His face was so flushed with blood that he looked sunburned. "I never saw anyone so angry," an eyewitness told the *News*. "You could almost smell smoke coming off him."

For his part, the president of Feathercombs was astonished to discover that he had approved the firing of a maniac. "What's this about?" he said.

It was a pointless question, and my grandfather disdained to answer it; he was opposed to stating the obvious. Most of the questions people asked you, he felt, were there to fill up dead space, curtail your movements, divert your energy and attention. Anyway, my grandfather and his emotions were never really on speaking terms. He took hold of the frayed end of the telephone cord. He wound it twice around his left hand.

The president tried to stand up, but his legs got tangled in the kneehole of his desk. His chair shot out from under him and toppled over, casters rattling. He screamed. It was a fruity sound, halfway to a yodel. As my grandfather fell on top of him, the president twisted himself toward the window overlooking East Fifty-seventh Street. He just had time to notice that passersby seemed to be crowding together on the sidewalk below.

My grandfather looped the cord of the handset around the president's throat. He had maybe two minutes before the rocket of his anger burned up its fuel and fell back to earth. That would be ample time. During World War II, he had been trained in the use of a garrote.* He knew that, done properly, strangulation was short work.

"Oh my God," said the secretary, Miss Mangel, making a late appearance on the scene.

She had reacted quickly when my grandfather burst into her office smelling, she would recall afterward, like wood smoke. She had managed to buzz twice before my grandfather grabbed the handset away from her. He picked up the intercom. He yanked the handset cord from the base.

"You'll have to pay for that," Miss Mangel said.

When he told this story thirty-two years later, my grandfather put a checkmark of admiration beside Miss Mangel's name, but with his rocket only halfway up the slope of its parabola he took her words as provocation. He threw the base of the intercom out the window of

---

* A length of piano wire, of all things, typically concealed inside a shoe- or boot-lace.

Miss Mangel's office. The chiming noted by the president was the sound of the intercom sailing through a spiderweb of glass into the street.

Hearing a cry of outrage from below, Miss Mangel went to the window to look. Down on the sidewalk a man in a gray suit was sitting looking up at her. There was blood on the left lens of his round spectacles. He was laughing.[*] People stopped to help him. The doorman announced that he was going to call the police. That was when Miss Mangel heard her boss screaming. She turned from the window to run into his office.

At first glance the office appeared to be empty. Then she heard the tap of a shoe against a linoleum floor, a tap, another tap. The back of my grandfather's head rose from behind the desk, then sank again. Brave Miss Mangel went around the desk. Her boss lay sprawled on his belly on the polished floor. My grandfather straddled his back, hunched forward, applying the impromptu garrote. The president bucked, and thrashed, and tried to roll himself over. The only sound was the toes of his cordovan bucks trying to get purchase against the linoleum.

Miss Mangel snatched up a letter opener from the president's desk and jabbed it into my grandfather's left shoulder. In my grandfather's reckoning, many years later, this action merited another checkmark.

The point of the letter opener sank only half an inch or so into meat, but the bite of metal blocked some meridian in the flow of my grandfather's rage. He grunted. "It was like I woke up," he said when he told me this part of the story for the first time, during the last week of his life. He unwound the cord from the president's neck.

---

[*] My grandfather knew only that the man he had accidentally beaned—fortunately, the intercom had only grazed his skull—declined to press charges. The *Daily News* identifies his victim as Jiří Nosek, head of the Czechoslovakian delegation to the august body that Alger Hiss had helped to charter. "This is the first time the high-ranking Red has been hit by a flying telephone," the *News* reported with a straight face, adding, "Nosek said that as a good Czech he was obliged to laugh off anything that didn't kill him."

He peeled it from the grooves it had cut into the flesh of his own left hand. The handset clattered against the floor. With a foot on either side of the president, he stood up and took a step away. The president flopped onto his back and raised himself into a sitting position, then sledded backward on his ass into a notch between two filing cabinets. He sobbed for air. When his face had hit the floor, he'd bitten his lower lip, and now his teeth were dyed pink.

My grandfather turned to face Miss Mangel. He plucked out the letter opener and laid it on the president's desk. When one of his rages wore off, you could see regret flooding his eyes like seawater. He dropped his hands to his sides.

"Forgive me," he said to Miss Mangel and to the president. I suppose he was also saying it to my mother, fourteen at the time, and to my grandmother, though arguably she was as much to blame as my grandfather. There was scant hope of forgiveness, but my grandfather did not sound as if he expected, or even wanted, to find any.

◑　　　◑　　　◑

At the end of my grandfather's life, his doctor prescribed a powerful hydromorphone against the pain of bone cancer. A lot of Germans were busy knocking holes in the Berlin Wall around that time, and I showed up to say goodbye to my grandfather just as Dilaudid was bringing its soft hammer to bear on his habit of silence: Out flowed a record of his misadventures, his ambiguous luck, his feats and failures of timing and nerve. He had been installed in my mother's guest bedroom for almost two weeks, and by the time I arrived in Oakland he was getting nearly twenty milligrams a day. He started talking almost the minute I sat down in the chair by his bed. It was as if he had been waiting for my company, but I believe now that he simply knew he was running out of time.

The recollections emerged in no discernible order apart from the first, which was also the earliest.

"Did I tell you," he said, lolling on his palliative cloud, "about the time I dropped a kitten out of the window?"

I did not say, then or at any point until he sank into the cloud for good, that he had told me very little about his life. I had yet to hear about the attack on the president of Feathercombs, Inc., so I could not point out to him that I sensed a motif of defenestration beginning to emerge in his autobiography. Later, when he did tell me about Miss Mangel, the intercom, and the Czech diplomat, I would choose to skip the smart remark.

"Did it die?" I asked him.

I was eating a cup of his raspberry Jell-O. Nothing else tempted his palate apart from a spoonful or two of the chicken soup my mother cooked for him, following the recipe of my late grandmother— born and raised in France—which called for a squeeze of lemon to brighten the broth. Even the Jell-O was not of much interest to him. There was plenty to spare.

"It was a third-story window," my grandfather said. He added, as if his native city were known for its adamantine sidewalks, "in *Phil-adelphia*."

"How old were you?"

"Three or four."

"Jesus. Why would you do something like that?"

He poked out his tongue, once, twice. That was something he did every few minutes. It often looked as if he were passing clownish judgment on something you had told him, but it was really only a side effect of the meds. His tongue was pale and had the nap of suede. I knew from a few precious demonstrations during my child-hood that he could touch the tip of it to the tip of his nose. Outside the window of my mother's guest bedroom, the East Bay sky was gray as the nimbus of hair around his suntanned face.

"Curiosity," my grandfather decided, and stuck out his tongue.

I said that I had heard curiosity could be harmful, in particular to cats.

As a boy, my grandfather lived with his parents, his father's father, and his kid brother, Reynard—my mother's Uncle Ray—in three rooms at the corner of Tenth and Shunk in South Philadelphia.

His father, a German-speaking native of Pressburg (now Bratislava), had failed in a series of dry goods stores and corner groceries throughout the 1920s and '30s. After that he abandoned hope of enduring ownership and played out the string as a sales clerk in liquor stores, watching other men's cash registers get robbed. In my grandfather's recollections his mother appeared as a strong back and a heart of gold, a "saint" indentured to the service of her husband and sons. In photographs she is a boxy woman, girdled with steel, shod in coal-black stompers, her bosom so large it might have housed turbines. She was all but illiterate in Yiddish and English but obliged my grandfather, and later Uncle Ray, to read to her daily from the Yiddish press so that she could keep abreast of the latest calamities to beset Jewry. From every week's household budget she managed to siphon off a dollar or two for the *pushke* can. Orphans of pogrom were fed, refugees berthed on steamships to freedom. Entire hillsides in Palestine bore the oranges of her compassionate embezzlement. "In the winter the laundry froze stiff on the clothesline," my grandfather recalled. "She had to carry it up all those stairs." Uncle Ray I knew as a playboy of the late 1960s in a sky-blue turtleneck and a gray tweed blazer. He drove an Alfa Spider and wore a raffish eyepatch over his gnarly left eye. Sometimes when I looked at him I thought of Hugh Hefner and sometimes of Moshe Dayan. As a boy, however, Reynard was studious and frail.

It was my grandfather, in the early days, who ran wild. Throwing a kitten out of a window was only a warning shot.

He wandered in the summertime from breakfast to dark, ranging as far east as the rancid Delaware and as far south as the Navy Yard. He saw an evicted family drinking tea on the sidewalk amid their beds, their lamps, their Victrola, a parakeet in a brass cage. He unfolded a packet of newspaper on the lid of an ashcan and found the eyeball of a cow. He saw children and animals beaten savagely and yet with patience and care. He saw a convertible Nash mobbed outside an AME church; Marian Anderson stepped out of it and lit up his memory, six decades afterward, with the crescent moon of her smile.

South Philadelphia was broadcast with Moonblatts and Newmans, those cousins who one day would people the weddings and funerals of my mother's and my childhoods. Their homes served as my grandfather's way stations. In threading his routes from one to the next, past blocks controlled by Irish and Italians, my grandfather laid the foundation of his wartime work. He cultivated secret contacts among the Italian bakers and grocers, running errands or working a broom in exchange for payment in pennies, lemon ice, or a twist of warm bread. He studied the nuances of people's ways of speaking and carrying themselves. If you hoped to avoid a beating on Christian Street, you could alter your gait and the cant of your head to look as though you were walking where you belonged. When that failed—or if, like my grandfather, you were not averse to scrapping—you fought dirty. Even Christian Street bravos squealed like babies if you hooked your thumbs in their eye sockets. Every so often, on the slope of a train embankment, behind the breast-shaped silos of the fertilizer plant, a battle would be pitched with bed slats, lengths of pipe, slingshots, and rocks. My grandfather lost a tooth, broke an arm, took uncountable stitches. On his left buttock he bore a pouty scar, the work of a beer bottle he sat on during a fight in a vacant lot behind the McCahan sugar refinery. Sixty years later the scar was visible whenever he used the bedpan, a silvery pucker, the kiss of violence.

His absences and injuries caused consternation to his parents, who made efforts to curtail them. Bounds were set, borders established; my grandfather subverted them. Resolute in his refusal to give details or name names, resistant to corporal punishment, willing to forgo whatever treat he was to be deprived of, he wore his parents down. In time they surrendered.

"Nothing can be done about a boy who throws cats out of windows," said old Abraham, my grandfather's grandfather, in his Pressburger German. Abraham ruled from his corner of the parlor that doubled as a dining room, enthroned atop his hemorrhoid donut among his books of commentary. It was nearly dark, one of the last free evenings of the summer.

"But what if he's lost?" my grandmother said for the thousandth or millionth time.

"He isn't lost," Uncle Ray said, issuing the finding that ultimately prevailed in the family Talmud. "He knows where he is."

He was trapped under a train car, one of six wooden boxcars on a stub at the far end of a storage yard by the river. The boxcars were used last to rush Baldwin-Felts men to the Paint Creek Mine War. Now they stood pastured against a hump of ground, and the mouths of a trumpet creeper devoured them.

He was hiding from a railroad bull, a big man named Creasey with a film on his left eye and patches of carroty hair growing on parts of his face where no hair ought to be. Creasey had already thrashed my grandfather soundly a number of times that summer. The first time he jerked my grandfather's arm up behind his back so hard the bones sang. The second time he dragged my grandfather by an earlobe across the yard to the main gate, where he applied his boot heel to the seat of my grandfather's trousers; my grandfather claimed the earlobe still bore the print of Creasey's thumb. The third time Creasey caught my grandfather trespassing, he strapped him thoroughly with the leather harness of his Pennsy uniform. This time my grandfather planned to stay under that boxcar until Creasey moved on or dropped dead.

Creasey stuck around, smoking cigarettes, pacing the weeds between the stub of track and the rest of the storage yard. My grandfather, flat on his belly, watched the bull's dusty boots through a scrim of dandelion and foxtail. Scrape, stop, pivot, return. Every few minutes a cigarette fell with a pat against the gravel and met its end beneath Creasey's right boot. My grandfather heard the twist of a bottle cap, a slosh of liquid, a belch. He had the impression that Creasey was waiting for somebody, killing time, maybe getting up his nerve.

My grandfather puzzled over it. Creasey was supposed to keep moving, sweeping the lots for hoboes, tramps, and pilferers like my grandfather, who had come to the Greenwich Yard that summer drawn by reports of coal for the taking, spillover from the cars as they trundled to the piers. The first time Creasey caught him it was because my grandfather had been weighed down by twenty-five pounds of coal in a sugar sack. Why did the man not carry on now with the work the Pennsylvania Railroad paid him to do? Inside the boxcar, over his head, my grandfather heard small animals in their nests, rousing themselves to their nightly business. According to his mother's natural history, he knew, that business was to bite young boys and give them rabies.

At last Creasey trampled his fifth cigarette, took another swig, and moved off. My grandfather counted to thirty and then slid out from under the boxcar. He brushed the grit from his belly, where the skin prickled. He spotted Creasey carrying a knapsack, making for one of the little stucco houses scattered here and there across the lots. On his first forays into the Greenwich Yard my grandfather had been charmed by the idea that railmen were cottaged like shepherds among the herded trains. He soon determined that the bungalows were no one's habitations. They had mesh grilles over their black-washed windows, and if you put your ear to their doors you could hear a thrum of power and sometimes a thunk like the clockwork of a bank vault. Until now my grandfather had never seen anybody going into one or coming out.

Creasey fished a key ring from his hip and let himself in. The door closed softly behind him.

My grandfather knew that he ought to head for home, where a hot supper and an operetta of reproach awaited him. He was hungry, and practiced in deafness and the formulation of remorse. But he had come here today to stand one final time at the top of one particular signal bridge that he had come to think of as his own, and tell another summer goodbye.

He cut across the storage yard and stole along a stretch of railbed to "his" signal bridge. He scaled the service ladder and clambered out along the catwalk to its midpoint, fifteen feet above the tracks. He raised up, holding onto the body of the central signal lantern. He jammed his feet in their canvas sneakers into the steel lattice of the catwalk. He let go of the signal lantern and stood balanced with arms outspread, hooked only by his ankles to the turning earth. Between him and the tenement on Shunk Street, the rail yard shuffled and sorted its rolling stock bound for New York, Pittsburgh, St. Louis. Trains and sections of trains clanged and rumbled and plowed furrows in the gloom.

He turned his face to the east. Darkness piled up like a thunderhead over New Jersey. Beyond the river lay Camden, beyond Camden the Jersey Shore, beyond the shore the Atlantic Ocean, and beyond that, Paris, France. His mother's brother, a veteran of the Argonne, had informed my grandfather that in the "cathouses" of that city a man might cross one further border, where silk stocking met white thigh. My grandfather took the signal lantern in his arms. He pressed his hips against its smooth encasement and looked up at the evening sky. A full moon rose, tinted by its angle on earth's atmosphere to a color like the flesh of a peach. My grandfather had spent most of that last Friday of the summer reading a copy of *Astounding Stories of Super-Science,* found among some other unsold magazines in the back room of his father's store. The last story was about a daring earthman who flew in an atomic rocket to the Moon's dark side, where he found ample air and water, fought bloodthirsty selenites, and fell in love with a pale and willing lunar princess. The Moon was a tough neighborhood, and the princess required frequent salvation by the earthman.

My grandfather regarded the Moon. He thought about the noble girl in the story with her *"graceful, undulating body"* and felt the swell of an inner tide reaching toward her, lifting him like Enoch in the whirlwind into the sky. He ascended the skyward tide of his longing. He would be there for her. He was coming to her rescue.

A door banged shut, and Creasey came out of the little house and rejoined his evening route. He was no longer carrying the knapsack. He crossed a set of tracks, a hitch of stiffness in his walk, and vanished among the cars.

My grandfather climbed down from the signal bridge. His path home did not run past the little house. But old Abraham had ruled correctly from his corner of the parlor: Nothing could be done for a boy who would throw a kitten out of a window onto a Philadelphia pavement just to see what would happen if he did.

My grandfather approached the little house with its gridded black windows. For a full minute he stood and watched it. He put his ear to the door. Over the electrical hum, he heard a human sound: choking, or laughter, or sobs.

He knocked. The sound broke off. The house's mysterious clockwork clicked. From the marshaling yard came the trumpeting of lashed-up engines, ready to drag a long load west. He knocked again.

"Who's there?"

My grandfather gave his first and last name. On reflection he appended his address. There followed a prolonged spell of unmistakable coughing from the other side of the door. When it passed, he heard a stirring, the creak of a bed or chair.

A girl peered out, hiding the right half of her face behind the door that she gripped with both hands, looking ready to slam it shut. The visible half of her head was a mat of peroxide tangles. Around the left eye, under a delicate eyebrow, paint mingled with mascara in cakes and blotches. She wore the fingernails on her left hand long, lacquered in black cherry. The nails on her right hand were bitten and bare of paint. She was wrapped loosely in a man's tartan bathrobe. If she was surprised to see him, she did not show it. If she had been crying, she was not crying anymore. But my grandfather understood Creasey the way you come to understand a man who repeatedly kicks your ass. The details of the hurt that Creasey might have done to this girl during his visit remained obscure, but my grandfather felt the outrage all the more vividly for his ignorance. He saw it in the ruin of her eye paint. He smelled it, a taint of Javela water and armpit in the air that leaked from behind the half-open door.

"Well?" she said. "State your business, Shunk Street."

"I saw him come in there," my grandfather said. "That Creasey bastard."

It was a word not to be used in the hearing of adults, especially women, but in this instance it felt fitting. The girl's face came out from behind the door like the moon from behind a factory wall. She took a better look at him.

"He is a bastard," she said. "You're right about that."

He saw that the hair on the right side of her part was cropped as short as his own, as though to rid that half of lice. On the right side of her upper lip she had raised enough whisker to form the handlebar of a mustache. Her right eye was free of paint, under a dense black brow. Apart from a shadow of stubble universal on either side of the chin, an invisible rule appeared to have apportioned evenly the male and female of her nature. My grandfather had heard but disbelieved neighborhood reports of sideshow hermaphrodites, cat girls, ape girls, four-legged women who must be mounted like tables. He might have reconsidered his doubt if not for the fact that he saw, filling both sides of the loose flannel wrapper from the neck down, only womanly curvature and shadow.

"The price of a peep is one nickel, Shunk Street," she said. "I believe you may owe me a dime."

My grandfather looked down at his shoes. They were not much to look at. "Come on," he said, reaching for her arm. Even through the flannel of her sleeve, he could feel fever on her skin.

She shook loose of his grip with a jerk of her arm.

"He won't come back this way for a while. But we have to go now," my grandfather said. There were whiskers on the chins of his own aunts: big deal. He was here by the power of a wish on an evening star. "Come on!"

"Aren't you funny," she said. She peeked out of the doorway, looked to either side. She lowered her voice in a show of co-conspiracy. "Trying to rescue me."

From her lips it sounded like the most peabrained idea ever conceived. She left the door hanging open and went back inside. She sat down on a cot and pulled a stiff blanket around her. In the light of a candle guttering on an overturned jar lid, panels of black switches and gauges glinted. Creasey's knapsack lay neglected on the floor.

"Are you going to take me home to your mama and papa?" she suggested in a voice that made him momentarily dislike her. "A drug-sick whore full of TB?"

"I can take you to a hospital."

"Aren't you funny," she said, more tenderly this time. "You already know I can unlock the door from the inside, honey. I'm not a prisoner here."

My grandfather felt there was more to her imprisonment than a lock and key, but he did not know how to put that feeling into words. She reached into the knapsack and pulled out a package of Old Golds. Something about the pomp with which she set fire to her cigarette made her seem younger than he had thought.

"Your pal Creasey already rescued me," she said. "He could have left me lying there right where he found me, half dead with my face in a pile of cinders. Right where those Ealing boys red-lighted me."

She told him that from the age of eleven she had been traveling in the sideshow of the Entwhistle–Ealing Bros. Circus, out of Peru, Indiana. She had been born a girl, in Ocala, Florida, but at puberty, nature had refashioned her with a mustache and chin fuzz.

"I went over big for quite a little while, but lately, I'm getting all this action from my girl department." She folded her arms under her breasts. "Body's been goofing with me all my life."

My grandfather wanted to say that he felt the same way about his brain, that organ whose flights of preposterous idealism were matched only by its reveries of unfettered violence. But he thought it would be wrong to compare his troubles to hers.

"I guess that's the reason I started on the junk," she said. "A hermaphrodite was something. It has a little poetry. There is just no poetry in a bearded lady."

She had been nodding, she said, dead to the world, when management at last saw fit to throw her off the circus train as it pulled out of the yard, bound for Altoona.

"Creasey found my valise where those assholes had pitched it. Conveyed me to these comfortable lodgings." She adjusted her legs and, before she gathered the blanket more tightly, caught my grandfather trying to see into the shadow between them. "Creasey is a bastard, true. But he brings me food, and smokes, and magazines. And candles to read by. The only thing he won't bring me is a fix. Pretty soon it'll be all the same to me, anyway. Meantime he doesn't charge me more rent than I'm willing to pay."

My grandfather contemplated the ashes of his plan. He felt she was telling him she was going to die, and that she planned on doing it here, in this room that jumped in the candlelight. Her chest blood was all over a crumpled chamois rag, and on the woolen blanket, and on the lapels of the robe.

"Creasey has his points," she said. "And I'm sure the folks on

Shunk Street would be happy to know that he has been kind enough to leave me in possession of my virginity. In the technical sense." She squirmed against the cot illustratively. "Railroad men. They are practical fellows. Always find a way around."

That started her barking into her scrap of chamois, which bloodied it some more. The violence of her coughing shook the blanket loose, baring her legs to my grandfather's inspection. My grandfather felt very sorry for her, but he could not keep his gaze away from the inner darkness of her robe. The spasm passed. She folded the bloodstained part of the chamois into the remnant that was still clean.

"Have a look, Shunk Street," she said. She hoisted the hem of the tartan robe, opened her legs, and spread them wide. The pale band of belly, the shock of dark fur, the pink of her labia would endure in his memory, flying like a flag, until he died. "On the house."

He could feel the turmoil in his cheeks, throat, rib cage, loins. He could see that she saw it and was enjoying it. She closed her eyes and raised her hips a little higher. "Go ahead, sweetheart. Touch it if you want to."

My grandfather found that his lips and tongue could not form a reply. He went over and put his hand against the patch of hair between her legs. He held it there, sampling it with rigid fingers like he was taking a temperature or pulse. The night, the summer, all time and history came to a halt.

Her eyes snapped open. She lurched forward and shoved him aside, covering her mouth with the bare hand while the painted one groped for the chamois. My grandfather took a crisp white handkerchief from the back pocket of his cutoff corduroys. He presented her with this evidence of the hopefulness invested in him by his mother, every morning afresh, when she sent him out into the world. The girl crushed the handkerchief in her fist without seeming to notice it was there. My grandfather watched her body tear itself apart from the inside for what felt like a long time. He worried she might be about to die right then, in front of him. Presently, she sighed and fell backward against the cot.

Her forehead shone in the light from her stub of candle. She breathed with caution. Her eyes were half open and fixed on my grandfather, but minutes went by before she took notice of him again.

"Go home," she said.

He eased the day's inviolate handkerchief from her fist. Like a road map he unfolded it and laid it against her brow. He sealed up the flaps of her robe around her and dragged the awful blanket up to her chin with its babyish dimple. Then he went to the door, where he stopped, looking back at her. The heat of her clung like an odor to his fingertips.

"Come back sometime, Shunk Street," she said. "Maybe I'll let you rescue me yet."

When my grandfather finally made it home well after dark, there was a patrolman in the kitchen. My grandfather confessed to nothing and provided no information. My great-grandfather, egged on by the patrolman, gave my grandfather a slap across the face to see how he liked it. My grandfather said he liked it fine. He felt he had earned a measure of pain through his failure to rescue the girl. He considered informing the patrolman about her, but she was by her own admission a drug fiend and a whore, and he would rather die than rat her out. Whichever course he chose, he felt, he would betray her. So he answered to his nature and said nothing.

The patrolman returned to his beat. My grandfather was subjected to lectures, threats, accusations. He bore up under them with his usual stoicism, was sent to bed hungry, and kept the secret of the two-sided girl in the train yard for the next sixty years. The following day he was put to work in the store, working before and after school on weekdays and all day Sunday. He was not able to make it back to Greenwich Yard until late the following Saturday afternoon, after shul. It was getting dark, and the weather had turned wet the night before. Along the tracks the reflected sky lay pooled between the wooden ties like pans of quicksilver. He knocked on the door of the little house until his hand rang with the pain of knocking.

I came into my patrimony of secrets in the late 1960s, in Flushing, Queens. At the time my grandparents were still living in the Bronx, and generally, if my parents needed to be free of me for more than a few hours, I would be deposited in Riverdale. Like the space program, my grandfather's business was then at its peak, and though later he became a strong presence in my life, in those days my clearest memory of him is that he was seldom around.

My grandparents and their Martian zoo of Danish furniture shared seven rooms in the Skyview, overlooking the Hudson. They lived on the thirteenth floor, though it was styled the fourteenth because, my grandfather explained, the world was full of dummies who believed in lucky charms. It was bad luck, my grandfather said, to be a dummy. My grandmother also scoffed. Though she personally had no particular fear of the number thirteen, she knew that bad luck could never be fooled by such a simple-minded stratagem.

Left to ourselves my grandmother and I might go to see a movie, one of the interminable candy-colored epics of the day: *Doctor Doolittle*, *The Gnome-Mobile*, *Chitty Chitty Bang Bang*. She liked to shop every morning for that evening's dinner; consequently, we spent a lot of time in grocery stores, where she taught me to look for tomatoes that still had a smell of hot sun in their stems, and then in her kitchen, where she taught me the rudiments and entrusted me with knives. If I have inherited it from her, then she must have found a mindful mindlessness in the routines and procedures of the kitchen. It tired her to read aloud in English, but she had a lot of French poems by heart and sometimes recited them to me in the ghostly language of her loss; I formed the impression that French poetry trafficked mainly in wistful rain and violins. She taught me colors, numbers, the names of animals: *Ours. Chat. Cochon.*

There were days, however, when being left with my grandmother was not very different from being left alone. She lay on the sofa or on her bed with the curtains drawn and a cool cloth folded over her eyes. These days had their own lexicon: *cafard, algie, crise de foie.* In 1966 (the date of my earliest memories of her) she was only forty-three, but the war, she said, had ruined her stomach, her sinuses, the joints of her bones (she never said anything about what the war might have done to her mind). If she had promised to look after me on one of her bad days, she would rally long enough to persuade my parents, or herself, that she was up to the task. But then it—something—would come over her and we would leave the movie theater halfway through the show, conclude the recital after a single poem, walk out of the supermarket abandoning an entire cart of groceries in the middle of the aisle. I don't think I really minded, exactly. When she took to her bed—and only then—I was allowed to watch television. Once she was down for the count, my only responsibility would be from time to time to run a little cool water on the washcloth, wring it out, and drape it over her face like a flag on a coffin.

Outside of the kitchen my grandmother's favorite pastime was cards. She detested the games Americans considered suitable for children: war, concentration, go fish. She found gin rummy dull and interminable. The card games of her own childhood were all trick-taking games that rewarded acuity and deception. When I was old enough to add and subtract in my head—around the time I learned to read—she taught me how to play piquet. It was not long before I could nearly hold my own against her, though when I was older my grandfather told me that she was always careful to make mistakes.

Piquet is played with a shortened deck of thirty-two cards, and before we could begin, my grandmother would strip a pack of Bi-cycles or Bees of all the cards from deuce to six. This was an oper-ation she performed with a certain heedlessness. When someone came home after a long day at the office, say, hoping to relax with a few hands of solitaire, and went to the drawer in the cabinet where games were kept, he was likely to find half a dozen plundered decks awash in an indiscriminate surf of pip cards. Those were the only occasions when I ever saw my grandfather openly express irritation with my grandmother, whom he otherwise coddled and indulged.

"It drove me nuts," he remembered. "I used to say, '*One deck!* Is that too much to ask? Could there be one goddamn deck that isn't ruined?'" He made a duck's bill of his lips, narrowed his eyes, hoisted his shoulders. "'*Boh.*'" I remembered this *echt*-gallicism of my grandmother's. "She *wasn't* ruining the deck, if you please, she was *correcting* it." He put on the Texan-in-Paris accent he used when-ever he spoke French. "*See-non, come-awn fair une pe-teet par-tee?*"

One afternoon when my grandmother sent me to get a deck so we could make a few *parties*, I discovered that since my last visit the drawer had been cleaned out and restocked with several new packs of poker decks, sealed and in their wrappers. It would be a worse outrage to my grandfather than usual, it seemed to me, to "ruin" one of these brand-new packs.

I opened some other drawers and poked around among the Yaht-zee and Rack-O and Monopoly boxes, looking for any of the decks that my grandmother had previously stripped. Inside a tin that once held Barton's almond kisses I found a deck of cards in a cu-riously drab box, pale blue printed with some words, which I took to be French, in a medieval-looking typeface like the one across the banner of *The New York Times*. It was thinner than an American deck, as if it contained fewer cards. Assuming that I had managed to locate an actual French piquet deck, I carried it into the kitchen, where my grandmother and I usually played.

I thought she would be pleased to see that I had found a way to keep my grandfather happy. Instead she looked alarmed. She was in the act of lighting one of the Wintermans cigarillos that she smoked only while playing cards, but she stopped with the match halfway to her mouth. My mother used to complain bitterly about the stink of my grandmother's cigars in my hair and on my clothing when I was returned after a visit, but I thought they smelled wonderful.

She took the unlit cigarillo from her lips and returned it to its little tin. She held out her hand, palm up. I surrendered the pale blue box. She opened its flap, tipped out the cards, and set it down on the table by the ashtray. She held up the deck and fanned it so she could see the faces. I saw only the backs, midnight blue patterned with crescent moons.

She asked where I had found the cards. I told her, and she nodded. She remembered having hidden them there long ago. She explained that she'd had to hide them because they were magical cards, and my grandfather did not believe in magic. I must not tell him about the cards, she said; it would annoy him and he would throw them away. I agreed to keep the cards a secret and asked my grandmother if she believed in magic. She said she did not but that, surprisingly, magic worked even if you did not believe in it. She seemed to have entirely recovered from her alarm at the thought that my discovery might be discovered.

She held up the blue box and told me that the words printed there were German, not French, and that, translated, they read FORTUNE-TELLING CARDS FOR WITCHES.

I asked my grandmother if she was a witch. I had the odd sensation that it was a question I had been holding at the back of my tongue for a long time.

She looked at me and reached for the cigarillo she had put aside. She lit it, shook out the match. She shuffled the cards a few times with her long pale fingers. She set the deck on the table between us.

In putting down these very early memories of my grandmother, I have so far avoided quoting her directly. To claim or represent that I retain an exact or even approximate recollection of what anyone said so long ago would be to commit the memoirist's great sin. But I have not forgotten my grandmother's two-word reply when I asked if the reason she owned a secret deck of magical fortune-telling cards for witches was that she was herself a witch:

"Not anymore."

I asked if this meant that she was no longer able or didn't remember how to tell fortunes. It was probably a little of both, she said. She would, however, be happy to show me how her magical deck of cards could be used to tell a *story*. All I had to do—she demonstrated as she explained—was cut the cards, cut them again, and then choose three from the top of the deck.

I have never had success in tracking down or identifying my grandmother's particular deck, the "Fortune-telling Cards for Witches," or "The Witch's Fortune-telling Cards," or however the name was translated. It may be that things I heard afterward about my grandmother's brief television career as a witch corrupted my recollection of the deck's name—maybe they were called "Cards of a Gypsy Fortune-teller," or "The Sibyl's Fortune-telling Cards." But I remember enough about the cards to conclude that it must have been a German variant on the standard "Lenormand" deck.

The first time I saw a classic Mexican Lotería deck with its iconic imagery (*El Sol, El Arbol, La Luna*), after moving to Southern California in the mid-'80s, I recognized its kinship to my grandmother's. Her deck had a card called the Ship that showed an old-fashioned argosy under full sail beneath a sky filled with stars. The House was white stucco with a red tile roof and a pretty green garden. The Rider in his red tailcoat rode a prancing white horse through yellow and green woods. The Child in its neutering nightdress clutched a doll and looked afraid. As on the faces of most Lenormand decks, a small oblong panel, inset at the top of each card above the Scythe or the Birds or the Bouquet, depicted a pip or court card with the German suits of hearts, leaves, acorns, and bells.*

I don't remember the first story she told me with her fortune-telling deck, or which set of three cards she drew it from. But after that first time, "playing with the story cards" became an occasional feature of our time together. There was no way to predict when the urge would come over her, though it came over her only when we were alone. In my memory of those occasions the day outside the windows of the apartment would be gray, cold, and wet; the weather may have played a part in putting her in the mood. Anyone who has spent time in the company of small children knows that a crushing boredom can unlock great powers of invention. My grandmother would be drifting gray and unfocused through an October afternoon, unsettled in the kitchen, wearying of my prattle. And then the cards would come out of their hiding place in the empty can of almond kisses, and she would say: *"Do you want me to tell you a story?"*

At this point I always faced a dilemma. I liked the *way* my grandmother told a story, but the characters who emerged from her witch's deck unsettled and frightened me, and the fates that befell them were dark. From the three cards I turned faceup on the kitchen table my grandmother's imagination would wind a cryptic path to the narrative she unfolded. The Lilies, the Ring, and the Birds, say, would not necessarily produce a story that had anything to do with either lilies, rings, or birds, and if it did, then it would reveal something terrible about them, some latent capability for malice or liability to perdition.

---

*Apparently, Lenormand decks owe their origin not to Mlle. Marie Anne Lenormand, the greatest if not the most fraudulent cartomancer of the nineteenth century, but to a game called *Das Spiel der Hoffnung*, played with dice, that with its thirty-six pictorial cards laid out in a six-by-six grid was a kind of hybrid of tarot and chutes and ladders.

In my grandmother's stories wicked children received grim punishments, hard-earned success was forfeited in one instant of weakness, infants were abandoned, wolves prevailed. A clown who liked to scare children woke up one morning and found that his skin had turned paper-white and his mouth had twisted into a permanent grin. A widowed rabbi unraveled his *tallis* and used the thread and some of his dead wife's clothes to sew their child a new mother, a soft golem silent as a raincoat. The stories gave me nightmares, but while she was telling them I found myself in the company of the grandmother I loved best: playful, exuberant, childlike, fey. In later years, whenever I recalled my grandmother to a close friend or a therapist, I would say that when she told a story, the actress in her came out. Her storytelling was a performance undertaken with ardor and panache. She did the different voices of animals, children, and men; if a male character disguised himself as a female, my grandmother would put on the funny, fluting voice that men affect in drag. Her foxes were suave, her dogs wheedling, her cows moronic.

If I hesitated before assenting to a story, my grandmother would rescind the offer, and weeks might pass before she offered again. So most of the time I simply nodded, unable to resolve the question of whether the company of the teller was worth the toll in bad dreams.

Almost fifty years later I still remember some of her stories. Bits of them have consciously and unconsciously found their way into my work. The stories I remember tend to be the ones I re-encountered in the plot of a film or in a book of folktales.* A few survived because some incident or sense impression of mine got tangled with or trapped inside the telling.

That happened with a story she told me about an encounter between King Solomon and a djinn. Afterward I remembered her introducing it as "from the Hebrew Bible," but that turned out to be

---

* I later recognized one particularly terrifying fragment as having been nicked from Tod Browning's *The Unknown*.

nonsense. Eventually I did find some Jewish folktales about Solomon matching wits with djinn but nothing like my grandmother's story. She told me that one day Solomon, the wisest king who ever lived, was captured by a djinn. On pain of death, the djinn demanded that Solomon grant *him* three wishes. Solomon agreed to try. He set a condition: Granting the wishes must cause no harm to any living person. The djinn therefore wished for an end to war; Solomon reminded him that if there were no war, the swordsmith's children would starve to death. Solomon helped the djinn to envision the disastrous outcomes of two more apparently benign wishes, and in the end the djinn was obliged to set King Solomon free. Typically the story did not quite have a happy ending, since afterward King Solomon himself could never again bring himself to wish for anything.*

I remember this story because after she was done telling it, my grandmother sent me to fetch something—a magazine, her glasses—in her bedroom. Maybe I was just snooping around. When I walked into the bedroom, I saw a shaft of afternoon sunlight, slanting in through a window, strike the eternal bottle of Chanel No. 5 on my grandmother's vanity. A djinn kindled in the bottle. It was the very color of the way my grandmother smelled; the color of the warmth of her lap and enfolding arms; the color of her husky voice resounding in her rib cage when she pulled me close. I stared at the flickering fire imprisoned in the bottle. Sometimes I found pleasure, warmth, and comfort in that fragrance, and sometimes when she dragged me onto her lap, her perfume dizzied me and brought on a headache. Sometimes her

---

* When I was in graduate school I was startled to find this story's source in *The John Collier Reader*—or so I have always believed until this afternoon, when I first riffled, then paged carefully, front to back, back to front, through the local copy (Knopf, 1972) and discovered no trace of such a story anywhere in the book. Either the encounter with my grandmother's borrowing came in the pages of some other collection or author, or else it happened in a dream, triggered perhaps by my reading Collier's "Bottle Party" with its deliciously malevolent djinn and immortal last line.

arms would be iron bands encircling my neck, and the scrape of her laughter sounded embittered and hungry, the laughter of a wolf in a cartoon.

◗   ◗   ◗

My five earliest memories of my grandmother:

1. *The tattoo on her left forearm.* Five digits encoding nothing but the unspoken prohibition on my asking her about them. The jaunty 7 with its continental slash.

2. *A song about a horse, sung in French.* She bounces me on her knees. Holding my hands in hers, clapping them together. Faster and faster with each line, from a walk to a trot to a gallop. Most of the time when the song ends, she folds me in her arms and kisses me. But sometimes when she gets to the last word of the song, her lap opens like a trapdoor and she tumbles me onto the carpet. While she sings me the horse song, I watch her face, looking for a clue to her intentions.

3. *The crimson blur of a Jaguar.* A Matchbox, a 3.4 Litre, the same color as her lipstick. She has bought it to console me after taking me to an ophthalmologist who dilated my pupils with drops of belladonna. When I panicked about the loss of vision she kept her cool, but now that I am happy again she gives way to worry. She tells me to put away the toy or I will lose it. If I play with it on the subway, one of the other boys riding on our train will envy it and steal it. The world is a blur to me, but my grandmother sees it clearly. Any of the shadows populating the 1 train might be a covetous boy bent on thievery. So I put the Jaguar in my pocket. I feel the Jaguar cool against my palm, the elegant taper of its lines, the words *jaguar* and *belladonna* that she will own forever afterward in my memory.

4. *The seams of her stockings.* Running true as plumb lines from the hem of her skirt to the backs of her I. Miller pumps as she feeds bones to a soup pot on the stove. Golden bangles stacked for safekeeping beside a floured marble pastry board on a countertop patterned with asterisks and boomerangs. The knob on the dial of her kitchen timer, finned and streamlined like a rocket.

5. *The luminous part in her hair.* Seen from above as she crouches in front of me, buttoning my pants. A ladies' room, maybe Bonwit or Henri Bendel, a periphery of foliage and gilt. I am—in English and French—her *little prince,* her *little gentleman,* her *little professor.* Her coat has a fur ruff that smells of Chanel No. 5. I have never seen anything as white as her scalp. My mother would have sent me into the men's room to do my own urinating and zip my own fly, but I am aware of no insult to my dignity. I understand that with my grandmother a different law obtains. A phrase I have heard comes to mind and along with it a sudden gain in understanding: *She will not let me out of her sight.*

IV

On December 8, 1941, unemployed, bored, and known as a shark in every pool hall within a hundred miles of the corner of Fourth and Ritner, my grandfather enlisted in the Army Corps of Engineers. Bequeathing his custom Brunswick cue to Uncle Ray—depriving the world, in time, of a *tzaddik*—he boarded a troop train for Rapides Parish, Louisiana. After six weeks of basic he was sent to a Corps base near Peoria, Illinois, for training in the construction of airfields, bridges, and roads.

His hustler's instinct was to underplay and advertise nothing, but among the raw recruits of Camp Claiborne and the bohunks and golems of Camp Ellis, he could not conceal the caliber of his game as a soldier and an engineer. He was strong and durable. His frugality with words got interpreted variously but to his advantage as manliness, self-possession, imperviousness. Inevitably word got around that he held an engineering degree from Drexel Tech, spoke fluent German, was all but unbeatable at pool,* and on intimate terms with motors, batteries, and radios. One afternoon when he and his fellow trainees were out butchering a meadow along the Spoon River, some idiot drove a truck through the line that connected their field telephone to the switchboard. My grandfather improvised a new connection using a nearby barbed-wire fence. When it started to rain

---

* He had put himself through Drexel by hustling games from New York to Baltimore and as far west as Pittsburgh. "I had no choice," he told me. "Everything my parents saved went to pay for that brother of mine."

and the wet fence posts grounded the line, he cut a spare inner tube into foldable bits and sent men down along the fence for two miles to insulate wire from wood.

The next day he was ordered to report to the commanding officer of his cadre. The major was a lean Princetonian, stained and yellowed by years of spanning chasms and draining swamps in malarial climes. His cheeks were all peeling skin and gin blossoms. He filled a briar pipe and took his time about it. Every now and then he sneaked a sidelong look at my grandfather, who stood uncomfortably at ease, wondering what he had done wrong. After the major had set fire to his pipe, he informed my grandfather that he was to be recommended for transfer to the Corps's officer candidate school at Fort Belvoir, Virginia.

The atmosphere of life as an enlisted man was toxic with disdain for officers, and from the first my grandfather had breathed that atmosphere freely, without need of filter or adjustment period.

"Sir," my grandfather replied after a moment of irresolution. He had nothing against this particular major. It was officers as a class whom he despised. "I'll swing a hammer until we've built a highway from here to Berlin. But, all due respect, I'd rather be a dancing chicken in a box on the Steel Pier than a commissioned officer. No offense, sir."

"None taken. I understand what you're saying, and between you and me, your dancing-chicken analogy is very close to the mark."

"Sir."

"All the same, are you aware that if you were to make the grade as a first lieutenant, it would add fifty dollars to your monthly soldier's pay?"

It happened that my great-grandfather's final enterprise, a lunch counter near Shibe Park, had recently gone under. He was working now at a package store, grappling in a hernia truss with steel kegs of Yuengling. For years my great-grandmother had taken in piecework, sewing ribbon and trim for a milliner. Now she had been obliged to get a job outside the house, boxing cakes and pastries in a bakery where the bakers, two half brothers, burned off their mutual contempt by abusing the counter help. My grandfather knew that his parents would shoulder any work and stomach any companions to pay the upkeep on Ray's education, in which they lodged their dreams.

"No, sir," he said, "I was not aware of that."

Two weeks later—the day before the men of his cadre boarded a train for Dawson Creek, BC, where they pitched in to work on the Alaskan Highway—my grandfather was ordered to report to the Corps OCS at Fort Belvoir. It was a bitter journey.

Far from the frozen north or the war's early battlefields, three hours from Shunk Street, more bored than ever, my grandfather began to brood. His years in poolrooms and classrooms inclined him to divide men into patsies, idiots, and shams, and there was little evidence at Fort Belvoir to debunk this taxonomy. Everywhere he looked he discovered laziness, incompetence, waste, bluster. In other soldiers' hearts such discoveries bred cynicism, but in my grandfather's there arose a more or less permanent state of aggravation.

Given the proximity of Fort Belvoir to Washington, D.C., it was only a matter of time before his exasperation generalized beyond the perimeter fence to encompass the seat of government itself. In spite of Pearl Harbor and the invasion panics it inspired, the capital had yet to lose its complacency toward enemies who were continents and oceans away. Anti-aircraft batteries were spotty. Elderly Curtiss biplanes patrolled sputtering overhead. A handful of Coast Guard tubs policed the rivers and bridges.

Walking the streets one afternoon on a one-day pass, my grandfather nursed his anger and amused himself by planning the conquest of Washington. For verisimilitude he enacted his role of *reichsmarschall* in his grandfather's Pressburger German, debating strategy with the added relish its glottals afforded. He ordered that crack commando units be trained to crew U-boats. He landed three hundred men on the Patuxent at the spot where the British had begun their invasion of 1814. His submarine jaegers blew up the Potomac bridges and electrical power stations, seized radio towers, cut telegraph and telephone cables. They entrenched the orderly street grid with grenade craters and razor wire, piled up chicanes across the approaches to the city. Thirty men sufficed to take the Capitol, a dozen to seize the White House. By the evening of the second day of his invasion, my grandfather stood in jackboots and peaked *schirmmütze* at the elbow of FDR, proffering his pen for the formal surrender.

He returned to Fort Belvoir that evening alarmed by the clarity and elegance of his plan. Before retiring for the night he formulated its essentials in a typed three-page memorandum to his CO, which was afterward mislaid, ignored, or possibly forgiven. In the darkness of the dormitory room he shared with an MIT-educated civil engineer named Orland Buck, he laid out the scheme again.

By pure chance, this Buck happened to be one of the few officer candidates not readily fitted onto my grandfather's three-part schema of humanity. Orland Buck was a Maine Brahmin whose father and grandfather both had died fighting to build heroic bridges, in Argentina and the Philippines. A history of raising hell in genteel institutions and the weight of his patrimony inclined Buck to the arts of demolition, and he zeroed in on that element of my grandfather's plan.

"One bridge would do," he decided. "Make it the Francis Scott Key and you would get their attention, all right."

Weeks passed without any acknowledgment of my grandfather's memorandum. Orland Buck and my grandfather spent their leave hours ostentatiously casing the Francis Scott Key Bridge with its arches in elegant cavalcade. Buck took documentary pictures of my grandfather taking pictures, unmolested, of the bridge's piers and abutments. Despite their efforts, no one questioned or even appeared to remark on the young men's fascination with the bridge, built by the Corps in the twenties, engineered by an associate of Buck's father.

In demolition training sessions, the Corps daily broadened their expertise, and at night Buck and my grandfather studied official copies of the bridge's construction plans in the base library.

"It will teach them a lesson," Buck said, lying on his bunk in the darkness. A radio, tuned low, brought news of Rommel's capture of Tobruk. "It will serve the bastards right."

My grandfather wondered how long ago, without his having noticed, his bunkmate had passed from the conditional to the future in talking about their plan. He didn't believe for a moment that Buck wanted to teach anyone a lesson or had the slightest interest in seeing justice done. Buck was not a sorehead, a perfectionist, or a nurser of grievances. He was in it for fun and only saying what he thought my grandfather wanted to hear.

"Don't get carried away," my grandfather told him.

"Who, me?"

In a strongbox at the back of an old Mack truck that stood rusting without engine or wheels under a tarp in the motor pool, Buck and my grandfather had stashed ten bombs of their own manufacture. The bombs' design was plausibly straightforward and effective: empty wooden ammo boxes stuffed with guncotton, which Buck and my grandfather had spirited away in amounts small enough to go unnoticed during demolitions training. A small amount of primer and Cordtex had been obtained in the same way, just enough for my grandfather to make his point harmlessly. Twisted to the end of each coil of Cordtex was a note typed by my grandfather that read NUR ZU DEMONSTRATIONSZWECKEN.*

"I don't like it when people get carried away," my grandfather said.

"Oh, no, neither do I," Buck said shamelessly.

On the night appointed for the exploit they strapped on tool belts, retrieved their store of demonstration bombs from the strongbox, zipped the bombs into four duffel bags, and went AWOL with an

---

* For demonstration only.

ease that bore out my grandfather's contempt for the way things were done at Fort Belvoir. They hiked through tall weeds and trash pine, across a service road, and into some woods that had been part of the original Belvoir plantation. They stumbled cursing in the dark of the forest until they came to the tracks of the RF&P, where they hopped a freight and rode an empty flatbed into Alexandria.

They jumped off just before the train entered the rail yard, in a neighborhood of low brick houses. From the Potomac Yard came a smell of diesel, an ozone scorch of pantograph sparkings. Those smells and the houses with their puzzled expressions stirred old yearnings and rancors in my grandfather's heart. He wondered, as in the past and for years to come, if this might be the night on which his life, his true life, began at last.

They found an old Model A pickup parked in an alley. The rear window glass of its cab had been replaced by a sheet of pegboard. My grandfather stove in the pegboard with a jab of his left elbow and wriggled through. He had never hot-wired a car before, but the principle was trivial and the Ford unresisting. It took him under a minute to turn the engine over. He unlocked the door and slid across to the passenger side. Orland Buck got in behind the wheel and pawed it for a second or two.

"You bastard," Orland Buck said happily. "God damn you."

"Drive."

A body slammed against the truck on Buck's side. Buck's window was filled with the eyes and red jaw of a dog. A man shouted from a house that backed onto the alley. Orland Buck laughed. He fought against the clutch and the gearshift. They lurched out of the alley under escort from the outraged dog before Buck hit the gas and they left the animal in their dust. The truck was not going to afford them very much in the way of stealth. As they turned onto the Jeff Davis Highway, it sounded like they were dragging a sack full of clocks behind them.

Orland Buck took himself in hand after that. He drove with care in the darkness, meeting the speed limit. They drove past the new airport, past the wasteland where they were putting up the new War Department building, past the cemetery where Buck's father and grandfather lay under their white crosses. They dragged their load of clock parts across the roadbed of their intended victim and turned left on the District side. Upriver a little way from Georgetown, near the old terminus of the C&O canal, Buck put the truck into neutral and cut the engine. They rolled into the gravel lot of Fletcher's Boathouse. Before getting out of the truck, they blackened their faces with burnt cork and pulled dark watch caps over their heads. Orland Buck was in heaven. My grandfather was obliged to admit that he was also enjoying himself so far.

"Now, did you ever paddle a canoe?" said Buck, a veteran of many Down East camps.

"I've seen it done," my grandfather said, thinking in particular of a silent version of *The Last of the Mohicans* he had taken in at the Lyric in Germantown. "If Bela Lugosi can do it, I can do it."

The hasp on the boathouse door broke at a tap of his hammer and chisel. My grandfather eased the door open a foot on its rollers and slipped inside. The darkness smelled of old canvas tennies. Buck found the canoe, lucky number 9, in which a War Department typist named Irma Budd once sucked him off. Bowed and loping, they ran it down to the boat ramp. My grandfather loaded in the duffel bags while Buck fetched two paddles. "Ready to have some fun, Lugosi?"

My grandfather dragged the canoe to the bottom of the ramp and climbed into the stern as the hull scraped, then slid free. It was not the type of question he would ever bother to answer.

In canoe number 9, silent as Piscataways, they breasted the Potomac. This was the part of the exploit that would expose them most to public view, and they had decided it would be better to get across and hug the Virginia bank, in those days still half wilderness. Adventure silenced Orland Buck. It brought out in him the sobersided Yankee, two wiry hands on a wooden shaft. For most of the crossing my grandfather was as useless as a Hungarian actor, though he did not give way to distress or embarrassment. By design they had chosen a moonless night, but the weather was clear, and over my grandfather's head the circuitry of heaven was printed in bright joints of solder. By the time Buck brought them around for the short downstream run to the Key Bridge, my grandfather was handling his own paddle with aplomb. He was as happy as he had ever been.

The bridge seemed to hold itself in tension, straining at its tethers as Orland Buck and my grandfather slid beneath its haunch. It thrummed with the passage of a car overhead. My grandfather shipped his paddle and crouched, rocking the canoe a little as Buck eased them to the foot of the abutment that buried its massive burden in the soil of Virginia. Buck reached out to steady the boat. My grandfather zipped open one of the duffel bags and took out the first bomb and a roll of adhesive tape they had boosted from the infirmary. Given time and actual malicious intent, they would have holed the concrete with a pick or borer to sink the bombs, to give the blasts some muscle. Concrete was a bastard, and my grandfather estimated that to bring the Key Bridge down in earnest might take a thousand pounds of guncotton. He taped the first bomb to the bridge's great concrete hoof. The strips of sticky tape as he unrolled them resounded in the arch like thunder cracks.

"Next," he said.

Orland Buck stroked at the water and they went farther in under the bridge. The water slapped against the canoe and against the abutment.

The Francis Scott Key Bridge has five arches, three that take giant steps across the water, one at either end to anchor the bridge to land. Orland Buck and my grandfather took turns taping three bombs to each of the four central piers, six bombs per man. When they had finished, it was nearly four in the morning. My grandfather looked up at the belly of the bridge. He admired the way the gap between the top of each arch and the flat bridge deck was taken up by a series of daughter arches, each inverted *U* obliged to descend farther from the deck than the last as the mother arch curved down and away. The whole space hummed as the wind passed through it. Beyond the vault of steel and concrete the vernal animals and heroes wheeled in the greater vault of the sky. Arch upon arch upon arch bearing up, craving the weight, crushed by the force that held it together. He looked down at Orland Buck in the stern of the stolen canoe. Buck was holding a time pencil and a 150-foot coil of Cordtex my grandfather had never seen and knew nothing about.

"You probably want to grab a paddle and put some distance between here and this boat," said Orland Buck.

My grandfather nodded. On some level he had suspected Buck was planning something of this nature. He sat down and deftly turned the canoe upstream. Buck paid out the coated cord with one hand, taking care not to dislodge the detonator pencil. When they had gone about a hundred and forty feet along the bank on the District side, my grandfather swung the paddle up out of water and ensured that it made solid contact with the side of Orland Buck's head. Buck fell onto his face. My grandfather twisted the time pencil free of the Cordtex and tossed it into the river. He sat Buck up, made sure that his friend was unconscious and not dead, and laid him out in the stern of the canoe. Then he paddled back to Fletcher's. When they got there, Buck was still out cold. My grandfather returned the canoe to the shed by himself, leaving three dollars to pay for the broken hasp. He shoved the empty duffel bags into a trash bin and loaded Buck into the cab of the stolen truck.

When they were crossing the Key Bridge, Orland Buck made a noise, and opened his eyes. He looked out the window and saw where they were. He experimented with his fingers at the site of his injury and groaned again. He shook his head. "Christ," he said with bitter respect.

"You got carried away," said my grandfather.

The next afternoon, when my grandfather returned to quarters after Maps and Surveying, there was an MP stationed on either side of his door. My grandfather braced himself to flee and then accepted his fate as it bore down on him. His cheeks, ears, and inner organs burned at the thought that his mother would now be obliged to let those two bakers shit on her head for the rest of her life.

The snowdrops in their spotless helmets held still as he approached them. They stared death, hatred, and tedium at him, and my grandfather stared those things back.

"Looking for me?" he said, stopping in front of the door, equidistant to each of their throats.

"No, son," said a voice from inside the room where he and Orland Buck had foolishly conspired to land themselves, my grandfather presumed, in Leavenworth. It was a rich man's voice, lilting and soft but accustomed to being listened to. "I'm the one that's looking for you."

A big man, past middle age, sprang up from the chair when my grandfather walked in. Broad at the shoulder like my grandfather, a bruiser gone old and fat. He wore a gray Glen plaid suit gridded with red, a red and silver silk tie, and wonderful black bucks. Though he looked like an English lawyer, my grandfather could smell the army on him. The man took the measure of my grandfather coldly and openly, top to bottom. What he saw appeared to confirm report or rumor. His eyes were extraordinary. Remembering them to me, my grandfather groped to define their color, comparing them first to sea ice, then to a lit stove ring.

"I am sure it will come as no surprise to you, soldier," the man said in his Park Avenue drawl, "to learn that you are in trouble."

"No, sir."

"No, indeed. How could it? You went looking for trouble, and you found it. Consistent behavior produces predictable results."

"Sir, I wasn't looking for trouble, I—"

"Don't bother to deny it. One glance at you and I know the whole story. You've been looking for trouble all your life."

"Sir—"

"Am I wrong, soldier?"

"No, sir."

"You stole equipment and materiel from the U.S Army. Went AWOL. Hot-wired a truck. Purloined a canoe. Planted live explosives on federal property."

"That part was not the plan," my grandfather said. "The live charge."

"No? Then how did it happen?"

It was clear that Buck had already confessed to everything, but my grandfather had not given up the whiskered girl in the train yard, and he was unwilling to give up his friend, even if his friend had turned out to be a rat.

"It was a breakdown in leadership," my grandfather confessed.

The eyes went abruptly from ice to fire. My grandfather had the disconcerting sensation of being loved by the beefy old man.

"Orlie Buck's father served in the Fighting Sixty-ninth as my aide-de-camp," the old man said. "He was always looking for trouble, too, and he knew that if ever he called out to me, I would hasten to his side and endeavor to get him out of whatever fix he was in, one way or another. I believe that is why, when those two snowdrops out there showed up to arrest him, Orlie reached out to his old uncle Bill."

A seine of anecdotes, genealogies, and dark allusions let out by Orland Buck over the past few months cinched together all at once in my grandfather's mind and caught a darting hope.

"Colonel Donovan, can you get me out of trouble, too?" my grandfather said.

"Well, my boy," Wild Bill Donovan said, "you know, the truth is I probably could. But as we've already established, that's not what you really want, now, is it?"

V

Following his arraignment on charges of assaulting the president of Feathercombs, my grandfather spent a week in jail. The bail was steep, and he had no collateral apart from a twenty-five-dollar reflecting telescope and a 1949 Crosley sedan.

Over that week he telephoned my grandmother twice. In the first call he misinformed her as to his whereabouts and said nothing at all about his arrest. The lawyer, Shulman, sent someone to pick up the Crosley from the garage on East Fifty-seventh and drive it back to New Jersey. The driver was instructed to tell my grandmother only that her husband planned to go by train on an urgent sales trip upstate.

On the fourth day of his stretch in the House of Detention, my grandfather phoned again. He provided my grandmother with memories not previously shared from a trip the previous August: a view from a motel window overlooking the rancid Susquehanna. An Italian restaurant that had served spaghetti in a green sauce called *pesto*. A long afternoon making sales calls in the heat. He had hated the job from the day he was hired, but now that he had lost it— demolished it—there was a retrospective charm in the tedium of those days spent barnstorming upstate beauty counters. Tears came to his eyes as he leaned against the outgoing-only pay phone in his gray jailhouse twills, eulogizing the wife of a pharmacist in Elmira who at first had taken only a case of Feathercombs but increased her order to three after he held up his demo mirror.

He never considered telling my grandmother the truth. She was already teetering; he was afraid the truth would push her over the edge. That was how he explained his subterfuge to himself, and to me thirty-two years later. It was not, in my view, a complete explanation. My grandfather never would have lied to exonerate himself, make himself look good, or evade responsibility. Unlike my grandmother, he did not seem to find pleasure or release in telling lies. But while he was a family man and loved us all in his wordless way, he was also, to the core, a solitary. If there was suffering to be endured, he preferred to withstand it alone. If he made a mess, he would clean it up himself. Unlike his wife, he was uncomfortable with make-believe, but his fetish for self-reliance made him secretive. So though it was true that psychiatrists, who got paid to know such things, had instructed him over the years to keep upsetting news away from my grandmother, it was also true that this advice suited his furtive nature. She was always threatening rain; he had been born with an umbrella in his hand.

The truth is that if he hadn't been so worried about his wife's mental state, my grandfather might have welcomed a couple of days in jail. Repentance is the most solitary of pursuits, and there could be no better place for penitence than shelved on a steel bunk in the Tombs. But scenarios of imminent breakdown and disaster at home began to obsess him. Though he hated asking for help more than anything else, in particular from people who loved him or would do it free of charge, my grandfather saw no alternative but to tell Shulman to try to track down his kid brother.

Uncle Ray had been ordained as a rabbi at the age of twenty-three, a wonder boy of learning. But sometime in the early 1950s my great-uncle had begun to reverse himself on questions of chance and divine intention. He had resigned his pulpit in northwest Baltimore and now made a good living hustling pool and poker up and down the Delmarva peninsula. To raise my grandfather's bail, Ray required a week's time, a supply of willing victims, and a surprise win by Hopeless Hope in the fifth at Hialeah.

My grandfather walked out of the Tombs with enough money for a shave, a bus, a Zagnut bar for my mother, and coffee and a donut for himself when he reached the Paterson bus terminal. Through Shulman, coached to represent himself to my grandmother as "a lawyer involved with your husband's business," my grandfather had arranged for his wife to meet his bus at ten-thirty.

At eleven-fifteen there was still no sign of her. He used his last dime to call the house.

"I'm here," he said.

"Here? Where is here?"

"In Paterson. At the bus."

"Paterson," she repeated. She might have heard rumors, her tone suggested, of there being such a place. She found her adopted homeland overburdened by places with preposterous names.

"Didn't Shulman tell you?"

"Shulman? Who is this Shulman?"

"The lawyer. Shulman."

"Shulman is the lawyer. Yes, I see." You would have assumed she was jotting the words down for subsequent study: *Paterson. Shulman. Lawyer.* "And now tell me, please, who are you?"

Only much later did my grandfather learn there had been a story in the *Daily News.* But he understood now that in spite of his efforts, word had spread.

"Look," he said. "I don't know what to say. I'm sorry."

"Are you? And why is that?"

"Darling, I know. I did a terrible thing, I'll sort it out. I swear. I could not be more sorry. I know how worried you must have been."

"Oh, but not in the least!" Because of her French accent, there was always a showiness to my grandmother's sarcasm. "Every time I'm starting to worry, then I think of you jumping out of the airplane, bringing emergency hair combs to the dishevel-ded ladies of Binghamtown, New York."

He winced, recognizing in this distorted version the lameness of the cover story he had concocted with Shulman. To sell it—as she clearly understood—he had been counting on the marginality of Binghamton to his immigrant wife's disorderly mental maps. But as usual she had seen through him and his stratagems. Like many of the spouses of "the lucky ones," my grandfather had observed that what got labeled *luck* was really stubbornness married to a knack for observation, a fluid sense of the truth, a sharp ear for lies, and a deeply suspicious nature. They'd had the same type of luck in South Philadelphia, but there you could do more with it than merely survive.

"Honey," he pleaded. "I just spent a week in jail. I'm filthy, I'm half dead, I'm in a bus station in Paterson. Please. Come get me."

"You have eaten something?"

"I had a donut. How is she?"

"She is at school."

He had not asked for my mother's whereabouts. They could be inferred from the time of day and the day of the week. But he let it pass. His question had been as pointless as any other.

"And this donut you ate," she said. "How big it was?"

"How big? It was a donut. It was donut-size. Darling—"

"But it filled up your stomach?"

"Sure."

"Good," she said just before she hung up on him. "Then you will have energy for the long walk home."

He pleaded with a soldier bound for Trenton on leave and wasted the dime on another call home. My grandmother had taken the phone off the hook. For the soldier's benefit he pretended, while listening to the busy signal, to hold a brief conversation with his wife in which he was forgiven and redeemed. He coughed to cover the clatter as the phone returned the dime, which paid for the bus to Ho-Ho-Kus. It dropped him on Sheridan Avenue.

He walked surrounded, for a long time, by tracts of new construction. Dirt lawns, planted saplings, houses like boxcars in snaking lines. When he drove past these new housing tracts at forty-five miles per hour on his way to work every day, they had appeared harmless, contained. On foot he could not seem to get past them. Houses oozed without limit in every direction. Cornfields, orchards, stands of oak and hickory that had seemed untouchable by time or steel had all been dragged under. My grandfather felt a stirring of unease that grew stronger the nearer to home he came. He worried that, in his absence, the ooze would have spread to overtop their white house on its little green hill.

He shook off the thought. He was irritated with himself for thinking it. But as he threaded his way among the housing developments, the image returned to plague him: his house, his wife and daughter, driven beneath the ooze. At last he turned off the county road onto a road paved with gravel and found himself safely among apple trees and shoots of corn. The panic subsided. But he could not seem to reassure himself that his family would not be drowned.

◑   ◑   ◑

The way I heard the story was that sometime after the fall of France my grandmother, unwed, not yet eighteen, and pregnant with my mother, had been taken in by Carmelite nuns in the countryside outside of Lille, where her family were prominent Jewish dealers in horses and hides. On learning that she was pregnant, and with the bastard of a Catholic—unappeased by knowing that the father was a handsome young doctor—her family had disowned her. It was the family of the handsome young doctor who had arranged things with the nuns. Shortly after my mother's birth, my grandmother's family was deported to Auschwitz, where they perished. After the handsome young doctor had treated the injuries of some local members of the Resistance, the SS had shot him.

All her life my grandmother's family looked askance at her interest in drama, poetry, handicraft. The nuns, by contrast, were sympathetic, aesthetic. They supported themselves by making and selling fragrant wreaths of laurel and dried flowers. They tended orchards and beehives and a meadow dotted with sheep. When I was eight or nine my mother had explained the concept of survivor's guilt to me, and told me that in her mother's case this was one of its sources: She had never been happier than with the sisters of the Lille Carmel.

My grandparents' farmhouse, on eleven acres outside Ho-Ho-Kus, New Jersey, had neither nuns nor sheep. But there was a meadow and an apple orchard, and my grandfather had spent their first winter building hives and honeycomb frames according to plans in a book from the public library. He had taken out a lease on the property in anticipation of my grandmother's discharge from her first hospitalization, from late 1952 to late 1954. He had hoped the place might carry her back to the remembered sweetness of the Carmel.

The apples had proved stony. The special-order French bees were prey to wanderlust and ennui. But from her first sight of the farmhouse, with its gingerbread, tangle of roses, and fresh coat of whitewash, my grandmother had conceded to my grandfather's logic. She emerged from that first time at Greystone in a fragile and quiet state, holding herself like an egg balanced on a spoon, but for the next twenty-eight months they lived on the farm in relative contentment. No angel inspired her to bare the prophecies of her body to fellow passengers on buses or trolley cars. She abandoned the bouts of prolonged fasting that rendered her skin translucent to an inner light equivalent in her mind to the Christ of her guardian nuns. She found work, taking leads in three productions at the prestigious Paper Mill Playhouse and being cast in a small role in a Broadway revival of *Ah! Wilderness* that closed out of town. Until the spring of 1957 the Skinless Horse had kept its gibes and railleries to itself.

Sometime during the week preceding my grandfather's rampage at Feathercombs, Inc., her cruel familiar returned to take up residence in a grand hickory tree in the house's front yard. The precise moment of its reappearance, like the reason thereof, remained unclear to my grandfather. In hindsight he recalled my grandmother once or twice having held herself very still, eyes closed, as if fighting down a bout of nausea. He remembered a shudder that she repressed, a smile that hung too long from the hooks of her face. For all my grandfather knew, the Skinless Horse might have been hanging around for months before it decided to occupy the tree fort my grandfather had built in the hickory tree as a thirteenth birthday present for my mother.

The day he got out of jail the first thing he saw, coming down the hill from the main road, was the tree. It was a sixty-footer, planted well before the turn of the century by the house's original occupants, a fellowship of free-love Christians. At the height of summer it would spread its leaves across the sky like a child's drawing of a tree, a perfect circle of crayon green. Hidden among its branches, the tree fort was my mother's galleon and keep. Now at the base of the tree there was a burnt blotch from which four jagged streaks extended upward. It looked like the print of a giant paw.

The eyeholes of the tree fort stared down at my grandfather as he circled around to the kitchen at the back of the farmhouse. They never used the front door. My grandfather hauled himself up the last three steps of his long walk home onto the back porch. The boards under his wing tips were new last summer. The previous porch was rotten and colonized by insects, and my grandfather had demolished it with a ferocity that approximated hope. Working alone or with my mother passing him nails from a bucket or bracing a plank with her bottom, he had cut, framed, and whitewashed the lumber of the new one, carpentering its Gothic lace under the guidance of another library book. The new porch felt sound and solid under the weight of him. Like the rest of the house, it was not and would never be his property, but in those years his ambition was not to own a piece of the world. Just to keep that piece from falling down or burning up around him would suffice.

The spring afternoon had turned cool, but the back door was open.

My grandfather smelled onions, bay leaf, simmering wine. He heard the "Trout" quintet bubbling on the record player in the living room. The kitchen windows streamed with vapor. Behind them darted the shape of my grandmother. She was an excellent cook, never more calm or present than with her hand on the rosewood grip of a razor-sharp Sabatier. In the early fifties, before her first hospitalization, she had been a frequent guest on WAAM's *Home Cooking*, giving lessons in French cooking to Baltimore housewives (those with tele-visions, at any rate) and briefly the host of her own program, *La Cui-sine*, which aired two mornings a week.*

"Look who's here," my grandfather said, coming into the heat of the kitchen.

She looked up from her bowl and whisk. She reached around to untie her apron. She had set her hair and put on her pearls. The pearls lay against the ruddy expanse between her throat and the cleft revealed by the scoop neck of her black sweater. The pearls seemed to radiate the absorbed heat of her skin. My grandparents forgave each other with the pragmatism of lovers in a plummeting airplane. There would be ample time for reproach in the event of their sur-vival.

"We have an hour before the school bus," my grandmother said.

My grandfather took off his shoes, his suit and tie, his curdled white shirt, his socks and garters. My grandmother helped him out of his undershorts. She led him naked up to the bathroom so he could wash away the Tombs.

Hot water was a pleasure, but he did not linger under the shower. When he came into the bedroom, my grandmother had unfurled her naked body on the bed, propped on an elbow. Knowing that he liked the look of it, she had retained the string of pearls.

---

* I still follow her recipes, typewritten on pale blue index cards, for *coq au vin*, cream of potato soup, and omelet. I lost or abandoned her impeccably seasoned omelet pan amid the wandering and confusion of objects that followed my di-vorce.

A photograph of my grandmother posed in a bikini, taken in Florida when she was in her mid-forties, shows a zaftig dame with impressive cleavage and dimpled knees. By then she had undergone the first-generation hormone replacement therapy (HRT) that softened her body and pacified her mind.* When she took my grandfather into her arms on the afternoon of his release from the House of Detention, her abdomen was rounded and firm under the watered silk of her stretch marks. Her waist remained narrow, her wrists and ankles thin. He took one ankle and used it to drag her across the bed. He pinned her upraised legs against him and entered her with his feet planted on the floor. The pearls shone against her skin in the failing daylight.

◗   ◗   ◗

As he was getting up from the toilet one morning in March 1990, in the master bathroom of his condominium at the Fontana Village retirement community in Coconut Creek, Florida, my grandfather heard something snap. He woke up bloody on the bathroom floor with a fat lip and a leg fracture. Later the broken bone would prove to be the result of a bone metastasis; it turned out that for the past six months, without telling anyone, he had been declining to undergo treatment for a carcinoid tumor in his gut. But at first all we knew was that he had fallen, and that someone would have to look after him as he recovered from a broken leg.

My mother, a public interest litigator, was in the midst of bringing a class-action suit against a pharmaceutical company whose popular second-generation HRT drug appeared to be giving thousands of women ovarian cancer and killing them before they turned sixty. My younger brother, embarked on a career as an actor in L.A., had just booked a TV pilot, a proposed reboot of the '70s show *Space: 1999*. I

---

* And killed her; she died of endometrial cancer in 1975, aged fifty-two.

was about to start a reading tour for the paperback edition of my first novel and was in the midst of an attempt, which turned out to be futile, to salvage something more than the material for a few short stories from the staved-in hull of my first marriage.

There was also the shadowy Lady Friend. Pooling information, we discovered that my grandfather had said little to any of us about her. Her name was Sally. She was an artist. She was a recent widow. None of us had a phone number or even knew her last name.

Sally called my mother on the day after my grandfather's accident and got right to the point: Though she and my grandfather had been dating only since September and were still getting to know each other, she was willing to help. But she had spent three brutal years nursing her late husband through his illness, decline, and recent death, and frankly, she was not sure she had the strength. My mother thanked Sally and said she understood. She had the sense that Sally already knew my grandfather well enough to imagine that he might not take to being nursed.

So my mother flew to Florida to fetch the man who had been her father since she was not yet five years old. She hoped that by bringing him to Oakland she would be able to arrange for his care and whatever therapy he needed and still be able to do her job. She booked him a first-class seat—over his strenuous objections—for the long trip west, so that he would be more comfortable. She arranged for his mail to be forwarded, and packed a suitcase with his clothes and papers. It was a big suitcase, with plenty of room for personal items, but my grandfather chose to bring only five:

1. *Rockets, Missiles, and Space Travel* by Willy Ley (3rd edition, Viking, 1957), a history of rocket flight up to 1956, combined with a detailed if ultimately mistaken prognostication of a manned mission to the Moon. I knew the book and its author were longtime favorites of my grandfather, but I had never seen this particular copy. It lacked a dust jacket and bore clear

evidence—tape stains, a tear on the pastedown where a pocket for the date card had been, NEW YORK STATE DEPT. OF CORRECTIONS rubber-stamped along the top edge—of its provenance. When I flipped through its pages, I noticed that throughout the book, someone—presumably my grandfather—had used a black marker to blot out certain words. I held up the defaced pages to the bedside lamp. Every blot covered an occurrence of one man's name: Wernher von Braun.*

2. A Zippo, known as "Aughenbaugh's lighter," which he had carried in his right pants pocket for as long as I could remember. He had quit smoking before I was born, but I'd seen him use Aughenbaugh's lighter many times to light charcoal grills, chimney logs, campfires. On a smooth oval, set into a nickel finish otherwise pebbled to hide scratches, you could make out traces of an engraved representation of an organic molecule, a linked pair of hexagons whose vertices were Cs, Hs, and

---

* My grandfather always made a show of his disdain for von Braun, said to have been one of the models for Southern and Kubrick's crypto-Nazi Dr. Strangelove. When he mentioned von Braun's name or quoted something von Braun was reported in the papers to have said, he would lay on a comedy German accent. My grandfather's company, MRX, had been the principal supplier of rocket and engine designs to Estes, Centuri, Chabon Scientific, and most of the other leading players during the heyday of model rocketry. MRX produced designs based on famous American rockets like the Vanguard, Thor, and Titan but never, in the dozen or so years of its existence, on the Redstone, Jupiter, or Saturn rocket families—all of which were developed by von Braun. This silent boycott endured throughout the Apollo era, when everyone wanted to fire a Saturn V. And my grandfather had shocked my parents and puzzled me when on July 20, 1969, after months of displaying fascination and mounting excitement about the imminent manned landing on the Moon, he had abruptly declined to join us and virtually the entire population of Earth in watching Neil Armstrong fulfill the lifelong dream that von Braun and my grandfather had shared. Only my grandmother seemed unsurprised by her husband's wordless departure from the room. "Apparently," I remembered her saying, nodding toward the television, "the way they have done it is totally wrong."

Os. Over the years I had asked him a few times what molecule was represented, but the answer I received ("Maltose"), or the reason for the answer ("Because it makes donuts taste good") struck me as so nonsensical and seemed to explain so little—my grandfather didn't even like donuts—that I finally concluded he was putting me on. As for the Zippo's eponym, my grandfather would only say that Aughenbaugh had been an Army buddy.

3. A black-and-white photograph of my mother, taken in August 1958. In the photo she was sitting bareback on a lean gray horse. She wore a beach towel around her hips and a one-piece swimsuit that she filled out more thoroughly than might be advisable for a girl not yet sixteen. She and the horse were angled away from the photographer, looking to his left. My mother held an archery bow with an arrow nocked to the drawn bowstring, ready to let fly at a target out of the frame. I had never seen the photo before it showed up among my grandfather's belongings. Neither he nor my mother would say much about it except that it had been taken at a hotel in Virginia Beach during the period of her life when she was remanded to the custody of Uncle Ray. My mother's hair was unkempt, and the look in her eyes, taking aim, struck me as murderous.

4. A model "moon garden," constructed from the lid of a to-go coffee cup, pieces salvaged from commercial model airplane and tank kits, a dozen small capacitors and four links of a metal wristwatch band, glued together and spray-painted Tamiya "Light Ghost Grey." It belonged to LAV One, my grandfather's scale-model lunar outpost, which he had spent the years since my grandmother's death building and reconfiguring. With its tunnels, pods, aerials, dishes, and domes, the LAV One model on its craggy scale-model lunar surface covered most of

the dining room table in his condo back in Florida. "He only wanted the Moon garden," my mother told me. "I had to kind of tweeze it out from the rest of it."

5. A publicity photograph, in a Lucite box frame, of the last crew of the space shuttle *Challenger*. In this photograph astronauts Michael J. Smith, Dick Scobee, and Ronald McNair sat at a table with their helmets in front of them like fishbowls from which they planned to draw lucky numbers. Behind them stood Ellison Onizuka, Christa McAuliffe, Gregory Jarvis, and Judith Resnik, cradling their helmets in their hands. The crew's flight suits, like the shiny cloth that covered the table, were a variation on the blue of the Florida sky in which they would soon be lost. Their seven smiles mocked them, at least to my eye. At one end of the blue table, like a human skull in a still life, stood a scale model of *Challenger* strapped to its fuel tank and booster rockets. In the photograph, the model shuttle looked like a child's toy, albeit a splendid one. It was hard to see the fine detail that my grandfather had put into this particular commission, how the cargo bay doors opened to reveal the remote manipulator arm, how the engine nozzles could be made to pivot. You could pull open the nose of the fuselage and look into the crew cabin, rendered in faithful detail down to the buttons and switches of the instrument panels and the "Sally Ride curtain" over the toilet.

Even if his scale model had not been selected by NASA for inclusion in the official mission portrait, my grandfather likely would have planned to attend the launch on January 28, 1986. He was a habitué of Cape Canaveral who drove up for almost every shuttle firing, as if trying to make up for his boycott—painful to him to have to maintain, I knew—of every Apollo mission. But that Tuesday corresponded to the eleventh *yahrzeit* of my grandmother's death.

At 11:39 A.M., when an O-ring failed and the shuttle began to break apart, my grandfather was at her grave in Jenkintown, Pennsylvania. He didn't learn of the disaster until he got back to his motor lodge in Center City and turned on the television.

He sat without moving, without blinking or breathing, as a flower of fire bloomed on a stem of vapor. In that and subsequent replays he watched fragments of the disintegrated spacecraft snake across the sky, wandering, doubling back, as if blindly searching for one another in the blue.

As soon as I heard the news—I was then in graduate school at UC Irvine—I tracked him down through my mother. I had expected that when I reached him, my grandfather might sound low, even mournful, but I ought to have known better.

"Too goddamn cold!" he said. "Thirty-six degrees at launch. Idiot bureaucrats."

"Why didn't they scrub it?"

"Because they're pencil pushers. Judy knew better than to launch in weather like that."

The astronaut Judith Resnik was a particular favorite of my grandfather's. She was a brilliant engineer who had, on a prior mission, become the first Jewess in space. Her tangle of wild black curls had enacted medusa feats in zero gravity.

"Poor Judy," my grandfather said. I could hear the voice of a television reporter in the background, shouting to be heard over the wind gusting along a stretch of Florida beach.

"I'm sorry I couldn't be with you," I said. "How was it?"

"How was the cemetery?"

"Dumb question."

"It was very festive."

"I'm sorry."

"Frankly? The grave looked untidy. I was shocked."

The wind whipped up along the beach on the motel TV.

"Grandpa? You there?"

"Yeah."

"You okay?"

"No."

"I know you miss her. I wish she were still here."

"I'm glad she isn't. If she saw what a mess her grave is, she'd be furious and she'd blame me. Because I insisted on that cemetery."

"Oh."

"Everyone else is already buried there, it was already paid for a long time ago."

I knew my grandfather didn't mean that he was glad my grandmother had died. I knew how much he missed her. I didn't know, because he had not yet told me, that inside the crew cabin of his *Challenger* model, one of the webbed panels enclosing the sleep niches could be lifted on a hinge to reveal two miniature human figures. They had been the original occupants of LAV One's moon garden before my grandfather enlarged the scope of that structure's function. A man and a woman, five eighths of an inch tall, lay together in a sleep niche, naked in each other's arms.* The male figure spread his body like a shield across the female; the female figure's long hair was painted a vivid shade of auburn.

My grandfather never revealed the intention behind this "Easter egg"—not to me, at least. It may have been a gag or, never one to let an empty grave or a $3.99 model kit go to waste, my grandfather may simply have been economizing. When I look at the *Challenger* mission photograph now, I don't see the seven smilers, pretty Judy Resnick, or even, really, the model itself. I see the hidden lovers, fates entangled like their bodies, waiting for release from the gravity that held them down all their lives.

◗   ◗   ◗

---

* Picnickers (minus blanket and transistor radio) lifted from a British OO-Gauge model-railroad kit called "Afternoon in the Park."

She touched his leg, and he woke up. The world around him was his bedroom and not a jail cell. My grandmother was taking her skirt and sweater from the valet on which she had neatly hung them. "Ten minutes," she said.

My grandfather put on a blue work shirt and a pair of chinos and went downstairs to find his mud-caked work boots. My grandmother had resumed work on her interrupted coq au vin. She stood at the stove with her head inclined over a wooden spoon that brimmed with steam. He came up behind her and touched his lips to her nape. She shivered. He felt that she expected him to say something. They had spoken very little so far, and he was not sure what he meant to say or what she needed to hear. He wrestled fiercely against the urge to say nothing at all. In his powerlessness to undo what had already been done or avert what lay ahead, he resorted to the usual inanity.

"We'll be fine," he told her. "It'll all be fine."

She did not contradict him, did not assent. She took a sip from the spoon. She made a sound that committed her to nothing. "Go," she said. "She is expecting to see you."

My grandfather waited at the top of the drive to meet the school bus, ready with the Zagnut bar. The sky was promisingly blue. To occupy himself, my grandfather constructed an almanac of nights lost to the House of Detention. The moon would be at three quarters and waning. Tonight, after he had eaten his wife's good coq au vin and dried and put away the dishes, he and my mother would rejoin Oliver Twist in his interminable sufferings. My grandfather would lie beside his daughter and then his wife, in turn, until their breathing gathered into sleep. Then he would go to the top of the hill behind the house, with his telescope and a thermos of tea, and lose himself for an hour or two in contemplation of the Sea of Serenity; Algol and Deneb; Eridanus, the river of stars.

"It will all be fine," he said aloud.

When the bus pulled up, he watched my mother, fourteen and lanky, slouch her way along the aisle, down the steps. When her feet touched ground, she burst into a run. He pressed his nose against her hair and breathed in her school smell, a smell like the flavor of a postage stamp. Against her better judgment, he persuaded my mother to devour the entire candy bar before they got to the bottom of the drive, where the hickory tree fingered the sky, awaiting my grandmother's next attempt on its life.

The candy bar spoiled my mother's appetite for dinner, but in the interest of peace, not wanting to betray my grandfather, she forced herself to clean her plate.

VI

My grandfather saw my grandmother for the first time in February 1947, at Ahavas Sholom synagogue.* She had been posed beside a potted palm, in a fox stole and sunglasses, under a banner that read TRY YOUR LUCK! The fur was on loan from the president of the Sisterhood. The dark glasses had been provided free of charge by the president's husband, an ophthalmologist, to treat a case of photophobia brought on by chronic malnutrition. I assume that the text painted on the bedsheet banner, part of the decor for Congregation Ahavas Sholom's inaugural "Night in Monte Carlo," was coincidence. The pose, however, had been calculated with utmost strategy.

Without consulting her, the sisterhood had decided that even though she was a widow encumbered with a four-year-old daughter, my grandmother, transferred safely to Baltimore from a DP camp in Austria, was the leading candidate for the position of wife to the new rabbi. Hebrew Immigrant Aid Society canteens and then the kitchens of Park Circle and Forest Park had conspired to ensure that my grandmother regained her shape, her color, and what the president always referred to as "that gorgeous head of hair." My grandmother was courteous, conversant with literature and art. She had ambitions and the talent, it was said, to be an actress on the stage. Her feline

---

* In its new digs on Reisterstown Road in Pikesville. Ahavas Sholom was among the first of the major synagogues in town to make the move from the prewar heart of Jewish Baltimore around Park Circle to the suburban wilds beyond Seven Mile Lane.

face and French accent, at times impenetrable, led more than one admirer to compare her to Simone Simon. In spite of suffering and loss, she laughed often, smiled easily. She strode into rooms with actressy shoulders and the humble swagger of a girl who had come of age among hardworking nuns.

A few times, it was true, she had come out with utterances that made no sense whatsoever, in French or English. It was also true that when she was not smiling, she fell into taut silences, seemed to listen for footsteps on the other side of doors, studied shadows in the corners of rooms. When taken to a Baltimore public library for the first time, it was reported, she had made straight for the recordings of Highland reels. The first two peculiarities were put down to her being a relative newcomer to English and a girl who had endured and survived the unspeakable. (Nobody could account for the love of bagpipes.) If one sometimes sensed a weird crackle around her, a scorching like dust on a solenoid, it was believed by the Sisterhood— and seconded by many of their husbands—that this mysteriously added to her allure.

The new rabbi, freshly graduated first in his class from the Jewish Theological Seminary, had charmed everyone with his brilliance and élan, his tailored suits and his faint delicious odor, unexpected in a rabbi, of gardenias. But he displayed a troubling streak of self-will. All his life he had been the pride of his family and the joy of his teachers. As a result he had learned to prefer his own ideas to those of other people, even with regard to subjects, such as the woman he ought to marry, about which he could be expected to know very little. Overt matchmaking attempts, each to a thoroughly eligible candidate, had not turned out well. The Sisterhood caucused and agreed to authorize the use of wiles.

To ensure that the target of the operation could not fail to notice her when he put in his scheduled appearance at "Night in Monte Carlo," the Sisterhood had posed my grandmother beside the rented palm tree just by the main door of the synagogue's reception room.

Two Sisterhood members were deployed here to pin my grand-mother down. Mrs. Waxman, married to a judge, had been the chief sponsor of my grandmother's petition for refugee status. Mrs. Zell-ner, among the first Jewish graduates of Bryn Mawr, spoke excellent French. Playing on my grandmother's sense of obligation and her hunger to speak her mother tongue, the women were prepared to hold her on the spot for however long it took the rabbi to arrive, at which point they would merely put my grandmother in his way, so that afterward—a key to the strategy—he could operate under the impression that he had discovered his future bride for himself.

The rabbi was late. The reception room filled with congregants who knew nothing of the Sisterhood's maneuverings and were eager for the evening to begin. The chair of the fund-raising committee stepped to the dais. He had prepared a welcome, studded with mildly off-color puns about spades and craps, but when the microphone gave him a mild electric shock, he was obliged to break off his speech. The Sisterhood president shoved her husband toward the dais, where the hired musicians, Jews dressed as fanciful Cubans, loitered with their instruments. The ophthalmologist crouched down beside the chairman of the fund-raising committee. He took the man's pulse and helped him unbutton his collar. Other male congregants offered assistance in the form of impromptu puns on the words *shock, cur-rent, spark,* what a re*volt*ing development this was, and so forth.

The fifteen-year-old sound technician struggled to locate and swap in a new mike, a task in which he was hampered by his moth-er's constant reminders that he ought to hurry. A scrum kicked up around the table of dairy appetizers, awakening old antipathies and reinforcing new ones. Meanwhile the thong of small talk and college French that the Sisterhood tiger hunters were using to lash their goat to its stake stretched ever thinner. A second microphone was found and tested. The board president was certified fit to conclude his speech.

"Please," he enjoined all those who had come to try their luck that night, "lose as much and as often as you possibly can."

The lights were lowered. The dance band generated a supper-club ambiance. Over the cha-cha-cha, the chatter, and the rattle of dice and roulette balls, my grandmother's handlers found it impossible to maintain their grip on her. She took a package of Herbert Tareytons from her borrowed beaded clutch.

"I find it is very warm in this room," she said, still unsuspecting her status as prey but conscious of the strain on the conversational tether. "Excuse me, please. Maybe I will have a look at the beautiful moon."

All at once the moon of Mrs. Zellner's face was suffused with delight. In her relief she may have tipped her hand slightly.

"*Mais voilà le rabbin!*" she cried.

◖　　　◖　　　◖

All day my grandfather had busied himself finding reasons not to accompany Uncle Ray to "Night in Monte Carlo." He was not ready to mix with "regular people." He was uncomfortable making small talk with strangers. He lacked the funds and the appropriate attire. He had no use for synagogues. He would just get in his brother's way. Each of these reasons, with the aplomb of a born dialectician, Uncle Ray discounted, dismissed, disarmed, or batted to one side. He appreciated the challenge a return to civilian life must represent, he said, but in the end you just had to hold your breath and jump into the pool. Nobody, apart from traveling salesmen and the people who accosted you in bus terminals, was comfortable making small talk with strangers. He would happily stake my grandfather for the evening, to be repaid by the winnings or at a later date. He owned a very nice blazer, Harris tweed, that was much too big in the shoulders for him. A synagogue, when you came right down to it, was only a building; great Jews from Abraham to Hillel had never laid eyes on one. And everyone, by design and almost by definition, was in a rabbi's way.

When the time came to leave for the synagogue, the only card my grandfather still held was to make himself disagreeable. Pick a fight and hope to be uninvited.

The problem with this approach was Uncle Ray's satisfaction with himself and his opinions. Whatever position you adopted, Uncle Ray alighted on higher ground. Attacks on his person or character could have no basis in fact; the kid just laughed them off. My grandfather hit him with surliness, scorn, wet-blanket inertia. Uncle Ray floated effortlessly above it all. But in the parking lot of Ahavas Sholom, as they were about to get out of his brother's brand-new Mercury coupe—Ray already had his door open—my grandfather, in his desperation to give offense, stumbled at last on a viable approach.

In the winter of 1947, no one—least of all Uncle Ray—was conscious of the creeping unbelief that afterward began to trouble my great-uncle and ultimately led him to exchange his pulpit for the pool halls and racetracks of Baltimore, Wilmington, and Havre de Grace. My grandfather seemed to have picked up on some early vibration of the crisis to come. From childhood he had suspected Uncle Ray of faking "the whole 'boy *tzaddik*' thing," to gain the attention and approval first of their parents, then of the greater Jewish world. A sibling's ESP guided my grandfather's hand as it reached for the quiver, let fly the shaft.

"You don't see the irony?" he said. "'Night in Monte Carlo'? You don't see how disingenuous that is? The whole joint's already a fucking casino, Ray. A sideshow tent. Remember, upstairs from Pat's Steak, that crew came in and opened a betting office? Those grifters from Buffalo who fleeced Frank Osterberg? That's you. You're running a wire store. Taking bets on races you're never going to have to pay off because you already know the result. The marks come in, you take their money. Promise them what, forgiveness, eternity, a line item in God's account book? Then you just sit back and wait for the blow-off. Give them a few last words of mumbo-jumbo, plant their chump bodies in the ground."

It was a long speech for my grandfather, who felt his argument take on more weight and conviction as it carried him along. Uncle Ray eased shut the driver's-side door with an angry punctilio. He twisted around in his seat to face my grandfather. His elbow mashed the Mercury's horn. His freckles vanished into the overall redness of his face. "How dare you?" he promisingly began.

With that opening horn blast and an encouraging flicker of guilt in his eyes, Uncle Ray mounted to the saddle of his high horse. He cited the humble piety of their long-suffering parents and grandparents, the good deeds and intentions of his congregants, the faithfulness and martyrdom of Jews the world over, the integrity of the rabbinate, the accomplishments of five thousand years. From there he moved on to Maimonides, Hank Greenberg, Moses, Adonai. Evidently pleased with the effect it made, he pounded the horn a couple more times for emphasis. At one point he grew so heated that his saliva flecked the lapel of the Harris tweed jacket my grandfather had borrowed. But then, having instanced the Lord God of Hosts, Uncle Ray paused. He narrowed his eyes. My grandfather, he realized, had offered no resistance or counterarguments. He just sat there with spiderlike patience, letting Uncle Ray rage.

"You almost had me." Uncle Ray grew calm, his tone measured. "You are coming in there with me," he said, "and you are going to be glad that you did. And do you know how I know you're coming in there with me?"

"How?"

"Because that is the Holy One's plan for you."

"Oh, really, God has a plan for me? About goddamn time."

Home a month, my grandfather was out of work, depressed, and scuffling. His college degree had been gathering dust for six years. His experience in Europe qualified him for nothing that was legal in peacetime. His Philadelphia homecoming had seemed to disappoint all participants, in particular his parents, whose keenest disappointment lay in discovering that, despite the captain's bars and the decorations for actions he could not discuss, they were still disappointed in him.

"Everything that has happened to you in your life before now," Uncle Ray said, "was part of the plan. And tonight it's all going to come together and make sense."

"You know this."

"I do."

"God slips you the inside dope."

Uncle Ray ran his hand along the tuck-and-roll upholstery under his thigh, his smooth chin adorned with the minute smirk of a man with a fix in.

"Christ, you are so full of it, Ray!"

"Yeah? So let's make a bet," Uncle Ray said. Only moments after his pious outburst, along the very lines my grandfather had employed to needle him, my great-uncle pointed unwittingly toward the exit door through which he and the custom Brunswick pool stick would afterward pass. "Five hundred dollars says you walk into that shul, in the first half hour—no, in the first ten minutes—the Holy One's plan for you will be revealed. The reason you needed to show up tonight."

"What horseshit," my grandfather said. "Brother, you are on."

His discharge pay had been snarled in red tape, and he didn't have anything close to five hundred dollars, but he figured you had to like his odds.

◑   ◑   ◑

My grandmother turned toward the doors of the reception room, curious to see the new-crowned princeling of Jewish Baltimore.

She caught a glimpse of a slender young man in a navy blazer with buttons like gold coins. Under a velvet yarmulke, also navy blue, he wore his ginger hair half an inch too long. Entering the room, he was mobbed by a group of men (among them Judge Waxman) who teased and fussed over him like uncles ushering a virgin nephew into a brothel. The rabbi was soon lost from view. Mrs. Waxman coughed up a Yiddish imprecation or description of what lay in store for her husband when they got home.

"I don't know," my grandmother heard the rabbi say. He was making a show of reluctance, letting the men pull him by the wrists into the room. "Gentlemen, I have my doubts."

As he was swept, redolent of gardenia, past my grandmother, she heard him apologizing for his tardiness. "It wasn't my fault," he said. "Blame my date."

"The brother," Mrs. Zellner said. She sounded doubtful of the identification, as if the visible facts did not conform with what she had been told. "A decorated war hero."

My grandmother saw my grandfather lingering in the hallway outside the reception room, looking as if he harbored doubts far graver than his brother's. He kept his hands straightjacketed so fiercely in his pockets that they had begun to pull open the fly of his trousers. His knit necktie was ill-knotted, and his brown tweed blazer, worn over a chambray shirt that needed ironing, was too tight at the shoulders. Everything—the music, the lights, the rattle of wheels and dice, the outbursts of joy or disgust from the tables, his clothes, his skin—seemed to fit the man too tightly. Only his eyes had found a way to escape. They leaped to my grandmother from the hollows of his face as though from the windows of a burning house.

"He could stand a little more decoration," said Mrs. Waxman.

◑   ◑   ◑

For all the resistance he had put up to attending that evening's event, my grandfather had given no thought to what it would be like when he got there. It was worse than he could have imagined. "Night in Monte Carlo"! A sequined half-moon, swags of ten-watt stars, paper carnations and potted palms, all carted in to cloak machinery that had been rigged to grind everyone down to zero sooner or later: To my grandfather, postwar, it seemed a ham-fisted synopsis of the world as he had come to understand it.

He sidled a little way into the room, hands stuffed into the pockets of his workman's pants, feeling fit for nothing. He lowered his head to avert his eyes from the gaudiness and blare, the unseemliness of his unscathed homeland and countrymen, the unseemliness of Baltimore and its thirty thousand well-fed Jews.

The girl in the black dress walked right up to him. He had not spoken to a desirable woman who was not at some level his enemy or a whore since 1944.

"I was not ready for her," he told me. "I was totally unprepared."

She was wearing sunglasses indoors, at night. Around her shoulders the remains of what had been a fox sank its teeth into itself. She came confidently but hedging a little, head cocked to one side, as if only eighty-five percent certain they had met before and prepared to acknowledge her mistake. Between the fox stole and the bateau neck of the cocktail dress (on loan from the board president's daughter) blazed an inch of bare white collarbone.

My grandfather heard Mrs. Waxman and Mrs. Zellner disconsolately calling after my grandmother as she bridged the final twenty feet of linoleum mock-parquetry that separated him from her. He registered the tick-tock oscillation of her hips, the amplitude of the curves divulged by the cut of the taffeta dress. During the war he had come to depend on his pool hustler's gift for taking rapid readings of other people's eyes, and her sunglasses unnerved him. They struck him as unlikely. He wondered if she was in costume, starring

later in a skit or pageant on the theme of "Night in Monte Carlo."
He surprised himself by smiling, which unnerved him further. The
girl's lips were painted red as Bicycle hearts and diamonds, and they
parted to reveal an Ingrid Bergman smile to go with the sunglasses.*
My grandfather heard a sound inside his head that he compared,
years later, to the freight-train rumble of an earthquake. He felt he
was standing in the path of something fast-moving and gigantic
that, in its blindness, was bound to carry him away. *Swept off his feet,*
he thought. *This is that.* At the last moment he managed to return
his gaze to his shoe tops and shook his head.

"Unbelievable," he said, aware that he was still smiling, and that
he owed his brother five hundred bucks.

○   ○   ○

Where the carport roof overhung the patio my mother had set out a
birdfeeder, a Lucite tube with an aluminum peg for a perch, packed
with birdseed, dangling on a chain. My grandfather liked to keep
an eye on the traffic through his window. He took particular interest in a squirrel he called "the momzer," which came every day
to raid the feeder. The momzer lacked grace, finesse, the power of
flight. Once it had scattered the sparrows, it would approach the
business end of the birdfeeder with a fierceness and a purpose
whose futility amused my grandfather. The momzer was subject
to gravity and the physics of a pendulum in ways a bird could not
understand. It would begin with bold resolve, clambering down the
chain from the overhang, hurling itself from a nearby trellis. But

---

* Her teeth had been painstakingly reconstructed with the compliments of a Liberty Heights dentist who afterward retired to Florida, where he turned up at a
reading I gave one night, at Books & Books in Coral Gables, to tell me that he
never entirely recovered from the shock of the ruin he found inside my grandmother's mouth.

within seconds it would find itself clinging by its forepaws to the metal peg, or to the bottom of the tube, its tail madly switching, while the birdfeeder bucked and gyrated and worked to shake the momzer loose. As though he had yet to exorcise the demon that, decades ago, had urged him to drop a kitten out of a third-story window, my grandfather burst into laughter every time the squirrel fell, with a meaty thud, onto the flagstones of the patio. Sometimes he laughed so hard that I would have to take a Kleenex and wipe tears from his eyes.

"All those ladies in the Sisterhood, putting out their birdseed to catch a little chickadee," my grandfather said. "But they caught a momzer instead."

○   ○   ○

According to my grandfather, my grandmother's first words to her future husband were: "Your head would look good on a fence."

She had approached him with an unlit cigarette scissored between her index and middle fingers, one eyebrow, just visible over the rim of her sunglasses, arched in entreaty. My grandfather got the immediate sense, from the dumbshow and from something else—a lack of gaucherie in her girlishness—that she might be a foreigner. He lit her cigarette with Aughenbaugh's lighter.

"Come again?" my grandfather said, the lighter's flame stopped just short of the tip of his own cigarette. He replayed the remark in his mind. He decided he had heard her correctly, that she had indeed told him his head would look good on a fence. "How so?"

My grandfather had seen human heads discarded or reposed in unusual places, though never, it was true, on a fence. Nevertheless, he felt this was a conversational gambit he would not have thought to attempt. Because he could not see my grandmother's eyes, he could not come to any solid conclusions about the spirit in which her observation had been offered. Only much later did he realize that in her weird way she had dispatched, with one stroke, the problem of making small talk with strangers.

"Oh, dear, I made a fault," she said. "I see you take offense."

"It's my natural expression," my grandfather said. "You'd look like this, too, if somebody stuck your head on a fence."

"*Wall*." The word burst forth from her, followed by a startling heehaw of laughter. She clapped a hand over her mouth. "I am so sorry. I mean to say wall, not fence."

"That changes everything," my grandfather said. His approach to the art of flirtation with women was founded on an impeccable poker face.

"Wait," she said, trying to hold back another of her braying laughs. "Have you ever seen a, how do you say, ca*thee*dral?"

With three sweeps of her white arms, she drew the walls, towers, and spires of a cathedral. She sketched with an efficiency of gesture that came as close as anything he remembered having seen to what poets and sportswriters liked to call grace. As her hands soared and dived, the coal of her cigarette shed glowing threads of tobacco. The orange sparks were reflected in the lenses of her cheaters. She finished by miming a rose window, encircling her fingers over her chest, a zone to which my grandfather's attention had already been drawn. Brassieres of the era were architectural affairs; in her bust, with its loft and scale and defiance of gravity, there was something cathedral-like that moved him. Then he saw that in gun-colored ink on the inside of her left arm, she bore the recent history, in five digits, of her life, her family, and the world. He read its brief account and felt ashamed.

"Yeah," he said. "I've seen some cathedrals."

"On the walls," she said. "The ancient walls." She pronounced it *hancient*. "You see faces in the stone. That is the kind of the face you have."

"Got it," he said. "I look like a gargoyle."

"Yes! No! Not a . . ." and she came out with the French word for *gargoyle,* which my grandfather after forty-two years could no longer retrieve. "Those are to catch the rain, and they are animals, monsters, they are ugly. That is not the kind of the face you have."

That was at least partly a lie. To one of her psychiatrists, she later confessed that she did think he was ugly, albeit in a way she found appealing, even arousing. When she first saw him, standing at the threshold of the reception room, contemplating departure before he had even arrived, she thought he had an American face, an American body. Buick shoulders, bulldozer jaw. Only if you considered his eyes would you be forced to conclude, and she did conclude, that he was beautiful.

"I am the one who look like the gargoyle," she said.

"Hardly."

"Yes," she said. "On the inside."

He let that one pass without comment, taking it for prattle, compliment-fishing; his first misjudgment, his first encounter with the voice of the Skinless Horse, speaking through her.

"Can I ask you to do something?" he said. "Would you by any chance be willing to take off those glasses?"

She stood very still, red lips pressed together. He wondered if he had made some kind of gaffe, if asking a Frenchwoman to remove her sunglasses violated a well-known Gallic taboo.

"The eye doctor said I am not supposed to," she said. Her voice faltered. "But I will." This came out barely louder than a whisper.

"It's all right," he said. "Never mind. You can just tell me what color your eyes are. That's all I really wanted to know."

"No," she said. "I will take them off for you. But also you have to do something for me. Let me to do something, I mean to say."

"Yeah? And what's that?"

I don't know how many people could have seen my grandparents, standing there in the hallway outside the doors of the reception room, whether anyone was paying any attention. But even if they had been standing in an empty room, I imagine that neither my grandfather nor the mores of 1947 can have expected my grandmother to do what she did next. Looking back at that night from inside the soft gray nimbus of Dilaudid, my grandfather could only close his eyes, the way he closed them that night, as she reached out to the fly of his trousers and, tooth by tooth, zipped him up.

"*C'est fait,*" she said.

When he opened his eyes, he found himself lost for the first time in hers. They were the color of twilight in Monte Carlo, when the stars come out to twinkle like ten-watt bulbs, and the quarter-moon fans her hem of sequins against the sky.

"Blue," my grandfather said, falling back against the pillow of the rented hospital bed in my mother's guest room. After that it was a long time, hours, before he opened his eyes again.

VII

Just before midnight of September 29, 1989, my grandfather completed the model of LAV One. It represented the latest thinking on lunar settlement design (the reason it had needed so many revisions), fourteen years' work, and about twenty-two thousand individual polystyrene pieces cannibalized from commercial model kits.* At the center of the model, amid the half-buried tunnels, bays, domes, huts, landing strips, and radar arrays, there was a hole about four inches in diameter. Looking down into this hole, you could see through to the plywood substructure of the model's molded lunar surface. If you asked my grandfather the purpose of the hole, he would always give you some variation on *You'll just have to wait and find out*; to be honest, there was not a lot of variation. After a while—no doubt according to his plan—I stopped asking.

He went to his workbench and took down a gaudy Romeo y Julieta cigar box. He removed a bundle of tissue paper from the box and unwrapped a circular structure fashioned from a take-out coffee-cup lid. He had initially completed the moon garden in May 1975, pillaging tiny N- and British OO-scale model train kits to fill it with flowering shrubs, rosebushes, and vegetables grown in hydroponic racks. With a careful thumbnail he lifted the lid's sipping flap, which he had reconfigured as an access hatch. He peered in to check on the family who had replaced the original lovers as occupants of the moon garden. On a sling bench and two sling chairs of his own

---

* Primarily military and automotive, purchased on sale or at a bulk discount.

design, enjoying moist and oxygenated air, sat figures representing my grandfather and grandmother, my mother, and my brother and me. The figures were posed stiffly (even for polystyrene people), as if for a formal photograph. Everyone safe and sound.

My grandfather lowered the flap. He carried the moon garden to the model of LAV One and fitted it into the hole that awaited it. He was not aware of any great sense of accomplishment. It was a job he had left undone for too long, a promise too long unkept, and what he felt most was relief.

Six months later he would be dead.

The next morning, well before dawn, my grandfather went out into the dense Florida darkness to load the trunk of his Buick LeSabre for a trip to Cape Canaveral. There had been no launches since the *Challenger* disaster nearly four years earlier. Now another shuttle, *Discovery*, was scheduled to lift off that morning at ten. He had filled a bait cooler with a freezer pack, a bottle of Michelob, a plastic food container of cut-up pineapple, and two meat salad sandwiches. Meat salad was a specialty of my grandfather's. You passed a piece of leftover roast through a meat grinder with some dill pickles, a couple tablespoons of mayonnaise, salt and pepper. Like many of my grandfather's specialties, meat salad tasted better than it looked or sounded, served on a nice challah roll. He put the cooler into the trunk with a pair of binoculars, a secondhand Leica with a brand-new telephoto lens, the latest issue of *Commentary*, a transistor radio, a gallon of tap water, and a reclining folding chair, complete with a footrest and a sun umbrella you could attach to the chair's frame. He had made the sun umbrella himself, surgically replacing the handle of a rain umbrella with a C-clamp.

Like any habitation of the elderly, Fontana Village was rich in insomniacs and early birds, but for the moment my grandfather had the morning to himself. Before closing the trunk of his car, he leaned against the rear bumper and listened to the silence. It was not perfect. It was never perfect. But he had come to appreciate how small or distant sounds could intensify it, the way a drop of blue paint intensified whiteness. The tick-tick of an insect or possibly a frog. A big rig downshifting out on I-95. Mist effervescing in the beams of the security lighting. Underlying everything, the low-pitched tinnitus that was the sound of Fontana Village itself, a compound hum of air conditioners, vending machines, circuit breakers, swimming-pool filtration systems, poorly insulated wire. A woman's voice, far away, calling out, "Ramon!"

My grandfather straightened up. He angled his head, his ear a dish attuned to the cosmic background radiation. He shuffled the short deck of Ramons he had encountered in his life. None of them lived in Fontana Village. There were some Cubans living at Fontana Village, and they sometimes had first names like Adolfo and Raquel, but they were Jews like everybody else, Goldmans and Levys come to the promised land of South Florida along a different branch of the river of exile. He did not know any of the Cuban Jews well. One of them might well be Ramon. Ramon Lifschitz. Ramon Weinblatt. From time to time some poor bastard with dementia went walkabout, and you would see his wife or the home care nurse running after him, shouting his name.

"Ramon! Hee-er, kittykittykitty."

The voice seemed to be coming from the direction of the Jungle, as the residents of Fontana Village called the wasteland that bordered the retirement village to the north and east. In the Jungle, nuisance plants and Bermuda grass gone feral had been at war with native stranglers since the late seventies, contending for ownership over five hundred acres that was briefly a golf course and country club. Somewhere in that tangle a devourer of pets, widely believed to be an alligator, plied its leisurely trade.

"Ramo-ohn!"

On the second syllable the woman's voice broke like a bar mitzvah boy's. There had been amusement in her frustration before, but that was gone now.

My grandfather looked at his watch, which he wore with the face on the inside of his wrist. It was already past five-thirty, and the trip north would take about three and a half hours, four if he stopped for gas and a toilet break. The return to service of the shuttle fleet had attracted considerable interest in the media, and traffic might be heavy. He really could not afford delay.

"God damn you, lady," my grandfather said.

He opened the well that held his tire-repair kit and took out the socket wrench without thinking about it or knowing why. He slammed shut the lid of the trunk. It thudded like a kettledrum in the humid air.

He crossed the parking lot, nervously gripping and renewing his grip on the shaft of the tire wrench, to a walkway lit at intervals. If you went right, the walkway led past the swimming pool that served this end of the complex. To the left, it wandered around the back of the cluster that included his own two-bedroom unit to a service area with a charging station for the carts that village residents used to get around. Past the service area, you came to a fairly wide strip of lawn backed by a running wooden rail about a foot high. After that, things became primeval.

My grandfather's leather sandals, imitation Birkenstocks of Israeli manufacture, slapped against the pavement. It was an angry sound. He was annoyed with Ramon, whom he pictured lean and cross-eyed, skulking into the Jungle to meet his death, just for a taste of rat or nutria. He was annoyed with Ramon's owner for coming out to look for Ramon when it was still pitch-dark and there was, at any rate, nothing to be done. There was nothing to be done, and yet off he went to try and do it; my grandfather was annoyed, most of all, with himself. The louder his sandals slapped against the pavement, the angrier he became. He found himself hoping that when he reached the edge of the Jungle, he really did encounter the alligator so that he could beat it to death with the socket wrench. That was the purpose, he now understood, for which he had taken the tool out of his trunk.

He crossed the northernmost of the lawns serviced by the groundskeepers of Fontana Village. The soles of his sandals kicked up pinpricks of dew that stung his shins. He was wearing khaki shorts, one of seven identical pairs he had purchased at Kmart, to go with the seven polo shirts and seven pairs of white tube socks, which he always wore with sandals, that constituted his daily uniform after my grandmother died. If it was somebody's birthday or some function he could not avoid, he would put on a Hawaiian shirt, decorated with bare-breasted hula girls, that I had given him as a joke. The shirt had scandalized some of his fellow villagers, but my grandfather had no regard for anyone who could be scandalized by a shirt.

Out here past the service area, it was too dark to see. My grandfather took out Aughenbaugh's Zippo and struck a light. Tiny beads of moisture in the air trapped the light before it could travel very far. Light enveloped his hand like a ball of St. Elmo's fire.

"Hello?" said the woman. "Who's that?"

"Your neighbor," my grandfather said.

The lighter grew hot against his skin and he snapped it shut. Retinal fire swam across the darkness. Then his eyes adjusted, and he found that he could see. Dawn was an abrupt business in Florida; in another ten minutes or so it would be morning.

"Mrs. Winocur claims to have seen it. She calls it Alastair," said the woman. My grandfather heard her introduce herself as Sally Seashell; later the last name turned out to be Sichel. "But do you think it's really out there?"

"Something's there," my grandfather said, never one to give false comfort. He thought Phyllis Winocur was full of shit, but he doubted that the cats and lapdogs of Fontana Village were vanishing voluntarily into the swamp in a bid for freedom, banding together out there like four-legged Seminoles. "How'd he get out?"

"My fault," she said, "I was dumb. I took pity on him. Back home he used to range so freely. He and I haven't been here long."

"Where's home?"

"Philly."

It crossed my grandfather's mind to observe that Philly could be tough on cats, too, but then he would have to explain. It had been a long time since he had attempted to explain himself to a woman. It felt like an insurmountable task.

"What part?" he said.

"Bryn Mawr."

"Bryn Mawr ain't Philly."

"Aha," she said. "Yes, I can hear it in your voice."

As it grew lighter, my grandfather came to see that Sally Sichel was a good-looking woman, tall, slender, but full-breasted. Dark complexion, long nose with a bump, a touch of Katharine Hepburn in the cheekbones. Maybe a couple of years younger than he was, maybe not. She wore a pair of men's pajamas, the kind that buttoned up the front, and duck boots coated in rubber the color of a New York taxi. She had not troubled to lace them up very well.

"Does he usually come when you call him?"

"Always."

"How long has he been gone?"

"All night."

"Hmm."

"I probably shouldn't say this," Sally Sichel said. "We just met. But that piece-of-shit cat is more or less my only reason for living."

My grandfather fought against an overwhelming impulse to say something along the lines of *In that case, maybe you ought not to have let him out of your house to be eaten by a half-ton reptile* or *For Christ's sake, lady, it's just a motherfucking cat.* He revised downward the favorable impression he had begun to form of her, an impression shot through with a surprising vein of lust; it had been a very long time. Anyway, you had to have reservations about somebody who walked around with her shoes untied.

"I know what you're thinking," she said. "He was only a cat."

"Not at all."

"It's just, I lost my husband very recently. And Ramon was really his cat."

"I see."

"They were very close."

"I understand," my grandfather said. "I lost my wife."

"Recently?"

"Fourteen years."

"Oh. Well, I'm sorry."

Sally Sichel started to cry. Standing there in her pajamas, arms crossed under her commendable breasts. Looking out at the Jungle that had taken her husband's cat, the architecture of her cheeks glazed with tears. Her nose began to run. My grandfather took a chamois, which he used to wipe his camera lenses, out of the back pocket of his shorts and passed it to her.

"Oh," she said, blowing her nose into the chamois. He remembered—as much in his loins as in his head or heart—the circus girl who had spread her legs for him in the cottage at Greenwich Yard, Creasey's bloody chamois clutched in her hand. "What a gentleman. Thank you."

He knew that it would also be gentlemanly to put a consolatory arm around Sally Sichel's shoulder. Not just gentlemanly; it would be humane. But he was afraid of what might happen down the line. A widow and a widower, easing each other's passage from grief to passion in the autumn of their lives: The very triteness of it seemed to ensure its likelihood.

From the time he'd moved to Florida in the mid-Seventies, the available women of Fontana Village had been giving my grandfather their best shot. While he turned out the beautiful and high-priced scale models that NASA and private collectors had commissioned, and explored the labyrinth of LAV One as it grew in intricacy and size on the dining room table, the available women of Fontana Village came to make their case. They sent scouts and embassies, plates of cookies and brownies and blondies, pots of soup, potato latkes at Hanukkah, cards, knit goods, pies, poems, oil paintings, cuts of meat, bottles of wine, and a dish of macaroni and cheese. I happened to be visiting when the macaroni and cheese showed up, and I thought it made a pretty strong case for its author, who had followed a recipe adapted from Horn & Hardart's.

As he'd been licking his fork, awash in memories of the Broad Street Automat, I'd thought my grandfather had looked more contented than I'd seen him in a long time. When the dish was empty, however, he had washed it out and dried it, dropped in a thank-you note scrawled on a scrap of legal paper, and left it on the woman's back patio at a moment when he knew she would be out. On a few occasions he had been cornered by some available and exceptionally persistent woman of Fontana Village, and just to get a little peace he had accepted her dinner invitation. More intimate invitations, some tempting, some issued with a frankness he could not help but admire, he had declined.

It was not that he wanted to be celibate. He got ideas. He missed the contact, the skin-on-skin warmth of it. The property manager of Fontana Village, Karen Radwin, had a way of touching your arm or your shoulder when she spoke to you, sometimes he would feel a jolt of current. And yet apart from one night in Cocoa Beach, Florida, in April 1975, my grandfather had kept his hands to himself since my grandmother's death.

You could say this or you could say that about the why or why not of it, but in the end it came down to this: He didn't feel like talking. He didn't feel like explaining himself. My grandmother used to complain sometimes about his silences, but only when there were other people around, when people started in with the banter and the repartee and the opinions on Agnew or Sondheim, as if she were embarrassed for his sake because his silence might be taken for disapproval or thickheadedness. *Don't worry about him*, she would say, *that's how he is—every time we start an argument I end up with a monologue.* Or *Some husbands take lovers, mine he take the Fifth.* Then she might put a hand on his knee and insist, reassuring herself maybe as much as whomever they were with at the time, *But he is listening.* After they had been married fifteen years—around the time I came into the picture—there was nothing he could tell her that she didn't already know. That was all he wanted: to be known.

He did not put his arm around Sally Sichel. He kept it where it belonged, by his side. Just to make sure, he transferred the socket wrench over to that hand as ballast.

Sally Sichel went to the low rail, put her hands to her mouth, and screamed, "RAMOOOOOOOON!" A yellow bird hiding in the brush nearby startled and took wing. She held the ragged note of the O. Lights came on in the units that overlooked the Jungle; calls were placed to the security office. My grandfather had not heard a woman scream that way—*holler* might be a more accurate characterization— for a very long time. Sally Sichel hollered for Ramon in precisely the way that a peeved older sister would holler from a stoop on Shunk Street when sent out to call her jackass brother home for supper. After the echo died away, Sally Sichel lowered her hands, stepped back from the wooden rail, and turned to my grandfather. She looked a little sheepish, but not very. With the coming of daylight, he could see the marks of care on her face, the shadows under her eyes, a taut- ness around her mouth as if she had bitten in to something mealy. A fine-looking woman, all the same.

She folded the chamois in half, smoothed it against the swell of her hip, folded and smoothed it again. She handed it back to my grandfather, and he returned it to the back pocket of his khaki shorts.

"Fucking alligator," she said. "He should choke on Ramon."

For that, Sally Sichel got a checkmark.

"Let me look into it," he said.

Sally Sichel stepped back and gave my grandfather a careful once- over. The opinion she had formed of *him* now appeared to be in need of emendation. Doubtless she had noted the baggy shorts, the san- dals worn over socks, the coral-pink polo shirt appliquéd, as if out of sensitivity to the fate of Ramon, with a leaping fox (or possibly a wolfhound) in place of the usual crocodile. He looked like the retired director of a Zionist summer camp. Now she considered his hair, silver turning to white, straighter and finer than in younger days but still a good head of it. She noted his suntanned, sinewy arms, his broad chest, the shoulders that over the years had borne up under the weight of pianos and other burdens. For some reason—she had not noticed until now—he was carrying a big iron wrench, his fingers flexing restlessly along its shaft as if he were itching to use it.

"Let you 'look into it'?" She laughed. It might have been a bitter or even a mocking laugh. Or maybe he had just cracked her up. My grandfather had spent his life saying things in earnest that struck people, women in particular, as funny. "What does that mean?"

My grandfather supposed it was a strange thing to have said. A more honest formulation would have been that he intended to see what could be done in the area of kicking an alligator's ass. But that also would have been a strange thing to say. At best it would have sounded like swagger, at worst like psychopathy. If he failed to kick the alligator's ass, it would be an idle boast. That was the problem, finally, with saying things, in particular things that were true. Yesterday his doctor had shown him a couple of numbers on a blood panel that looked "a little off," and said it might be nothing serious or it might be very bad. He wanted my grandfather to see a specialist. He had written down a name and a number on a card. The card was stashed inside the *Commentary*, keeping company with an unflattering caricature of Hosni Mubarak.

My grandfather was seventy-three. Over the course of his life, the definition and requirements of manhood had been subject to upheaval and reform. Like the electoral laws of his adopted home state, the end result was a mess. A patchwork of expedients, conflicting principles, innovations nobody understood, holdovers that ought to have been taken off the books years ago. Yet in the midst of modern confusion, fundamental kernels of certainty remained: Representative democracy was still the best way to govern a large group of human beings. And when some lady's dead husband's cat got eaten by an alligator, a man looked into the matter. Even an old man who wore socks with his sandals and needed to see a specialist because something was off in the numbers that told the story of his blood. A man would see what there was to be done.

"I could research what the proper procedure is with alligators," my grandfather said. After all, alligators were dealt with every day in a variety of ways. They could be trapped, snared, hit with tranquilizing darts. They could be shot, butchered, skinned, and turned into steak and boots. "I mean, if you like. I realize it won't be any help to Ramon."

Sally Sichel started to laugh, but this time she caught that my grandfather wasn't joking, and her mouth snapped shut. Her cheeks turned bright red, but it was not out of embarrassment, because she looked him straight in the eye. "Why not?" she said.

There was the whirr of an electric cart. My grandfather looked toward the service area. It was Devaughn, the night guard, coming to find out who had been making all that noise. Devaughn was almost as old as the people he was paid to protect. He had been born and raised in the part of Florida that was really Georgia and Alabama. No one was sure if he was white or black—it could have gone either way—and those residents of Fontana Village who were deputized or inspired to ask found that in his presence, their nerve failed them or the relevance of the question dwindled away. He had been taught as a boy to regard the occasional Jewish salesman who passed through his native swamp as belonging to a race of lesser demons, horned and dealing in wonders. His manner toward the residents of Fontana Village was suitably tinged with wariness.

Devaughn listened to the story of Ramon and the alligator, and it was not long before he started shaking his head. At first my grandfather took Devaughn's head-shaking for an expression of regret, commiseration, or disgust. But it turned out that Devaughn felt there was schooling that needed to be done.

"That is not no alligator," he said. "Been telling Ms. Radwin almost two years now. I have seen its bowel movements. I know how a alligator bowel movement supposed to look. And I know how a snake bowel movement supposed to look."

"A snake," Sally Sichel said. "A snake that can eat a cat or a dog? Does Florida have snakes like that?"

"It's probably somebody's pet boa constrictor that escaped," my grandfather said. Once when I visited him, we had watched a program on channel 12 (the only channel my grandfather watched) about the problem of invasive animal species in the state of Florida. Boas, mynahs, feral pigs, rare aquarium fish had escaped captivity or been deliberately released into the wild, where generally they had done well for themselves. The program had been an hour long, but my grandfather waited in vain for a discussion of what was to be done about the invasive species that was really the cause of the problem. "If it's a boa constrictor, it could get big enough to eat a pig or a deer."

Sally Sichel, my grandfather, and Devaughn looked at the Jungle. The idea of a giant snake that could strangle a pig or a deer and then swallow it whole slid cold and coiling through their hearts. Then Devaughn got into his cart and whirred away, back to the security desk in the Village Center. Let the day man worry about giant snakes and crazed old Jewesses wandering out into the weeds at the crack of dawn, hollering when they were supposed to be sleeping.

"Speaking of eating a pig or a deer," Sally Sichel said, "I could make you some French toast."

My grandfather looked at his watch and his heart seized. He had forgotten all about the launch. If he left now, drove fast, and didn't stop, he would probably, with a little luck, just make it in time. He had been planning for months, since the Return to Flight was first announced, to do this trip up to the Kennedy Space Center. He knew the names and ranks of all five members of *Discovery*'s crew. He could tell you the fields of their graduate and post-graduate work, their mission histories, their hobbies and foibles, their relationships and personal ties to the lost crew members of *Challenger*. He had followed the investigation into the cause of that disaster acutely, delving into its minutiae. During the visit of mine that had featured such a fine dish of macaroni and cheese, all my grandfather wanted to talk about was O-rings, ceramic-tile heat shielding, and Dr. Richard Feynman—always referred to by full name and title. In Feynman's relentless common sense, my grandfather saw rare evidence of hope for the world.

For months he had felt that it was not just the shuttle program that would be at stake when *Discovery* blasted off. It would be an entire vision of the future, shared by all the fading partisans of space flight, for whom the launch held the promise of collective redemption. Now my grandfather understood that his interest in the loss of *Challenger* and the fate of *Discovery*, his obsession with the modifications that had been made to its solid rocket booster, or to Commander Rick Hauck's vintage Corvette, amounted to nothing grander than Sally Sichel's feeling that she was living only to care for her late husband's cat. There was nothing collective about it. It was purely personal, a seal to stop his heart against a leak of sorrow. Seen in that light, the whole business struck him as much less interesting.

"I already ate," he told Sally Sichel. "I really ought to get on the road."

"That's why you were up and about. I wondered. Where are you off to?"

My grandfather checked his watch again. Almost ten to seven. The darkness of his predawn kitchen, the hum of the electric clock on the wall, the faucet dripping as he cranked out a brown dollop of meat salad, felt like a long time ago.

"Nowhere," he said. "Never mind."

"French toast? Still no French toast. All right. How about a cup of coffee?"

"I wouldn't want you to go to any trouble."

"I promise I won't," said Sally Sichel. "Anyway, I get the feeling trouble is your department."

VIII

For a while after my grandfather got out of jail, the Skinless Horse appeared content merely to stalk my grandmother. When her daughter or husband happened to be around—and my grandfather, out of work and facing trial, happened to be around a lot—she drowned its nickering in a flood of chitchat and palaver. When she found herself alone in the house, she had a record of Highland reels and marches that she played very loud, because for unknown reasons the sound of bagpipes kept the creature at bay. At all times, alone or in company, she fought to avert her face from windows that overlooked the hickory tree. When her strength failed, the Skinless Horse would be there, sitting on one of the lower branches, baring its square teeth, stroking its enormous bloodred penis.

◑   ◑   ◑

"Was it a horse, though?" I asked my grandfather on the second or third day of my visit home. "Or just a man with a horse's head?"

"I never saw it," my grandfather said dryly. "I guess it must have had hands."

"And a penis."

He stuck his tongue out at me a couple of times. He stared out his window at a skein of fog wound around the eucalyptus and arborvitae trees. "The penis looked like a raw turkey neck," he said. "Or so she said."

To a psychiatrist who treated my grandmother in the late fifties, she once attributed the physical appearance of her tormentor to a picture-book painting of Bottom and Titania that haunted her childhood dreams. Another time she described having witnessed the gelding of a draft horse in the stable of her family's tannery, and once she speculated about the weird comminglings of men and bleeding hides she had watched come and go across the tannery yard. In the pit of her worst ravings she often claimed to have been raped by a stallion or a man with a stallion's head. There was a timelessness in these ravings that made it seem as if the childhood violation were ongoing, happening still.

"She cooked up all kinds of theories," my grandfather said. "She used to read Freud and Jung." He pronounced it *Young.* "Adler. All those guys. So she could tell the doctors what she thought they wanted to hear."

My grandfather often felt frustrated or baffled by my grandmother's illness, but when it came to the origins of the Skinless Horse he thought he understood. The Skinless Horse was a creature sworn to pursue my grandmother no matter where she went on the face of the globe, whispering to her in the foulest terms of her crimes and the blackness of her soul. There was a voice like that in everyone's head, he figured; in my grandmother's case it was just a matter of degree. You could almost see the Skinless Horse as a clever adaptation, a strategy for survival evolved by a proven survivor. If you kept the voice inside your head, the way most people did, there could really be only one way to silence it. He admired the defiance, the refusal to surrender, involuntary but implicit in the act of moving that reproachful whisperer to a shadowy corner of a room, an iron furnace in a cellar, the branches of a grand old tree.

◑　　　◑　　　◑

On the eve of the preliminary hearing of charges in the Feathercombs case, my grandfather took his telescope and a thermos of tea up to the top of the hill behind the farmhouse to have a look at the full moon. In his heart, he said, he knew that the Horse was lurking. He could see the signs. There was the stream of observations, questions, and imponderables that had begun to pour out of his wife, drowning out silences almost before they could begin. Once, nearing home with the car window rolled down, he'd heard a ghostly skirl of bagpipes on the air. Another time he had caught my grandmother turning from the living room windows that looked out on the tree with a violent bloom of color in her cheeks and throat.

He had been outside with his telescope for two hours, in his fur hat and Pendleton jacket, when wood smoke reached his nostrils. At first he registered the smell without attributing or even identifying it. His right eye had full possession of his brain and was busy dazzling it. He had just pointed his telescope at Reiner Gamma, near the southern coast of the Sea of Storms.

Of all the celestial bodies available for viewing to the backyard astronomer, the Moon was the only one you could see in enough detail to imagine living there, ranging those quicksilver mountains in seven-league moon boots. Naturally, my grandfather knew the Moon was inhospitable to life. When it came to astronomy, he might have been a layman, but he had worked throughout the late forties and early fifties as an aerospace engineer, first for the Glenn L. Martin Company, then briefly at a firm of his own, Patapsco Engineering, designing inertial guidance and telemetry systems. The need for a guaranteed paycheck after my grandmother's first breakdown in 1952 had obliged him to sell his interest in Patapsco.* Since then the recession of 1953, bad luck, and—in my grandfather's view— the white-shoe, genteel anti-Semitism that pervaded the aerospace industry had forced him gradually down the economic ladder and,

---

* In 1962 the Martin Company, now Martin-Marietta and well along in its development of the Titan rocket, purchased Patapsco from my grandfather's former partner Milton Weinblatt for, according to my grandfather, "maybe two hundred times what Weinblatt paid to buy me out."

at spare moments, ever deeper into the world inside his telescope's lens. In his imagination, he built my grandmother a city on the Moon and escaped by rocket with her and my mother to settle there and live in peace.

At first it was a domed city to afford a stunning view with every earthrise of all the strife and unhappiness they had left behind. Over the years, as he read and researched, its configuration changed. To account for cosmic rays, he put buildings inside of craters and in tunnels underground. To assure reliable sunlight, he put my grandmother's moon garden in a bright spot near the North Pole. But two principles, two rules of the game, endured: On the Moon there was no capital to grind the working moonman down. And on the Moon, 230,000 miles from the stench of history, there was no madness or memory of loss. The thing that made space flight difficult was the thing that, to my grandfather, made it beautiful: To reach escape velocity, my grandmother, like any spacefarer, would be obliged to leave almost everything behind her.

A moment after he smelled smoke, he became aware of a flicker at the edge of his field of vision, light leaking in. For a few seconds he ignored it. Then, with a jolt, he connected the orange flicker to the smell of firewood. He looked up from the oculus of the telescope, blinking away the ghost on his retina of Reiner Gamma, a luminous fish.

In the yard beyond the farmhouse, the hickory tree stood rigged in sails of fire. The windows in the face of the tree fort shone with a malign glint.

My grandfather's first reaction, after disbelief, was annoyance with himself. On his return from jail, in the wake of the first fire, he had gone through the house from cellar to attic, rounding up combustibles and locking them in the toolshed. But he had relaxed his vigil, and his wife would have had ample time to replenish her stock of hair spray, lamp oil, paint thinner. (In fact, it would emerge that she had improvised, showing an ingenuity he could not help but admire, by using a kitchen spoon to fling cotton balls larded in Vaseline, like tiny gouts of Greek fire, directly into the treehouse.)

The second thing my grandfather felt was rage. The persistence of his wife's madness was an insult, an act of defiance, a repudiation of the past two years of relative peace in their marriage. From the top of his hill my grandfather shouted my grandmother's name like God summoning a prophet to a mountain of reckoning. Even five hundred feet from the roar of the flames, his voice in his own ears sounded thin and feeble. Its very feebleness increased his anger.

He strode down the hill at a vengeful clip. If he didn't find her already burned up and dead, then he intended to kill my grandmother. He held off on making the decision as to how the killing would be done until he got his hands on her and discovered which method promised the sweetest deliverance.

By the time he reached the bottom of the hill, the tree was englobed in gases, spewing a long orange jet. It looked, my grandfather said, like a comet on an old map of the heavens. Between him and the tree hung a curtain of heat that turned his cheeks red for days afterward and singed the tips of his hair. His anger dissipated as he contemplated the shimmering curtain, a heart of fire pumping its lifeblood into the sky. There was nothing for him to do but stand there and marvel.

◑   ◑   ◑

My mother remembered none of this.

"Just the next morning," she said. "The tree was this shriveled black stump. Like a burnt wick on a candle."

She had changed out of her work pantsuit into a turtleneck and jeans. She had more work to do on the class-action suit, but she was taking a break to knit a stocking cap for her father, who often complained that his head felt cold. When she was through, it would have gold and crimson stripes and a green pom-pom. It was not the kind of hat anybody would want to die in, but maybe that was the point.

Every night after work my mother came in and sat with my grandfather while I cooked dinner and got a tray ready for him with some Jell-O and a cup of lemon tea. My grandfather had expressed impatience at the constant presence by his bedside of one of us or the night nurse. He understood we were there because we were afraid he might die when no one was in the room. He had promised us that he would cling to life, in spite of pain and all cancers primary and secondary, until at last, one day, the doorbell would ring, somebody would have gone to the toilet, and we would be forced in spite of our precautions to leave him unattended. Then, and only then, would he permit himself to die.

"Your mother dosed you with Benadryl," my grandfather told her. "You slept through the whole thing. I think she used to put a pill in some pudding. She was always knocking you out, any time you couldn't sleep."

I watched the truth of this surface in my mother's eyes.

"Wow," she said. Her recollection of these years was riddled, an empty quadrant of space lit by infrequent stars. "I used to eat a *lot* of tapioca pudding."

I could tell she thought this explained why she had lost so much history from that period of her life, but I wanted to point out that amnesia, whether induced by drugs or by trauma, did not explain everything. It did not explain, for example, the constant gaps and erasures that she introduced into her accounts of the things that she did remember. My brother and I had grown up knowing that the destiny of our family was tied in some way to that of Alger Hiss. We knew that our grandfather had gone to prison, our grandmother to a state hospital. We knew that the time our mother had spent in the care of Uncle Ray had left her with a grasp of the intricacies of pari-mutuel betting, a couple of gaudy trick shots at nine-ball, and an abhorrence for racetracks, poolrooms, and their denizens. Those were all things worth knowing, I supposed, but they didn't add up to much. If her children studied her silence as she had studied their grandfather's, they could hope to learn only that silence, that old folk remedy, was at best a partial antidote to pain.

"Where was Mamie?" I asked my grandfather. "While the tree was burning down?"

My grandfather looked at my mother and out came his tongue, as if in distaste at my idiotic question. "She was watching it burn," he said.

❍   ❍   ❍

Like most wonders, the fire in the hickory tree was of short duration, and when its meal was through, it winked out like a candle snuffed. The suddenness of its departure, my grandfather said, was a measure of how thoroughly it had consumed the available fuel. One minute it was there, a comet plunged to the earth, dazzling the January darkness, its heat so intense that it stopped my grandfather in his tracks. The next minute it was gone, along with the tree fort, the tree, and the cult of gentle New Jersey ecstatics who had planted it long ago. A few flames crackled here and there along the nubs that once were branches. Then they flickered out, too, leaving smoke, a whistle of steam, and a light snowfall of ashes.

My grandfather found my grandmother sitting barefoot on the porch steps in a thin nightgown, outside the front door that was never used. Her cheeks were gray with ash, her eyelashes and eyebrows singed, her mouth expressionless.

"Never mind," he said to her and to himself. He sat down beside her on the top step of the porch. The skin of her bare shoulders was cold, but she took no notice of the chill or of the arm that he put around her. After a while he got up and called the fire department.

Then he came back and sat with her until the truck showed up, lights and sirens and seven men in boots and helmets with nothing in particular to do.

"Well, *somebody* went bananas," one of the firemen said.

As my grandfather recalled the fireman's diagnosis, so many years later, his eyes filled with tears, as if to drown the fire of his own bitter memory. He closed his eyes against them.

"Dad?" my mother said after my grandfather had been lying still and quiet for a while with his eyes closed. Resting, sleeping, scudding across a soft gray sky of Dilaudid. We watched his chest with practiced eyes for signs of respiration. "Are you tired? Do you feel like eating something?"

"Grandpa," I said, trying to sound chipper. "Come on, let me make you something."

He opened his eyes. I saw that the fire of memory had returned, inextinguishable.

"Tapioca pudding for everyone," he said. "And lots of it."

IX

I remember my mother telling me, when she was in the midst of settling my grandfather's estate, that fifty percent of a person's medical expenses are incurred in the last six months of life. My grandfather's history of himself was distributed even more disproportionately: Ninety percent of everything he ever told me about his life, I heard during its final ten days. Out of a scant handful of memories that he had shared with me when I was growing up, one of the few I heard more than once was of his first glimpse of my mother. He always put it more or less the same way: "The first time I saw your mother, she was crying her eyes out."

This hardly qualified as reminiscence, since he never really enlarged upon it or added any detail. It was offered more in the way of an ironic commentary on some fresh instance of my mother's stoicism, pragmatism, or levelheadedness, of her being a *tough cookie*, a *cool customer.*

"They think they can crack her," I remember him saying during the days she was fighting (with his assistance) to disentangle herself legally and financially from the mess my father had made of our lives, "but she won't crack." After a pronouncement of this kind my grandfather would often shake his head and add, savoring the irony, "Hard to believe the first time I saw her, she was crying her little eyes out, poor thing."

The first time my grandfather saw my mother was a Sunday afternoon in early March 1947, a couple of weeks after "Night in Monte Carlo." He rode the number 5 streetcar from his brother's house in

Park Circle to Ahavas Sholom, which was about to begin its observation of Purim. Technically, Purim had fallen on a Friday that year, but due to some Sabbath pettifoggery and the city of Baltimore not having been walled during the time of Joshua, it was to be celebrated today.

My grandfather had no interest in the Jewish calendar or Uncle Ray's explanation thereof, and as for Purim itself, he could take it or leave it. Unlike the other Jewish holidays, it had been fun when he was a kid, and he still gave it credit for that. But somewhere between the Ardennes and the Harz mountains, my grandfather had lost the taste or the capacity for celebrating an enemy's defeat, and it struck him as cheap and painfully mistaken to draw all the neat parallels that Ray planned to draw in his sermon between the would-be exterminator Haman and the bona-fide exterminator Hitler. Jewish wiles and bad luck (aka "God") had put a stop to Haman's plans; Hitler had simply run out of time.

The annual celebrations of God's mercy, justice, and power, the feasts or fasts undertaken in praise of His Name, the miracles He was supposed to have thrown our way over the centuries—in my grandfather's mind, it was all nullified by the thing he had not yet learned to call the Holocaust. In Egypt, in Shushan, in the time of Judah Maccabee, God had intervened to deliver us with a mighty hand and outstretched arm; big deal. When we were sent to the ovens, God had sat with His outstretched thumb up His mighty ass and let us burn. In 1947 there was, to my grandfather, one reason to continue calling oneself a Jew, to go on being Jewish before the world: as a way of telling Hitler *Fuck you.*

He was not on his way to Ahavas Sholom to celebrate Purim, endure his brother's preaching, or stamp his feet every time Haman's name was read from the Megillah. He was not even going for the *hamantaschen,* though naturally, he would not say no.* He was going

---

* He was particularly partial to the ones filled with poppy seed, that dollop of *mon* glowing lustrous as a spoonful of little black pearls.

to the synagogue that afternoon because Uncle Ray had assured him that my grandmother would be there, and my grandfather was hoping to get into my grandmother's panties. The woman had passed through the fire without being consumed, but she had, my grandfather understood, been damaged. So he had decided that he was going to save her. Getting into her panties was a necessary first step.

From the first that was a part of his attraction to her: not her brokenness but her potential for being mended and, even more, the challenge that mending her would pose. He thought that if he took on the job of loving this broken woman, some measure of sense or purpose might be returned to his life. He thought that in mending her, he might also be mended. Ever since the late winter and spring of 1945 my grandfather had been suffering from a form of spiritual aphasia. No matter how many times he pored over them, he had trouble assigning sense or value to the things he had seen and done during the war. He had been assured many times by experts and authorities that his wartime actions had served a larger purpose and, furthermore, that some new purpose would be found for him in the after-war. Until the night he met my grandmother, he had put no credit in such assurances; now, as he returned to the synagogue on a mission of lust, he was more inclined to believe them. His lust itself felt like a form of belief.

He understood that it was possible to define the word *fool* as "one who takes on a job without knowing its true extent or difficulty," but after all, that had been standard procedure in the Army Corps of Engineers. If there was anything like wisdom to be gained in this world, maybe it was to be found in the hopeful, hopeless motto of the Corps: *Essayons*. So, he didn't know how big or hard a job he was getting himself into with this woman. At least he knew where to begin: with her hips pressed against him, her legs wrapped around him, her body encompassed by his arms.

Since "Night in Monte Carlo," my grandfather had seen my grandmother three times.

The first time was as the result of a kind of reverse ambush engineered by Uncle Ray. Mrs. Waxman, recovering swiftly from the failure of the Sisterhood's first plot to ensnare the new rabbi, had invited him to a "casual supper" at the Waxmans' floor-through apartment in the Riviera, on Eutaw Place, to which, secretly, she had also invited my grandmother. Uncle Ray was hip by now to the conspiracy against him, however, and aware that his brother had blundered head over heels into the trap the Sisterhood had laid. Accepting the invitation, Uncle Ray showed up with my grandfather in tow, counting on a display of brotherly solicitude for the decorated vet with the thousand-yard stare to earn him the forgiveness of the Waxmans.

Awkwardnesses followed. A seating arrangement devised for pre-dinner drinks in the intimate drawing room of the vast apartment, where two Joseph Urban armchairs encouragingly faced an exceedingly narrow Hagenbund love seat, was spoiled both visually and tactically by the hasty interpolation of a crewel-work Eastlake side chair from the front parlor. Also, a leaf and a place had to be added to a kitchen table that was just the size, and had been set, for four. Also, the cook was obliged to reapportion fifty exorbitant grams of beluga caviar on the toast points with cream cheese that were the *hors d'oeuvre*. But the greatest awkwardness that night, undoubtedly, was my grandfather. Positioned alone on one side of the kitchen table, across from his brother and at an angle to my grandmother, he barely spoke, introduced food into his mouth at mechanical intervals, and stared at my grandmother without art or restraint. When she caught him staring, he would even more artlessly look down at the food on his plate with a show of puzzlement, as if he kept forgetting what supper was and how it was supposed to work.

What puzzled him, in fact, was my grandmother. When an engineer encounters his destiny or doom, it always takes the form of a puzzle.

The elegant girl he remembered from "Night in Monte Carlo" had been lively and cosmopolitan but odd and flighty and possibly a bit of a nut. She had, for God's sake, zipped up his fly in a synagogue! The woman at the Waxmans' kitchen table was no less beautiful than that girl but otherwise completely different in manner, in style, in energy. No more interested in the young rabbi than he was in her, she had chosen to wear a drab woolen suit-dress of an outmoded military cut. She filled it out nicely but could not enliven it. Her conversation was measured, tentative, careful, even grave. It gave no evidence of nuttiness. It was more polished, couched more in American English than two weeks before.

The absence of playfulness and flirtation in her manner brought out the languid solemnity of her feline face and eyes. The tangles of her hair had been combed and pinned close to her scalp and seemed more russet than auburn, with a sheen like the coat of a chestnut horse. The laugh he remembered as raspy, verging on braying, was a demure chuckle. At "Night in Monte Carlo," my grandfather had pegged (maybe even a little bit dismissed) her as a fetching but scatterbrained gamine trying to relinquish her dark and painful history into the hands of hairstylists, dentists, and couturiers. A bird of passage, hollow-boned. The woman he met at the Waxmans' that second evening seemed heavy at her core, subject to some crushing gravity. She was a vessel built to hold the pain of her history, but it had cracked her, and radiant darkness leaked out through the crack. When the conversation touched on the Carmelite convent where she had been hidden during the war, my grandmother's voice grew husky. It throbbed with sadness. Uncle Ray passed her his handkerchief, and they all watched her dab at her eyes as the kitchen filled with silence and the smell of gardenia.

My grandfather was troubled and fascinated by this alteration from the girl of ten days before. Had the flirtatious gamine in the Ingrid Bergman sunglasses been a pose adopted for the evening, while this shapely vessel leaking sadness approximated something closer to the truth of her self? Or was it the other way around? Maybe neither version was the "truth." Maybe "self" was a free variable with no bounded value. Maybe every time you met her, she would be somebody else. He became vaguely aware that he was experiencing pain, a pulsing in his left shin, and realized that his brother was kicking him under the table. Inferring or registering that Mrs. Waxman or Judge Waxman had just asked him a question, my grandfather looked helplessly from one to the other. No help was forthcoming from either direction. Uncle Ray was obliged to intervene.

"Electrical engineering," he said in a dry tone of voice, sounding exasperated but not unamused. "He has a BS from Drexel Tech. And yes, Judge, he is very much looking for employment, sensitive as he is to the fact that his long-suffering kid brother would dearly love to have his couch back."

Until very recently, my grandfather, on hearing this remark, would have shot back with something along the lines of *Hey, you know what? I can be gone tomorrow,* and would have meant it. For weeks he had woken up on Uncle Ray's couch every morning not knowing why he was still in Baltimore, and lay down on it again every night telling himself it was time to move on.

"I'm interested in rocketry," he was astonished to hear himself declare. "Inertial guidance systems, telemetry. I'd like to find work out at Glenn Martin, if I could. I hear they might be starting to do some things in that area."

Mrs. Waxman looked impressed, or maybe she was just taken aback; it was by far my grandfather's longest utterance of the evening. Judge Waxman said that, as it happened, one of his former law partners had a brother who was a vice president of the Martin Company. Perhaps there was something he could do to help my grandfather.

"Are they building space rockets out there?" Uncle Ray said. During the war, Glenn Martin had built a vast plant at Middle River in the northeastern wastes of Baltimore to manufacture thousands of B-26 Marauders and Mariner seaplanes. "Because let me tell you something, this brother of mine, with his inertia and his telepathy? He might look like a chunk of cement with a flattop. But he wants to fly to the moon."

Apart from this and my grandmother choking up about the sisters of Carmel, my grandfather had no clear recollection, forty-two years later, of anything else said by anyone at the table that night. The only other conversation he remembered came after dessert and coffee had been served. His feelings about my grandmother at this point were a confusion of curiosity, pity, ambition, desire. He felt that he needed, for the sake of clarity, to escape her gravity for a minute or two, for as long as it would take to smoke a cigarette. He slipped away from the table and, looking for some kind of back stair or terrace, found his way to a large porch enclosed with glass. It was unheated but furnished with wicker and an étagère to hold plants and on a spring afternoon must be a pleasant place to sit and have money and be a judge. It had a closed-up smell. He opened one of the casement windows, hoping to find some purchase in the cold night air.

He had just lit a Pall Mall when the door clanged open. It was my grandmother, cloaked in a thick fur coat, sleeves dangling empty at her sides. The coat, like Mrs. Waxman, came enveloped in a formidable vapor of Tabu. It must have cost the judge as much as the 1947 Cadillac Sixty he had sent around to pick up his guests.

"Hello."

"Oh, uh, hiya."

She looked longingly at the cigarette between his lips. He passed it to her and lit another for himself. When he looked up again from the spark and flare of butane, still a little cross-eyed, he saw her shudder once, a traveling wave that passed from her hips to her shoulders and then across her face in a ripple of dismay.

"You okay?"

My grandmother made a funny sound, somewhere between embarrassed laughter and a yelp of pain, then ducked out from under

Mrs. Waxman's coat like it was on fire. At the same time she tossed it in the general direction of my grandfather like *she* was the burning building and it was up to him, a fireman waiting with his life net, to save it. He caught the coat by the collar. She put a hand to her chest, swallowed, and took a drag on the cigarette. She looked sheepish.

"I'm so sorry," she said. "Only I really don't like fur."

"Oh?"

"When they cut away the skins . . . ? I have seen it."

"Yeah?"

"And I never liked it."

That was the first time she told him about the family tannery, in Lille, near the Belgian border. In her schoolgirl English, with almost nothing in the way of expression or emotion, she depicted a childhood haunted by blood and putrefaction and the piss stink of the tanning vats, by horses in the slaughter lot screaming like girls. She described the flaying of hides in terms of vivid color. Silver blade. Red blood. Blue membrane. Golden fat. White bone.

He held the coat up between them. In the moonlit dark of the glassed-in porch, it seemed to shimmer with a ghost of animal motion.

"That is *hotter*," she said.

"Oh, yeah?" He had no idea what she was talking about but felt abruptly that he was back on familiar territory with her, with the girl from "Night in Monte Carlo" telling him how his head would look good on a fence.

"Many hotters. Mrs. Waxman says it takes fifteen or twenty hotters."

My grandfather could not help it. He laughed. "*Otters*," he said.

"You know what this is, a hotter?"

"I'm pretty sure that was otter in the soup tonight."

She frowned, less with her mouth than with her thick Jennifer Jones eyebrows. He liked what her eyebrows did, particularly when she frowned.

"Oh, you are teasing me," she concluded.

"I'm sorry."

"No, teasing me is not bad."

"Really?"

"Yes, when you do it. I like if you do it."

My grandfather felt himself blush. The only light came from moonglow and a lamp at the far end of the drawing room. He wondered if it was enough for her to see that he was blushing.

"I like *you*," he said.

"I like you, too." She said it in half a second and then added less than half a second later, "I have a little girl, did you know this?"

"Right," my grandfather said, caught off guard. So there were two of them, two who would need saving. *Essayons.* "How old?"

"Four years. Five years in September."

"And your, uh, the father?"

"I murdered him." When she saw my grandfather's face, she burst out laughing, then covered her mouth with her hand. She started to choke on the smoke of her cigarette. "No! I'm sorry . . . !" At first she kept on laughing, but as the coughing fit persisted, it seemed maybe she had started to cry. My grandfather couldn't tell. She held her breath, let it out. She pulled herself together. "That was a joke but not funny, so why I was laughing?"

That was a tough one to answer. My grandfather let it pass. She stubbed out the cigarette in a pot on the étagère that held dirt and a withered stalk.

"The father is dead," she said. "In the war."

She walked over to the casement window my grandfather had opened and put her face through into the cold air. She looked up at the Moon, a day or two past its first quarter. She was convulsed by another shudder, then another. She was definitely crying now, and probably cold as hell. He slung the fur coat over one of the wicker chairs. He took off his blazer. It was the same one he had borrowed from his brother to wear to "Night in Monte Carlo." He lowered the blazer over her shoulders. She leaned in to it as if it were a stream of hot water from a shower head. She kept on leaning backward until she fell against him. He felt the shock of contact. The weight of her against his chest felt like something she had decided to entrust to him. He wanted badly, wanted only, to be worthy of that trust, although apparently his penis, stirring, had its own ideas on the subject.

"I want to fly to the Moon, too," she said. "Take me with you."

"Sure thing," my grandfather said. "I'll figure it out."

The next time he saw her, she was coming out of Silber's bakery holding a box tied with candy-striped string. She did not see him. He followed her down Park Heights to Belvedere and then to the ragged lower end of Narcissus Avenue, keeping a careful distance, and watched her disappear with the box into the upstairs unit of a two-family house that was better maintained than its neighbors (and turned out to be a rental property of Judge Waxman's). The following night, around two in the morning, he got up off of Uncle Ray's couch, where he could not sleep for thinking of her. He got dressed and took the keys to his brother's Mercury and drove over to the two-family house on Narcissus. There was a light on in a window upstairs. His heart caught on some hook inside him. He nosed to the curb, and cut the lights. It was another chilly night, but the lighted window was open and she was leaning on the sill, smoking a cigarette and looking up at the Moon. He wondered if she was looking at the Moon and feeling the cold air and remembering the promise he had made her, his chest unyielding against the weight of her.

My grandfather heard a child's calling voice, too faint and far away for him to hear distress or complaint or urgency in it. My grandmother turned her head sharply toward the room behind her, stubbing out the cigarette against the windowsill. Sparks rained down into the shrubbery below.

◑   ◑   ◑

As he approached Ahavas Sholom that Purim Sunday with a clear sense of mission if not of operational plan, he saw a little girl sitting alone on a stone bench outside the glass doors, knees pulled to her chin, arms encircling her legs at the ankles. She was rocking back and forth, no more than three degrees in either direction, and making low sounds that at first, from a distance, my grandfather took for singing. She had on a green dress, green tights, and black patent-leather Mary Janes. The dress had cap sleeves that left her arms bare, and even with the tights she must be awfully cold—my grandfather was wearing a hat, a scarf, and a wool topcoat over a cardigan sweater. He supposed that when he was three or four years old he might have felt like crying his eyes out, too, bare-armed in forty-degree weather on a cold stone bench, but he liked to think that he would have had the sense to get up and go inside where it was warm.

One of the synagogue front doors banged open. The girl stopped rocking and sat up straight. A Jew came out of the building, holding a small loden coat. The Jew had on an enormous *shtreiml*, a black caftan whose hem swept the concrete, and a beard like Edmund Gwenn's in *Miracle on 34th Street*. My grandfather was surprised to see a Jew of this variety attending services at Ahavas Sholom, where the women sat with the men and the rabbi was a fast-talking dandy who could not even raise a decent five o'clock shadow. The Jew in the big fur hat ignored or seemed not to hear my grandfather coming up the walk, and the girl ignored the Jew except to the degree that she was no longer crying her eyes out. She was no longer crying at all.

After a moment the Jew draped the loden coat over the girl's shoulders, settled the lapels around her neck with a few deft movements, and went back into the building. When the Jew opened the door again, a gust of air lifted the hem of the caftan, revealing a pair of bright red slippers with upcurving toes. My grandfather was even more surprised by the slippers than by the Jew's presence at Ahavas Sholom, but you could have filled a book with the things he did not know or frankly care to know about Orthodox Jews and what went on underneath their clothing.

"I didn't realize they made Jewish Eskimos," my grandfather said to the little girl when he got to the front door of the shul.

She looked up at him. Heart-shaped face, lips chapped and puffy, upturned little shikse nose. Bottle-green eyes dry of tears. It must have been the cold after all.

"What?" she said.

"Aren't you cold?"

She slid her arms into the sleeves of the loden coat. She nodded.

"So why are you sitting out here?"

"I'm not allowed inside for two hours."

"Oh? Why is that?"

"Because I was bad."

"So you have to sit outside in the cold for two hours?"

"Yes."

"You must have been especially bad."

"Yes."

Two hours in the cold for a misbehaving kid seemed excessive, but he knew even less about the disciplinary habits of these people than he did about their footwear. He looked through the glass door for the Jew in the big fur hat, thinking he might have a word. The walls of the lobby or vestibule, a large spartan expanse with an angled modernist ceiling, had been papered with cutout onion domes and pointed arches to evoke a Persian mood. A large banner slung between two raked poles just inside the entrance read THE ROAD TO SHUSHAN in mock-Arabic script. A few people were milling around by the door to the sanctuary, among them the Jew in the hat. A slender young woman stood beside the Jew, got up like a sideshow Salome in bangles and veils.

"You need me to put in a good word for you?" he said to the little girl. "I got an in with the warden."

"What?"

"Who said you have to sit out here in the cold for two hours?"

"I did."

"*You* did."

"Yes."

"Because you were bad."

"Uh-huh."

"So you're punishing yourself."

She nodded.

"What did you do that was so bad you had to punish yourself?"

"Mama said I was discourteous."

"Who to?"

"The rabbi."

"Really? How were you discourteous?"

"I asked him why he wears the same perfume as our downstairs neighbor Mrs. Poliakoff."

"Oh-ho."

"What?"

"What kind of perfume does Mrs. Poliakoff wear?"

"Jungle Gardenia."

My grandfather laughed, and after a moment, with a degree of caution, the girl laughed, too.

"It's funny," she suggested.

"It is to me. Very."

"Yes, it's very funny."

The door opened again and the Jew with the big fur hat was there, wearing a dime-store Santa beard and a Chinatown mandarin coat.

"Look, all of the bad little children are here."

My mother stopped laughing and looked away.

"You know, I'm pretty sure Ray does wear Jungle Gardenia," my grandfather said to my grandmother. "I think this one has paid her debt to society. Maybe we can let her come back from Siberia, huh?"

"I have been out here three times telling this to her!" my grandmother cried. "There is nothing you can tell to this one. I said to her, 'You were rude, please, for two minutes, go and sit in a chair over there—inside of the room, not outside of the *building*. For two *minutes*! She says, 'No! I am so bad, I am going to sit *outside* for two *hours*.' I have been *begging* to her, please, come inside, you are going to catch a pneumonia!" My grandmother pronounced the initial *p*. She turned to my mother. The beard flapped up and down. "Do you want to get sick and go to the hospital? Do you want to die?" She sounded exasperated, even angry, and yet at the same time there was a theatrical trill in her voice, as if she were only playing the part of an exasperated mother at her wits' end. Maybe that was just an effect of the comedy beard. "Is that what you want?" she said.

"No," my mother said.

"I'm glad to hear that, because if you die, then I will have to kill myself, and I don't want to die, either."

My grandfather thought this kind of talk might be carrying things a little too far, but he wasn't sure. He seemed to remember his mother engaging in rhetoric of this sort with him when she was at the end of her own wits. He was not sure how he felt about such talk, or he knew that he disliked it; but on this woman, it fit. In her pain and her vividness and her theatricality, she seemed to have access to some higher frequency of emotion, a spectrum of light invisible to his eyes.

At the mention of suicide, my mother looked up at her mother, intrigued. "Why will you have to kill yourself?" she said.

"Because without you I will have no one, and I will be totally alone, so what is the point then, I might as well die."

"Okay, okay," my grandfather said. "Nobody's going to kill themselves, and nobody's going to be alone." He looked down at my mother. "I've been telling the rabbi he smells like Mrs. Poliakoff since before the war. And I don't even know Mrs. Poliakoff. You think maybe I ought to spend the next two hours out here with you, punishing *myself*?"

"No," my mother said. "I'll come in."

"Then so will I," my grandfather said. He opened the door to the shul. "Come," he said. He held out his hand to my mother. He was not certain he had ever held out his hand to a child in this way. He wanted my grandmother to see that he could hold out his hand to her daughter and that, when he did, her daughter would take it. If he could get the kid to relent and come in from the cold of a Baltimore afternoon, that would be another way for him to begin to mend what the war had broken.

For a second or two my mother seemed to consider taking his hand. In the end, though, she just got up and scurried inside. My grandfather was disappointed, and disappointment filled him with resolve. He would work at the kid. He would do what he needed to do until he had gained her trust and hopefully her affection.

"I'm sorry," my grandmother said. Even through the fake beard with the preposterous hat, her eyes sought his, and searched his face, and saw his disappointment and his resolve. My grandfather was not sure anyone had ever looked at him like that unless they were hoping to clean his clock. At the possibility of truly being seen, something in his chest seemed to snap open like a parachute.

"It's fine," he said. He pointed to the beard, the caftan. "What's this?"

"I am playing the part today of Mordecai, obviously. In the *purim-spiel*."

"That explains the shoes."

"Your brother is Vashti."

"In the veils." That was Ray flouncing around outside the door to the sanctuary, vain and imperious as a queen of Persia. "Typecasting. Hey." He put a hand on her arm. Even through the sleeve of the Chinese coat the charge of contact was there. "Doesn't that thing bother you?" he said.

He pointed at the *shtreiml*. As he recalled, a proper *shtreiml* was made with the tails of some furry little animal, a marten or a mink. My grandmother looked confused by the question.

"You got something like eighteen mink tails on your head there."

She did not look horrified by this information. The memory of screaming horses and peeled hides did not rack her like a fever. Instead she looked . . . It was hard for my grandfather to describe. It would have been easy enough for him, considering what came after, to recall the look that passed across my grandmother's face that afternoon as one of embarrassment, discomfiture, the look of someone caught out in a moment of self-contradiction. But in the end the word that he settled on was *impatient*. She pursed her lips and gave her shoulders a little Gallic shrug, as if to suggest that he must already know the explanation for her tolerating the touch of death against her skin.

"It's for the play," she said.

Five minutes before the end of Devaughn's next shift, my grandfather showed up at the security desk wearing rubber waders over
stained chinos, holding an empty one-quart Ziploc. He carried a
blue NASA knapsack, meant for children, into which he had placed
a thermos of lemonade, a first aid kit, and a field guide to snakes and
reptiles from the Coconut Creek branch of the Broward County Library. In his right hand he carried a blackthorn walking stick, never
used, that Sally Sichel had bought for her husband, Leslie, when
his fatal disease first enfeebled him. Until yesterday afternoon the
walking stick had been surmounted by a sterling silver duck's head.
In the Fontana Village metal shop my grandfather had (with Sally's
permission) removed this and replaced it with the iron head of a
three-pound maul. As he walked across the grounds from his unit,
swinging the stick, my grandfather had ignored a number of puzzled looks and two direct queries. But Devaughn understood at once
what my grandfather had in mind.

"It was me?" he said, "I'd go with a machete." Devaughn chopped
at his left wrist with the edge of his right hand. "You want to deca-
pacitate it, clean and quick."

My grandfather made a mental note to see Perfecto Tiant, the
chief of the landscaping crew, about borrowing a machete when the
time came. He held up the Ziploc bag. "You said you saw its droppings," he said. "I'd like you to help me get hold of some."

"Right now." Devaughn looked skeptical.

"Isn't your shift over at eight?"

"Yes, sir, it is. But then, see, I'm kind of on Devaughn time."

"Yeah? And what happens then?"

"On Devaughn time?" Devaughn rolled his eyes to the ceiling. He seemed to be consulting a long menu of pastimes and pursuits. "Well, for one thing? Not picking up a snake bowel movement, putting it into a baggie."

"Never?"

"No, sir."

My grandfather and Devaughn stared at each other. The mechanism in the clock on the wall behind the counter advanced with a loud thunk into the next minute of their lives.

"I suppose I might be willing to pay you for your trouble," my grandfather said.

Devaughn smiled. He found it a comfort to see a show of miserliness in a Jew. He assumed that my grandfather was a millionaire. "How much?" he said.

"Twenty-five. But only if I get something to put in this bag."

When the day man came in, Devaughn pulled on his billed cap with the Fontana Village logo and picked up his zippered nylon briefcase. My grandfather followed him to his car, a 1979 Cutlass Supreme. It sat creaking in the employee lot, vinyl top bleached and peeled by years in the heat of Florida. Devaughn opened the trunk and put in his briefcase, minus a peanut butter and potato chip sandwich that he folded over twice and rammed with a fingertip into his mouth. He unbuttoned his uniform shirt and hung it on a hanger from the valet hook inside his car. His belly sloshed in the wineskin of a ribbed undershirt. His bare shoulders were ivory-yellow and densely freckled. The freckles, like his hair and eyelashes, were the color of a Nilla wafer. He stuffed the billed cap into the briefcase and, from atop the rear dash, took out a straw cowboy hat whose brim curled up sharply at the sides. At the very back of the trunk, under the rear dash, he opened a toolbox of molded plastic and dug around until he found a machete as long as his forearm, in a leather sheath. Balancing it flat across his upturned palms, he contemplated my grandfather. He was still chewing the sandwich, lips pursing as his jaw worked up and down. "Doubt you going to need it this morning, but," he said. "You welcome to borrow it if you want."

"I don't like to borrow," my grandfather said. "I'll rent it from you."

"Suit yourself, then."

My grandfather got into the car. It was an oven. He rolled down the window, and the trim of the handle burned his fingers. The air-conditioning wheezed. Its breath smelled of mildew tinged with peanut butter and potato chips.

"Time I really got a good look around in there?" Devaughn said. "It was with Finlay Gadbois, you remember Finlay?"

My grandfather recalled a blond pompadour behind a motocross magazine, two black brogues propped up on the security desk.

"Finlay's brother was a investigator for some real estate lawyers got tangled up in the whole mess over there for a while? Took me and Finlay for a tour one time, we went right in the front gate. The, uh, droppings was all over the, like, the front porch of the clubhouse."

"Show me."

"It's all chained up, though."

"Show me."

"With a padlock."

My grandfather settled the NASA backpack on his lap and looked out the window at the expanse of Fontana Village. The scene never varied except for the transit of rain, people, and golf carts across it. Shadows of eaves and dormers moved slow as hour hands across the blank faces of the units. Stucco, palm trees, concrete walks, lawns that never seemed to grow or fade. Inverted over everything a glass bell of sky. Shake the whole thing a couple of times and you would stir up a flurry of glitter. My grandfather was tired of looking at it, to a depth of his soul that made him wonder if there might really be something wrong with him. The name and number of the specialist were still keeping company with Hosni Mubarak in the latest issue of *Commentary*. As soon he had taken care of this snake problem, he told himself, he would make that appointment.

"When I feel like I've got my twenty-five dollars' worth," my grandfather said, "then I'll stop telling you what to do. Show me."

Devaughn put the car in gear. He drove out of the gates of Fontana Village. They made three left turns, bending around a vast South Florida city block. Devaughn turned in to the driveway of the abandoned country club. Grass crazed the driveway. They did not get far before they had to stop. The property had been fenced all around with chain-link drowned in a surf of kudzu. Rusted signs warning away trespassers had been fixed to the fence by the city and by the defeated successors to the original losers of the country club. Among the warning signs stood a gate cabled and locked with a heavy padlock.

My grandfather got out of the car and notched the walking stick up under his arm. He took off his belt and fed it through the loop on the machete's holster. He put the belt back on. He didn't think he was going to need it this morning, either, but you never knew. Sometimes a hunter could get lucky.

Beyond the gate, the driveway carried on to an arch in a pink stucco wall. Kudzu had strung its green banners across the archway and worked its fingers into a thousand cracks in the pink stucco. On a frieze over the arc, between a pair of cartographic dolphins, a plaster triton sat on a compass rose, blowing a conch trumpet. The triton had lost its face. The leering dolphins were blackened with grime or mold. The name of the country club was Mandeville.

"That's where you want to look for him," Devaughn said, pointing at the cracked blacktop between the chain-link gate and the archway. "Middle of a nice hot road like that, end of the day when the air's starting to get cool."

"Where's this clubhouse?"

"Through the arch, up the road. You can kind of almost see it, something pink there? Long way to go."

"I see it."

A shard of pink in green shadow. A forlorn pink, the pink of a tattered flamingo in a roadside zoo.

"Look there!" Devaughn was pointing to the left of the gate, just beyond the fence, under a sprawl of rhododendron.

My grandfather grabbed the hilt of the machete. His hand craved the bite of its blade into muscle. But there was no snake drowsing in a coil under the rhododendron. There was only what appeared to be a scrap of upholstery batting, a rude nest woven of gray twine and ashes. At one edge it devolved into a tuft of down that might once, my grandfather supposed, have been Ramon. It lay on the far side of the fence about three feet beyond the limits of either my grandfather's or Devaughn's reach.

My grandfather handed Leslie's stick to Devaughn.

"What you call this thing?" Devaughn said, hefting it.

"It's a snake hammer."

Devaughn nodded knowledgeably. He got down on his belly and poked the stick under the fence toward the twist of scat. Grunting and cursing, he steered its steel tip to within an inch of the scat but no closer. He let go of the stick on the wrong side of the fence and it slid away from him. His body went slack against the ground. "Shit." He looked at my grandfather, awaiting reproach.

"Decent snake hammer's going to set you back more than twenty-five bucks," my grandfather said.

He took Devaughn's place on the ground and managed, straining, to retrieve the stick. His arms were long in proportion to the rest of him, but he had no better luck than Devaughn in reaching the remnant of Ramon. He stood up. Vertigo swept over him. Fire drew arabesques at the back of his eyes. "Shit," he said.

"Name of the game," Devaughn said.

My grandfather sat in the car with the door open and drank some of the lemonade from the thermos. A small plane droned toward the Atlantic, trailing a banner lettered in red capitals. He struggled to make out the distant text with an urgency he knew to be misplaced.

"Sea and Ski," Devaughn said.

My grandfather nodded. He took out his wallet and paid Devaughn in full.

"Sorry it didn't work out," Devaughn said.

"Care to make it fifty?" my grandfather said.

Devaughn drove my grandfather to a hardware store and waited in the car. My grandfather bought a Yale padlock that appeared to be nearly identical to the one cabled to the chain-link gate. He gave some thought to a pair of bolt cutters, but they were expensive and bulky and he knew the sight of them would spook Devaughn. As it was, Devaughn eyed uneasily the paper bag in my grandfather's lap.

When they got back to Mandeville, my grandfather climbed out of the car and shut the door. The temperature was ninety-five degrees. Across the feral golf course on the other side of the fence, a million insects played a one-note tone poem entitled *Heat*. My grandfather leaned in through the window on the passenger side. "Go park the car down the street," he said. "By the lawn and garden store. I'll meet you there in two minutes."

"What you going to do?"

My grandfather walked over to the fence. He matched the padlock to the business end of the snake hammer.

"No," Devaughn called. "No way."

"Two minutes."

"It's crazy. Why you don't just go in from the Fontana Village side?"

"Fence."

"Have to have a hole in it somewheres. All them pets get inside no problem."

"What do I look like? A shih tzu or an old man?"

"A old man."

"Here's where there's a paved road. You told me yourself they like to lie on hot pavement."

"So you going to just walk in there in broad daylight."

"I'm going to need to come back. Probably a number of times." He hefted the brown paper bag with the lock inside it. "I want to make that easier to do."

"You going to get us arrested," Devaughn said. "I can't have that. I'm an old man, too, and I need this job. I didn't plan for no financial future like y'all."

"Two minutes. If I get caught, I'll say I walked here. I won't say a word about you."

"They might put you in jail."

"I've been in jail," my grandfather said. "I got a lot of reading done."

Devaughn looked surprised. His gaze drifted down to my grandfather's feet in the rubber waders and back up to his blue-and-white canvas bucket hat, souvenir of a visit to an Israeli kibbutz that he and my grandmother had made not long after the Six-Day War.

"I might like to re-estimate my opinion of you," Devaughn said. He leaned across to roll up the passenger window, then backed the car down the driveway.

My grandfather watched Devaughn pull away. He raised the head of the walking stick and brought it down on the padlock. The impact rang up his arm to the elbow. The lock held firm. It took seven more smacks with the hammer to crack it. He yanked it open. He tried to swing aside the chain-link gate, but the kudzu vines held it fast. He pried it open an inch or two with the shaft of the walking stick but not enough to squeeze through. He unsheathed the machete and brought it down. The tendrils snapped like guitar strings. Pain twanged in my grandfather's shoulder. The gate swung open without a sound.

My grandfather found his fingers trembling as he tore open the packaging of the new lock. After he put the new lock into place, he stooped to pick up some bits of the shattered one. He fitted them into the blister of the packaging with the rest of the old lock and put it in the paper bag. Then he stepped into the snake's domain. He looked around, listening for a dragging sound, a pop of twigs. He was under the impression that snakes gave off a musk, and he sniffed the air. Twice dapples of sun on shade stopped the blood in his veins. He lowered himself to stoop for the snake hammer, then walked over to the rhododendron and crouched down beside it. He used the tip of the walking stick to slide the scat into the Ziploc bag.

When he tried to stand again, his knees had locked. He planted the stick in the gravel and, grateful not to find himself mocked by the smug expression of a sterling-silver duck, pulled himself up along its length. On his feet once more, he made for the gate and locked it. He slipped the key into an outer pocket of the knapsack, alongside the baggie. Then he walked down the street to the lawn and garden store to settle his account with Devaughn, and to inquire about the going day rate for a machete.

◑   ◑   ◑

"What was it for?" I said. "What did you do with the snake poop?"

"There was a professor at Miami. In the biology department. A herpetologist. He agreed to take a look at it."

"And?"

"He felt confident it was not the fecal matter of a boa constrictor."

"So it was an alligator."

"It was a python."

"A *python*? Don't pythons get really big?"

My grandfather shrugged. The shrug said, *Define big.* It said, *Compared to an ankylosaurus? Not so big.*

"Can they get big enough to eat a cat?"

He stuck out his tongue once, twice. I handed him a mug of apple juice and he took a measured sip.

"A python can swallow a deer," he said.

"Jesus."

"A cat? To a python? Like a handful of nuts."

I resisted the urge to point out that snakes did not have hands.

"So, last year," I said, "like, right after I visited you? And we watched that PBS thing about exotic pets taking over the Everglades? You basically went out into the jungle. And started hunting a python."

Another shrug: It passed the time.

"So did you use one of those, like, noose-on-a-stick things they had?" I mimed the thrust-and-tug action of the snare tool a park ranger on the program had employed to bag a boa constrictor.

"I had no interest in capturing him," my grandfather said. "I wanted to kill him."

"With a gun?"

My grandfather screwed the left side of his face into the comedic half-mask he adopted when he was trying to conceal his disappointment in you.

"Maybe you should be taking notes," he said. He handed back the mug of apple juice. "I had a snake hammer. Why would I need a gun?"

XI

For their sins, Wild Bill Donovan recruited Orland Buck and my grandfather into the Office of Strategic Services. They were sent to study mayhem and spycraft at Area B, an OSS training facility in the Maryland mountains on the present-day site of Camp David. The U.S. military had long disavowed the practice of espionage and deception as beneath its gentlemanly dignity; many of the instructors at Area B were Brits. They had spent their lives subverting insurrections and infiltrating rebellions. They did not care if you forgot to salute them. They thought that training to shoot at a target while standing straight up with your arm sticking out like a turnstile was about as useful as learning how to joust. They were unobtrusive and ferocious men whom my grandfather could not fail to admire.

He learned to work with a compass, a garrote, and a onetime cipher pad, and to crawl a long way on his belly under live machine-gun fire. He learned to forge and alter documents, to hide intelligently, and to parachute off the top of a ninety-foot platform (though he never jumped from an actual plane). For a while he was the target of Jew hate by a couple of bigots in the class. Buck pleaded with him to get a little bit carried away just this once. The next day during hand-to-hand training, my grandfather broke the jaw of one of his tormentors, and after that the other ran out of things to say.

On graduating Buck and my grandfather were given three days' leave in Baltimore, where Buck got my grandfather so drunk that he was able to directly experience, if not to communicate, some of the unlikelier effects on time and space called for by Einstein's Special and General Theories of Relativity. They said goodbye at Baltimore Penn Station, where they boarded trains bound in opposite directions, Buck for New York City, my grandfather for Washington. A week later Orland Buck was dropped by parachute into Italy to cause trouble ahead of the Allied invasion. This he did, moving north and east with violence and aplomb until December 1944, when he and some Titoist partisans inadvertently blew themselves up along with a bridge on the Kuba River.

One of the few people ever to have really seen my grandfather's potential, Bill Donovan had "something different" in mind for the other principal in the Key Bridge Affair. In a memo recommending him to the deputy director for special projects, Stanley Lovell, Donovan portrayed my grandfather as "capable, it might be, of genius-level thinking, [. . .] calm and analytical in temperament, if bloody-minded."

With the invasion of Italy under way and plans for the invasion of Normandy being drawn up at COSSAC headquarters in London, Donovan foresaw a need for men qualified to go in behind the eventual invasion force and pick Germany's pocket. The prize would be German scientists, engineers, and technology—miles ahead, in many areas of research, of anyone or anything in the U.S. at the time. The ideal agent would have both the technical knowledge necessary to fathom the secret laboratories and proving grounds of the Reich and the operational skill to find and loot them. My grandfather, Donovan wrote, "suited to a 'T,'" but until the invasion could be arranged, he would need to be "distracted, his mind kept activated, lest he get himself killed out of sheer boredom."

From the middle of 1943 until just after D-day, when he was assigned to one of the new "T-Force" units and sent to London for training in the high arts of plunder, my grandfather worked for Stanley Lovell in research and development, which occupied the cramped basement of the OSS campus at Twenty-third and E. Donovan had recruited Lovell, a chemist and patent lawyer, to equip clandestine

OSS operatives in Europe, North Africa, and the Far East. Lovell and his R&D team set to work devising the fountain-pen pistols, lipstick cameras, and cyanide-filled shirt buttons that have featured ever since in the panoplies of movie and television spies. They found new approaches to infiltration, sabotage, and secret communication. They hit on ways to kill the enemy with cunning and panache, with exploding pancake flour and incendiary bats.*

I jotted down some of the names of the devices and tools my grandfather remembered having contrived during his time at Twenty-third and E. It was a fairly long list, with many annotations, scrawled inside the front cover of the book I was reading that day, Salinger's *Nine Stories*. Decades later, having recommended "For Esmé—with Love and Squalor" to my elder daughter, I went looking for *Nine Stories*, one of a number of titles that had been duplicated on the shelves of my first marriage, in graduate school. At the sight of the cover with its grid of colored blocks, the memory of that afternoon returned to me: a slant of submarine light through the eucalyptus outside the guest bedroom, my grandfather's brown face against a white pillow, the sound of his Philadelphia vowels at the back of his nose like a head cold. But when I opened the book, the inside cover was blank. In making our terminal inventories, my ex-wife and I must have exchanged copies. I had lost to estrangement and carelessness the only document I possessed of the week I am now trying to reconstruct. And I can recall only five of the projects my grandfather claimed to have originated:

I. A crystalline compound, dubbed "whizzite," that, when mixed with an operative's own urine and added to the fuel tank of an airplane, truck, or panzer, caused delayed but complete and irreparable damage.

---

* Flying mammals, not sporting gear.

2. A small irregular pyramid of steel that, when wedged against a rail along a stretch of track from which the opposite rail had been loosened—not even removed—was guaranteed to derail any locomotive moving less than thirty miles per hour.

3. A flexible, expandable garrote made of piano wire sheathed in an ordinary shoestring. "Fairly reliable," my grandfather remembered.

4. A pair of "convertible bifocals," the lower half-moons of whose lenses were ground in such a way that, with a few twists of the frames, they could be arranged to form a serviceable spyglass.

5. A "magnetic paint" that would, for example, permit a limpet mine to be affixed to wood or glass. "That one never quite came together," my grandfather said. "Could've made a fortune if it had."

My grandfather enjoyed his time with Lovell, for the most part; kept out of the action once again, he welcomed the chance to lose himself amid solutions to the novel technical problems that crossed his desk every day. It was important work, in its curious way. But ultimately, it was an office job in the world capital of office jobs, a city whose bureaucratic fecklessness my grandfather once dreamed of repaying with conquest and shame. No one was more thrilled than my grandfather when the news came from Omaha Beach that it was time at last for his war, for his life, to begin.

◑   ◑   ◑

After Glenn Miller's set—one of the last the bandleader played before his plane went down over the English Channel on December 15, 1944—Lieutenant Alvin Aughenbaugh returned to the billet he shared with my grandfather, the smallest flat with the fewest windows on the highest floor of the Mount Royal Hotel, Oxford Street, London. He was whistling "Moonglow," and there was a telltale bulge at the hip pocket of the cardigan his sister had knitted for him. They were orphans, Aughenbaugh and his sister; she was like a mother to the guy. He took off the sweater only when directly ordered to do so. The commanding officer of their unit was regular army, but he understood that he had been put in charge of a bunch of oddballs, and for the most part the sweater never left Aughenbaugh's body. It had a shawl collar, toggle buttons, and a sash that Aughenbaugh left untied because he felt self-conscious about having womanly hips. When he wore it, he looked, fittingly, like an engineer with a Ph.D. in food production from the University of Minnesota. His field of expertise before the war had been the mass manufacture of donuts, or what Aughenbaugh called "industrial-grade edible tori." He spoke German and French, read Russian and Latin. He was two hundred pages into the writing of an analytical biography of August Kekulé done entirely in limericks, entitled *A Rolling Autophagous Snake*. Apart from one or two professors at Drexel, he was the first intellectual my grandfather had met who was not a pool hustler, a criminal, or a rabbi.

"Lo, I bring you tidings of great joy," Aughenbaugh said. "So put down the pornography, Rico."

My grandfather put down the book he was reading, a bound edition of the *Zeitschrift für angewandte Chemie* for 1905 containing a key text in the history of gas warfare chemistry, J. F. Haber's *Uber Zündung des Knallgases durch Wasserstoffatome*. He lay uniformed but for necktie and shoes. "Find something good?"

"I only drink the best." Aughenbaugh's alcoholism was riddled with morality. He believed it was less sinful to drink good liquor than to drink hooch. "As you know." The supply of good liquor, like the supply of everything else, was subject to gluts and shortages. Lately, it had been tough to come by. "Given a choice." He fished a fifth of something out of the hip pocket of the sweater his sister had knitted.

"Where'd you get it?"

"I distilled it myself, as a matter of fact." Aughenbaugh uncapped the bottle, stuck it under his nose, inhaled. "From a fine mulch of bomb debris and uneaten portions of creamed mock kidney on toast."

Aughenbaugh often resorted to false cheeriness in the bleak hours between dusk and inebriation. He was by nature a cheerful man, but he was homesick. He missed his dog, his cat, his books, his record collection, ice fishing, and his sister, Beatie. The world had been plunged into fire and darkness, and a scarcity of good liquor imperiled his soul. On top of all that there was English wartime cuisine, which substituted plentiful inedibles for scarce ones with vile inventiveness. In the canteen at lunch today, in the maze of Great Cumberland Street where their mission was headquartered, the role of creamed kidneys had been played by something called neeps, seethed in a cornstarch slurry.

"Best neeps yet, I thought," Aughenbaugh said.

"The neeps were top-notch."

"I would have sworn those kidneys were unmock."

"Well, they use real urine," my grandfather said. "Gives it that tang." He folded his hands behind his head and flexed his toes pleasurably in his regulation socks. Unlike cornstarch and neeps, grain coffee, or beetroot fudge, Aughenbaugh's ersatz cheer was a reasonably effective substitute for the real thing.

"Speaking of urine," Aughenbaugh said, "it's time for your sample, Rico."

He looked around in vain for something to pour the whiskey into. The firm that supplied the Mount Royal with glassware and crockery had been hit by a doodlebug. The flat's ration of monogrammed MR glasses had been pilfered by a WAAF of my grandfather's brief acquaintance named Marigold Reynolds. Beakers were requisitioned from a lab at Great Cumberland Street, but then Aughenbaugh had needed them for an ongoing in-house experiment aimed at devising a cure for airsickness. He had spent the flight over from Langley with his face in a pail and the color of his uniform shirt, making sounds that were variations on the theme of his last name. He was dreading the short hop to Paris tomorrow.

"Oh, shish kebab," he said. "I meant to swipe a couple of glasses from the bar."

Shish kebab. Sugarloaf. Sheboygan. Whenever life called for foul language, Aughenbaugh broke into a reserve of quaint midwestern euphemisms. There seemed to be hundreds, rarely repeated. My grandfather had met few Lutherans. He wondered if they were handed some kind of list to memorize as children.

"Right, then." Aughenbaugh set the bottle down on a dresser. "See if I can't scare us up a couple of tankards, what?" he said, putting on his C. Aubrey Smith voice. "Do something about that beastly sobriety of yours."

"Just one tankard," my grandfather said. He patted the *Zeitschrift.* The Haber paper was eight pages long. He had been reading it for a month. Each of its sentences, dense with formulae, was a mile that must be crawled across shards of glass. My grandfather was on page six. "Got to keep my wits about me. I might need to conjugate the future perfect of *deisobutanisieren.*"

"Nonsense, old boy, wouldn't hear of it."

Aughenbaugh went back out to the flat's sitting room, where the experiment in antiemesis was under way. My grandfather heard him say, "*Fudge-bucket.*"

"I'd suggest you just drink from the bottle," my grandfather called. "But I wouldn't want civilization to collapse."

Stoppers popped. A pipette chimed. Glass clinked against glass like a lovers' toast. Aughenbaugh came back into the bedroom holding three beakers, each half-filled with sludge of varying translucence and color, from roast beef drippings to crank case fluid. One key stage in the preparation of the antiemetic had involved boiling some old ginger snaps with a handful of weeds Aughenbaugh had found growing in a bomb site.

"Is it ready?"

"Has to be." Aughenbaugh set the beakers down on the dresser beside the bottle of whiskey. He poured off the contents of two beakers into the third, leaving their bottoms tinged with a glaze of anti-puke formula.

"How was the show? Glenn say hi?"

Whenever he and his wartime band of soldier musicians came through London, Major Glenn Miller also lived in the Mount Royal Hotel and played nightly. Over the past few months Aughenbaugh had managed to engage his hero in two or three short conversations, all touching on the London weather, about which of course it was best to say nothing. For Aughenbaugh these had been encounters with a mahatma. They brightened his existence for days afterward.

"The show was depressing," Aughenbaugh said. "To be honest. I can't explain why, exactly."

"Playing was off?"

"Note-perfect. The great Jerry Gray arrangements, those pop-popping short phrases. Everything as tight and good-sounding as that time at the Mayflower." He poured two precise fingers of whiskey into each of the beakers. "I don't know what's wrong. I'd almost say the heart seems to have gone out of old Glenn. You better have a word with him, Rico. Set him straight."

Training with their T-Force unit, my grandfather, as was his habit, had offered very little in the way of information about himself, even to Aughenbaugh. The tale of his career before his recruitment to this arm of U.S. intelligence was a farrago of quarter-truth and rumor. It was said that he had worked as an enforcer for various New York and Philadelphia gangsters; that, as a rite of Mob initiation, he had shot himself in the stomach with a bullet rubbed with raw garlic to make the wound more painful. He had been known, it was reported, to bite off the ears of his enemies and feed them to stray dogs. And if he ever smiled at you—this rumor was Aughenbaugh's personal favorite—that smile would be the last thing you ever saw. Aughenbaugh had made my grandfather smile often enough to laugh at this hyperbole and with enough intimacy to tease him for the seed of truth it contained. There might or might not be something menacing in my grandfather's reticence—that was really up to you—but when he did speak or show emotion, it had a persuasive effect. It was Aughenbaugh who had nicknamed my grandfather after Cagney's gangster hero in *The Public Enemy*. As far as I know, this was the only nickname my grandfather was ever given, or ever tolerated.

"I'll see what I can do," he said, realizing that the heart might be going out of Aughenbaugh and wondering what he could do.

"Now, then," Aughenbaugh said, giving each beaker of whiskey a stir with the pipette to mix in the dash of airsickness dope. He handed a beaker to my grandfather. "Drink up."

My grandfather took the beaker and set it down on the nightstand between his bed and Aughenbaugh's. He picked up *Zeitschrift für angewandte Chemie*.

"Darn it, Rico, now, come on." Aughenbaugh tugged the book out of my grandfather's hands and tossed it over his shoulder. It opened in flight with a rustle of indignation and smacked against the wall. The wallpaper was patterned with moderne circles and lines that often tormented my grandfather by seeming to diagram the structures of impossible aromatics and polymers. "You're seeing phantom heterocyclics in the wallpaper again, aren't you?"

"No."

"I'm serious, man. Any other night. Not tonight."

"What's special about tonight?"

Aughenbaugh composed himself. His forebears, with patience and faith, had endured crop failures, cattle plagues, and iron winters. He could handle one exasperating Philadelphia Jew. "Well, let's see. For one thing. Tomorrow they are strapping your Heinz 57 into a C-47 and shipping it off to a place called Germany, where, from what I've heard, it is very likely to encounter a large number of armed men who will try to decorate it with a swastika made out of bullets."

"That's tomorrow."

"We are talking about one drink, for gosh sakes."

My grandfather shook his head.

"Why not? And don't give me that bullwhiz about how you don't like to lose control."

"I don't."

"There is no control."

Aughenbaugh knocked back the beaker of whiskey. He sat on the edge of his bed and set the empty beaker on the nightstand. He picked up the one he had poured for my grandfather and toasted my grandfather's health. He knocked that one back, too. He let out a sigh that did not sound entirely bereft of pleasure.

"Good?"

"Wonderful." He put down the beaker and rose, looking heavy on his feet. He went to pick up the book that he had thrown. He smoothed its pages and handed it back to my grandfather. "It's just the illusion of control," Aughenbaugh said with his accustomed gentleness. "You know that, right? There is no actual control. It's all just probabilities and contingencies, wriggling around like cats in a bag."

"Yes, I know that," my grandfather said. "But when I'm sober, I never have to think about it."

There was a thump, a pressure felt somewhere deeper than the eardrums, rooted in the ground. It was like the turbulent boom that rumbled windows, walls, and floorboards when a bomb hit the house down the street, the office block next door, but it could not have been a bomb. A bomb gave warning of its approach. It heralded its own arrival. It fell whistling from the belly of a Junker, or keening, or humming, or with a yell of inhuman high spirits that got louder and more ecstatic as it fell. If it was a buzzbomb, a doodlebug, then it prowled overhead, restless and muttering to itself, before its counter hit zero and its servo was cut. Then you heard a loud silence as the doodlebug surrendered to gravity and fell to its appointment with fire and destruction.

My grandfather just had time to think *rocket!* when the unheralded explosion gave way to a roar and a clatter like the Central pulling in to Marble Arch station. A second boom unfurled across the neighborhood, an uncoiling peal of thunder with a stinger in its tail. At four times the speed of sound, the concussion and the turbulence of the rocket's approach would always show up late for its detonation.

"We heard it," said Aughenbaugh. "That means we aren't dead."

My grandfather laced up his boots and tied his tie. They got their topcoats and hats. Aughenbaugh grabbed a camera. They took the stairs down to the basement of the hotel to avoid whatever hysteria might be loose in the lobby. They went down a long hallway with a checkerboard floor. Through the open door at the end of the hallway you could feel the heat of the fire and the cold of the night. Cooks and dishwashers in their white coats and black trousers were going in and out, speaking French and Polish and English. Into the kitchen, out the door, out of the kitchen, into the street. It looked purposive, a relay, a bucket brigade, but they were just wandering around like idiots with nothing to do. A fat cook stood in the doorway looking out. There was firelight on his belly and his face. My grandfather pushed him out of the way. He and Aughenbaugh ran out into Oxford Street and unoriginally stood there like idiots with nothing to do.

The physics of the rocket's detonation had sucked the show windows from the front of Selfridges. The windows had been decorated for the season with ice floes and ice mountains of pasteboard and sequins. A frolic of pasteboard Eskimos and penguins. The aurora borealis or australis in arcs of colored foil. A mannequin Father Christmas in Scott Expedition drag. Now the sidewalk was buried in snowbanks of shattered glass. Christmas trees lay scattered like tenpins. Their needles drifted down onto my grandfather's hat and the epaulets of his greatcoat. When he hung up his trousers that night before bed, cellophane snowflakes snowed down from the up-turned cuffs. Pasteboard Eskimos and penguins, headless, torn in half, continued their inaccurate cohabitation. Father Christmas was found the next morning in a dovecote on a nearby rooftop, intact and unharmed apart from a holiday frosting of pigeon shit.

Selfridges was not on fire, but the building beside it was. A fire brigade came around the corner in a wheezing old calliope of a pumper, followed by two teams of air raid wardens in Crossleys. The wardens in their shaving-bowl helmets made their way back along the street toward the corner, barking at hotel guests and patrons of the ballroom, telling them to get out of the way and please let the crews do their job. An ambulance nosed its way in among the bystanders and ruination. It was driven by a breathtaking young woman, blue eyes, black hair tumbling from under a narrow-brimmed hat, packed hastily into some man's shirt and trousers under her green WVS coat. He never saw her again, but forty-four years later, my grandfather remembered her vividly, her necktie, the swell of her breasts under the shirt, her gabardine trousers into the tops of her wellingtons. She told him and Aughenbaugh that the spirit of volunteerism was commendable, but it would be best for them just to get out of the way and let her mates and her do the job that the ARP and the Jerries had trained them to do. It was a harrowing job. If blood and pieces of what had until recently been citizens of London were something you wanted to see, you could see them.

"Penguins with Eskimos," Aughenbaugh said contemptuously. Remembering this line, years later, my grandfather burst out laughing, even though it literally hurt to laugh. "What the hell are we fighting for, Rico?"

They went back inside and up to their room. Aughenbaugh poured more whiskey into the beakers and passed one to my grandfather. It was graduated in milliliters. The whiskey went to ninety-two. My grandfather raised it and proposed a toast. "Cats in a bag," he said. He drank it all in one swallow and held it out for Aughenbaugh to fill again. "Probabilities and contingencies."

"It's a metaphor," Aughenbaugh said. "The bag is Newtonian physics."

"I missed that," my grandfather said.

XII

Sometimes they would roll into a town or village so hard on the heels of the armor and infantry that they encountered people uninstructed on the difference between liberation and surrender. An old man in a clock tower with a deer rifle, say, or five murderous Boy Scouts sharing a burp gun, or the last joker in town with a death's-head on his hatband, insisting with tedious punctilio on standing them to a round of pointless slaughter. Lives and time would be lost trying to clarify the matter.

"This is bullshit," said Diddens.

He was talking about the arrow in his left foot. It was a fine piece of pine and goose feathers. A second arrow had lodged with a thunk in a window box several feet wide of my grandfather, just before he dragged Diddens to cover behind a pile of rubble in the main thoroughfare of Vellinghausen. It had taken Diddens a minute to get past incredulity.

"I mean, what kind of thing is that?" Diddens was squatting on his right haunch with his left leg stuck out in front of him. He was an Alabaman, a chemist who had worked in Dow's pesticides division before the war. He was not prone to hysteria, but the arrow had him a little keyed up. "A fucking arrow?"

"At least it makes a change from bullets," my grandfather said.

"Fuck you, it's not sticking out of your foot!"

"You have a point."

"This is bullshit!" Diddens said again. This time he yelled it, but his cry had nothing to resound against and it failed to carry. Vell-

inghausen had undergone a week of shelling by both sides, followed
by a pitched two-day tank battle before the Germans conceded the
town for good to elements of the 8th Armored Division. Almost all
the buildings were badly damaged. Most of the main street of Vellinghausen was gray sky.

"Calm yourself," my grandfather said. He understood that from
Diddens's point of view, it seemed absurd to have come across France
and four hundred miles into Germany without being touched by artillery or small-arms fire only to be shot with an arrow. On the other
hand, there was a venerable school of thought that taught when a
conquering army showed up in your hometown at the head of a trail
of death and destruction, you were supposed to do what you could to
make conquest expensive, using whatever came to hand. That type
of behavior was the stuff of poems and heroes. In the past three
months my grandfather had seen poetry and heroism of this nature
cost the lives of several Germans, three first-rate jeep drivers, two ra-
diomen, and Lieutenant Alvin P. Aughenbaugh, Ph.D. This Diddens
was Aughenbaugh's replacement, and he was all right, but I don't
think my grandfather ever recovered from the loss of Aughenbaugh.
He would not tell me the circumstances of his friend's death other
than to say that it came in the back of a jeep while my grandfather
was trying to keep him upright and talking until they could find an
aid station.

"Did it hit bone?" my grandfather asked Diddens.

"I— " The question seemed to give Diddens something to focus
on. He gritted his teeth and studied his heavy boot. He was moving
his foot around inside it. "No, I don't think so."

"Can you put weight on it?"

Diddens put a hand on my grandfather's shoulder and raised himself off the ground. He drew in his left leg and lowered himself onto
the left foot. He gasped. "Uh. No." He stuck his foot back out. This
time he just sat down flat on the cobblestones, as if now were any
kind of time to take a rest. "Ah, jeez. It really hurts. I think the point

must be coming out of the bottom. Is it coming out of the bottom? Can you see?"

My grandfather frowned. They were already behind schedule. Vellinghausen was not even supposed to be a stop on their route. They were supposed to be following the 3rd Armored Division, but a map failure, a moonless night, and unexpected panzer movement south of Lippstadt had entangled them with the 8th. Forward regiments of the 3rd were already a day or more ahead of them, headed for Paderborn. A day or more closer to Nordhausen.

My grandfather reached for the gun at his hip. At the same time he bent over and grabbed hold of the shaft in Diddens's foot. He jerked the arrow backward. It slid loose with a moist pop. The head emerged streaked with purple from the hole it had made going into the boot, just to the left of the laces.

Diddens let out a yawp of outrage and shock. "What?" he said.

My grandfather stood up and came out from behind the heap of plaster chunks, roof tiles, and plaster dust that had been hiding them. He raised the gun and swept the street with his eyes, thinking about angles and sight-lines. He noted without lingering on them a black and orange cat, a bicycle that concussion had twisted around a hitching post to symbolize infinity. Behind the rubble pile Diddens clutched his foot and diverted his thoughts from the pain by describing in Alabaman detail the unnatural use that my grandfather had made of my great-grandmother. Up the street on the right, a bakery occupied the ground floor of a stucco townhouse painted the color of lemon custard. The houses this side of it had paid off the tank gunners' luck with jackpots of rubble like the one they had taken cover behind. My grandfather traveled his gaze up the pale stucco to the third story. Its paired windows seemed to be at about the limit of the effective range of an archer.

"What are you doing?" Diddens said. "Get down, are you fucking nuts?"

My grandfather knew he was taking chances. In general it was

best, for example, not to try to remove a sharp object from a punc-
ture wound because it might be acting to plug the hole it had made
in some major vein or artery. But there were no major veins or ar-
teries, as far as my grandfather knew, in the human foot. As for
stepping into the middle of the street when you knew somebody out
there was trying to kill you with a bow and arrow, he had decided to
test a personal theory that since the arrow had gone into Diddens's
foot and not his head or his throat, the archer must not be much of
a marksman.

"No," my grandfather said. "Just in a hurry."

In the ruins of Köln he and Aughenbaugh had interviewed a captured Wehrmacht truck driver—irrespective of what it said on their
bills of lading, all truck drivers carried information—who reported
having hauled a shipment of machine parts in mid-March to a group
of "professors" at Nordhausen. One of the professors he claimed to
have seen there was a thickset young blond whom the driver described as clearly the man in charge.

As it happened, my grandfather, along with all the other hunters
in the unit, was recently issued a detailed inventory of thousands
of leading Nazi "professors." It was code-named the Black List and
was said to have been compiled from a German original found by a
Polish janitor at Bonn University, half-flushed down a toilet in the
mayhem of the German retreat from that city. My grandfather's
orders were to track down the scientists, technicians, and engineers
whose names appeared on the Black List and capture them before
the Russians could. At the top of the Black List was the name of a
physicist said to be the inventive mind behind the V-2 rocket, one of
which had come close to killing my grandfather and Aughenbaugh
that night in London. According to the limited intelligence the Allies
had on him, this rocket man was a beefy blond fellow.

My grandfather had never wanted anything more than he wanted
to be the man who brought in this Wernher von Braun. Or maybe at
that point—he told me—what he wanted more than anything was to

see one of von Braun's rockets. That desire was, at the moment, the only certainty he possessed, apart from a strong intuition that one of the Russian hunters traveling west from Poland behind the fast-moving Red Army would never sit around crying because he had an arrow in his foot.

Something whispered in my grandfather's left ear, and just behind him a mallet struck a block of wood. The flower box, planted only with mud and ash, had taken another hit. The time had come to test his hypothesis about the archer's marksmanship. So far the man was shooting one for three.

The fourth arrow hummed in low and whistling and clattered against the cobblestone street about fifteen feet in front of my grandfather. It skittered along, struck some jut in the cobbles, and bounced. Its vector was deformed by the impact, and it shot up at an eighty-degree angle to the street. It tumbled interestingly through the air toward my grandfather, end over end and moving slightly to the left of him. He reached out as it came cartwheeling and managed to snatch it as it went by.

○   ○   ○

It was not that my grandfather felt no fear.

"I was afraid the whole time," he told me. "From the minute I got there. Even when no one was shooting at me or trying to drop a bomb on my head. But whenever they did shoot at me, what happened was, it made me angry, too."

"And the anger trumped."

"It was, you know, it flooded over me."

"Yeah."

"It just washed everything else away. That was the time . . . In my whole life, that was the time I got some use out of it. When somebody was shooting at me." He twisted his mouth. "But I didn't know until that day it worked with arrows, too."

◗   ◗   ◗

He caught the arrow in midflight and turned to the yellow house, looking up. Swagger in the angle of his head, taunting the archer, a red needle of Philadelphia climbing inside him. He saw a flicker of white in one of the third-story windows: a shirtfront. A brown sleeve. A pink hand. A gaping mouth. A man leaned out of the window, propped at the hip against the window ledge, half-bracketed with a dark brown bow. Something loose and careless in the way he was hanging himself out the window suggested that he was not much older than my grandfather. He dangled an arrow like a long cigarette between the fingers of one hand. He nocked the arrow and shifted himself a little. My grandfather raised the gun and then, to satisfy the strange code duello of Vellinghausen, they fired off their respective shots.

A sharp hammer, or maybe a pickax, took a sudden whack at my grandfather's helmet, front and center. The archer sagged and let go of the bow. It dropped and hit the street with a twang. The archer listed and hung balanced on the window ledge for what felt to my grandfather like a very long time, as if making up his mind whether to go after the bow. Then he tumbled from the window and hit the cobblestones with a doubled sound: a drum crack, a carpet beater smacking against wool.

My grandfather holstered his gun and took off his helmet. It looked like the prop from a movie comedy, some kind of farce in which GIs fought Indians. He turned the helmet upside down. The arrow had pierced to a depth of not quite an inch. Later he would find a dot of dried blood beaded at the center of his forehead.

He yanked out the arrow and put the helmet back on his head. He walked up the street to the bow and picked it up, then turned to the young man. My grandfather guessed he might be about Ray's age. He lay twisted into a swastika under the bakery window. His skull leaked blood at the back where it had smacked against the stone street. He wore dark suit trousers, a dark tie, and a shirt with a tab collar and pearl snaps. There was nothing about his clothing or face to suggest that he was the kind of man who would try to kill you with a bow and some arrows.

My grandfather was about to kneel beside the young man to see if he was dead when he heard from behind a long, soft exhalation that might have been despondent, angry, or both. There was no time to draw the pistol, so he raised the bow and fitted the nock of the arrow he'd caught to its string. He was ready to let fly. He had never shot an arrow, but he was willing to try. He had managed okay, after all, with a canoe.

It was an old priest in a cassock that reached almost to the tops of his pointed shoes. White dust patterned the black cassock in big splotches like continents or the spots on a cow. He was standing by the white bicycle that the shock wave of a bursting shell had wrapped around a pole, mourning its loss. He reached out to run his spider hand along the tubes of its frame. He might have been bidding it farewell or trying to puzzle out the geometry of its torsion. He did not seem aware that in principle he was within arrowshot of an American soldier.

"Good morning, Father," my grandfather said, lowering the bow.

The white-haired priest looked up. His mouth fell open. He took note of the bow and arrow, and his eyes went a little dull with understanding. He closed his mouth. His gaze traveled the street until it found the body of the archer. "Is he dead?" the priest said.

"I don't know. I think so."

The priest approached the body. He moved quickly for a man of his age and with a doctor's officiousness. Screwing up his face, he worked himself into a crouch alongside the body and laid a ruddy hand on the archer's chest. He lowered his head to the archer's until his left ear nearly brushed the archer's lips.

My grandfather heard a scrape behind him. Diddens limped up the street, his left foot printing the paving stones with roses. "He dead?" Diddens said.

There was a first aid kit back in the jeep with the driver, who had completed his medic's training. Unless of course the driver had been killed by an arrow, or a blunderbuss, or some retired merchant seaman with a blowgun.

The archer opened his eyes, two pannikins of water stained with two blue droplets of gouache.

"Apparently not," my grandfather said.

The archer's face was aimed at the sky, but he fixed his pale eyes on the old priest's head, the pink pate, the milkweed-tuft hair. This gave the archer a downcast or shy expression. The old priest's ear was angled to catch the sentences emerging from the archer's lips in softly popping bubbles of blood. The words were spoken too low for my grandfather to hear and, in any case, seemed to be in the local dialect, which gave my grandfather difficulties. The old priest nodded, said something, nodded again. He folded the archer's hands between the bones of his own, clasped them, and began to speak. It was not a reply, or not a direct one, at any rate.

The old priest spoke the requisite Latin and drew a hasty cross with his fingertips curled at his chest. He reached into a slit in his cassock. His hand moved around inside the dusty fabric. He wore the universal expression of a man searching his pants pocket for something that must be there. When his hand reemerged, he was holding a small brown medicine bottle with a black cap. His right hand shook as he worked to get the bottle unstoppered.

In the gray and cold of that place, the smell that came from the little bottle alarmed my grandfather. It was overripe as fruit and acrid as summer. It made the heart leap. It smelled the way the word *sacrament* sounded.

The bottle shook as the priest dripped a dime of golden liquid into his left palm. Now the left hand started to shake. The oil trembled. It found a crease in his pink palm that drained it all down the side of his hand. It drizzled down onto and stained the dying man's white shirt.

"Shit," said the old priest. Aughenbaugh would have been scandalized. "Idiot."

The priest smeared a thumbprint of oil onto the dying man's forehead. The archer made a sound of animal contentment.

As a young man, my grandfather seems to have had no higher regard for religion than he displayed in the days when I knew him. I have his old black hardback copy of *The Magic Mountain*, his favorite novel. Across its front flyleaf in block capitals, under his name and the date (March 11, 1938), as though announcing to the world some kind of solemn verdict or choice, my grandfather printed the word HUMANISM. By the spring of '45 he had lost that all-caps certainty about his choice of worldview. Cold, hunger, darkness and blood, and the random assignment of death as the coefficient to victory and defeat alike had conspired to bankrupt his humanism. The only choice that seemed to remain, seven years after he inscribed his copy of *The Magic Mountain,* was a choice between faith and numbness.

At close range, he had been exposed to the horror of the human body's fragility, its liability to burst open, to be ripped in two, to deliver up its pulp through a split in the outer peel. He had suffered bombardment, gun barrage, loneliness, foolish commanders, and a two-month case of the GIs. He had lost Aughenbaugh. He had killed a boy who was shooting at him with a burp gun. Apart from the fact that he was, as a result, still alive, that was one person more than he ever wanted to kill again. Along the way he had captured or had a hand in the capture of men of science—one who had taught chemistry at Princeton before the war, another whose medical research had been funded by a Rockefeller—in laboratories and proving grounds dedicated to the cultivation of fatal toxins and missile-borne plagues.

In the face of all that, my grandfather had come down on the side of numbness. Even when Aughenbaugh had died in the back of that jeep, blood soaking his cardigan, calling for his sister, Beatie, in a voice of boyish plaintiveness, my grandfather had permitted himself to shed only a few tears. Now, watching the old priest comfort the dying man in low, musical Latin, my grandfather felt some inner tether come unlashed. His cheeks burned. His eyes stung. For the first and only time in his life, he felt the beauty that inhered in the idea of Jesus Christ, in the message of comfort that had managed to survive, reasonably intact, despite having been so thoroughly corrupted and profaned over the past two thousand years by Christians.

Relief spread across the face of the dying man. He closed his downcast eyes. The old priest looked up at my grandfather without apparent reproach or emotion of any kind. He tried to get up from the paving stones beside the corpse but did not seem to have the required flexibility. My grandfather offered his hand and hoisted the old priest to his feet. The priest studied my grandfather's face for a moment, his jowls powdered with plaster dust, his expression unreadable but not unfriendly. He reached again into the slit of his cassock, felt around. My grandfather took a step away, thinking this time the priest might be reaching for a gun. He reached back to put a hand on Diddens's chest, ready to shove the Alabaman to safety.

The old priest's hand reemerged from the slit in the cassock holding a white handkerchief, ironed flat with crisp corners. He passed it to my grandfather. The fresh linen smelled of lavender.

"I'm sorry," said my grandfather. He meant to apologize for spoiling the handkerchief, but it came out sounding like regret for the body at their feet. That was all right with my grandfather.

The priest looked at the damp bit of linen and then searched my grandfather's face. "Keep it," he said.

"What was he saying, Father?" Diddens's German was more correct but less fluid than my grandfather's. He pointed to the dead man. "What was he telling you?"

The old priest glanced over his shoulder at the body of the archer. "What was there to say?" he said.

XIII

The old priest's name was Father Johannes Nickel. He had been the rector of St. Dominikus-Kirche until the Lord, in the form of an 88mm shell from a King Tiger, had seen fit to deprive him of his home and place of employment. For the past week he had been living with his aged sister, a widow, on her farm a few miles to the northeast of Vellinghausen. The farmhouse was a long walk for an old man but not so far—here Father Nickel heaved another sigh—on a bicycle.

My grandfather offered the services of their jeep and driver, Private Anthony M. Gatto, who was susceptible to spasms of prayerfulness. Gatto and Father Nickel solemnly shook hands.

"It will be dark soon," Father Nickel said. "I invite you to stay the night with my sister and me. There is no room in the farmhouse, but you would be more than welcome to sleep in the hayloft. The straw is clean and you would be warm."

In his fitful eastward progress through Belgium and Germany that winter, my grandfather had shared all manner of billets: with dogfaces and officers, in misery and in comfort, in attack and in retreat, and pinned down by snow or German ordnance. He had bedded down under a bearskin in a schloss and in foxholes flecked pink with the tissue of previous occupants. If an hour's sleep were to be had, he seized it, in the bedrooms or basements of elegant townhouses, in ravaged hotels, on clean straw and straw that crawled with vermin, on featherbeds and canvas webbing slung across the bed of a half-track, on mud, sandbags, and raw pine planks. However wretched, accommodations were always better or no worse than those on the enemy side. If that was not written down in the field manual or stipulated by some tribunal in Geneva, it was nevertheless an iron law. When Allied soldiers came knocking at the door of a German farmhouse, they would not be planning to sleep in the hayloft. If the farm folks did not relish a night in the barn, there was always the cellar.

"That is very kind of you, Father," my grandfather said. He found the old priest's self-regard oddly touching. "Unfortunately, we need to keep on."

"Your friend's foot is injured."

"Nevertheless."

"When I left the house this morning to come here and look for my bicycle, my sister was killing a chicken. I believe she plans to cook it in a stew. There are carrots and potatoes and a bit of flour for dumplings."

My grandfather turned to consult Diddens and Gatto, knowing what he would find in their faces yet surprised all the same by the depth of its canine abjection.

"Lieutenant's foot is hurting pretty bad," Gatto said.

Diddens nodded. "Ow," he said.

"It's better not to travel after dark," my grandfather said.

The Germans were in retreat north and east, and the general feeling was that they would not be returning to Vellinghausen anytime soon. The town was held by some bone-weary somnambulists from the 7th Armored Infantry and a few bewildered-looking sappers from the 53rd Combat Engineers. Troops were few and scattered, and to a passerby it might appear that the invasion had been conducted not by soldiers but by clouds of smoke, the gray sky pouring into the roofless houses, and a hunger so profound it had gnawed the houses to their foundations and the trees to stumps. Here and there a baker or a butcher had opened for business, but this apparent optimism or bravado was nothing more than the robotics of habit. There was nothing to buy, nothing to sell, nothing to eat. Smoke had left the eye sockets of houses with black eyebrows of astonishment. Cats hugged corners leaving brushstrokes of ash on the stucco.

Gatto steered their jeep around the blown carcass of an M4 tank, a human leg (German) in a gray pant leg and a black boot, a bathtub with its feet in the air, and an erect dame whose high-button shoes and widow's weeds must have dated from the Franco-Prussian War. The old lady had her hands over her mouth. She was staring at a heap of rubble, pipe, and wire that to the observer looked no different from any of the other heaps that artillery fire had spilled into the street. Staring old people, staring children, staring women and girls. Staring amputees on crutches. The stares did not seem hostile, sullen, or resentful. Nor were they the stares of people watching their fondest wish come true. Some people smiled. Others turned bright red as though fighting tears or shame. Some did both at once.

One night the month before, back on the other side of the Belgian border, Aughenbaugh had delivered a lecture on the etymology of the word *war*. He said that he had looked it up and it came from an ancient Indo-European root signifying *confusion*. That was a foxhole night, bitter cold. The 5th Panzer Army was making its last great push west. You had to hand it to those Indo-Europeans, my grandfather thought, rolling through Vellinghausen. Confusion shone on the faces of the townspeople. War confused civilians every bit as surely as it did the armies who got lost in its fogs. It confounded conquest with liberation, anger with heartache, hunger with gratitude, hatred with awe. The 53rd Combat Engineers looked pretty confused, too. They were milling around at the edge of town, contemplating the long stretch of road between there and beautiful downtown Berlin, trying to figure out if they ought to mine it or clear it of mines.

In a smaller square a little to the north of the main street, the priest begged Gatto to stop the jeep in grave but halting English. The square was pegged with the stumps of what might have been elm trees. The stumps were cut clean and all to the same height. They had been felled by ax and not artillery. The cuts looked recent but not fresh.

"We've had a very cold winter," the old priest said. He was sitting up front, next to Gatto. Everyone agreed that this was unquestionably the case. "I gave out the pews and reredos and so forth. The beautiful oak pulpit, which a professor-doctor from Tübingen dated to the thirteenth century. I told them to take the crucifix, too. It was quite large. Used prudently, it might have heated a dozen homes for a night or two. But there they drew the line. They were shocked, I think. I tried to explain that if He would give His life to save their souls, He would not mind parting with His image to warm their bones." He shook his head, looking at the ruin of his church. "Of course, in the end it went to waste."

The stray 88 had knocked the square tower off the shoulders of St. Dominic's Church. The beams holding up the roof, which was clad in metal, had collapsed and caught fire. In their collapse, the roof beams had formed a kind of bowl or funnel into which the metal roof, now a molten pool, had poured. The glowing drizzle had burned a hole in the sandstone floor, then flowed through to fill the crypt. What missed the hole spread in ripples across the floor, setting fire to everything it touched that was not made of stone. The dislodged tower, with lacework iron steeple, had slid onto the parsonage behind the church, landing square on its four corners like a gymnast sticking a dismount. Half the old half-timbered house had been flattened, killing the old priest's housekeeper but sparing Father Nickel for as yet unknown purposes. When the tower sat down, the counterforce of its impact with the ground had sent the steeple heavenward in a skewed arc that ended, as with so much of St. Dominic's business over the centuries, in the churchyard. The steeple broke into three large and many small pieces, some of which still smoldered in the churchyard. Smoke rose in plumes to haunt the gravestones.

"So He is in there, buried under all of that," Father Nickel said.

"Saying, 'Tsk, tsk, silly people, now, why didn't you burn me when you had the chance!'"

The American soldiers exchanged looks. Private Gatto helped the old priest down from the jeep, and Father Nickel promised to return in a few minutes with something they would be happy to have for the celebration. He had decided that the German retreat across the Ruhr meant the war was over, and he was not interested in counterargument. He dismissed Diddens's halfhearted insistence that in fact they were still enemies, saying he could not speak for Diddens but that a priest could not have enemies any more than a hog butcher could be a vegetarian.

He had gone half the distance to the gate of the churchyard when he seemed to remember something, a possible difficulty. He turned back to the jeep, considering the three Americans. He pointed to my grandfather. "You will find a shovel in the toolshed," he said. "An excellent shovel with long experience."

The iron gate of the churchyard hung half-hinged and twisted, like the bicycle, into a glyph signifying something unknown. Father Nickel lifted the latch nevertheless and swung it open with a certain ceremony. My grandfather went to fetch the gravedigger's shovel from the toolshed.

One of the headstones was engraved with a name and dates that made some kind of learned Latin joke, one my grandfather did not understand. My grandfather hesitated a moment when the old priest encouraged him to start digging at its foot. He was concerned not about desecrating a grave but about detonating a possible mine that this old coot knew to be buried here.

"You speak German with the accent of Pressburg," Father Nickel said. "I was born in that city in 1864, under the reign of Emperor Franz Josef I."

My grandfather explained that his grandfather and father had been born in that city as well, though he was unable to provide dates.

"Did they tell you that a Pressburger is incapable of deceit?"

My grandfather was forced to confess that they had neglected to mention this fact. Nevertheless, he started to dig. The hole he dug was not wide and before long the shovel struck metal, less than two meters down.

"Well?" said the old priest.

"Excellent shovel," my grandfather said.

The minute Father Nickel heard that Allied soldiers had set foot on German soil, he had sent for his former sexton and gravedigger, Alois. Alois had grown up a ward of the parish. It had been his job as a boy to prepare the church's most valuable relic, a bone from the body of Saint Dominic, for its yearly presentation. At eighteen Alois had enlisted and been shipped east to Smolensk, where a *limonka* had taken his left ring finger and pinkie and his left eye. He was returned to Vellinghausen suffering from shell shock that gradually deepened into black depression. He would not return to his former employment at St. Dominikus-Kirche. Every night he drank himself into unconsciousness and slept where he fell. While drunk, he would repeat foul blasphemies he had learned in the army. These did not offend Father Nickel, who had heard everything, but he knew that God was less forgiving, and he worried about the fate of his former protégé's soul. Hoping to distract the young man as much as to protect the church's treasures, he had asked Alois to build a strongbox that could be buried in the churchyard, disguised as an actual grave. Alois still had a strong back and clever hands. Despite his injury, he could wield a hammer and shears.

To the old priest's delight and relief, Alois, guided by lingering reverence for his former charge, the holy relic of Saint Dominic, had accepted the commission. He persuaded the late housekeeper, Maria, to part with an old cedar chest. Then he went to the parish henhouse, which had stood empty for over a year, and pried loose the corrugated sheets of zinc that roofed it. He cut the zinc to measure and nailed the pieces to the outside of the cedar chest. He had carved the jocular headstone to Father Nickel's specifications, then buried the strongbox, filled with the wealth of St. Dominikus-Kirche, at its foot. Now the chest sat looking impregnable and snug at the bottom of a six-foot shaft dug with machined precision to fit it exactly.

"How heavy is that thing, Father?"

"Seventy-three kilograms."

My grandfather started to question the precision of Father Nickel's reply, then realized: "Alois weighed it."

"He made a complete inventory, which I mailed to the Congregation for Divine Worship at the Curia for safekeeping."

My grandfather felt that he would have liked to meet this tragic but admirably methodical young man. He hesitated, believing he already knew the answer to the question he was going to ask. "Maybe Alois has some thoughts about digging up the box," he said. "Where is he?"

"No doubt he would have done," Father Nickel said. "Unfortunately, the young man you killed today, in the street . . . to whom I gave extreme unction . . ."

"Ah," said my grandfather. "I'm sorry about that."

"I was able to comfort him at last," the priest said. "As you saw."

My grandfather had seen something he was not prepared to concede or even acknowledge. He managed a nod.

"He had been shooting at you. With the bow."

"That's right." My grandfather nodded back toward the jeep. Diddens appeared to have fallen asleep. "Diddens got an arrow in the foot; I had to remove it."

"Alois was a fine archer. You're lucky that the injury to his hand spoiled his aim. You have some Russian trooper to thank for your life."

My grandfather nodded. Then he and Father Nickel went back to staring down into the hole in the ground. My grandfather made out a groove running down the right side of the shaft. There was a similar faint groove down the left side. "He used a block and tackle. The one he used for the coffins. He passed it around the bottom of the chest, through those grooves."

Father Nickel nodded. He anticipated my grandfather's next question. "It was made chiefly of wood," the old priest said with an air of regret.

"Ah."

"I'm afraid we also burned the rope."

My grandfather had Gatto back the jeep through the churchyard gate and around the edge of the burial ground. Gatto threaded the gaps among headstones until he was alongside the hole. Outside Bonn, Aughenbaugh and my grandfather had come upon the wingless but otherwise intact fuselage of a small flying bomb—a guided missile, we would call it today—jammed into a frozen pond like a cigar butt into the sand of an ashtray. It was of a design no one had ever seen. It was stuck fast in the ice. So Aughenbaugh and my grandfather had gotten hold of a welding torch and improvised a winch out of salvage, spare parts, and a length of chain. They freed the Enzian—as it later would turn out to have been code-named— packed it up, and shipped it back to Wright Field.

Now my grandfather paid ten feet of chain from the drum mounted to the front of the jeep. He tossed it over the limb of a bare chestnut tree that must shade the church wonderfully in summer, then passed it around Gatto's waist a few times. He cinched it at the back, leaving about seven feet free at the end. He tied a piece of stiff fence wire to the loose end of the chain and gave it to Gatto. He and Diddens picked up Gatto and turned him upside down so that he dangled headfirst from the branch of the chestnut.

A dagger trimmed in nickel with a black scabbard fell out of Gatto's pocket and hit the ground with a thump. It was decorated with a silver eagle. Diddens got in the jeep and backed it up a little closer to the tree. Gatto swung over the hole. A silver ring ornamented with a death's-head fell out of his pocket, and then a wristwatch whose face, when my grandfather retrieved it, had a pair of lightning bolts in the twelve spot.

"I'm sorry," Gatto said. "Tell him I'm sorry."

Father Nickel said that it was nothing, but my grandfather thought the old priest looked scandalized. My grandfather wrapped his arms around Gatto's hips and aimed him. Diddens paid out more chain, and Gatto's head went into the hole.

"No," Gatto said. "No, god damn it. I can't do it. Take me out!"

They winched Gatto back up out of the hole. He was crying. My grandfather took his place. Diddens and Gatto turned him upside down and fed him down into the hole. His shoulders barely cleared the sides and his body blocked most of the light. My grandfather thought he could smell spring stirring in the darkness of the hole. It was a meaty odor, a smell of worms. He dangled from the taut end of the chain. He put out his hands. His fingers touched the cold zinc that clad the chest. He braced himself with his left hand and, with the right hand, fed the wire through the groove in the right wall of the shaft. He poked it through the underside of the chest and then kept pushing until the tip of it emerged through the groove in the left-hand wall. He tied a knot in the chain and called out that he was ready.

Nothing happened. He called out again, louder. He kicked with his heels at the chain that held him suspended. It thrummed meaningfully. Still he dangled, a Jew on a chain sharing a strait grave with the bone of a saint. The smell of worms began to cloy. It had the wet-blanket heaviness of his own exhalations. He was suffocating. The Luftwaffe had been all but knocked out of the fight, but every once in a while a stray Messer would fly overhead with its MG-131s chattering and flashing. Maybe Diddens, Gatto, and Father Nickel had been strafed. Maybe the old priest had decided to punish him for killing Alois, and Gatto for looting the corpses of dead SS men.

But as blood filled his head, it seemed to bring an odd tranquility. Suffocation was reputedly gentle and quick so long as you did not struggle against it. He thought about the sense of profound relief that had spread across Alois's face as he was dying in the street. Then he felt a painful jerk at his waist.

In under a minute he was out and on his feet. The evening was upon them in the west. In the east the sky was going from gray to black.

○　　○　　○

The jeep hit a pothole. My grandfather's head jolted against something metal. In his dream he was a boy knocking a soup can off a fence post with a brickbat. He woke up. The tires were spattering fresh mud onto the old snow along the roadside. The road skirted a broad stream or narrow stretch of river. Call it the Ruhr. On the opposite bank of the stream, my grandfather could make out the remnant of a railway line. The tracks had been raked up badly by ordnance: artillery, bombs, or both. They would need to be repaired. That was something for the engineers to tackle once they had resolved the road-mining conundrum.

My grandfather had not eaten in nearly three days. He had not slept more than four hours at a stretch since leaving London. He was dehydrated. Likely he was in a kind of delayed or ever compounding shock. The idea that the 53rd Engineers would soon be called upon to repair that stretch of track on the opposite bank of the Ruhr became confused in my grandfather's mind with memories of the Corps of Engineers training camp in Illinois long ago. The thought that he was going to be handed a maul or a mattock and put to work was more than he could face just then. There was so much torn-up track, and Berlin was still so far away.

He went back to sleep. When he woke up the second time, he was sitting propped in the softest bed in Germany, on the cleanest sheets. Father Nickel was at his bedside, smoking a GI cigarette. The heavenly bed was built in to an alcove of a candlelit room that turned out to be the only room in the house. The bed alcove took up a quarter of the premises. The kitchen and hearth, with a wooden table and dining chairs, took up another quarter. The rest was books in crates and piles. A refugee kingdom of books hastily evacuated after the collapse of St. Dominic's, a library in exile.

"Ah," Father Nickel said when he saw that my grandfather was awake again. "Here he is."

"Hey!" A chair leg scraped. Diddens loomed out of the flickering shadows. His face was veiled in steam from a bowl of chicken stew that he held in his palm. In his other hand he gripped a steel spoon. The stew smelled leafy, a meadow smell, almost like mint. When my grandfather encountered it again in my grandmother's cooking, it turned out to be an herb called summer savory.

"You okay, Rico?" Diddens said.

"Fine," my grandfather said. "How's the foot?"

"The old lady patched me up."

"Yeah?"

"Yeah, her name's Fräulein Judit."

My grandfather nodded at the stew. "Pretty good?"

"Oh, yes," Diddens said. He went a bit teary-eyed.

"Don't worry, Lieutenant, we left you plenty," Gatto said. He was hunched over his own bowl at the table. "Have some."

A smaller, stouter, older version of Father Nickel rose up from the darkness beyond Gatto, her head wrapped in a dark kerchief. She was reaching toward my grandfather, holding out a bowl and a spoon.

"Perhaps in a minute, ma'am," my grandfather said, nodding to the old woman. Her nose and ears were pinches of bread dough, her dark eyes two currants in poked holes. "Thank you."

"Yes, in a minute," Father Nickel snapped. His tone softened as he turned back to my grandfather. "First a little of something very nice."

The old priest had been sitting on the chest from the churchyard. Now he crouched beside it the way he had crouched beside Alois dying in the street. With an air of tenderness, he lifted the lid on the crate. He took stock of the situation within. When he emerged from behind the lid, he was holding a big green bottle with a long neck and a squat bottom.

"It is cognac," Father Nickel said. He pronounced the word with reverence and a French accent. "Very wonderful cognac."

He handed the bottle to my grandfather. The label was all heraldry and the kind of clerical script you saw lettering diplomas and pound notes, a bunch of French verbiage. Lean and raffish lions flanked a quartered escutcheon. The vintage was 1870. "Before the phylloxera," my grandfather said.

Father Nickel sat back down on the crate. The muddy skirt of his cassock rode up. The soles of his high black boots were holed and patched with tarpaper. His high socks were hand-knit and curiously festive, socks that might have been worn by the grandfather in *Heidi*.

"That's right," he said. "Just before. So, you take an interest?"

"Purely scientific," my grandfather said. He shook his head and handed the bottle back to Father Nickel. "But you go right ahead, please, Father."

Father Nickel seemed to consider taking offense. "You think I put poison in it."

"I want to see it properly enjoyed," said my grandfather.

Father Nickel took a small oblong glass with a wide foot from a hutch by the table. He filled it halfway with cognac. He took a long swallow. He gasped pleasurably. When he lowered his head to my grandfather again, the offense seemed to have been forgiven. "Your friends are too trusting. They ate the soup. They took some wine."

The old priest filled a second glass with cognac and handed it to my grandfather. Diddens and Gatto raised their glasses. There was a dark green wine bottle on the table between them. If it had come out of the ground with the cognac, it must be something special. Diddens and Gatto appeared to find it palatable.

My grandfather took a sip of the cognac. It came on crackling and hot, like the first hard pulls on a cigar as you were getting it lit. After the blaze of a flavor like tobacco, he tasted something between butter and walnuts, and finally, a bittersweet sparkle on his tongue, like a squirt of oil from a crushed grapefruit peel.

"Well?"

"Wonderful," my grandfather said.

"The real treasure, eh?" The old priest tapped the crate between his legs. "The rest of it isn't much. Some old silver plate. A telescope. A gold monstrance. An old Bible bound in wisent leather. Beautiful but so fragile it can't even be opened, let alone read. All of it the work of men. But cognac . . ." He took another long swallow. He did not need to finish the sentence. His expression made clear his belief in the divine provenance of champagne brandy.

"What about the relic? Saint Dominic's bone?"

"Ah, yes," the old priest said. "The left stapes of Saint Dominic. No doubt, no doubt. A very precious treasure indeed." It sounded halfhearted. His hand caressed the cognac bottle.

"A telescope," my grandfather said. "Is that what you said?"

"Yes, my son."

"Is that a relic, too? Is it some kind of holy telescope?"

"No. It is a Zeiss telescope. It is my personal property." He smiled. "I did not wish it to fall into enemy hands." The old priest poured another glass of brandy that had been put into a cask seventy-five years ago.

"Are you an astronomer?"

"An amateur," Father Nickel said. "I have contributed a few insignificant observations. Chiefly lunar."

"I also take an interest in astronomy."

"In addition to vine blights."

"That's right."

"Then you come under the protection of Dominic, my son."

"How is that?"

"Saint Dominic de Guzman is the patron saint of astronomers." The old priest looked a little melancholy. "As to the value of that protection at this juncture, I would not care to hazard a guess."

XIV

The soldiers slept in the bed, each in his one-third share of heaven; it was the barn for the old woman and the priest. Diddens had taken pains to calibrate the amount of wine he consumed so that it counterbalanced the pain in his foot. Courageously, Private Gatto had volunteered to scout ahead, as it were, and locate the point where analgesia gave way to excess. Now my grandfather lay staring at the darkness as Gatto and Diddens took shifts working the stops and pedals of the pipe organ they appeared to have smuggled into the bed. Whenever they fell silent for a few minutes, there would be no sound but his own tinnitus and the intermittent booming of the war at night. It sounded very far away. My grandfather could take no comfort in that distance. He was accustomed by now to feeling grateful that when death settled like a flock of birds around him, it was other men and not him on whom it perched. This gratitude never had anything to do with happiness.

After what felt like two or three hours, he gave up. He extricated himself from the dogpile of Gatto and Diddens and climbed down from the bed in its niche. In the profundity of the rural dark, he groped for his trousers, his boots, somebody's overcoat. At sunset the weather had shown promise of clearing, and my grandfather thought about opening the crate to look for the telescope the old priest had mentioned. He found the top-front edge of the crate with his shin. He knelt beside it and felt for the hasp. In the end he could not bring himself to lift the lid, discouraged in a way that he found mystifying by the presence of St. Dominic de Guzman's stirrup bone. He went out into the yard between the barn and the farmhouse. Father Nickel sat hunched on a tall stool, his telescope pointed at the sky.

For a city boy like my grandfather, the number of visible stars had always been only a dim fraction of the five thousand or so he knew were visible to the naked human eye. Even in Rapides Parish there was ambient light enough to conceal the true madness of the heavens. On a clear night in blacked-out countryside, in between bomber runs, when the tracer fire ceased and the searchlights went dark, the stars did not fill the sky so much as coat it like hoarfrost on a windowpane. You looked up and saw *The Starry Night*, he told me; you realized that Van Gogh was a realist painter.

Tonight, however, as my grandfather joined Father Nickel at the telescope, the stars were lost in the dazzle of a full moon. Also, of course, a large swath of Westphalia was on fire. Smoke cobwebbed the vault of night.

"You should rest."

"No doubt."

My grandfather reached into the left hip pocket of the coat he was wearing and found a ten-pack carton of Luckies. So it was Gatto's coat. He tore open a pack and offered a Lucky to Father Nickel. Neither of them had a light. My grandfather crept back into the house with a piece of straw and lit it in the embers of the hearth. Once he got his cigarette going, he lit Father Nickel's and carried it back out to the priest. They looked up at the Moon hung from the sky like a mirror.

"Permit me to show you my little mountain," Father Nickel said.

My grandfather hunched over the oculus of the telescope. It was an old but excellent telescope, lovingly maintained. Father Nickel had fitted the eyepiece with a lunar filter to reduce the glare of moonlight. The resultant detail came as a shock. The rays of craters were sharp as cracks starring a mirror. The edge of the lunar disc was toothed like the blade of a circular saw. Somewhere in the center of the Montes Apenninus, according to the old priest, rose little Mons Gallienus.

"You see Mons Huygens?" he said. "You know it?"

"I . . . Yes. I see it."

"Now, look perhaps three degrees of arc to the southeast. You will see a shadow, a patch of gray. To my mind it resembles the print of a deer's hoof."

"Right."

"Now from there look, let us say, two degrees of arc to the northeast."

"Okay."

"It is there."

"Right."

"It has an almost castellated appearance."

"Ah."

"You see it?"

"Yes."

Father Nickel clucked his tongue. "You don't see it," he said, not without a trace of bitterness. In fact, due to the earth's rotation, the image of the Moon had already drifted out of the eyepiece. The telescope would have to be slewed.

"I'm sure I did," my grandfather said, standing up. "*Castellated* is the perfect word."

Father Nickel grunted. They lit two more cigarettes from the ends of the first and smoked them. They looked at the Moon with their unaided eyes. My grandfather shivered and worked himself more deeply into Gatto's overcoat. The snoring was faintly audible from the house. In a coop at the far corner of the farmyard, the remaining chicken, a rooster, muttered to itself, their comrade in insomnia. My grandfather heard a sound like a breeze through treetops, but there was no breeze, and after a moment he decided it must be the river he had glimpsed earlier from the back of the car. The war, a thud of gunnery, was something he felt rather than heard, a pulse at the hinges of his jaw. My grandfather, taking Father Nickel's long silence for hurt feelings, regretted his failure to see Mount Gallienus and was about to apologize, but it turned out that Father Nickel's thoughts were elsewhere.

"In the twenties there was a kind of rocket mania here," the old priest said. "In Germany. The newspapers and magazines were filled with rockets. Rockets to deliver mail. Rockets to the Moon. Fritz Opel built a rocket car. Every tinkerer and charlatan was going to the Moon."

My grandfather mentioned Hermann Oberth, whose *Die Rakete zu den Planetenräumen*, published in 1923 and discovered in the OSS library during the months he worked for Lovell, had comforted him when, on the hooks of his restlessness, being safe and comfortable and well out of the fight was the worst fate he could imagine.

"His book was the start of it, I believe," Father Nickel said. "All the rocket madness. Hermann Oberth, yes, a remarkable man, a very advanced thinker." And then, as if the next words followed logically: "No doubt he is now dead."* He tap-tapped his cigarette as he pronounced the words *todt ist*. Glowing orange threads of tobacco scattered from the end of his cigarette. "Oberth worked with Fritz Lang, yes? To make a film, *Frau im Mond*. A silly film in many ways but technically impressive. The particulars of a rocket voyage to the Moon were presented in a way that made the business seem credible. Not at all far-fetched. After the film, oh, well." He shook his head. "For a moment, Germans, to the left, to the right, it didn't matter. Everyone lifted his gaze, just for a little moment, to the heavens." The old priest squinted up at the brilliance of the Moon. "There was earnest discussion about the imminence of lunar travel. One felt that it might come very soon, in a matter of a few decades at most. Certainly I felt this way."

My grandfather had seen the Lang film in the early thirties, under its American title of *By Rocket to the Moon*, at the Model Theater on

---

* In fact, Oberth, awarded the *Kriegverdienstkreuz* ("*mit Schwerten*") for extraordinary bravery during and after the massive 1943 Hydra raid on Peenemünde, emigrated after the war to the U.S., where he worked on both the Atlas and Saturn rocket programs, became a prominent early UFOlogist, retired to Germany and died at the age of ninety-five, surviving my grandfather by eight months.

South Street. In the film the lunar journey had been effected by the means of a multistage rocket, just as described by Hermann Oberth (with what turned out to be remarkable prescience) in *Die Rakete zu den Planetenräumen*. Problems of payload, the earth's gravitation, and the weightlessness of space were presented and solved by ingenious and plausible means. If my grandfather had heard someone predict, as he walked out of the theater on that winter afternoon at the bottom of the Great Depression, that it would require as many as "a few decades" to conquer the Moon, it would have struck him, then eighteen or nineteen, as absurdly pessimistic.

"It was very well done," he agreed.

"At that time, I prepared a memorandum," the old priest said. "I wrote to the Curia, proposing that the Mother Church ought to prepare itself for the eventuality of a human presence on Luna. I suggested that, at every level from the liturgical to the eschatological, profound questions must arise from mankind's attainment of that neighboring world. Does the papal doctrine of discovery, for example, apply to the Moon as it did to the Indies in the time of Columbus? What will be the fate of the souls of the first Catholic lunar colonists—almost certainly no more than a handful, to begin with—if the sacraments, Holy Communion, Confession, and so forth are not available? When we speak of *Rex mundi* or *Salvator mundi*, is it to be made explicit, or is it already implied, that we intend to say *Salvator mundorum*? If we should encounter Selenites—though, given the Moon's apparent barrenness, that seems unlikely, but very well—let us say that having made use of the Moon as a way station, humanity proceeds outward to the planet Mars, where it encounters sentient, civilized creatures. Let us say, furthermore—I am quoting myself, you understand. The words of my memorandum."

My grandfather said that he has assumed as much.

"Let us say, then, that in outward form, and even in the internal construction of their organs, these Martians are not so very different from us. Indisputably, they are part of God's creation. Presumably, they are in possession of immortal souls. Can their salvation be assured or even conceived on a world whose feet have never been trod by the feet of Christ? And if it can be conceived, and if we might assure it, then is it not our urgent and solemn duty to carry the word of the Lord across the black gulf of ignorance and damnation as soon as possible? And so on and so forth."

"Interesting," my grandfather said.

"Oh? Do you really think so?"

"Well, that sort of speculation, it's not something I ordinarily go in for, but—"

"It was all rubbish."

"Ah."

"Pretext, I should say. Any nonsense I could dream up, any sophistry that might persuade the Curia to put its considerable resources into sending a holy mission to Luna. At that moment, as I said, such a voyage seemed far from impossible or impractical. It seemed to be only a matter of time. Naturally, I proposed myself as the prelate of this mission, despite my age. I was strong and healthy. I still am, considering. And to fly in a rocket through the void of space to the Moon, like a hero out of Verne or Wells? To stand there, gazing up at the fat turquoise globe in the heavens? My calling to the priesthood came only in my twenties. A trip to the Moon is something I have longed for all my life!"

For the first time in what felt like years but could have been no more than five weeks—since two or three minutes before Alvin Aughenbaugh caught the bullet that killed him—my grandfather laughed.

"Please, laugh," Father Nickel said with a show of generosity. "Laugh at your foolish old enemy."

My grandfather saw moonlight welling in the old priest's eyes. He put a hand on Father Nickel's shoulder. "The only difference between you and me, Father," my grandfather said, "is that I never wrote it all down."

XV

Somewhere out there, beyond the tempered glass visor of his helmet, a fire bell clanged. This did not concern my grandfather. There was no oxygen here to feed a fire or to carry the vibration from the tongue of a bell. Here the enemies were cold and silence. He was warm in his moon suit, however, and he could hear his own heart beating. Bounding along the lunar surface in long arcs, half a million miles from the earth and its fires and alarms. Let it burn. Let it melt, let its rafters give way, let the whole thing collapse under the weight of its own sad gravity. The only thing spoiling his lunar idyll was the infernal itching at the back of his neck where the helmet attached, impossible to scratch in his suit and gloves of rubberized silk. And that rich smell of compressed air from the tanks on his back, so oddly reminiscent of warm dung. . . .

"Herr Lieutenant."

My grandfather opened his eyes in the dark. A recent disturbance among the cows below reverberated in the clanging of their bells. A straw from the bale he had been using for a pillow was jabbing him in the neck. He discerned Father Nickel's head and neck peeping over the edge of the loft, hands gripping the ladder. My grandfather scratched the back of his neck. He was glad to have been wakened, contemptuous as ever of the happiness to be found in dreams, displeased with himself for having fallen prey to it once again.

"I am sorry to wake you, Lieutenant."

There was something concealed in a fold of the old priest's voice.

My grandfather sat up, shaking loose the last lunar strands of gossamer. "Diddens?"

"Asleep. Private Gatto, too. They are both well, do not worry."

My grandfather looked around for the old woman. When he had climbed into the loft a few hours earlier, he had tried without success not to wake her. He had apologized, and with the twang of the local dialect, Fräulein Judit had apologized for her brother's rudeness. She referred to Father Nickel as "the little pasha." She said that having been born a baby and finding he enjoyed it, he had never bothered to stop. The light of the Moon filtering in through a chink painted two portraits of itself on the old woman's eyes. "He will die without ever having spent a night on anything but goose down," she had said.

My grandfather had assured her that the switch was all his idea. "The bed is much too comfortable," he had explained. Evidently, there had been truth in this, since after spreading Gatto's overcoat across his body, he had immediately fallen into sleep with all its treacheries. At some point the old woman had crept out of her blankets and down the ladder without his even noticing.

"She went to draw water," Father Nickel said. "She will have our breakfast for us when we get back."

"Oh?" my grandfather said. "Are we going somewhere?"

"That is up to you."

In the darkness my grandfather could not read the expression on Father Nickel's face. The tone of the old priest's voice was hard to interpret. Anticipation might be doubt. Urgency might be mischief. It sounded as if the old priest had made up his mind to do my grandfather a kindness that he feared he would live to regret.

"Come," he said. "I have a gift for you. Come see."

He lowered himself back down the ladder. My grandfather reached for his boots and dragged Gatto's coat to the edge of the loft. He swung his legs over but then sat without moving at the top of the ladder. Reason, common sense, and experience conferred and came to the conclusion, not without regret, that the night was taking a decided turn toward the fucked up. Regardless of how long ago the cognac you had drunk was put into its bottle and how many chickens had died for the sake of your stew, the war was not over. Father Nickel was the enemy.

"I'm sorry, Father. Unless you tell me right now—"

"It's a rocket, fool!" the old priest said. "A damned rocket!"

My grandfather climbed down from the loft and pulled on Gatto's coat. The cows made way, pots and pans, a bovine fart. The old priest went out. My grandfather followed, wondering if his ability to smell something off about a situation had deserted him.

The night, an hour before dawn, was very cold. My grandfather buttoned up the coat and jammed his hands into the pockets. Father Nickel appeared to be headed toward an outbuilding at the back of the farm, a garage by the look of it. My grandfather relaxed a little. The rocket that the old priest intended to show him must be a bit of handiwork. Solid fuel, battery ignition, welded from a section of pipe, the kind of thing they printed plans for in *Popular Mechanics*. The story began to write itself in my grandfather's imagination. For a year, two years, five years, the old priest had waited for some response to his memorandum from the Curia. And then one day, just as hope began to tip into disappointment, he had run across the article in a magazine or a Sunday newspaper: "The Fascinating New Hobby of Amateur Rocketry." Detailed instructions, step-by-step photographs, a list of materials. Like a group of exiles re-creating a lost homeland in a few city blocks, the old priest had been able to replicate his lost hope in miniature, to build a scale model of his dream. And now all this nocturnal hugger-mugger because, with the outbreak of war, as was the case in Britain, the Nazis had outlawed amateur rocketry. My grandfather felt a renewed squeeze of affection for this lonely old humanist, holing up night after night in his sister's garage to engineer—at least in his imagination—the means of transport and escape.

Just before they reached the old garage, Father Nickel cut abruptly to the right. He tramped past the ruins of a pig pen, past a squat water tank, past a garden whose beds were still cloaked against the winter in sheets of burlap. At the edge of the farm, what appeared to be a large forest stretched away into the distance of the night. Pine and fir trees stood together as if conspiring to keep out the moonlight, hiding a profound darkness behind their backs. Father Nickel headed directly toward those trees and that darkness. Some trick of the moonlight made it appear to my grandfather's suddenly spooked imagination as if the trees had all at once, just a moment before, stopped in their tracks. They held an air of restless hesitation. My grandfather came to a halt. Half of the American soldiers killed or wounded since D-day had come to grief in woods like this.

"What rocket?" he said. "Whose rocket?"

"Your rocket, my son," Father Nickel said. When he saw that my grandfather continued to linger, he said, "Listen. I know you are hunting for rockets."

Now? said experience, common sense, and reason. *Christ, you idiot, what the fuck is it going to take?*

Gatto kept a carton of Lucky Strikes in the left hip pocket of his overcoat. In the right hip pocket, apparently, he kept a looted Walther PPK, wearing its sharklike leer. My grandfather had never held one before. You could feel the homicide trapped inside it.

He had told the old priest nothing about his work, the mission, unless he had blabbed about it at some point in his sleep. That was the kind of thing that happened in spy novels and romances—muttered revelations of conspiracy, adultery, crime—but it struck my grandfather as unlikely. A creation of novelists and screenwriters, like total amnesia and hand-to-hand combat between men who were carrying guns. In his experience the things people said while they were asleep were even less intelligible than the things they saw. At any rate, except for the occasional appearance put in by his Yiddish-speaking mother, my grandfather dreamed in English. It was hard to imagine that if he had talked in his sleep, the words would have come out as German.

There was no telling, however, what Diddens or Gatto, drugged on chicken stew and drunk on wine, might have confessed. After a certain number of years, a priest probably came to elicit confessions without even trying.

"Apologies." *Entschuldigung*, to my grandfather's ear always the most beautiful of German words. Away to the north and northeast, the war pulsed at my grandfather's temples and the hinges of his jaws like a headache coming on. "I must insist, Father, that you tell me where you are taking me. Now."

In the moonlight he could not be entirely certain, and no doubt his conscience or forty years of accumulated retrospective tenderness influenced his impression, as reported to me, that when Father Nickel saw the gun in my grandfather's hand, he looked heartbroken. But he simply nodded, and when he spoke, his tone was patient and forgiving.

"In the winter, you see, in December or January, they started to route the trains this way. From somewhere up in the Harz Mountains, I believe, to the rail yards at Soest and thence west. At some point they were loading them on the beds of special lorries, camouflaged under netting, and driving them within range of Antwerp and, of course, London. For the trains to deviate this far to the south before turning west, well, it's very much the long way around, isn't it? I presume the more direct routes were bombed. And then, when the retreat from Belgium began. There was no other way. In time things became chaotic around Soest, which has been bombed very heavily, very heavily. Often the trains passing this way were obliged to stop; there is a siding along the river just down the hill from here. They would sit and wait on this siding for an hour, two hours. And then, you see, one night when the train carried on, one of them had been left behind. Abandoned. I still do not know why. I must assume that it was damaged in transit or found to be somehow defective. No doubt they are fragile. Deadly things often are. Come."

"You're saying that, on the other side of these woods, there is a V-2."

"Yes."

"An intact V-2 rocket."

If this turned out to be true, it would be, as far as my grandfather knew, the first such capture by any of the Black List teams. It would be a spectacular prize.

"Yes, yes!"

"Through these woods."

"And then down the hill. There is a path, with the snow all gone it's nothing, a walk of twenty minutes, perhaps, for a young man. Twice that, since you shall be in my enfeebled company. Come."

Just before he followed the priest whose ward and beloved sexton he had murdered only a few hours before, into the darkness at the back of the trees, my grandfather took a look up—a last look up, it might be—at the stars. The Moon was down, and they had reclaimed the whole of the sky.

At that hour all across Europe, if the local skies were clear, people who believed, knew, feared, or hoped they were about to die were looking up at the stars. From Finland to the Balkans, from the Black Sea to the doorstep of Africa, across Poland and Hungary and Romania. Looking up, maybe, through a pane of Perspex, or through lenses that corrected for myopia. Through a tangle of razor wire, a gun slit, a grid of tracer fire, the blown hatch of an M1. Standing, stumbling, kneeling. Dead on their feet or running for their lives. From open fields, street gutters, and foxholes. Atop a pile of rubble, in a fresh-dug ditch, on a Turkish carpet in a house that had no roof, on the deck of a ship on fire.

No doubt some of these people looking up at the stars sought the lineaments of God's face. Many saw no more than what was to be seen: the usual spatter of lights, cold and faraway. For some the sky might be a diagram captioned in Arabic and Latin, a dark hide tattooed with everyday implements and legendary beasts. At least one man, looking up at the stars that night from the edge of a forest in the Westerwald, saw an archipelago of atomic furnaces in a vacuum sea, omnidirectional vectors of acceleration radiant from a theoretical point of origin that predated humanity by billions of years, as unperturbed by mechanized mass slaughter on a global scale as by the death of one individual.

This was my grandfather's line of thinking, and he found both comfort and guidance in it. He could trust or mistrust Father Nickel; either way the outcome would mean nothing to the stars. So why not, for one night, lay down the weary burden of mistrust? For an hour, say, and no longer. Just long enough to see the rocket. After that he would shoulder the burden again.

◑   ◑   ◑

"So, what happened?" I said. "What'd he do?"

I had been schooled by now in the ways of South Philadelphia and the world that was, in my grandfather's view, its macrocosm. I was expecting treachery, mischance, one debt incurred when another was repaid.

"He showed me the rocket," my grandfather said.

"A V-2. You saw a V-2 rocket."

"I saw more than one. This was just the first."

"And?"

"And . . . ?"

"What was it like?"

He pursed his lips and angled his face toward the window. He considered the question for long enough that I began to wonder if he had forgotten it.

"It was tall."

"Tall?"

"The old man said it was as tall as the steeple of his church."

"Okay," I said. I hadn't pictured them as being so tall. "But, I mean . . . how did you feel? What did you think?"

"I don't know how to put it into words."

"Were you disappointed?"

"On the contrary."

"Afraid?"

"Of what? It wasn't going anywhere."

It occurred to me that neither disappointment nor fear was an emotion my grandfather ever really struggled to express. Both could be stated plainly and left behind.

"Did it make you happy?" I said.

The word seemed to catch him a little off guard.

"Something like that," he said.

* * *

In children's drawings, all houses have chimneys, all monkeys eat bananas, and every rocket is a V-2. Even after decades of stepped-back multistage behemoths, chunky orbiters, and space planes, the midcentury-modern *Enterprise*, the polyhedral bulk of Imperial star destroyers and Borg cubes, the Ortho-Cyclen disk of *Millennium Falcon*—in our deepest imaginations the surest way to the nearest planet remains a trim cigar tapering to a pointed nose cone, poised on the tips of four swept-back axial fins. By the time I became conscious of rockets—and I grew up at the height of the space race, surrounded by the working models and scale models my grandfather's company manufactured, by photographs and drawings of Saturns and Atlases and Aerobees and Titans—they had progressed well beyond von Braun's early masterwork, in design as in power, size, and capacity. But it was a V-2 that would carry me into the outer space of a fairground ride, that labeled the spines of the public library's science fiction collection. A V-2 was the "weenie" or visual anchor of Walt Disney's Tomorrowland. In the V-2, form and purpose were united, as with a knife, a hammer, or some other fundamental human tool. As soon as you saw a V-2, you knew what it was for. You understood what it could do. It was a tool for defeating gravity, for escaping the confines of earth.

For my grandfather, I believe, the war was everything that happened to him from the day he enlisted until the moment he walked into a clearing in the woods outside Vellinghausen, Germany, in late March or early April 1945. It was everything that resumed happening, the awful things he saw and the revenge he contemplated, from the moment he walked out of the clearing until the German surrender six weeks later. The thirty minutes or so that he spent with the rocket in the woods, however, was time stolen from the war, time redeemed. He would leave the clearing with that half hour cupped in his memory like an egg kept warm in the palms. Even when the war had crushed it, he remembered the pulse, the quickening of something that might break free and take to the sky.

When they walked into the clearing, the old priest sat down on an upended packing crate, crossed his legs, and lit a cigarette. The far-off pounding of artillery came to a momentary halt, and in the interval before the first birds, as the darkness deepened, some power seemed to enter and flow across the clearing. After a moment my grandfather identified that tide as silence. Then a bird sang, and the sky lightened, and you could begin to see the rocket aspiring to heaven on its mobile launch table. My grandfather divined its purpose with an upward leap of the heart.

Of course my grandfather knew that, from the point of view of German command, of Allied command, of Hermann Goering and General Eisenhower and the people at whom it was to have been launched, the rocket was still—was only—the war. The clearing had been cut by soldiers, the rocket had been transported here by soldiers. Soldiers would have armed, primed, aimed, and fired it. Like its fellows—around three thousand between September 1944 and March 1945—it had been fitted with a warhead that contained two thousand pounds of a highly explosive form of TNT that would detonate on impact. Its manufacture had been ordained and carried out not to bear humankind to the doorstep of the stars but to atomize and terrorize civilians, destroy their homes, shatter their morale. If some unknown mischance had not intervened, this rocket would have joined its fellows in racing the sound of its own arrival toward the city of Antwerp, where, on December 16, to take the worst example, a V-2 had fallen on the Rex Theater in the middle of a showing of *The Plainsman*, killing or injuring nearly a thousand people.

None of that, however, could be blamed on the rocket, my grandfather thought, or on the man, von Braun, who had designed it. The rocket was beautiful. In conception it had been shaped by an artist to break a chain that had bound the human race ever since we first gained consciousness of earth's gravity and all its analogs in suffering, failure, and pain. It was at once a prayer sent heavenward and the answer to that prayer: *Bear me away from this awful place.* To pack the thing with a ton of amatol, to hobble it so that instead of tearing loose once and for all from the mundane pull, it only arced back to earth and killed the people among whom it fell, was to abuse it. It was like using a rake to whip egg whites, a dagger to pick your teeth. It could be done, but to do so was a perversion. Furthermore, ineffective. As a weapon, a tool of strategy, it was clear to everyone by now that the V-2 had failed. Yes, four or five thousand hapless Frenchmen, Belgians, and Englishmen had been killed by the rocket bombs. Tens of thousands more had been left wounded, homeless, or afraid. But in the end, bombs of the ordinary variety had killed, maimed, and frightened people in far more terrible numbers. And now here were the Allies, deep into Germany, and the rockets were impotent and no longer fell.

My grandfather felt sorry for Wernher von Braun, whom he could not help envisioning as shy, professorial, wearing a cardigan. His pity for and anger on behalf of the imaginary von Braun tapped the reservoir of his sorrow over the loss of Aughenbaugh. Alvin Aughenbaugh, with a hint of Paul Henreid. The poor bastard! He had built a ship to loft us to the very edge of heaven, and they had used it as a messenger of hell.

"Lieutenant?" Father Nickel said. He put a hand on my grandfather's shoulder.

My grandfather averted his face. Automatically, he moved to shrug off the old priest's hand, but in the end he left it where it was. Between him and Father Johannes Nickel, as between two stars, lay unbridgeable gulfs of space-time. And yet across the sweep of that desolation each had swum, for a moment, into the other's lens. Poor von Braun! He needed to know—my grandfather felt that he must find him and tell him—that such a thing was possible. Scattered in the void were minds capable of understanding, of reaching one another. He would put his hand on von Braun's shoulder the way the old priest's gnarled paw now lay benedictive on his own. He would transmit to von Braun the only message lonely slaves of gravity might send: *We see you—we are here.*

XVI

In 1972 Uncle Ray recruited my father—then employed as team doctor to the Washington Senators—to invest in his latest under-taking, a chain of fancy "billiards clubs" called Gatsby's, that served liquor and welcomed female customers with Tiffany-style lamps and foofy cocktails. At its peak—just preceding its complete extinction—the chain encompassed five locations in Washington, Baltimore, Philadelphia, and Pittsburgh. In decor the clubs combined elements of gentlemen's club, traditional chophouse, and the then-popular "fern bar." In concept the undertaking combined elements of pipe dream, tax dodge, money-laundering scheme, and irretrievable mis-take. Uncle Ray was not entirely forthcoming to my father about the identity of their silent partners, and my father was not entirely forth-coming, it seems, about the extent to which he was already a focus of attention for having failed to report income to the IRS. Anyone who cares to waste a few hours among the archives of the *Post, Sun, In-quirer,* and *Post-Gazette* may trace the fragmentary outlines of their disaster, which cost my great-uncle a beating that left him hospital-ized for weeks and made my father a quasi-fugitive for the rest of his life.* I don't have the space or the stomach to go into the details here, and anyway, the Gatsby's debacle was barely a footnote, if that, in the history of the Philadelphia Mob.

---

* "That was just his excuse," my mother observed on reading this manuscript, in a dry deadpan that sounded a lot like my grandfather. "He was in hiding from the day we met."

In my family, naturally, it proved of more significance. With Uncle Ray facing criminal charges and my father in the wind, my grandparents and my mother were left holding a variety of bags. My grandfather constructed a defensive array of high-impact lawyers, but even with this shield in place there were penalties, liabilities, and liens. To raise the necessary funds, he forced a reluctant Uncle Sammy to buy out his interest in MRX, and the happiest (or at least the most productive) period of his life came to an end. Less than a year after he lost the company he loved, he lost my grandmother, too.

By the time he met Sally Sichel, almost nothing of value was left apart from the condo (which my grandmother had been able to visit only once after its purchase) and fifty-seven model spacecraft built to a rigorous scale from premium materials. From his private stock my grandfather culled ten of the best, including a sweet little Sputnik PS-2 that obliged you, if you lifted a hinged panel, to contemplate the awful fate of a tiny Laika (a modified husky pinched from an N-scale Alaskan Railroad kit).

Three days after meeting Sally, he sold all ten of the rockets to the Bluestein twins up in Cocoa Beach. He used the proceeds to pay Devaughn and purchase the supplies he would need to hunt down the snake that had eaten Ramon.

Every night at nine except Sunday, Devaughn would meet my grandfather at a Waffle House, drive him to Atlantis, and drop him at the gate with its gaffed lock. My grandfather would shlep off into the darkness laden with his gear—canvas sack and work gloves, flashlight, and the panoply of special tools he had crafted: snake hook (vinyl-coated storage hook welded to the end of an old golf club), snake stick (a length of narrow-gauge PVC pipe fitted with a noose of nylon cord), and, of course, snake hammer. Precisely two hours and thirty-five minutes later he would return carrying his waders so as not to muddy Devaughn's car. Then Devaughn would drive my grandfather back to the Waffle House before starting the midnight shift at Fontana Village.

"Every night?"

"Except Sunday. Sunday Devaughn went to church."

"I must have talked to you during that time, right? I'm on the phone with you, and you're telling me you had rice pudding for dessert or whatever, and meanwhile you're getting ready to go *snake hunting*."

He registered my pointless question and then looked away.

"Fine," I said. "Why?"

"You saw the show. *Alien Invaders*. It wasn't eating just pets. It was eating a wide and troubling variety of native birds and amphibians."

"Oh, really?"

"Endangered species."

"And house cats."

"It was an alien invader. It didn't belong there."

"Humans don't belong there, either," I said. "Why didn't you hunt them?"

"I don't know," he said. "I guess I never get around to it."

"But, I mean, it was really all about Sally, wasn't it?"

"What was about Sally? What are you talking about?"

"The snake had been eating pets for months, you didn't care. Then you met Sally, all of a sudden you want to kill the thing. You were doing it for her sake."

"Was I?"

"Grandpa. Come on."

"Maybe."

"Totally."

"Well," my grandfather said. "There are worse reasons for killing, believe me."

०   ०   ०

My grandfather took Sally to an overpriced crab house in Boynton Beach, a rope-trimmed tourist trap that my grandmother had despised. On the way home, as though her ghost had poisoned his chowder, my grandfather experienced cramps. As a rule, he avoided shellfish and pork because, while he had long since left his religion in the Neolithic, where he felt it belonged, he retained, in his words, "a kosher belly." The trouble in his stomach embarrassed him obscurely, so he kept it to himself. It would be a matter of getting to a toilet as soon as possible. On the way home from the crab house, he obliged himself to drive patiently. The effort required kept his mind off the pain.

"Good lord, I just remembered," he said. He had parked the LeSabre and they were walking toward Sally's cluster of units through the luminous Florida dark. She had invited him to come have a look at her place. Curiosity about the interior arrangements of one another's units was a kind of currency at Fontana Village, one in which even my grandfather traded. There was not necessarily anything more to her invitation, he had decided, than that. "I think I might have forgotten to unplug my soldering iron."

That afternoon he had recapped a buzzing old Zenith at the request of his neighbor Pearl Abramowitz. There was nothing he had been able to do for Pearl's other complaint: that increasingly, all the people singing and talking on her radio seemed to be doing so in Spanish. He had, however, remembered to turn off the soldering iron. It was not even a question of remembering; he had made a habit of it. That was the purpose of habit, in my grandfather's view: to render memory unnecessary.

He could see that he had let Sally down, but she covered it with a joke. "I've only known you three days," she said. "But that doesn't sound like something you would forget."

This was undeniable. "No, but if I don't check . . ."

"Of course. I totally understand."

"I'll be over in ten minutes. Five minutes."

"Go."

He hurried back to his unit and repaired to the bathroom, where fighting, though fierce, was mercifully brief. He washed up and discharged three precise bursts of Alpine Summer air freshener. He went back out to the living room. The yellow sofa, the whitewashed wicker étagère, the expressionless walls had a disintoxicating effect on his imagination. He saw the elaborate scale model of LAV One on its mound of simulated lunar surface, on which he had lavished thousands of hours and dollars, for what it was: five pounds of painted plastic scrap sitting on ten dollars' worth of plaster cloth and chicken wire. What was he doing, chasing after Sally Sichel? "Asking her out," so improbably, on a "date"? The recliner they'd had since Riverdale, in which my grandmother used to sit, watching *Jeopardy!* and yelling deliberately incorrect guesses at the screen, as though trying to throw the contestants off their game, leveled its mute reproach.

Sit, it seemed to implore him. *Stay. Slacken. Vegetate.*

The telephone rang. It was Sally.

"You all right?" she said, and for a moment he thought she had inferred from a grimace, a sharp intake of breath, the uproar in his belly. Had he groaned or, God forbid, farted without realizing it? "Did your house burn down?"

"I'm fine," he said. "I had turned it off."

"I see." Her tone was distinctly disbelieving. This irked my grandfather for a moment until he recalled that in fact he was lying to Sally. She was an observant person, a noticer. There was no human quality that my grandfather held in higher regard. "Well," she said, "that's too bad."

"It's too bad?"

"Yes. A little fire might help with the cold feet."

This remark puzzled my grandfather—his feet were fine—but then he understood: Sally had no idea that his dinner had given him a cramp. She supposed he was just running away from her, that he was afraid of having, as he put it to me, "feelings in that direction." Once he understood, he was shocked. It came as a worse shock to discover, on searching the feelings he was afraid of having, that Sally's supposition was correct. There had been nothing wrong with his stone crab chowder apart from too much salt. The cramp was a case of nerves, not food poisoning.

"Okay, okay," he said, glaring back at the haunted recliner. "I'll be right over."

The unit did not belong to Sally but to an old friend who was living now with a daughter in Tel Aviv. The friend and her late husband had bought the unit, remodeled it, and furnished it with lots of raffia and glass, and then a week after they moved in, the husband had keeled over on the Fontana Village tennis courts and died. Everything that was not raffia or glass had been painted, covered, or tiled in soft tones of rose and ash-gray, a modish palette that Sally didn't care for. A bedsheet had been tacked to the large white wall by the patio doors, where it struck a discordant note, because it was patterned with green and gold dandelions, and because it was a bedsheet.

"You have one of your paintings under there?"

Sally shook her head. She turned to the bedsheet on the wall and lifted it with both hands. My grandfather went and stood underneath this impromptu canopy to look. It was a large photographic portrait in black and white, mounted and matted in a black metal frame. It was a close-up shot of a moonfaced beauty and a handsome fellow with satyric eyebrows, both around his age. They were posed with their heads together, their eyes twinkling with acceptance and wisdom.

"Little did they know," my grandfather said.

She nodded. They stepped out from under the bedsheet and she let it fall. "I have to keep it covered," she said. "I don't have the patience for hindsight."

"Too much like regret," my grandfather said.

A viable moment had arrived. Sally leaned in to kiss him. He got a late start and then misjudged her angle of approach. There was an unfortunate encounter between her teeth and his chin. She clapped a hand to her mouth, her cheeks ablaze, and made an adjustment to her dental work.

My grandfather dabbed at the bite mark on his chin, checked his fingertips for blood. "Wee wow," he said.

"Shit," Sally said, having restored order in her mouth. "Is this going to be a disaster?"

My grandfather had a hunch about it, but he kept it to himself. She reached out and took hold of his chin and examined it, then used her purchase on his chin to guide her mouth toward his. There had been pink grapefruit in her salad at dinner and he thought he could taste it on her lips.

"How about we give it one last try?" Sally said.

"If you wouldn't mind," said my grandfather.

But thirteen minutes later, when she emerged from the master bath having made it plain that she intended to fuck him, the expanse of her naked body, lavishly freckled and presented without modesty, overwhelmed my grandfather. An inner coaxial was cut, and his head filled with white noise, and then he passed out. When he came to his senses, he was on his back on the bed in possession of what felt like a monstrous erection. Stretched out alongside him, Sally reached to take hold of it. Before her fingers even brushed against his skin, however, my grandfather came. The spurt was so abrupt and unadvertised that it had the character of a practical joke. Sally flinched and looked slightly offended. My grandfather's sense of humiliation was acute. It took everything he had not to get up and leave. Pack his car, drive to California without stopping. Only California would not really be far enough.

Sally went back into the bathroom. This time when she came out, she was wearing a robe.

"I'm sorry," said my grandfather. "Maybe it was a little too soon."

"Too soon is better than too late, dear."

"Yeah? What if it's too soon *and* too late?"

"Oh, it is," Sally said. "Definitely. Too soon for that type of talk."

She sat down on the bed beside him and gave him a brief but not perfunctory kiss on the lips. "And too late for backing out now, because I like you."

"Sally . . ." Now was the time at last to talk to her, to tell her about the blood panel and Dr. Mubarak, as my grandfather had come to think of the specialist. Now, before like turned to something stronger and it really was too late.

"How do you feel about rum raisin ice cream?" Sally said.

"I'm the only person I know who likes it."

"Not anymore. How about Spencer Tracy?"

"In my opinion? The best."

"I agree. So, channel twelve is showing *Boys Town* at nine."

"Yeah? You know, I remember when it came out, it was showing at the Stanley. But somehow I missed it."

"That's what I'm telling you," Sally said. "It's never too late."

XVII

Many years later, when my mother was packing up to move out of the house where my grandfather had died, she came upon some liquor boxes in a crawl space.

"It's just lot of your old junk," she reported when she called me.

Knowing that I had a weakness for old junk in general but especially my own, she brought the boxes over one afternoon* to consign them to the mercy of my nostalgia. The first one I opened was a Captain Morgan rum carton that held fifty or sixty letters and postcards from friends, lovers, and writing teachers of the 1980s. Buried under the old mail were some cassette recordings I had made from a friend's father's collection of Bob and Ray albums, a baggie that held a loose joint, a Hot Wheels Beatnik Bandit, and my brother's vinyl copy of *Moving Pictures*.

"Good box," I said.

In the next one—Gilbey's gin—I found a plastic shopping bag from New Rose Records in Paris. It once held either *Fire of Love* or a Johnny Thunders live album, depending on which visit to New Rose it was from. Now it contained a floppy black felt hat with a wide brim. That, an unopened box of blank TDK cassettes, and an "Aquarian" deck of tarot cards bought at Spencer Gifts in the Columbia Mall when I was thirteen turned out to be all there was in the Gilbey's box. I scowled at the hat, trying to place it.

---

* I had long since become a resident of Berkeley, California.

"Blond," my mother said, tweezing a long strand from the nap of the wide felt brim.

Simultaneously, we recalled having seen this hat on the head of my fair-haired ex-wife.

I pointed to the third carton, which once held a dozen bottles of Old Crow. Its cardboard was more brittle than the others', its typography antiquated, its cartoon crow a raffish Jazz Age dandy. It had been sealed with old-fashioned packing tape, the kind you used to have to moisten with a sponge.

"I'm pretty sure that one's not mine," I said. "It looks really old."

"Oh," my mother said, slicing through the packing tape with her house key. "Huh."

I thought I caught a note of unease or at least wariness in her voice, but that may be a detail contributed by hindsight. The first thing to come out of the box were some children's books, small hardcovers without jackets: *The Black Stallion, Misty of Chincoteague* and *King of the Wind, National Velvet,* and one called *Come on Seabiscuit!* Beneath these lay a manila folder and a zippered fabric pouch. The folder was full of color photographs of thoroughbreds clipped from magazines, pasted onto cardboard backing, and cut out to make horse paper dolls. The zip pouch held the moldering remains of miniature tack my mother had fashioned for her paper horses out of bits of lanyard and leather thong and scraps of what looked like brown Naugahyde.

"That's what Velvet did," my mother explained. "In the book. So I made my own. But then your grandpa made these for me." From the Old Crow box she took nine little wooden horses, each balled up in a page from *The Baltimore Sun* for November 12, 1952. As she unwrapped each one, she set it on my kitchen table. The horses stood about three inches at the shoulder, carved—the first two with a pocketknife, my mother recalled, the rest with a set of carving tools— from soft lightweight wood. Each had been fitted with a mane and tail made of brush bristles, then painted: bay, chestnut, brown, dappled gray, dun, black, white, piebald, midnight blue. The modeling of the brown and the bay was crude, simplified almost to the point of abstraction, but after the first two my grandfather's skill had improved along with his tools. There was real likeness if not realism in the arcs of the other horses' necks, in their streamlined heads and balletic poses.

I held up the blue horse. "Kinda whimsical for Grandpa."

"That's Midnight. He knew how to fly."

"Midnight," I said. "Ooh."

I flew Midnight in a figure eight over the heads of the other horses and brought him in for a landing. I was surprised to discover at this late date that some part of the business of her girlhood had been conducted in my mother's imagination. When she told a story from those days, it was usually an account of something observed, overheard, endured, or undertaken, as though her formative years had been spent entirely in the world outside her own head. In self-portrait she was a child without daydreams, without fears, fantasies, doubts, longings, or unaskable questions. When I was a boy, my most routine flights of fancy and invention always seemed to leave her shaking her head, looking up at God or the kitchen ceiling, making a face that said something along the lines of *Where does he get this shit?* When I heard about Midnight, it made me wonder if she had been sandbagging all this time, pretending to be ignorant of a language in which she was conversant if not fluent. Concealing her origins, safely assimilated into a daylight country of earthbound horses.

"What else you got in there?" I said.

She glanced into the Old Crow box and looked away. She swept up all the blown blossoms of newsprint and shoved them crinkling down into the box.

"Well," she said, and I understood that there was something else in the box.

She turned to the little painted remuda on the kitchen table. Her eyebrows tangled above the bridge of her nose, and her mouth was pursed as though the horses presented her with a problem. At first I thought she might be debating whether or not to make a present of them to my younger daughter, who was then on the cusp of the Velvet Brown years. But my mother's eyes seemed too faraway and fretful for that.

"Well," she said again. She folded the flaps of the box and picked it up. "I can leave all that here for the kids, if you think they'll want it."

"Great."

"What?"

"No, nothing."

"I know," my mother said. I saw her push herself to say the next word. "Horses."

"A whole box of them."

"You think that's weird. Because of my mother."

"No, I . . . I mean, 1952? So you were ten when all this got packed up?"

"Yes. I went to live with Bubbe and Zayde." These were her names for my grandfather's parents, dead long before I was born. "They were over in Camden by then. It was only supposed to be until he found work, but I ended up finishing the school year in Camden. It took him a while to get a job. He ended up in New York."

"On Radio Row, right? Where the World Trade Center is."

"He worked for Arrow as a store manager, and then when Arrow started selling parts to companies, he went into sales because the money was better. I went to live with him in Queens."

"Where was Grandma?" I said, though I guessed the answer to my question the moment I asked it.

"November '52," my mother said. "That was the first time."

"Ah."

"They dropped me with Bubbe and Zayde and then he took her to the hospital. She was really, you know. Something was really out of whack."

She was looking at the midnight-blue horse. The bristles of its mane and tail were ivory white. Its head was angled skyward as though in aspiration. Any kid could have seen, I thought, that it was the magic one, the one that might be able to fly.

"I mean, *all* girls have the horse thing around that age," I said. "Ten eleven twelve. It's super-common."

"Mm-hmm," my mother said, but it didn't sound like she was agreeing with or even humoring me. She was pitying me. She thought that I was kidding myself, in denial.

"Because, I mean, did you know about the Skinless Horse?" I said. "Before she went into the hospital the first time?"

She set the box back down on the kitchen table. I started the teakettle. I had some Drambuie on hand. I assured her that it was not too early in the day to add a slug of the stuff to one's cup of Earl Grey.

"Before that?" she said. "Did I *know?* Did I know. I mean, I . . . *sensed* . . ." She paused, reluctant to carry on in this vein, trucking with things that could merely be sensed. "I knew she was afraid of something I couldn't see."

I poured tea from the pot into her mug and doctored it to her specifications. She took a sip and then, a moment later, took another, longer sip.

"Good," she said. She didn't say anything else after that, and she probably would have liked to move on.

"So when you were ten," I said, "November 1952, you packed it all up in that box."

"Yeah."

"It kind of looks like you never unpacked it again."

"I never did."

"How come?"

"Because I stopped liking horses."

"Because you found out about the Skinless Horse?"

"No," my mother said. She drained the cup of spiked tea. Then she opened up the flaps of the Old Crow box again and started rooting down through the crumpled flowers of Baltimore to the bottom. "Because I saw it."

◑   ◑   ◑

My grandmother was an on-air personality—*star* would be overstating the case—on station WAAM from around 1948 to 1952. In those years relatively few Baltimore households owned television sets. Growing up in the Baltimore area twenty years later, I rarely encountered people who had seen my grandmother on TV. From time to time when I was a kid, a former housewife of the fifties might recollect the pert, impeccably coiffed ménagère who calmly disjointed rabbits or whacked cutlets with a tenderizer while wearing pearls and a Dior dress supplied by Hutzler's, the sponsor of *La Cuisine*. My mother is now my only surviving authority for channel 13's having aired a French-language instruction program taught by my grandmother on Sunday mornings after *The Christophers*. And nobody ever seemed to remember Fay Beau the French Weather Maid, promising sunshine or warning of storm fronts on *News at Noon* in her black livery and starched white cap and apron.

To this day most of the people who remember my grandmother on television were kids at the time, my mother's age or a little older, and what they remember is a mass of dark hair teased into a feathery cowl around a dead-white face, eyebrows like a raven's wings, dark sleeves restlessly flapping and swooping in a dry-ice fog as my grandmother stalked the set of *The Crypt of Nevermore*, an antebellum Gothic fantasia of toppled columns, tilted headstones, and iron gingerbread. They remember her as "Nevermore, the Night Witch," and they are unanimous in recalling that if you were allowed to stay up late on a Friday night during those years, and tuned in to channel 13 for the forty-five minutes before WAAM's twelve-forty-five sign-off, my grandmother would freak you the fuck out.

Television's first "horror host" is generally agreed to have been

Maila Nurmi, aka Vampira, who emerged a couple of years afterward from some murky Hollywood borderland of cheesecake soft porn and Maya Deren–esque surrealism to introduce and heap ridicule upon Z-grade thrillers on KABC in Los Angeles. Others in other cities—Zackerley in New York, Ghoulardi in Cleveland, Marvin in Chicago—emerged toward the end of the decade, after the classic Universal horror films were packaged for television, and though they had their own gimmicks they all more or less followed the pattern laid down by Vampira: camp, innuendo, and the airing of movies ripe for mockery by the host of the show.

Nevermore, the Night Witch, wasn't like that. She didn't show movies; there were no horror movies licensed to be shown on television, and if there had been, the brothers who owned the station— more friends of the ubiquitous Judge Waxman—would not have seen the value in acquiring them.

"She hammed it up pretty good," my grandfather told me. "But she played it straight, not for laughs. The accent helped. She lived in the Usher family crypt, that was the shtick. Name over the door." He closed his eyes, and they sank into the purple shadow that surrounded them. He reran the grainy kinescope of memory. "She's there shpatziring around the graves, she turns and looks at the camera, '*Oh!*'" His voice went half an octave up and took on a certain slinkiness. "'*I see you have dared to return!*' Right? Then she invites you in. The camera, what do you call, zooms in on the iron gate of the crypt, meanwhile she has to quick run around to the other half of the set, where it's supposed to be the inside of the crypt. Cut to the other camera, she comes in, sits down in a chair, more like a throne, I think they got it from a church. She picks up a book and she reads. Out loud. Ghost stories. Weird tales. That type of thing. Never my cup of tea."

The Crypt of Nevermore, broadcast live, aired weekly from October 7, 1949, the centennial of Edgar Allan Poe's death, to October 24, 1952.

Baltimoreans who sat down at midnight on October 31, 1952, to watch the Night Witch's presentation of Poe's "Metzengerstein," as promised by TV listings in the *Sun*, were surprised to find only a static shot of a jack-o'-lantern posed on a wooden stool in a fog of CO_2. The holes of its face had been hacked in haste with some dull tool, and as its candle guttered and flared, the jack-o'-lantern displayed an expression of torment that many viewers, according to a subsequent report in the *Sun*, found disturbing; there were complaints. On the following Friday at midnight an old *March of Time* newsreel was shown. Neither *The Crypt of Nevermore* nor my grandmother ever returned to the air.

Around five-thirty that Halloween Friday my grandfather was in the kitchen of a rented house on Maine Avenue, in Forest Park. On first walking in the door that evening—home early for a change—he had wrapped three potatoes in foil and stuck them in the oven. Now he had a steak frying in a cast-iron skillet and a pot on the boil for some wax beans. He stood at the range, sleeves rolled, still in suit pants and necktie, wearing an apron patterned with tomatoes on a background of yellow plaid. Pancake turner in one hand, tumbler of Scotch in the other. Every Friday night he poured two fingers of Johnnie Walker over an ice cube. That would be the extent of his consumption for the week.

As he cooked, he lost himself pleasantly in the task of trying to find flaws in a completed design for an improved accelerometer feedback circuit that he and Milton Weinblatt, his partner at Patapsco Engineering, had been working on for the past several weeks. Six months earlier Weinblatt and my grandfather had quit their jobs in the instrumentation division of the Glenn L. Martin Company to open their own shop. Jews, malcontents, and restless men, they were frustrated by the timid pace of iteration at Martin and by having been passed over for promotion year after year while gentiles of lesser ability were made project managers and department heads. He and Weinblatt had sunk all their savings into their venture. The technology of inertial navigation systems, which enabled a rocket or missile to navigate and make course corrections on its own without external input or guidance, was in a fairly primitive state. Weinblatt and my grandfather were betting that the pace of innovation in computer circuit design, already rapid, was going to increase, soon making it possible to build nonmechanical, solid-state, or (as we would say now) digital navigation systems. If their bet turned out to be correct, Patapsco would be ready to take advantage of the innovations, and its proprietors would cash in.[*]

My grandfather felt in the soles of his feet that there were people climbing the front stoop of the house. The doorbell rang. It was a little early yet for trick-or-treaters, but he presumed that as she had done every Halloween since her first as the Night Witch, my grandmother intended to answer the door in costume. He slid the wax beans into the boiling water and forbade himself to touch the steak until his internal timer had registered the passing of another two minutes. He was aware of a thread of anxiety pulling at his belly when he thought about this year's front-stoop theatrics, but the truth was, this made him anxious every year. He was uncomfortable with the whole *Crypt of Nevermore* situation in general. The weird sexuality of the Night Witch (and of the stories she presented on the program, Blackwood, Le Fanu, Lovecraft: Freud would have a field day with the stuff) reflected a little too closely the nature of my grandmother's sexuality as he experienced it and, worse, the importance of that weirdness, that *witchiness*, to the hold that she had over him.

The doorbell rang again. He heard a buzz of little voices from the stoop. He flipped the steak and turned down the flame. He went to the front door. The vacant living room troubled him, unaccountably. There was no reason for the living room not to be vacant, but it did not feel *empty*. The luminous dial grinned on the front of the

---

[*] In later life Milton Weinblatt endowed chairs in avionics engineering at Stanford, Cal Tech, and his alma mater, the Stevens Institute.

big RCA console. Its automatic tonearm return did not always work properly, and he heard the stylus worrying the record label *skrch-skrchskrch*. Record sleeves lay scattered across the top of the console.

The record spinning on the RCA's platter was a ten-inch LP by Pipe Band of His Majesty's Scots Guard, 2nd Battalion, from an album called *Marches, Strathspeys and Reels*. Lately, my grandmother had been in the grip of a mania for bagpipes; he did not even attempt to begin to understand it. He lifted the tonearm and switched off the console.

"Honey?" he called up the stairs.

He had not seen my grandmother or my mother since walking in the door, but that was not unusual. Each of them seemed to spend increasingly longer periods alone, my mother in her bedroom, my grandmother in the room that my mother remembered as a "studio" and my grandfather as a "sewing room." When he was home they would hang around whatever room he happened to be in, but when he was not around they seemed to avoid each other.

He opened the front door, where the cast for an impromptu *Peter Pan* had assembled by chance: a pirate, an Indian princess, a fairy, and a little fellow in green whom my grandfather supposed was meant to be Robin Hood but made a serviceable Pan.

The accidental Neverlanders offered to withhold from committing a ritually unspecified act of mischief in return for a bribe of candy. My grandfather was ill at ease with this custom, relatively novel in the early 1950s. In the South Philly of his childhood, Halloween was a night when masked Irish hooligans threw eggs and flour bombs and wrote obscenities and slurs in soap on people's windows. He looked for the bowl, filled with loose pieces of Brach's Autumn Mix of candy pumpkins, corns, and cat's-heads, that ought to have been placed by the front door. It was not there.

"Just a minute," my grandfather said to the trick-or-treaters.

He called again for my grandmother and my mother but got no answer. Maybe they had gone to the store for candy at the last minute.

"Huh," he said. "I don't know what to tell you kids."

The children regarded him with careful and, in the case of the fairy, sharp expressions. My grandfather got the idea that his enactment of confusion struck them as insincere. He took his coin purse out of his pocket. He found four quarters inside it. In 1952 a quarter could buy five candy bars. The children went away content.

Back in the kitchen the steak was nearly done. He turned up the gas for another minute, gave it a poke with his finger, then slid it onto a plate. He returned the pan lacquered with amber drippings to the fire and glugged some Johnnie Walker into the pan. There was a hiss and a billowing of vapor that stung his nostrils. He took out Augenbaugh's lighter and ignited the vapor. As the whoosh of ignition faded to a simmer, he heard somebody scream. The sound arced like a skyrocket and burst with a yawp, almost a sob. My grandfather decided not to be alarmed. It had been an implausible scream, a Hollywood coloratura. Somebody having fun of the season. One of the neighbors scaring the evening's foot traffic with a haunted house sound effects record album.

He gave the bubbling reduction a couple of stirs to deglaze the pan. He listened. The scream was not repeated or followed by a creaking crypt door, a howling wolf, chains dragging across a dungeon floor. He poured the whiskey reduction over the steak on the plate, buttered the wax beans, and snatched the potatoes out of the oven with a mitt.

Once again there was no reply when he called out, this time adding the information that supper was ready. He had cut the steak into three pieces and buttered his baked potato when my mother—two months past her tenth birthday—walked in, wearing old dungarees and a loden shirt with the tails untucked. He was a little surprised to see that she was not in her Halloween costume: Velvet Brown, winner of the Grand National, in her jodhpurs and her gold and magenta silks. No doubt she had reckoned correctly that if she showed up at the table to run its steeplechase of sauces, condiments, and other hazards in the beautiful costume my grandmother had sewn for her, she would have been sent back to her room to change.

"Where's your mom?"

My mother glanced at the plate of bleeding steak between the two of them and looked away. Her features were arranged to give an effect of unconcern, but it was easy to see she was upset about something. He recalled that she had planned to go to school as Velvet Brown, for a parade around the neighborhood. He wondered if the costume had suffered some mischance. Maybe she had been teased. Behind the effort of her indifference he sensed consternation. If the problem was the costume, her eyes said that it had been spoiled. Her eyes said that it had been taken from her and torn to shreds.

"What happened?" he said.

She watched his hand and the fork it held convey her chunk of steak to her plate. She shook her head. "Nothing."

"I thought you would have your costume on."

Tears rolled like beads along her eyelashes. They scattered when she blinked.

"Did something happen to it? Did you get it dirty?"

"Nothing happened. I changed my mind."

"What? You don't want to be National Velvet? Why?"

Her reply was rapid and muttered so as to render it unintelligible, but there was nothing unusual in that. Lately, she did not really speak words to him so much as spirit them hastily and furtively out of her mouth like a bank robber tossing his gun and stocking mask out the window of a getaway car.

"Mumblemumblemumble," he said, as if quoting her.

"I said I'm not going trick-or-treating! Okay?"

She was regarding the bleeding steak on her plate with unconcealed revulsion. She looked like she might be about to throw up.

"So I heard somebody scream about maybe ten minutes ago," my grandfather said. "Now I'm wondering if that might have been you."

◗   ◗   ◗

That morning my grandmother had sent my mother off to school with an assurance that Velvet Brown would have her Pie. Even as the promise was tendered, my mother could not help feeling that something dreadful lay coiled at its bottom. Her mother, she knew, had endured terrible things during the war and after. She had been taken from her family, and then her family had been taken from her. The Nazis had also killed the handsome and heroic young doctor who was my mother's real father and who was usually played, in her imagination, by James Mason. Her mother had fought her way through the confusions and indignities of life as a refugee, through homesickness, shock, mourning, professional struggle, and the storms of exaltation and fury that blew through her head with the inconstant rhythm of hurricanes. All this while never losing the air of cheerful bitterness that, for my mother, defined bravery. When my grandmother promised my mother a "Hallowsween horse," her tone had been terribly cheerful. She would allow that she was not wild about horses—"I don't have to love them," she would tell my mother, "because you love them enough for both of us"—but my mother suspected that in fact my grandmother had a horror of them.

If my grandmother was walking downtown and saw that a mounted policeman or an arabber with his horse-drawn fruit wagon lay in her path, she would cross to the other side of the street. When she could not avoid contact with horses, my grandmother would hold herself still the way people did when it hurt too much to move, and take breaths in small sips through her nostrils until the animal had passed her. If they happened to pass on a drive one of the many horse farms in the countryside around Baltimore, my grandmother would lower her voice or stop talking entirely, as if she thought the horses in the pasture might be listening.

All day at school—my mother was in Mrs. Hampt's fourth grade class at Liberty Elementary—though she tried not to think about it, her thoughts kept returning to the horse she had been promised or, rather, to the dread that mysteriously was its passenger. It was like when you lost a tooth and your tongue kept finding and probing at the tang of blood in the gap. She knew from experience that whatever its nature, the horse her mother constructed for her would manage to be both beautiful and disappointing. She hoped (though this seemed unlikely) that it would not also be strange.

Parading with her classmates in her gaudy silks through the streets of Forest Park after lunch, Velvet Brown had felt an odd bereavement, an emptiness between her knees. She felt *unhorsed*. For this sense of loss my mother blamed my grandfather, who had made the original promise to provide her with a Pie for Halloween.

"I didn't even *want* a horse," my mother told my grandfather. She was lying facedown on her bed, having abandoned her supper, still in her dungarees and wool shirt. "I was *fine*."

"I apologize," my grandfather said. "I thought that I would have the time."

Emboldened by his success with the set of carved and painted horses, my grandfather had proposed to complete my mother's costume that year with a stick horse whose wooden head would be modeled on that of the horse from the movie version of *National Velvet*. From the start the impulse was unduly freighted with guilt. Back at Martin my grandfather's work had often cut in to his time with my mother, but since going out on his own, he was almost never home. The theory behind the stick horse was that if my mother consulted on her horse's design and helped with its construction, my grandfather would no longer be neglecting her. Like many promises born of a guilty conscience, this one had fallen prey to the failing it was intended to rectify. The push to develop a closed-loop accelerometer meant that my grandfather rarely got home before eight, usually closer to eight-thirty, my mother's bedtime. In the last two weeks, as he and Weinblatt found their designs taking a promising tack, his work on the Pie had all but come to a halt.

"A stupid head on a stupid broomstick," my mother said. Her eyelashes were soaked with tears, and fury blotched her cheeks. Filaments of snot cobwebbed her face to her pillow. "Like I'm a baby. Like I would ever want my friends to see me with that."

"I know." My grandfather was standing by the side of bed, looking down at her. "I'm sorry."

"You and your stupid idea—"

"Enough."

"I was fine without a horse!"

"*Enough.*"

My grandfather rarely raised or felt the need to raise his voice with my mother. As if to compensate for the erratic and unpredictable behavior of my grandmother, my mother had fashioned herself, by will and instinct, into the most tractable child in the city of Baltimore. She left off yelling at him and lay crooning into the crook of her arm.

"What happened?" my grandfather said. "Where is your mother?"

"I don't know." Now the poor girl just sounded tired. "She wasn't here when I got home. A record was playing. Her handbag was gone. I did my homework. I cleaned my room. I heard you come home. I wanted to see what she made. I went to look."

"And?"

My mother pressed her lips together. Her chin trembled. She shook her head and then buried her face in the pillow. She was not giving anything else away.

My grandfather stood a moment, looking down at her. He wondered if the bigger misfortune was to have the crazy woman for a mother, or the father who was crazy enough to love her. He wanted to stroke my mother's hair or give her shoulder a pat, but he felt angry with her for throwing his failure in his face. His hands dangled at his sides like inoperable tools. He knew he was being selfish and unfair to a child whose only mistake had been to put her trust in him.

"I'll look into it," he said to the back of my mother's head. He wondered if he had ever said anything so useless.

My grandmother's domain was a room off my grandparents' bedroom that must have been a porch once. It was small and low-ceilinged, with a ribbon of mullioned windows running around three sides. My grandmother had found room in it for a sewing machine, a small worktable, a floor lamp, and a dressmaker's dummy.* To the left of the door as you came in, my grandfather had built some shelves for my grandmother's notions, her supplies, and her disorderly row of paperbacks, most with French titles. On the wall to the right of the door, over a steel typist's table, hung a bulletin board shingled with art postcards and photos clipped from magazines. Neither my mother nor my grandfather could provide me with much in the way of specific works or artists (apart from van Gogh and a Delacroix tiger), but they remembered the imagery of the postcards and clippings as "creepy" (my mother) or "typical" (my grandfather): still lifes of meat, coin-operated automatons that told fortunes, a family of musical dwarfs who had survived Auschwitz. One morning the previous June my grandmother had found a luna moth expiring with languid wingbeats on a tree in the backyard. That got stuck to the bulletin board, too, its viridescence fading with time to dull dollar green.

The relative order or disorder of my grandmother's "studio" was as reliable a gauge as any of the tenor of her mind. There were others: whether or not she greeted him by name when he walked in the door or called out a goodbye on her own departure. Whether she was in the middle of her cycle or a week before the end. If she brought him coffee in bed, that was a good sign. If she felt appreciated by the world. If there were cut flowers in the vases and jars; if the flowers were fresh: good signs. Empty vases were bad and dead flowers worse. If she touched her fingers to the back of his neck as

---

* In spring and fall, when the latest ready-to-wear designs arrived from Paris, my grandmother would haunt Hutzler's with a marbled pad that she furtively filled with sketches so that she could re-create the clothes for herself at home.

though noticing it for the first time—as though noticing him for the first time—that could be a good sign. If it was not February. If she did not get out her deck of fortune-telling cards and waste hours laying them out in crosses and grids. If she did not linger in the cave mouths of Catholic churches but only passed them by. If she was not lost for the hundredth time in Vincent's letters to Theo or the *Fioretti* of Saint Francis. If it was not a Sunday; Sundays were the worst.

Every day had been a Sunday during that summer of 1952. Days of lassitude, nights of insomnia. Horrific dreams whose contents she refused to divulge, swallowing them whole on waking like a spy who feared capture. The sewing room filled with stacks of magazines she never got around to clipping, with sacks of grapes and cherries that rotted when she forgot to eat them and left the whole upstairs of the house smelling of vinegar. She would hang an old shawl across the doorway and stay in there for hours at a time. With a show of black humor, she would confess that she was in hiding but would never say from what or whom and did not really seem to be joking.

She checked out the usual bunch of weird records from the Pratt library—Indonesians banging on the local plumbing with hammers, G. I. Gurdjieff droning away at his harmonium, those fucking bagpipes—and played them over and over on a portable record player. She rarely ate and never cooked. When she emerged from behind the shawl and went out, she became a magnet for proselytizers and truth possessors. Copies of *The Watchtower* and *The Theosophist*, tracts and pamphlets dense with references to soul travel and *vril*, replaced the sacks of rotting fruit. In late August my grandmother covered the sewing room's windowpanes with squares of black paper so that she could not be observed by the shadowy whickering thing of which my grandfather then knew relatively little and understood less.

The night before my mother started fourth grade, two policemen had brought my grandmother home, barefoot and wearing a man's fishing jacket. Somebody had seen her, partly unclothed and moving erratically, down by the harbor and thought she might be contemplating or risking suicide. Just as the police had arrived on the scene, she was seen to set fire to the pages of a book and throw it into the water. From the description supplied by the witness to police, my grandfather recognized the book as having been one of the marbled notebooks in which his wife's sketches of the latest Paris prêt-à-porter looks alternated with her notes, reflections, and dreams, jotted hastily in French and reading, as far as my grandfather could tell, like hallucinatory telegrams. The cops thought about bringing her to Hopkins for observation. Once she'd set her notebook on fire and thrown it into the harbor, however, she no longer seemed distressed or unbalanced. She was cool, contrite, embarrassed by her behavior and state of undress, and lovely. One of the policemen recognized her from television. He loaned her the fisherman's jacket, and they brought her home. After that night she had seemed distinctly sane and unburdened. She lost herself in mothering. She returned to my grandfather's bed and opened her legs to him with her accustomed readiness. She had tidied up her sewing room.

Now, abruptly, it was a mess again.

Three empty bags of Brach's Autumn Mix lay on the floor, slit open, amid mounds and scatterings of vivid candy. The worktable was strewn with her fortune-telling cards, the ones she had been given in the DP camp at Wittenau by the requisite old gypsy witch woman never seen again. Faceup, facedown in a flat pile, as if built into a tower and then knocked down. A snarl of brown fabric jammed the platen of the sewing machine. A full cup of tea with milk, the surface opalescent with congealed fat. An open bottle of aspirin. Three inches of ash that had been a cigarette, preserved in the notch of an ashtray like fossilized proof that my grandmother had abandoned the job in haste.

Incomplete on the floor in the center of the room, amid the scattered candies, lay the Pie. At the moment it looked more like a kite than a horse, a strange coracle of brown oilcloth stretched over bent tomato stakes. An oval frame that curved upward at one end, partly covered in oilcloth skin. The green stakes slid into and were held in place by thin sleeves my grandmother had sewn into the fabric. They were lashed together at key junctures with wire ties.

In its partial state it took my grandfather a moment to understand: the oval of the body, the upcurving of the neck. It was something you might see in some old-fashioned mummer show, a pantomime horse to be worn around the hips. My grandfather had just formu-lated the thought *I wonder what she planned to do for the head* when he noticed the bucktoothed skull sitting on the typist's table under the bulletin board. A bone zeppelin, bleached, splintery as driftwood. Formerly the property of a small horse or pony.

XVIII

"It's really just the eyes," I said. "Mostly."

My mother didn't say anything. She was looking down at the horse skull on my kitchen table. She pinched her chin between three fingers as if to keep from averting her face.

"I mean, it's all of it, obviously. But especially the eyes."

The skull lay on the outspread towel in which it had spent the past fifty years, folded and stuffed into the Old Crow box, under my mother's books and the painted wooden horses wrapped in newspaper. The towel must have been white once, but time and humidity had dyed it with streaks of brown and rust red. A broken nib of mildew had spattered it with black.

In the sunlight coming through the kitchen window against the dingy towel, the unwrapped thing was radiant with strangeness. The incisors protruded to form a cruel beak, as if the skull had belonged to some monster bird of the Pleistocene. The jaws on either side, with their ridged molars, grinned like a pair of gaping zippers. The nose bone narrowed over the nasal cavity to a wicked prong. And into each orbit my grandmother had socketed a millefiori paperweight, multicolored cells honeycombed within a dome of clear glass. When I was a kid, the millefiori glass my grandmother kept around her apartment had always reminded me of bright handfuls of fancy hard candies. Cast in the unlikely role of eyeballs, however, the paperweights were like the kaleidoscopes of madness itself.

"I can't believe she thought you would *wear* it," I said. "How was it even supposed to attach to the neck?"

"I don't know if it was."

"But didn't she make it for your costume?"

"That's what my father thought."

"But you didn't?"

"If you were making someone a horse costume out of sticks and fabric, is that how you would do the head?"

"No. But maybe this was, like, how she saw it. Her version. The Night Witch version."

My mother was having none of it. "The silks she sewed me were so pretty! Perfect copies of the ones Elizabeth Taylor wears in the movie. They didn't have, I don't know, batwings on them or anything."

"Yeah, no, I get it."

"They were beautiful. I loved them. She knew how to make me a Pie."

"So if it wasn't part of the costume, what was it for?"

"At the time, I think what I thought was that my mother, she sort of . . . She had all these pamphlets and tracts lying around that she had collected. Religious tracts, Catholic prayer cards, but also things about Atlantis, Mayan religion, the, what is it, 'transmigration of souls.' All kinds of nonsense like that. It felt to me like that thing"— she pointed vaguely at the skull—"came out of all that religious mystical crap."

"You mean, like, it was almost kind of a, something she *prayed* to? An *idol?*"

"Not, I don't know, I mean, I was ten years old, I guess I thought—"

"You thought she was worshipping a horse god."

"I don't know if I went quite that far in my thinking."

"But now?"

"Now I don't think about it."

"Yeah, I know."

"You don't approve. You think I should just keep dredging it all up all the time."

"Not all the time. Just, like, every ten years or so."

My lame attempt to lighten the moment failed. She was looking at the skull straight on, and I saw that it was simply hateful to her.

"Mom," I said. "Forget it."

She made a Gallic noise of my grandmother's for which there is no good onomatopoeia, so I suppose *harrumph* will have to do. If she were a woman of my generation, she might have said *As if.*

"I understand," I said.

"Oh? Okay."

"That sounded patronizing."

"You want to know what I think now?"

She surprised me by grabbing the skull, swooping it off the table, and shoving it toward me, snout first. I jumped back, knocking over a kitchen chair. It's possible that I may have screamed.

"She wasn't *worshipping* the Skinless Horse with this thing. She was trying to ward it off."

"Whoa," I said. "Mom." I picked up the chair I had knocked over. "You scared me."

"Right," my mother said.

○   ○   ○

On the fir floor in the upstairs hall at the edge of the Chinese runner, my grandfather noticed a drop that looked like blood. It took the print of his finger and left a taste of salt on his tongue. In the doorway to the upstairs bathroom, a droplet had starred the wooden transition strip between fir and tile. In the bathroom across the grid of black and white tile, four asterisks pointed like the handle of the Dipper to a blood Arcturus in the space between the toilet and the bathtub. My grandfather's heart lurched. He turned to confront the bathtub.

It appeared to be empty, clean, and dry, but he forced himself to stare at it long and hard. He felt that if it contained my grandmother's body steeped in a tea of her lifeblood and Baltimore tap water, he could not trust his eyes to report nor brain to comprehend the fact. Shock could be a kind of plate armor. He gave horror, pain, and loss all the time they needed to pierce it. But there was nothing, only the shine on white porcelain and her flask of Emeraude bath oil, its note of benzoin a lingering sting in the air.

My grandfather went to the toilet and lifted the seat. On the underside of the left-hand branch of its *U*, at the tip, he found a comma, a little fish of blood. He folded some toilet paper, dipped the paper in the bowl, and wiped away the little fish. He ran some water on a washcloth and wiped away the stains on the floor. Then he stared down at the crossword-puzzle tile. Ruminating, only half aware that he was also taking a long-deferred piss, he considered clues and hints. He ransacked his store of experience of my grandmother and her behavior. He penciled in a few possibilities:

1. My grandmother had been attacked, in or just outside the bathroom, and carried off by some intruder. She had suffered internal injuries or fought back and bloodied her assailant. In the absence of other physical evidence, this did not seem a likely scenario, yet even after he had searched the house from cellar to attic, finding no sign of intrusion, he could not shake the feeling that there had been someone in the house.

2. My grandmother had injured herself, accidentally or on purpose. She was not accident-prone, but she had gone through periods during which she bit her cuticles or scratched her shins with her fingernails until she bled. On one occasion she had plucked her eyebrows clean, and though this produced no blood, it had struck him at the time as a kind of self-injury or, better, self-vandalism.

3. She had been surprised by the onset of menstruation or by a flow that was unusually heavy. If she was menstruating, and in particular if more heavily than usual, this might have triggered

some kind of psychological disturbance to explain both her absence from the house and the presence in her sewing room
of a horse skull with paperweights for eyes. It had long been
apparent to him, though at a level of consciousness too low for
observation and plotting of data, that there was some kind of
association between his wife's monthly cycle and the ebb and
flood of her sanity.

Following on this third possibility, he caught the flickering of a
fourth at the horizon of his thoughts, but like a lightning strike, it
was gone by the time he looked its way. In the meantime, in some
other part of his mind, my grandfather's pessimism and the brute-
force denial that he deployed in place of optimism contended over
the question of whether he was making a mountain of a molehill
here. Big deal, a few drops of blood, a hastily improvised and un-
happily conceived horse costume, an absence that was not usual but
hardly unheard of, especially when my grandmother had a show to
do that night . . .

He shook off this line of thinking and its appeal to his reptile-
brain optimism. Something was wrong, *felt* wrong. He had known
it as soon as he'd seen the bagpipe records on the console. In general, my grandmother in the grip of a mood was inclined to hole up,
shut down, or curl inward. But sometimes the woman would just
bolt. Taking off that night when the police picked her up, ill-shod,
ill-dressed, booking along the sidewalk with a forward cant and her
arms held fixed at her sides, conversing with invisibilities of pain,
presenting like a classic urban nutcase, flying her Night Witch hair
like the flag of madness.

My grandfather went back into my mother's bedroom. She was
sitting up, rocking back and forth at the edge of her bed, holding the
carved horse that, working in the driveway one evening long after
dark, he had inadvertently painted blue instead of black. He had
been annoyed by the fuckup; naturally, that one turned out to be the

favorite, the one on which she bestowed the power of flight. The girl was a labyrinth to him; only by chance and error did he ever stumble blindly into her heart.

Her face was puffy and she wore a stoical expression. The rocking reminded him of the little girl he had met for the first time on a bench in the cold outside Ahavas Sholom. Defiantly serving out the inhumane term of a punishment she had imposed on herself, confusing obedience with rebellion and vindication with endurance.

"Come," he told her. "Put your costume on. We'll find your friends and you'll go with them."

My mother shook her head.

"I have to go out," he said. He decided to lie to her. "Your mother's up at the studio, she forgot the book she's going to read tonight. I need to take it to her."

"I'll come with you."

"Eh, you know, Pat'll be working the desk tonight, you know how he is about kids hanging around."

"I'll wait in the car."

"You don't want to go trick-or-treating?"

"No."

"Okay, listen. I tell you what. Your behavior, recently, your manners. Your schoolwork. I've been meaning to tell you. They've really been very good."

He realized as he offered this praise that he had no idea if it was accurate. She had never been anything but compliant and well mannered, however, and he assumed, though he had not paid much attention lately, that this remained the case. Her first-quarter report card had boasted the usual cordillera of As.

"So," he said, "if you want to go with your friends, because you've been such a good girl lately, how about we say, whatever you bring home, you can eat. No matter what. As much chazzerai as you can stand. All right? You can have it for breakfast, lunch, and dinner. All of it. Until the whole bag is gone."

Before the razor blade scares of the 1960s, before industrial confectioners cottoned on to the market for small, individually wrapped pieces of brand-name candy, the loot a kid brought home from trick-or-treating was made by the lady of the house where it was given out: popcorn balls, candy and caramel apples, cookies, marshmallow treats, toffees. Such items quickly went stale or lost their appeal and, after a week or two, whatever a kid had not managed to consume was ready to be thrown away. Since, as a firm rule, my mother was never permitted more than one treat per day, the bulk of what she collected on Halloween ended up in the garbage can. My grandfather's extravagant offer had no precedent. It was transparently a bribe.

"What's wrong with Mama?" my mother said. Her voice deepened to a woeful contralto.

"Nothing."

"I know it's something bad."

"Nothing is wrong, she forgot her book."

My mother nodded as though reassured. She shuddered. My grandfather handed her a handkerchief. She wiped her eyes and blew her nose and handed it back to him. He put it, snot and all, into his pocket.

"I know you're lying to me," she said.

"Oh, is that right?"

"And I'm not going."

"No?"

"I don't want to. I hate candy apples, anyway."

"So you'll trade with your friends. You like popcorn balls."

"It's bad for your teeth. Your saliva turns the sugar to acid, the acid dissolves the enamel, and you get a cavity and have to get a filling, with a drill and a bunch of shots in your mouth, I don't want that."

"So you'll brush."

She held the blue horse up to her face at eye level and moved it through the air in arcs and dives. She half closed her eyes, a technique he remembered from his own childhood, making the horse and its flight more real through some enchantment of perspective and the lensing effect of lids and lashes.

"Look. Honey. I have to go out, and I can't leave you here alone. With all the people coming to the door? You don't know who's going to show up. All kinds of hooligans out causing trouble tonight, you remember last year they smashed every pumpkin on the block."

The blue horse dipped and banked through the air between them. She was finished with the conversation. Where other, less tractable children might have openly rebelled or thrown a tantrum, my mother had learned to withdraw, to abstain, to retreat from a scene of conflict without moving a muscle.* My grandfather knew better than to waste any more breath trying to persuade her. When she checked out, there was nothing to be done but compel her physically or else back down. My grandfather loved my mother and was reasonably certain that she loved him in return, but there was some negotiated basis to their relationship that she understood more clearly than he did. His fatherhood was a kind of grant that she bestowed on him, a tenancy of which she was the lessor.

"Actually, the sugar gets eaten by bacteria that live in the mouth," my grandfather could not prevent himself from pointing out before he turned and left her alone in the bedroom. "The bacteria excrete the acid that eats the teeth."

He went downstairs to the kitchen and made seven telephone calls. The first call was to the switchboard of WAAM; no one at the station had seen my grandmother since Tuesday morning's broadcast of La Cuisine. Next he dialed the number on a card left behind, in case they ever needed any help, by Officer Sharkey, the policeman who had loaned my grandmother his Pendleton fishing jacket and

---

* It was an art at which she only improved over the years, as a wife and a mother. "Oh no, don't do that!" I can remember my father shouting as my mother gathered her cloak of absence around herself and another argument devolved inexorably into a harangue. "Look at me, God damn it!"

kept her out of the psych ward. Officer Sharkey had the night off. The next five calls my grandfather made, in turn, were to a pool hall in East Baltimore, a bar in Fells Point, the home of a woman who sounded disgracefully drunk, the home of a woman who sounded abominably sober, and, thanks to the latter, another pool hall out in Dundalk.

A knock on the door, a carillon of little voices on the porch.

The candy still lay scattered on the floor of the sewing room. My grandfather knew that he ought to take a bowl up there and retrieve it, but he did not want to have to look, or avoid looking, at the horse skull. He dug around in his trouser pockets. He was out of quarters. He had three nickels and four pennies, but there turned out to be four trick-or-treaters, the Grumman children from two doors down, disguised as a shepherd and his three-sheep flock. Clifford Grumman, accurately, was fleeced in black. My grandfather pocketed the nickels and deposited the pennies in the children's palms, taking no notice of whether the Grummans went away pleased or not. In 1952 a penny could buy you a piece of bubblegum, a candy cigarette, or a licorice whip.

He found three fifty-cent rolls of pennies in a kitchen drawer. He put on his suit jacket, made sure he had his wallet and car keys, and went out to the front porch to wait. He sat down on the metal glider, lit a cigarette. The hinges of the glider were rusted and creaked atmospherically in the dark.

In the half hour that followed, three cowboys, two Indians, a Mad Hatter and White Rabbit, Jesse and Frank James, a queen ("Just a queen"), and a number of hoboes, along with five mothers, two fathers, and a dog wearing a Pierrot hat came tripping up the porch steps. Once my grandfather had gauged the pace of visitors, he increased his payment to two pennies per trick-or-treater, flicking them from the roll with his thumbnail into each waiting palm. He did not consider but in hindsight would concede that he might not by his manner or his fare be spreading waves of Halloween joy.

My grandfather had just lit his fifth cigarette when the first in what became a long series of unreliable red roadsters, a brand-new Jaguar XK120, rumbled onto the street and stopped in front of the house. Its driver cut the engine and then sat as if marshaling patience or resolve.

Uncle Ray was two years free of the pulpit that had fit him as poorly as the clothes he was wearing now, some kind of English hunting get-up, baggy tweed pants and a tweed jacket with large front panels of plaid wool. In later years he would switch to Alfas and more of a Mastroianni resort-wear vibe, but in snaps from the early fifties, he looks like he's planning to go off and shoot some partridges or appease Hitler.

Uncle Ray lit a cigarette of his own and then came up the walk to the porch. The smirk and the swagger that had unaccountably chosen this man as the vehicle for their conquest of the world or at least the Delmarva Peninsula had reached some kind of new pinnacle of insufferability.

"So where is she?" he said as he and my grandfather shook hands.

"I don't know."

"She didn't leave a note?"

My grandfather shook his head. He stood up and fished his car keys out of the hip pocket of his jacket.

"Where's the kid?"

"Upstairs."

"She ready to go, get her uncle some taffy?"

"Says she doesn't want to."

"She's upset." Uncle Ray opened the front door. "Hey, Velvet!" he called out. "Post time!"

"Ray, I have to go."

"So go."

At that moment another party of trick-or-treaters approached the house, followed by another, and by the time my grandfather was through dispensing pennies, his brother had returned.

"She's getting her costume on," Uncle Ray said. He looked down at the split roll of coins. "Pennies."

"No candy. It got spoiled."

Uncle Ray took the half-roll and the two intact ones, and my grandfather started down the steps.

"So where are you going?"

"Hospital."

"You think she's hurt?" He spoke in a whispery rasp. "You think she hurt herself?"

"I don't know," my grandfather said, lowering his voice, too. "What happens when you have a miscarriage?"

"She was pregnant?"

"I . . . I wouldn't know."

"You wouldn't know?"

"I didn't know. I don't know."

"Were you trying?"

My grandparents had been trying to produce a child almost from their first night together, Purim 1947. At the beginning it was an unarticulated hope expressed only in a mutual disregard of birth control, a hope shared by many survivors of war and calamity to counter general death with a particular life, to light a candle in the universal night. Once they were married, they embarked on the project openly and deliberately, with a fixity of purpose that over time had faded in vigor as it became more awkward and painful to them both. The thought that my grandmother might finally have conceived their child was so welcome, so eagerly anticipated for so long, that for an instant the joy of it outweighed the concomitant dismay of understanding that, in this instance, a pregnancy would be only the necessary condition for its loss.

"It's been discussed," my grandfather said.

"So she's upset about that, it's natural. She'll just need a little time."

"I know, I know. I'm sure you're right."

The idea returned to him, more clearly, that the state of her mind was connected in some way to her menstrual cycle. Had the improvement in her mood since September been caused by an unsuspected pregnancy? Abruptly, he remembered her having woken him last night. She was sitting up, speaking French, with the odd clarity of someone asleep and dreaming. When he asked her what was the matter, she had switched to English and told him they had to call someone to come take away the furnace in the basement right away. She could not or would not tell him why, but he must trust her that it had to be done or something very bad would result. In a patronizing tone it now made him wince to recall, he had assured her that he would put someone on the task of removing the furnace the very next morning. My grandmother had nodded and a moment later was lying down again, easing back into normal sleep. Or so my grandfather had assumed; certainly *he* had gone back to sleep. But what if she had been up for the rest of the night after that, poor thing? What if her midnight outburst had marked the ebbing, along with the incipient life inside her, of whatever chemical benefit that pregnancy bestowed? He thought of her lying there, feeling herself sliding inexorably back to the place she had been last summer, frightened, alone, making disordered plans of escape, and it made his heart hurt. What did she think was happening in the basement?

"You look worried," Uncle Ray said. "Don't worry."

"I'm not worried," my grandfather said.

"About what?" said my mother, coming out to the porch. She was wearing some old corduroy overalls over a pair of long johns, carrying a burlap sugar sack. Bare feet, an inverted metal saucepan for a hat.

"No shoes?" my grandfather said.

"I saw the cartoon," my mother said. "He was barefoot."

"In this weather."

"Take it up with Walt Disney."

"What a little brat you are," Uncle Ray said tenderly. "Candy Appleseed."

My mother reached into the sugar sack and took out a book, worn black boards, no jacket. "Here," she said to my grandfather.

"What's this?"

"Mama's book? For you to take to the station? The one she forgot?"

It was a tattered hardback copy of *Tales*, with the marvelous Redon illustrations, that my grandmother used when she read Poe on *The Crypt of Nevermore*.

"Right," my grandfather said.

Uncle Ray's ear was attuned to the coded conversation of hustlers, cheats, and their confederates. "Nothing against Johnny here," he said. "But what happened to National Velvet?" He looked from my mother to my grandfather and back. "What?"

"Sore subject," my grandfather said.*

---

* She was not just changing her costume, I pointed out to my mother, she was ridding herself, as completely as she could imagine, of the need for a horse. Except for maybe the Wandering Jew or Diogenes, no figure was more famous than Johnny Appleseed for being a pedestrian, for walking around everywhere on his shoeless feet. The very next day she had packed up her horse books, the carved horses, and the skull. It was called magical thinking, I told her. Children who believe they are to blame for their parents' misfortunes believe they have the power to abate them. My mother thought about it. I waited for her to congratulate me on my insight. "Where's the magical part?" she said.

XIX

In 1952 in Baltimore an autumn haze was closer to smoke, and though the Moon was high and nearly full, its light hung diffuse and opaque as if moonlight were only an inferior brand of darkness. As he patrolled Forest Park in his car that Halloween, looking for my grandmother—a check of nearby hospitals and police stations had turned up nothing—most of what my grandfather saw was shadow. Then, into a cone of streetlight or a lighted porch, there would burst a doctor and a dead man and a robot and a carrot and Abe Lincoln and a werewolf and a pharaoh and a fly. My grandfather had never seen so many kitchen-broom witches, bedsheet ghosts, popgun sheriffs. A giant baby holding hands with a pint-size gorilla, a tramp with a monocled millionaire. A dreamlike river of children coursing in and out of shadow, pooling on stoops, and out there somewhere a woman with a crack in her brain that was letting in shadows and leaking dreams.

He sat stopped at a traffic signal. A turbulence of historic personages, zoo animals, and career aspirations boiled surrealistically through his headlight beams, Viking horns, a giraffe's neck, a pink tutu, a Mountie's campaign hat. My grandfather rolled down his window and called to ask if anyone had happened to see Nevermore, the Night Witch. Of course, they thought he was kidding around.

"Ah!" said the giraffe, dipping its papier-mâché head to sprint the rest of the way across the street in halfway-mock alarm. "The Night Witch!"

"Don't scare me!" said the Viking.

With every corner my grandfather turned, his hope of spotting my grandmother would rekindle, and at the end of every block his heart would sink anew. After a while he noticed that the coveys and duckling chains of little kids were starting to give way to lurking platoons of older boys without costumes who loped crookedly, dragging cartoon-burglar pillowcases from house to house and flicking furtive eggs at passing cars. When an egg was thrown, there would be a burp of tires, shouts of grievance and malediction, coyote yips of laughter. The night turned authentically menacing. My grandfather could not bear the thought of my grandmother abroad in it. Hurting from the inside. Emptied out. She had been pregnant and she had miscarried and then the voice or the thoughts or the memory that tormented her had returned: her hidden history of loss, loss upon loss upon loss unending, flooding back into her body as that tablespoonful of life leaked out. Her true companion. Her lover with his bleached bones showing and his maddened eyes.

The view through the windshield swam. My grandfather pulled over to the curb, blocking someone's driveway, and cut the engine. He fought against the tears. They were nothing but tears of panic, and of all the emotions there was none more contemptible. He closed his eyes so that he would not have to see his breakdown witnessed by a world that had the strength to make him cry. After a minute he opened his eyes again. He lit a cigarette, and the nicotine seemed to organize his mind. Aughenbaugh's lighter was cool against his palm, and from its engraved face a comforting gaze seemed to stare back at him through the pince-nez of maltose, the imperturbable gaze of the man who had passed the lighter on to him, two glucose rings hooked together by a glycosidic bond.

He lit another cigarette and began to conduct a review of methodology, as if it were not a lost woman he sought but simply a better means of seeking, a heuristic against loss. The effectiveness of a search of this kind depended on the amount of information available about the area to be searched, the number of searchers, and the cost in time elapsed. He knew Forest Park and the surrounding neighborhoods well enough, but he was alone and in a hurry. Was it best to start at some arbitrary perimeter and work inward toward an indefinite center, or to proceed by quarterings? The grid of streets to be covered was a mishmash of orthogonals and diagonals, and searching it posed interesting problems in topology. Clearly, any useful algorithm for maximizing the number of individual blocks searched at the lowest cost in time would have to integrate a Euclidean metric of distance as covered by transverse streets with a non-Euclidean metric of the zigzag distance imposed by square city blocks. In this instance the topological problem was complicated by the likelihood that the goal was not stationary and, indeed, at this moment might be riding the 33 streetcar or getting into a murderer's Pontiac or lying like a smashed kite at the foot of the Bromo-Seltzer Tower or sunken, drowned, tugged along the bottom of the Patapsco River by the tide. In the meantime it was almost eleven P.M. He had been driving around uselessly for hours.

He decided to head toward the studios of WAAM. Even when she was struggling with her moods, he thought, the woman never lost sight of her duties and commitments. In a dark period, her pain was usually intensified by the consciousness of falling down on the job as a mother, a wife, an employee, a friend. Sometimes knowing that she had someplace to be or someone depending on her was enough to lift her above the darkness for an hour, for a day, for as long as the job was not done or the errand unaccomplished. However near to the edge of the map she might have sailed today, it was always possible that her Friday-night gig was beacon enough to turn her back. Maybe she was there now, whitening her skin with a sponge of pancake makeup, painting ragged feathers along the ridge of her eyebrows.

As he drove, he lit another cigarette with the flare of the lighter and his thoughts found their way back to heuristics—algorithms that offered shortcuts to solutions of complex problems—and an article he had read in *Scientific American* about a problem in the mathematics of graphing.

You were a traveling salesman whose territory obliged you to cover n cities, with your heavy sample case and your fallen arches and your weariness of diner food and hotel beds. Because you missed your wife and your daughter, you wanted to visit each city in your territory only once and then return home, having traveled the shortest distance in the least amount of time. There were $(n\text{-}1)!$ possible routes, and if n wasn't too big, say five towns, you could sit down with your map and your distance table and your pencil and your incipient case of heartburn and add it all up and see which of the twenty-four possible routes was the shortest. But once n got up into even the low two digits, the job of calculating the distances for each possible route, even if you were superhumanly quick with a sum, might take hundreds or thousands of years. With only fifteen cities, there were a trillion possible routes. What you wanted, poor wandering and footsore salesman, was some kind of algorithm, an operational shortcut that would let you find the most efficient route without doing a thousand years of math.

So far, it turned out, there was no such algorithm. But my grandfather had read that a cash prize was being offered by the RAND Corporation in Santa Monica to the first person who came up with a workable heuristic that would solve the Traveling Salesman Problem. Its solution, RAND felt, would open up all kinds of possibilities in the burgeoning field of operations research, a field that, as it happened, overlapped with the work he and Weinblatt were doing. He felt the faint stirring of an idea then, an approach to inertial navigation systems that would involve the heuristics of topological algorithms. It was a marvelous idea, and he backed away from it, giving it space; you could blow on a fire to stoke it, but if you blew on a little flame, it would go out.

He headed up into Woodberry toward the studios of WAAM. He imagined that he was the one who solved the Traveling Salesman

Problem and collected the cash prize. Clearly, the answer lay in the mathematics of linear functions. He might brush up on his Hamiltonian mechanics, dust off his knowledge of set theory. He saw himself accepting a check for the prize winnings and then—it was not at all unreasonable to imagine—a job offer from his awestruck fellow boffins at RAND. *Please,* they would beg him, *come out to Santa Monica, we need you. Come and work on this application of topology to navigation.* Would he go? He pictured them, my grandmother, my mother, and himself standing on the wooden deck of a house near the ocean. California. Nothing but sunshine and horizon, a place without shadows, far from the darkness of Europe and its history, that endless Halloween. He saw them, walking down the beach with their trousers rolled. A child, their child, ran ahead of them, a brash little boy scattering seagulls. His heart swelled. It was all very pretty. It was as pretty as the solution to a problem in topology that would never be solved.

He had reached the television studio up on its hill at the heart of town. It was a composite building, two boxes shoved together, a windowless stucco packing crate that held the studio floor next to a brick shoe box built in the style favored at the time for public schools and libraries, the bricks in long horizontal courses, the windows a horizontal strip. At this hour most of the windows were dark. There were only two cars parked by the entrance; the crew parked in a garage at the back.

In the lobby the night man, Pat, ignored a banquette sofa and a coffee table shaped like a footprint with no toes. A selection of trade publications and magazines lay scattered across the coffee table. Pat was dressed like a policeman but in gray, with a peaked cap and a black necktie. With his blue eyes, gin blossoms, and dignified bearing, he reminded my grandfather of a seedier Bill Donovan. Pat took his job very seriously, believing, according to my grandmother, that when the local cadre got the word from Moscow, they would have orders to seize control of WAAM. To repel the attack, poor Pat had been entrusted with only a letter opener in a leather pen cup, a flashlight, and a key ring (though tonight his arsenal had been supplemented with a pumpkin and a sheaf of Indian corn), which likely explained why he was always kind of a sourpuss.

"I've been at my post since eight o'clock, sir," Pat informed my grandfather. "I have not seen your wife. And you are not the first to come asking. Mr. Roberts been out here twice, see if she got here yet. Mr. Kahn, too."

My grandfather asked Pat if maybe he could speak with Mr. Roberts (the floor manager) or Mr. Kahn (the director) or, seeing as how they were busy men who already had enough to worry about, if maybe he could just have a look around. Maybe his wife had come in earlier, to find some prop or a music cue in the record library, and fallen asleep in a chair in the artists' room. He believed in this possibility as he offered it, but as soon as it left his lips, it sounded unlikely and Pat's face told him that he was talking nonsense. My grandfather had not only come here expecting to find his wife, he reminded himself. He had also come, complementarily, to strengthen the case for her having really disappeared. My grandfather remembered the book.

"She's going to need this," he said. "When she gets here. She's on her way. Be here any minute." He held up the collection of Poe.

"Yeah?" Pat said. "What's on tonight?"

"'Metzengerstein.'"

"Never read him, he any good?"

"Tune in tonight," my grandfather said. "Judge for yourself."

He pointed to the big twenty-one-inch RCA television mounted in a heavy oak cabinet behind Pat's desk. Permanently tuned to channel 13, presently showing a movie my grandfather didn't recognize. John Wayne was underwater, bare-chested, fighting a giant octopus with a knife.

"Oh, I don't watch your missus anymore," Pat said. "I have to turn down the sound when she comes on. Nice lady. *Pretty* lady. But she gives me a fantod. Meaning no offense."

"Pat. Please. I need to find her."

"Well, all right, then, you have a seat," Pat said. "I'll go find Mr. Kahn."

Pat went through the door that led to the main corridor running between the two halves of the TV station. My grandfather lingered at the counter, running his fingers across the tuck-and-roll surface of the pumpkin. He wondered why one hemisphere of a pumpkin always seemed to be as smooth as polished stone while the other was always streaked and warted with some mysterious cement.

After a minute Pat had not returned. My grandfather went to the banquette with its legs of bent rebar, and though sitting was the last thing he wanted to do, he forced himself to sit. He shuffled through the magazines: *Broadcast News, Sponsor, Advertising Age,* a *Ring,* a couple of old *New Yorkers.* One *New Yorker* somebody had left open to an advertisement with a cartoon drawing of a dismayed fisherman reeling in a boot. My grandfather sympathized. Then, in the column of text that ran down the page alongside the advertisement, his gaze caught on the hook of a capital *V,* separated by a hyphen from the numeral 2.

The article was entitled "A Romantic Urge." Its author's name was Daniel Lang. Over the course of several pages in the middle of the issue for the week of April 21, 1951—over a year and a half ago—Lang revealed to the literate, Dunhills-smoking, Triple Sec–drinking American public that the man behind Germany's fearsome V-2 rocket was now living happily in Huntsville, Alabama, and working as a top scientist along with many other former Nazi "men of science" in the U.S. Army's guided missile program. My grandfather had heard reports of something like this, with no mention of Wernher von Braun, and they had been vague enough for him to dismiss from his mind. It appeared, however, that not only von Braun but the better part of the German rocket program— more than a hundred men captured by the U.S. military's wartime Operation Paperclip—had been transplanted to El Paso and then to Huntsville, where they were now being paid excellent salaries, learning to eat tamales and grits, driving around in their Chevys wearing cowboy hats and providing the United States with a missile capable of putting a nuclear warhead in the middle of downtown Moscow. Lang characterized Operation Paperclip as having been a treasure hunt and its operatives as "talent scouts."

Lang was charmed by von Braun, with his blond hair and his buoyant manner and his protestations of innocent indifference to the strange ways of generals and führers. Von Braun was quoted to the effect that it made as much sense to blame a rocket scientist, who had wanted only to "blaze a trail to other planets," for the deaths and destruction caused by the V-2 as it did to blame Einstein for the A-bomb. Lang characterized the man my grandfather knew to have held the rank of *SS-Sturmbannführer* (major) as a civilian, a man of peace, a reluctant warrior with his head in the clouds; he referred to the mechanized slave pit Nordhausen where the V-2 rockets had been assembled as a "production plant" staffed by Russian POWs.

"This is not good," Barry Kahn said. My grandfather looked up. The director was a good-looking kid, one of those new postwar intellectual young Jews who dressed like a hoodlum in motorcycle jackets, rolled dungarees, never a tie. Behind him Pat stood shaking his head, looking at once reproachful and satisfied, as if he had predicted that nothing good would come of him going off to look for Mr. Kahn, or of my grandfather marrying a woman like my grandmother. "Where the hell is she, man? What am I supposed to put on the air in twenty-five minutes?"

The telephone behind the reception counter rang and rang again. Pat went around behind the counter and answered on the fourth ring, "WAAM." He listened. His yellowed eyes, forked with pink, rolled toward my grandfather. "He's right here." Pat handed my grandfather the receiver. "It's your brother."

Less than a minute later, having spoken fewer than five words to the individual on the other end of the call, the husband of Nevermore, the Night Witch, hung up the phone. He turned to Barry

Kahn. The tough-looking young Jew took a step backward, stumbling a little in his haste. His gaze was fixed on the point of the letter opener my grandfather held in his right hand. The blade of the letter opener was smeared, as with gore, with a film of orange pulp. "Easy, now," said Barry Kahn.

In 2014, when I interviewed Kahn at his daughter's home in Owings Mills, Maryland, the phrase he used to describe my grandfather at this moment was almost identical to the one employed by the anonymous witness who would be quoted on May 25, 1957, in the New York *Daily News*: *I've never seen anyone so angry in my life.*

My grandfather took a folded handkerchief from his hip pocket and used it to wipe the pulp from the blade of the letter opener, then dropped it back in the leather pen cup. He turned to Barry Kahn and handed him the pumpkin. "Here you go," he said. While he'd been on the phone hearing the news that Uncle Ray tracked him down to pass along, my grandfather had used the letter opener to carve— punch out, really—a ragged parody of a human face. It had holes for eyes, a slit for a nose, a bent, moronic leer.

"What's this?" Kahn didn't want to take the pumpkin. He took it nevertheless.

"Her understudy," my grandfather said.

He went to the coffee table and picked up the April 21, 1951, issue of *The New Yorker*. He held it up and took Aughenbaugh's lighter from his pocket and set fire to a corner of the magazine. When the magazine had caught, he dropped it in a metal wastebasket by the station's front door. "Happy Halloween," he said.

A fire blazed up in the wastebasket. The metal rumbled with heat and then fell silent as the flame died away.

◑   ◑   ◑

The Carmel, corner of Caroline and Biddle. An eminence of brick behind an iron gate in a high brick wall. Windows like slits behind heavy jalousies, steep roof castellated with dormers. A house of refuge or penitence but either way a house built to estrange its occupants from the world. On the roof the tall white cross, that high diver with arms outspread.

My grandfather had been instructed to use the back door. He parked the car on Caroline and found the alleyway promised by the prioress of the Carmel. It was an old East Baltimore alleyway paved unevenly in stones that made him wobbly at the ankles. The prioress had said to look for a steel door with a granite step. Beside the door he would see a little crank for the doorbell; on no account was he to crank it. At this hour of the night, she had told him, the Carmel was ruled by silence, or under a rule of silence, or words to that effect. They would hear him coming before he even had time to knock.

The prioress had struck him over the phone as a woman accustomed to taking matters in hand. "It was hard to know how best to serve your wife when she got here," she had told him when he'd called the number she'd left with Uncle Ray. "I settled on a cup of tea and a pillow."

Everything was as the prioress had promised: steel door with a sheen of moonlight, wide stone step for the leaving of deliveries, donations, and foundlings. Crank like the handle on a pepper mill below a plaque that bore the duplicitous suggestion TURN. As my grandfather raised his hand to knock, a bolt slid back and the door swung inward. In the open doorway, surrounded by shadow, a round face hung pale and disembodied, a full moon painted on a theater drop.

"Mother Mary Joseph?"

The face twisted with amusement, annoyance, or disdain. Its owner drew back a step, and my grandfather saw that she was barely out of her teens and likely nobody's mother in any sense of the word. It was the flowing brown scapular that had made her face seem to hang bodiless in the dark. The scapular gave off a clean smell of lavender and steam. The young nun invited him in with an awkward chopping gesture, like someone trying to wave away a bee. He stepped over the threshold of the Carmel.

Snow shovels, sandbags, a hand truck, rolls of strapping tape, some old bicycles, all labeled, everything stacked on shelves or hung from hooks. A menagerie of overshoes, Wellingtons, and galoshes. And a second nun, an ancient woman, swarthy and whiskered and crooked like a finger. The moment my grandfather came through, this tiny personage hurled herself at the heavy door and shoved it to, and the young nun drove home the deadbolt. With the breach sealed, the air in the Carmel's basement corridor seemed to thicken with silence. It was like putting in a pair of earplugs. You could hear yourself swallowing, the click of your neck bones. The nuns slid past him, keeping their eyes downcast, away from the service entry.

"I'm here to see my wife," my grandfather said.

His voice was a blare, a racket. He started to apologize, but the nuns were moving away from him down a hallway of painted cinder block. Bare bulbs, a green and white chessboard of linoleum polished to a high shine, as from constant sweeping by the hems of habits. The nuns were heading toward a stairwell at the far end. They went with a kind of slow urgency, like they were carrying iron kettles full of boiling water. At the bottom of the stairwell they stopped. This was as far as they planned to travel in my grandfather's company. The old nun unbent one gnarled hand and uplifted its palm. My grandfather nodded; pointlessly, since they had yet to look at him. He started up the stairs. The unspoken apology lingered at the tip of his tongue.

"I'm sorry," he said when he reached the first-floor landing.

The prioress was waiting for him, a handsome woman tented in a great volume of brown serge like a pylon planted in the doorway to block his path. Her voice was barely louder than a whisper yet not the least bit soft. It carried. It expected to be heard.

"Are you now?" she said. "And why would that be?"

She had three inches and thirty pounds on him, and she looked him right in the eye. She wore a pair of men's eyeglasses, circular black frames with thick lenses.

"For the intrusion," my grandfather said. "For the late hour."

"There's nothing to apologize for. I told you to come."

He followed her down another hallway. The flooring here was some kind of hardwood, spotless and redolent of beeswax. Her habit trailed the same good smell of serge freshly laundered and ironed. She led him past unmarked doors, a radiator, a statuette of some naked martyr in ecstasy or torment, a framed portrait of a beautiful nun interrupted, while writing in a book with a quill pen, by the appearance of a giant human heart in the blue sky over her head. The airborne heart was being pierced by a giant arrow; maybe she was writing about that. The pipes of the radiator rang with steam hammers, and the hallway was uncomfortably warm. Down toward the end of the hall was a door with a tin plaque that read INFIRMARY, black letters on white enamel.

"Wait," the prioress said. Again she interposed her body between my grandfather and the place where he needed to go. She opened the infirmary door enough to look in, and gave a little grunt, somewhere between enlightenment and annoyance. She closed the door and turned to face my grandfather. Behind the lenses of her eyeglasses, the look in her eyes was compassionate without being friendly. "Come with me, please."

"Is she in there?"

"Yes. Come with me."

"Sister—"

"Please." She was pointing to the next door down the hall. It stood ajar. "You have a decision to make and right now too little information for making it."

By chance or instinct, she had hit on the type of reasoning that could move my grandfather. After a moment of hesitation, he gave in and followed her into the room next to the infirmary. It was un-marked. She switched on a bare light overhead, revealing a desk and two bentwood chairs, a tall shelf crowded with dull-looking texts, an empty mesh wastebasket, and a metal filing cabinet. The surface of the desk was bare but for a blotter, a dreadnought telephone of the 1930s, and a framed photograph of that era's pope sitting smugly on a throne, wearing a hat that looked like a white yarmulke. My grand-father took the seat across from hers.

"It's a very long time, I've no doubt, since a man set foot in this room," she said, her tone disapproving and a touch melancholy. "Or-dinarily you and I ought to be separated by a screen of some kind."

"Is that the information I'm going to need to make my decision?"

The smart remark seemed to take them both a little by surprise. The prioress looked at him through half-lowered eyelids. "Maybe so," she said mysteriously after a moment. "Now, I gave your wife some tea."

"You mentioned that."

"Valerian tea. It has sedative properties."

"Yes."

"And now she's gone and fallen asleep."

"Ah."

"She was wrung out. I know you're anxious to see her, my friend. But tonight we must let her sleep."

"Sister—"

"Of course it's inconvenient, you came all the way over here, and I'm sure you're very concerned. Of course you are. I see it on your face. But you'll agree, won't you, that it would be an unkindness to wake her? Please. Go home. Come back in the morning or as soon as you can tomorrow. We'll look after her until then."

"Sister, I, uh, truly, I appreciate the concern and the care you've already taken with her. But I just want to take her home. Tonight. Now."

"I see. And are you sure that she'll want to go home with you?"

"What are you getting at?"

"Don't take offense, please. I may be a nun, but I am also a woman and thus very sure that I know much more about men in general and husbands in particular than you do. My question was reasonable. If she wants so very much to be at home with you, then why isn't she there at home with you right now?"

It was a fair question, he had to admit.

"She went out, she, uh, left. She was upset."

"Friend, let me tell you something. Your wife wasn't 'upset.' She was out of her cotton-picking mind." She seemed to listen to the echo of the phrase as it faded. She looked satisfied by the sound of it. "Did you actually *see* her, did you witness her behavior, at any point this evening?"

"No."

"Did you *hear* her? Did you hear the language that came flying out of her mouth?"

"I was at work," my grandfather said. "When I got home, she had already left, I didn't realize right away."

"I see," the prioress said. "Listen, do you know how I found you tonight? How I happen to know your name, how I came to have your telephone number?"

"I assumed . . . I figured she asked you to call."

"She did not say one word about you, as a matter of fact. Not in my hearing. I knew your name because, hmm, when was it, maybe two or three months back, your wife left a check for five hundred dollars in our charity box. Drawn on your joint checking account. I never cashed it. It was so much money. I felt it might be taking advantage. In any case, I kept the check. Your name was printed on it. That's how I knew how to reach you."

"You're saying she's been here before."

"Your wife has been coming to our special 'Sisters in Prayer' service, it's open to all women of faith, one Sunday a month for, oh, it must be a year now."

The compassion that had never entirely left her eyes, even when she was exercised and aggravated with my grandfather, now seemed to give way to outright pity.

"You didn't know," she said.

"No."

"But you do know . . . Forgive me, my friend. You do know that your wife isn't just 'upset.' You do understand that she's mentally ill?"

He did understand it, but he had never said the words, aloud or to himself, or even permitted himself to squarely think the thought.

"The things she was saying tonight, oh!" The prioress closed her eyes and shook her head a little. "Calling herself a witch. A 'night witch,' if you please. Calling herself liar, bad mother, whore. And worse. Telling me, 'I killed my baby tonight.' Saying she had, if you please, been violated, sexually, by a *horse* that had no *skin*, and that after it was over, she went to the toilet, and looked in, and saw her baby floating in there." These words came out in a rush as if the prioress could not wait to get them out of her mouth and be done with them. "You've never heard talk like that from her?"

"She never . . . She never put it . . . like that."

"Finally, well, I had enough, I suppose. I'm sitting with her, right beside her. I give her the tea, and I tell her, 'Now, that's *enough*. No more of that talk. And she does calm down. And she looks at me, and she takes my hands in hers. 'I feel safe here,' she says. 'I *only* feel safe here. I want to stay. I have a vocation, Mother,' she says. 'I'm called.'"

My grandfather surprised both of them. He laughed. "That is crazy," he said. "First of all, she's married, to me. Second of all, she has a daughter who's eleven years old. And third, she's a *Jew*."

The prioress wanted to remind him that many women born Jewish had lived out their lives in orders.* He could see it on her

---

* She was undoubtedly aware of the life and martyrdom of her sister Carmelite, Teresa Benedicta of the Cross, born Edith Stein in Breslau, gassed at Auschwitz, and eventually canonized in 1998 by Pope John Paul II.

face. No doubt there were plenty of nuns who had children, and ex-husbands, too.

"It's not *necessarily* crazy," the prioress said. "But in this instance, I happen to agree with you. She may very well have a vocation. It isn't for me and you to say if she does or she doesn't. She can't stay here, though, not like this. And yet, please, my friend, let's be honest with each other and with ourselves: She can't go home, either."

My grandfather started to protest, but she raised a pale hand. Her palm at the base of each finger was studded with callouses like ivory buttons. My grandfather closed his mouth.

"I'm not a psychiatrist," the prioress said, "and you are her husband, and so naturally and rightly it must be your decision, and I will defer to it as I must. But I *am* a trained nurse, I'll have you know. And I do have experience in these matters. And I can tell you without a nickel's worth of doubt that your wife needs to be under a doctor's care. A *psychiatrist's* care. Your wife needs to be in a mental hospital, friend, getting medical treatment, while I and all the sisters in this house pray for her recovery."

A floorboard creaked. The prioress looked up and my grandfather turned to the door. A nun stood in the doorway, small, thin, something mouselike in her long nose and the front teeth that showed in the parting of her lips. She lowered her eyes to the floor when my grandfather looked at her.

"Is she awake, Sister Cyril?"

Sister Cyril nodded. "And she seems . . . happy!" She looked up, a flash of defiance in her voice, and met my grandfather's gaze.

"Sister Cyril!"

Sister Cyril lowered her head again. "She says she wants to tell him . . . about her vocation."

The prioress regarded my grandfather, who sat in the chair knowing that he needed to get up and go to his wife and grab her and take her out of this place, unable to proceed any further in his thought or action than that. He didn't know where to take her. He did not have the faintest idea where a woman like my grandmother could ever possibly belong.

"What do I do?" my grandfather said. "What do I say to her?"

The prioress waved a hand at Sister Cyril. "Sister Cyril, please return to your duty."

"Yes, Mother."

"You may tell her that her husband will be in shortly to see her."

The prioress waited until Sister Cyril had retreated from the room and the creaking of the floorboards in the hallway had faded away.

"What do you say to her? Well, friend, not as a matter of policy, but just for the moment," Mother Mary Joseph said, "I might encourage you to lie."

◖   ◖   ◖

The small room was all crosshatchings of shadow like a lesson in shading a sphere, an arc of darkness wrapped around a circle of gray with a bright spot a bit off-center. The bright spot was my grandmother; all the light in the sad little room seemed to be radiating from her. She was sitting up in the iron infirmary bed, hands reposed on the bedsheet where it had been folded back over the wool blanket. No makeup. Hair tied back with an unmistakable severity. He had never seen her look more beautiful.

"You really do understand?"

"Yes, darling. Of course."

"This is the only place I can be safe."

"I know."

"I want us all to be safe. I want our daughter to be safe."

"Yes."

"It is too dangerous when I am outside of this place."

"I understand."

"Yes, you are a soldier. You understand about a calling. One have to make a sacrifice."

He knew he ought not interpret or take to heart anything she said while in this state. He could almost hear the prioress advising him so. He knew my grandmother was under the delusion that she was about to take orders as a Carmelite novice, and that the sacrifice implied was of worldly ties and not of their daughter, as on some pagan altar, daubed with the blood of a mare. He could not keep the image out of his head, a knife, my mother's pale throat. He shuddered. "Okay."

"It's really okay?"

"Of course."

She lifted her arms from the bed and he stepped into them. A smell of castile soap. A hint of mothballs.

"You are so good," she said. "Thank you."

He stood hunched over, a crick in his neck. Her cheek was wet against his. On a chest of drawers by the bed, next to what he recognized as her copy of the *Fioretti*, there was a portrait of Jesus Christ. It was a modern litho, rendered with photographic realism, propped up in a metal eight-by-ten frame. Jesus looked like Guy Madison with a beard and Lauren Bacall's hair. His gaze was leveled at my grandfather. No doubt his expression was meant to be compassionate, but to my grandfather it looked merely pitying. He remembered how, in the war, he had watched an old priest administer last rites to a dying German civilian and been moved by the Latin words and the message of peace he could sense encoded in them. But this pretty-boy Jesus just gave him the creeps. *You had your shot, buster,* this Jesus seemed to be saying with those smoldering Guy Madison eyes. *You lost her.*

My grandfather worked himself free of her arms and drew back until he could look her in the face. If her expression had been vacant, the way books led you to expect—"nobody home"—it might have been easier to bear or at least to accept. When something was gone, it was gone. But my grandmother's eyes were not vacant, they were filled to overflowing. Her face was busy with all the usual traffic in intelligence and feeling. At some level, surely, she must know that all this vocation business was nonsense, impossible, a charade. She must know that tomorrow, next week, after a couple months of rest and soothing chats with a top psychiatrist, it would pass.

"You know this will pass," she said, stopping his heart. "I see how you are so sad. Jesus sees, too. He will comfort you."

"No need," my grandfather said, resisting the urge to address the picture of Jesus. "I'm fine. We'll be fine. I'll see you tomorrow."

She laughed. She thought that was adorable. "It doesn't work that way, silly."

He couldn't take any more. She held on to his hand.

"I want to show you something."

"What's that?"

"It's our sweet baby," she said.

She reached for the little brown *Fioretti* and allowed it to fall open between her hands, to a place marked by a playing card. Blue-backed with a pattern of white crescent moons. Deftly, her fingers dealt him the card, but he did not care to see its face and would not turn it over.

◑   ◐   ◐

When he got home that night, my grandfather found Uncle Ray and my mother asleep on the couch in front of the television set. It was long past sign-off. Random-sample ants of wild signal swarmed the screen. All the lights were out, and the gray radiance of television static bled the room of color. Uncle Ray was sitting up at one end of the couch with his chin sunk to his chest. My mother lay across the cushions in her corduroy overalls, knees pulled to her chest, head in Uncle Ray's lap. Her lips were stained a dark shade of what my grandfather presumed, judging from a half-eaten candy apple that lay upside down and stuck to the coffee table, to be red. Uncle Ray's outstretched right arm lay along the length of my mother's body from her shoulder to her hip.

It was an innocent, tender scene; it disturbed my grandfather. The glow of the television disturbed him. It made him think of will-o'-the-wisp, the radiance of decay. *Ignis fatuus:* the light of an old magazine full of old news burning in a trash bin; the flicker of genius insight that had caught in his mind that evening as he was driving around Forest Park looking for my grandmother. He tried to rekindle it now. A phantom boy scampering down the beach at sunset. The RAND Corporation, the Traveling Salesman Problem. Topographic heuristics applied to the problem of dead reckoning in inertial guidance. He chased the foolish fire a moment longer, verging on it . . . and it winked out and was gone, never to return.* What did it matter? It was going to cost a fortune to hospitalize my grandmother, get her the care she needed. The adventure of Patapsco Engineering was over for him. He would have to get Weinblatt to buy him out and find more reliable work, a regular paycheck.

He went to the television. Just before he switched it off, the foam of entropy brimming from the screen seemed to reverse, to organize itself into a familiar pattern. For a few seconds my grandfather stood motionless, the hair standing up on the back of his neck, as a coherent image appeared on the television's screen. Holes for eyes. Nose a slash of black. Jagged jack-o'-lantern grin. When he read in the paper afterward that for the final transmission of *The Crypt of Nevermore*, Barry Kahn had taken the butchered pumpkin, put a candle inside, and let the play of the little flame fill the next forty-five minutes of dead air, my grandfather wondered. He wondered if an image could be retained by the phosphor coating of a cathode tube, or if it had bounced off some angle of the atmosphere and returned, an electronic revenant.

He switched off the television. The face lingered in negative on

---

* "I was almost ahead of my time," my grandfather observed when he recounted this incident to me. Solutions and heuristic approaches to modified versions of the Traveling Salesman Problem are today at the heart of advanced robotic navigation research.

his retinas until, like a will-o'-the-wisp, like a flash of insight, it faded and winked out. After that, until his eyes adjusted, the room was dark.

◑   ◑   ◑

"Remember that book I used to love, *Strangely Enough*?" I asked my mother that afternoon at my kitchen table as we stood looking down at the grinning horse skull with its mad mandala eyes. *Strangely Enough* by C. B. Colby, a nonfiction collection of pieces about "unexplained" incidents and paranormal events, had been a staple of the Scholastic Book Club in the 1960s and '70s and among the key texts of my childhood. "There was a piece in there, something kind of similar. A transmission, the call sign of a TV station in Houston, Texas, appeared one day out of the blue on televisions over in England, I think it was. But, like, *years* later, after the station that broadcast it had gone out of business. Nobody knew where the signal came from or where it was before it reappeared."*

"Huh," my mother said.

"So maybe what Grandpa saw was something like that."

My mother looked at me. She'd had a couple of slugs of Drambuie by then, and the look in her eyes did not trouble to be merciful.

"Maybe not," I said.

She put the skull back into the middle of the stained towel and wrapped it up. She set the bundled skull into the Old Crow box. I found a roll of packing tape, and she sealed the box along every seam as though to prevent any future exposure, or possibly escape, of its contents. She left with the box under her arm and I have not seen it, and we have not discussed it, since.

---

*The KLEE "phantom call sign" incident related as fact by *Strangely Enough*, and widely reported as fact in newspapers of the mid-fifties, turns out to have been part of a hoax, a midcentury electronic variation on the old "money-printing machine" scam, perpetrated by an enterprising British con artist.

There were a lot of painters living at Fontana Village. They painted detailed oil portraits of World War II aircraft, still lifes with seashells, nostalgia-brown scenes of shtetl weddings. They exhibited their work in the lobby of the Activity Center, at the annual holiday art fair.

Sally Sichel was not that kind of painter. She had studied at Pratt and taught painting at UC Davis with Arneson and Thiebaud. Joan Mitchell was the bridesmaid at her first wedding. Her work was not well known—my grandfather, whose idea of great painting began with Winslow Homer and ended with *Analog* magazine cover artist Kelly Freas, had never heard of her—but she was hardly unknown. Her canvases hung in museums and on the walls of collectors as far away as Japan. Back when SFMOMA was still in the War Memorial Veterans Building, they used to keep a small Sichel in a dim corner, where I paid it a visit once not long after my grandfather's death. Like most of Sally's work from the sixties, it seemed to be rooted in some dense and private mathematics. Its lacework of parabolas and angles—red-orange against titanium white—confused the eye. Retinal afterimages turned the white regions to jumping blue-green neon.

When she met my grandfather, she had been a widow for less than two months, but she had been alone and grieving for much longer than that. Leslie Port, her third husband, had succumbed, slowly at first and then in a dizzying rush, to an unspecified disease that, my grandfather only later came to realize, must have been AIDS.

The disease was poorly understood at the time, and Leslie's care was a prolonged bout of expensive flailing. Though Les had worked for years at Hewlett-Packard—he helped to invent the screen-and-button interface used by ATM machines and gas pumps all over the world—and made a good living, in time his treatment devoured his savings, along with all of Sally's mental and emotional resources. Along the road to his death were wild switchbacks in diagnosis, prognosis, and prescription. Leslie's first wife and three adult children, with their spouses and ex-spouses, formed a repertory company of guilt, cluelessness, and resentment that seized upon each reversal to stage marathon productions. Sally told my grandfather she had not touched a paintbrush in three years. "I haven't had the time," she said. "Or if I had time, then I didn't have the energy. I was too tired. I'm still tired."

They were lying on their backs in my grandfather's bed, a queen. My grandfather lay on the side (the left) that had been the haunt of his insomnia, dreams, and cares for all the years of his marriage and then widowerhood. In that long-desert region of the mattress there was now, astonishingly, the warm body of a woman and a smell of amber and cloves. It was their second night together. She had begun with her head nestled against his shoulder, but his shoulder was too bony and her cheek was too hot. The name of her perfume was Opium and he found the smell of it alarming, but he liked the rasp of her low voice in the dark. She had been telling him her life story in scattered chapters with footnotes and asides. Her story was seventy-two years long. He still had not made an appointment with the specialist, nor said anything to Sally about the funny numbers on his blood panel—that was all she needed, another sick man on her hands—but he had a feeling he would not live to hear the whole megillah.

"Do you miss it?" my grandfather said. Sweat prickled on his skin as it evaporated in the air-conditioning. He shivered and moved a little nearer to her.

"Not really." She stopped talking. My grandfather regretted having interrupted the flow of her autobiography with an unnecessary question. Then she said, "I take it back. I do miss it. How interesting, I didn't realize until you asked me."

"Sorry."

"For what?"

"Giving you something new to miss."

"That's all right," Sally said. "God knows it's better than missing Ramon."

The next day he drove her to an art supply store in Fort Lauderdale. She bought an easel, a dropcloth, a roll of canvas, stretchers, gesso, brushes, several tubes of cadmium, alizarin, and cobalt paint, and two cartons of titanium in pots, one bleached, one unbleached. He lifted the cartons out of her shopping cart and set them on the counter for the cashier to ring up.

"What's with all the white?" he said.

Sally raised an eyebrow. Her hair was tied in a scarf patterned with blue and green Matisse cutouts, and she was wearing a faded shirt with a button-down collar, blue pinstripes on white. The collar was unbuttoned enough to betray the scalloped lace trim of her brassiere.

"Think I'm just going to come out and tell you?" she said. "Just like that?"

It had been years since my grandfather had been competently teased by an attractive woman. This turned out to be a thing he had not known that he was missing.

"Is it a secret?"

"Of course it's a secret. Don't you know anything about art?"

"Art Carney."

"Oy. You promised no puns."

"I know next to nothing about art."

"Even I don't know the reason, why all the white. That's how secret it is."

They drove back to Fontana Village and my grandfather helped Sally carry her supplies into her house. The still-unfurnished guest bedroom had a sliding glass door that filled it with morning sun. They put all of the supplies in there in an orderly jumble. Sally laughed her raucous laugh.

"This is such bullshit," she said. "Come back in two weeks, I guarantee you it will all be sitting there like that. Untouched."

"So long as *you* don't go untouched that whole time."

"My God, you are such a pervert. Stop. Go kill your snake. No."

My grandfather put his arms around Sally's hips and pulled her toward him. She was wearing a pair of loose white pasha pants with an elastic waistband. His hands plunged past that and the lace waistband of her panties. He availed himself of two handfuls of her ass. It was not an inordinately large ass, yet the heft of it seemed to connect him to an immense source of gravitation, one for which he was belatedly grateful, as though for a long time he had been weightless and drifting.

"I was planning to feed you first," Sally said.

"All right," said my grandfather.

He reached out with a foot to hook the canvas dropcloth, bundled into its plastic package. He slid it across the floor and eased himself down onto it, kneeling on this impromptu cushion at her feet.

"Good Lord," Sally said, and then, "Oh, my."

He pulled down her pants and panties and contemplated the graying hair that thatched her belly. It grew sparse but long and very soft against the fingers. He put his cheek to her belly. The soft gray-blond hair rustled in his ear. The smell of her cunt reached his nostrils, not yet familiar, no longer strange. He tried and failed to compare it to the remembered smell of my grandmother's cunt. It had simply been too long, too goddamn long.

"Feed me," he said.

"No puns," Sally reminded him, lowering herself with a certain careless care onto the floor of the borrowed condominium. "You promised."

XXI

My grandfather took Diddens to see the rocket in the clearing and reported the basic details of its location and condition. He indicated that he planned to act on further V-2 related intelligence without mentioning von Braun, and left Diddens in charge of bagging and tagging the rocket for shipment west. He left Diddens in ignorance of his actual plans as much and as long as he could. He told himself he would move faster and smarter alone, but the truth was that he was grieving for Aughenbaugh, and like a lot of grieving people who keep a habitual distance from their emotions, he thought that being alone was what he needed.

He shook hands with the old people in turn. He put two cartons of Chesterfields and a cigar of unknown provenance into the old priest's hands. The priest kissed my grandfather on the cheek and blessed his journey in rapid Latin. Fräulein Judit received two cans of sweetened condensed milk, a box of saltines, and the February 7, 1944, issue of *Life*, which had mysteriously appeared in my grandfather's rucksack the day after he and Aughenbaugh followed the 104th Infantry into Köln. The cover was a picture of George Bernard Shaw. In return my grandfather received a cold stare, a granite handshake, and a small, dusty wheel of cheese.

"What the hell?" Diddens said. "Where are you going?" He had woken feeling tender and green at the gills but, having thrown up a few times in the pigsty, polished off the last bottle of wine, and had a tramp through the woods to see the magnificent beast of legend, he seemed back to his old querulous self.

"I'll be back," my grandfather lied. "I just want to have a look around. You wait for the transport crew to show, help them get the firecracker loaded."

My grandfather had given Diddens credit for the find; it was the arrow in the foot that led them to the priest who had led them to the V-2.

"You have a job to do," Diddens warned my grandfather. "Only reason you're here in the middle of all this shit."

"I'm going to get that von Braun," he said. "That's my job."

"Yeah? What are you gonna do when you find him, hey? Kiss him on the lips?" He put on a Southern-belle voice. "'Sweet Wernher, baby, your rocket gives me such a hard-on. Let me suck it!'"

"Probably."

"'Oh, Wernher, your *von* is so *braun!*'"

My grandfather never saw Diddens again. He walked out of the farmyard and down the road as far as the first crossroads. Almost immediately, he heard the rumble of engines and the crunch of a truck transmission being skillfully abused. Two half-tracks, an armored car, and a deuce-and-a-half mess truck belonging to the 869th Field Battalion of the 65th Infantry Division rolled past. They had become separated from the rest of the division in the night and were heading to Paderborn, where the cooks riding in the deuce-and-a-half had orders to provide every GI they could find with a pancake breakfast. Paderborn was more or less on the way to Nordhausen, the last known whereabouts, to my grandfather at least, of von Braun. My grandfather climbed into the back of the deuce-and-a-half with sacks of flour, stacked cartons of powdered eggs, two steel drums of corn syrup. He fell asleep before he could even finish cautioning himself not to fall asleep.

When he woke up, the truck was grinding and bucking and he could hear the driver swearing up in the cab. When he'd flagged down the deuce-and-a-half, my grandfather had noted the insignia painted on its front passenger door, a red spot on a gold shield. Beneath this a legend crudely lettered in white paint informed the curious that this truck, whose name was *Big-Leg Woman*, had been driven continuously since June 1944, from Omaha Beach to the Ardennes, by Corporal Melvin Fish, of the Red Ball Express. Corporal Fish would be accustomed to driving on fucked-up roads by now, but this one seemed to be giving him trouble.

My grandfather poked his head out of the back of the truck. It appeared that some brave tactician had decided to toss a stray unit of motorcycle infantry over his shoulder to cover the SS retreat from the neighborhood. Two or three dozen bikes with sidecars, a couple of squat Kübelwagens. A unit of 105mm Priests on a hilltop to the west had caught the German cyclists on a stretch of open ground. For a hundred yards the road was a chicane of wrecked machines and dead men sunk in a churn of mud. It had not rained for several days, and this was not natural mud; it had been compounded by truck tires and caterpillar treads from dust and blood and whatever home-brew sauce the Krauts were putting in their engines as it leaked from busted fuel tanks to puddle in the ruts. There was hair in the mud. The soldiers, insofar as my grandfather could distinguish their features in the impasto of their bodies, had been the greenest of boys.

For the moment my grandfather was more interested in the condition of the motorcycles. Even before the artillery got to them, they must have been a sorry sight, fruit of the scrap yard, hybrid freaks. Bicycle parts pressed into ad hoc service, a sidecar that seemed to have been formed from a galvanized steel washtub, tires piebald with patches. Bicycles, arrows. Soon they would be throwing bricks and rocks. They were already throwing the bodies of their children.

A little way up the grassy slope that had served the gunners for a bowling alley, a German officer sat on his bike. As *Big-Leg Woman* skidded and fishtailed past him, his left eye seemed to fix on my grandfather, hanging out of the back of the truck. The right side of the officer's skull and most of his face, apart from the staring eye, had been shot away. A spray of fine hair clung like dry grass to the blackened cliff of his parietal bone, fluttering in the breeze. His caked boots were planted solidly on either side of what appeared to be a nicely intact motorcycle, low-slung and painted an incongruous shade of khaki. He had a grown man's build, broad shoulders drawn back to lend his posture a hint of defiance. His gloved fists were locked around the grips of his motorcycle's handlebars. Maybe he had peeled away from his unit up the rise, hoping to draw the fire of the guns, or had hoped to rally his teenage fusiliers for a suicidal uphill charge toward them. As the convoy of trucks weaved and ground their way through the wreckage, one of the GIs predictably took offense at or could not resist the remnant of that blond head on those arrogant shoulders. He drew his Colt and took a few halfhearted potshots, to no effect. Then he got serious and the head burst into red mist. The carcass with no head stayed smartly upright, straddling the motorcycle.

My grandfather jumped down from the back of the truck, sinking into the grim slurry to his ankles. Like the mud itself, the stench of the mud was an amalgam only war could concoct, like the smell when MP delousing crews made POWs take off their clothes and boots, and the rancid butter gas of unwashed feet combined with armpit and the naphtha burn of bug spray. My grandfather found Corporal Fish's puzzled face in the right-hand rearview mirror. He waved his thanks for the lift.

The road sucked at his boots. He reached the shoulder and scrambled up to the headless officer. A dense mesh of flies busied themselves in the air just above the decapitated stump as if attempting to weave themselves into a makeshift head. Apart from the stump, which revealed more than my grandfather cared to learn just then about the structural anatomy of the throat and upper vertebrae and the appetite of flies, there was nothing to suggest that the officer, a lieutenant like my grandfather, was prepared to relinquish the motorcycle. Even without his head, he maintained his rigid posture, his air of having dug his heels in.

"Enough already," my grandfather said. "We get it."

He took a breath. He worked his arms around the upper torso from behind, turning his face away from the meat and the frenzy of flies. Powerful impulses of his nervous system urged him just to yank the carcass loose and drop or even hurl it to the ground. He forebore. He worked the hands free of the grips with a few gentle twists. He eased the carcass off the seat, hoisted it up, and swung it until the farther leg came away free. He laid the body supine on the grass like he was helping a drunk to bed.

Still holding his breath, my grandfather stripped the body of rifle, cartridge box, and gloves. Black leather gauntlets, heavy and cuffed, very Nazi. He pulled them on. The black leather was spattered with blood. He wiped his hands on the dead officer's uniform trousers.

He went back to take a look at the motorcycle, a Zündapp. It was filthy but appeared to have been well maintained. It was an uncompli-cated machine, engine and gearbox hung on a skeleton like the spread finger bones of a bat. A shaft drove the rear wheel and, he noted, the sidecar's wheel. Ignition on the gearshift mount. Four speeds. Canvas cover over the sidecar as if the late operator had been accustomed to solitary rides. Apart from the black rubber grips, the seat and tires, and the steel caps of the jerricans, the whole thing was painted a matte shade of desert tan. Stenciled on the nose of its sidecar, a cute little white palm tree hid modestly behind a white swastika. The Zündapp had an air of misplacement, a Central Park polar bear in August. In 1990 as in 1945, my grandfather was willing to devote a minute to pondering the mysteries of the Zündapp's journey from the Maghreb to the Westerwald and the long downward journey of the Wehrmacht itself from the days of Rommel and the Afrika Korps.

He climbed on. The driver of a passing Willys tapped his horn and my grandfather lifted a gloved hand. He sat a moment, coming to terms with the bulk of it between his legs. He turned the ignition switch, opened the throttle, stepped on the kickstand. The engine rattled to life.

Within ten miles of setting out, he had fallen in love. He had driven a motorcycle only once, for an hour during which he never got comfortable on the BSA belonging to a pool player from Jersey. He remembered contending with alarming phenomena of pitch and torque. There had been a constant sense of lurching. Vibrations were transmitted directly to his bones and joints.

This bike, poised on and steadied by its third wheel, just went. It flowed through upshifts and hugged the road in tight turns. The engine was loud but did not weary the ear. The ride was bouncy but not jarring. The fuel tank between his thighs was nearly full with potato-peel ethanol or distilled shoe polish or whatever it might be. It was an excellent machine, though it had done nothing to help its previous owner hold on to his head. Later my grandfather would re-member thinking, as he headed for Nordhausen, that he could not wait to show it to his new friend Wernher von Braun. They would tool around the autobahns of a postwar Germany, von Braun riding in the sidecar like a gentle-natured bear.

꩜   ꩜   ꩜

"Was he still there?"

"No."

"No?"

"He was gone by the time I got there. Long gone."

"But you found him."

He didn't answer. He was sitting up, face angled toward the window. His breathing looked steady, but it was past lunchtime, and he had not eaten anything all morning but a few bites of Jell-O. I figured he was feeling a little weak. "Grandpa? You okay?"

"Fine."

"Want a little soup? Mom made you some."

He kept his eyes on the window as if something interesting were happening at the birdfeeder, out of my line of sight, another doomed attack by the momzer. Only he wasn't smiling.

"I'm talking too much," he said after a while.

"I'm sorry. We can stop. You should rest. Rest your voice."

He made a face, dismissing the suggestion. He was not talking more than he had voice or strength to handle. He was talking more than he believed to be wise or suitable. Since, in his view, he reached the limit of conversational daring at the end of a three-minute jeremiad on the world's failure to recognize the superiority of the Wankel rotary engine, I didn't take this admonishment, or self-admonishment, too seriously. I felt like it was, if anything, a tad melodramatic.

"I'm glad you're talking," I said. Melodrama was all right with me.

"That's just why I shouldn't be."

"What? Why?"

"You're too glad."

"I'm too glad?"

"Too interested."

"Oh no, I'm bored out of my skull," I said. "Really, I'm just being polite."

On the street a crew was topping trees to open a view for somebody higher up the hill. All that afternoon a chainsaw started, stopped, started again. Views in the Oakland hills are graded on a scale of visible bridges from one to five: the San Mateo, the Dumbarton, the Bay, the Golden Gate, and the Richmond. My mother's living room and bedroom scored a respectable two. From my grandfather's bed, however, the only visible span was the swag of black coaxial cable strung from a corner of the house to a telephone pole up by the street.

"You think this explains everything," my grandfather said. He freighted the word *explains* with as much contempt as it would bear before exiling it from his mouth. "Me and your grandmother. Your mother. My time in prison. The war." He turned from the window.

In his eyes, through the haze of hydromorphone, I saw a flash of something I took, based on the historical record, for anger. "You think it explains *you*."

"It explains a lot," I said.

"It explains nothing."

"It explains a little."

"It's just names and dates and places."

"Okay."

"It doesn't add up to anything, take my word for it. It doesn't mean anything."

"I get it," I said.

"Oh, you get it? What do you get?"

"I get that you're a big ol' fuckin' nihilist."

That raised a smile; or maybe the momzer was back.

"Richard Feynman," I said. "Doctor Richard Feynman."

"What about him?"

"All he wanted was to find the answer to the question 'Why did *Challenger* explode?' Right? And that answer was never going to be 'Because it was all part of God's plan' or, I don't know, '*Challenger* exploded so that some little kid somewhere would get inspired to grow up and become an engineer and invent a safer, more durable propulsion system for spacecraft.' Or even, like, 'Because humans and the things they make are prone to failure' or 'Shit happens.' The explanation was always going to be something like 'Because the weather was too cold, so the O-rings became brittle and failed, and fuel leaked from the fuel tank and ignited, which caused the shuttle to accelerate beyond its intended structural tolerance so that it broke apart.' The answer was always going to be dates, and names, and numbers. And that was good enough for Feynman, because the point was to find out. The meaning was in the inquiry."

"It was the solid rocket booster," my grandfather said. "Not the fuel tank."

"Right."

He kept on looking at me without speaking, but whatever had blazed out through the cloud cover was gone. A tear rolled down his cheek, and he turned his face to the window again. I got up and pulled a Kleenex from the box. I started to try to wipe away the tear, but he pushed my hand aside. He took the Kleenex.

"I'm ashamed," he said.

"Grandpa . . ."

"I'm disappointed in myself. In my life. All my life, everything I tried, I only got halfway there. You try to take advantage of the time you have. That's what they tell you to do. But when you're old, you look back and you see all you did, with all that time, is waste it. All you have is a story of things you never started or couldn't finish. Things you fought with all your heart to build that didn't last or fought with all your heart to get rid of and they're all still around. I'm ashamed of myself."

"I'm not ashamed of you," I said. "I'm proud."

He made another face. This one said that what I knew about shame —what my entire generation, with its deployment of confession as a tool for self-aggrandizement, knew about shame—would fit into half a pistachio shell.

"Anyway, it's a pretty good story," I said. "You have to admit."

"Yeah?" He crumpled up the Kleenex, having dispatched the solitary tear. "You can have it. I'm giving it to you. After I'm gone, write it down. Explain everything. Make it mean something. Use a lot of those fancy metaphors of yours. Put the whole thing in proper chronological order, not like this mishmash I'm making you. Start with the night I was born. March second, 1915. There was a lunar eclipse that night, you know what that is?"

"When the earth's shadow falls across the Moon."

"Very significant. I'm sure it's a perfect metaphor for something. Start with that."

"Kind of trite," I said.

He threw the Kleenex at my head. It bounced off my cheek and fell on the floor. I bent to pick it up. Somewhere in its fibers, it held what may have been the last tear my grandfather ever shed. Out of respect for his insistence on the meaninglessness of life—his, everyone's—I threw it into the wastebasket by the door.

"So," I said. "You went to Nordhausen."

He shook his head, but he was going to give way. We both knew it.

"Yes, God damn it, I went to Nordhausen," he said in a tone that sounded more defeated than angry. At that moment I knew—knowing nothing—that it had been the worst place on earth. And a part of my nature that had lain dormant for a long time snapped open like an eye.

I had been raised among quiet people who repressed their emotions. I knew my father to have been "a big talker," "a bullshit artist," and (an epithet I remembered hearing my grandfather throw in his face) "a loverboy," but that was hearsay and, given his record, distinctly an argument in favor of repression. I was aware that in some remote age, my grandmother had been a source of fire, madness, and poetry, but those days were misty legend; one could only infer them from traces in the geological record. In my family, in my lifetime, we preferred to leave the business of feeling, and talking about feeling, to people with nothing better to do.

Youthful rebellion, therefore, had required my wholehearted embrace of poetry, fire, and madness, and of all those—Rimbaud, Patti Smith, Syd Barrett, the girls I went after—who trafficked in them. Long after rebellion cooled, I flew the flag of self-expression. I had emerged into adolescence toward the end of the seventies, that great unbuttoning. As I came into young manhood, the ascendant Recovery Movement was at work normalizing the idea that redemption lay in the sharing of experience and feeling, and that in denial there was something like damnation. Right up to that afternoon at my grandfather's bedside, prodding him to tell me about Nordhausen and the beefy young blond man, I believed (and for the most part believe still) that silence was darkness, and that naming shone a light. I believed that a secret was like a malignancy and confession a knife, a bright hot beam of radiation that healed as it burned. I believed it was good—this being among the few things that truly did go without saying—to "get it all out."

Then I heard the bitterness of defeat in my grandfather's voice when he said that he had gone to Nordhausen.

I thought about how, when I was a kid, as my big-talking, sweet-talking, fast-talking father was in and out of courtrooms, tax dodges, marriages, and my life, the constancy of my grandfather's silence had been just that: a constant. It was, like him, something I could always rely on. And really, where was the proof that two decades of national yammering, of getting it all out, had brought about an increase in collective national happiness? I had recently read something in *Scientific American* about the Roman city of Herculaneum, buried by Vesuvius, uncovered by archaeologists; how exposure to light and air was destroying what centuries of darkness had preserved. And radiation treatment? A textbook example of a situation where the cure was worse than the disease. On balance, most of the time, in the ordinary course of life, it was probably best to say what was in your heart, to share what was on your mind, to tell the people you loved that you loved them, to ask those you had harmed to forgive you and to confront those who had hurt you with the truth about the damage they had done. When it came to things that needed to be said, speech was always preferable to silence, but it was of no use at all in the presence of the unspeakable.

"I think maybe I'll have a little soup after all," my grandfather said.

I went into the kitchen and ladled some of my mother's chicken soup into a bowl from the big Tupperware in the refrigerator. While the soup heated in the microwave, I opened the legs of the breakfast tray and wiped it down with 409. I folded a napkin and set a spoon on the napkin. I found the salt and pepper shakers shaped like terriers, one white, one black. Sometimes my grandfather liked to sprinkle his soup with those little yellow Israeli soup croutons—he called them *mandelen*—and so, for the extra calories, I poured a handful into a saucer and set that on the tray. When the soup was hot, I eased it from the microwave to the tray and carried the tray to the bedroom. The broth was gold. The carrot and celery and onion were gems. A filigree of golden fat adorned the surface. In the steam coming off the bowl of soup was the hint of lemon, a memory of my grandmother. Really, it smelled very good.

We got him propped up and into position. Then I set the tray across his body and tucked the napkin into the collar of the long T-shirt he wore.

He leaned forward to put his face, his nostrils, in the path of the steam coming off the bowl. He closed his eyes and inhaled. He picked up the spoon, and I watched him put away most of the bowl. The taste of it seemed to come as a kind of relief.

"Okay," he said. He put down his spoon. "Wernher Magnus Maximilian Freiherr von Braun." After the name, he added something acrid in Yiddish.

"All I got was onion," I said.

"Something your great-grandmother used to say. A Yiddish curse. 'He should grow with his head in the dirt, like an onion.'"

"That what's going on there?" I picked up the copy of *Rockets, Missiles, and Space Travel*, purloined thirty-odd years earlier from the library of the Wallkill prison. "In the Willy Ley book, you— well, somebody—like, blotted von Braun's name out over and over again."

"Me," he said, adding dryly, "It didn't work."

He sprinkled a few mandelen onto the soup and took another spoonful. I heard the tiny crackers crunch between his teeth.

"And then . . . I remember how you wouldn't watch the moon

landing. How you got up and left the room. Even though that was pretty much something you had been waiting your whole life to see."

"Yah."

"Did that have something to do with your feelings about von Braun?"

"Yah."

"So, obviously? Something must have happened . . . ?"

Another spoonful of soup went into his mouth. He swallowed it. His eyes were fixed on mine, watchful and withholding, challenging me to justify the logic of my inference.

"Because that morning, when you took off on that motorcycle, it sounded like, at that point, you were feeling almost like . . . like you and von Braun were . . ."

"'Kindred spirits'?"

"Yeah. But then later, at a certain point . . ." He was still watching me, with less apparent tenderness than I could ever remember having seen in his eyes. He had put down his spoon. "It kind of seems like you pretty much decided you hated the guy's guts."

"Pretty much," he agreed.

"Why?"

When I was a boy and fell prey to what he regarded as an inherent weakness for stating the obvious, my grandfather had a certain voice he would use to repeat whatever I had just said. To me it sounded like the voice that Mel Blanc used to do dimwitted bloodhounds, Yetis, and musclebound dumb-asses in the old Warner Bros. cartoons. My grandfather probably thought of it as the voice of Lon Chaney, Jr., playing Lennie in *Of Mice and Men*. I had not heard it in a very long time, but now it resurfaced: stammering, at once low-pitched and infantile.

"'Something must have happened,'" he said in his moron voice.

I waited. He picked up the spoon and tilted the bowl toward himself. It looked like he was going to polish off the rest of it. I imagined the account I would make to my mother when she got home from work: *He loved the soup. I got him to eat a whole bowl.*

There was a clang as he flung down the spoon. In a man so frail and narcotized, the gesture felt inordinately violent. He pushed the bowl away. Later I would find a chip missing from its rim.

"You want to know what happened at Nordhausen?" he said in his regular rasp. "Look it up."

XXII

When my mother got home, I went down to the library, a storybook-style cottage on Mountain Boulevard that stayed open late on Thursday nights.

I started with *Gravity's Rainbow*, which I had read at UC Irvine for Mike Clark's graduate seminar on the modern novel, and which was the (accurately researched, it turned out) source of most of the little I had ever known about the V-2. I spent an hour flipping through and skimming the relevant passages, starting with the book's epigraph, then following its secondary character of Franz Pökler, a young engineer whose career traces the history of spaceflight in Germany: the Weimar period of "Rocketport Berlin" and the starry-eyed *Verein für Raumschiffahrt,*[*] *Frau im Mond* and the rocket craze, the militarization of rocket research that came with Hitler's rise, Peenemünde, and—I was jolted to discover—Nordhausen, where the book's protagonist, Tyrone Slothrop, also turned up at one point. I remembered having read these passages—some absurd, some harrowing—set in and around the rocket's mountain lair, but the name of the site in the Harz Mountains had gone out of my memory completely. I wondered if my grandfather knew or had ever tried to read *Gravity's Rainbow*. I wondered how he would have felt about the book's depictions of the

---

[*] The Spaceflight Society, of which my grandfather's favorite author, Willy Ley, had been a founding member and the wealthy young Baron von Braun a kind of boy-genius mascot. Ley, a vocal opponent of Nazism and of the militarization of rocketry, fled Germany for the U.S. in 1935.

European theater of operations, the horror of Nordhausen, the experience of rocket attacks, and so many other things Pynchon had never lived through or seen. It all felt convincing to me, but what did I know? Apart from so-called hard science fiction, which he read (as with *The Magic Mountain*) for its artful packaging of big ideas, my grandfather regarded most fiction as "a bunch of baloney." He thought reading novels was a waste of time more profitably spent on nonfiction.

Beyond the Pynchon there was not a lot. A brief *Britannica* entry on Nordhausen and its Mittelwerk rocket factory, cross-referenced to entries on the V-2, the facility at Peenemünde, and the Dora-Mittelbau concentration camp. Mentions of Peenemünde, the Mittelwerk, and KZ Dora-Mittelbau in a few general histories of World War II. Some of the grimmest pages, toward the end, in a book about the 3rd Armored Division's yearlong slog from Normandy to Dessau. A Pentagon-approved 1971 book on Operation Paperclip that made careful reference to the 1947 acquittal, on charges of war crimes, of a V-2 project middle manager named Georg Rickhey. Finally, the jackpot, an article in *The New York Times* from March 1984, which I read on microfilm. It summarized an exposé of Operation Paperclip in the latest issue of *Bulletin of the Atomic Scientists*. The author of the exposé, the *Times* said, had made extensive use of formerly classified documents released under the Freedom of Information Act to establish in detail that the postwar history of American technological accomplishment, particularly in the realm of biological warfare, aeronautics, and spaceflight, had been rooted in heinous Nazi war crimes and an elaborate American cover-up of those crimes. Following decades of inaction and denial, the article said, the U.S. government had stripped the citizenship of a prominent rocket scientist, Arthur Rudolph, and deported him to his native Germany. Rudolph had declined or been unable to contest direct evidence linking him to numerous atrocities during his tenure as managing director of V-2 production at Nordhausen. Along with Wernher von Braun, the article said, Arthur Rudolph had been the lead designer of the mighty

Saturn V, the rocket that had borne the Apollo missions toward the Moon.*

Altogether it was not a lot, but I got the general drift.

Until August 1943 the plan was for V-2 rockets to be manufactured, once they became operational, at the same top-secret facility, on the remote island of Peenemünde off the German Baltic coast, where their research and development had been carried out. The prototypes and test rockets had all been manufactured in Peenemünde's workshops by hundreds of "foreign workers"—prisoners, housed in an adjacent concentration camp, most of them Poles. The prisoners had already begun construction of a new factory when, during the full moon of August 17, Peenemünde became the target of a massive Allied air raid. The secret of Peenemünde had been discovered, intelligence gathered, reconnaissance carried out. The aim of the raid, code-named HYDRA, and the hope of its planners— among them Churchill's son-in-law Duncan Sandys—was to strangle the V-2 (or A4, as it was known then) in its cradle. To that end, six hundred Lancasters, Halifaxes, and Stirlings dropped two million kilograms of high-explosive bombs in what was believed to be the general vicinity of the workshops, the experimental stations, and the living quarters of the scientists and engineers.

At that time the science of bomb targeting was less than precise. As the raid unfolded over Peenemünde, errors—navigational, calculative, aeronautical—compounded. While measurable damage was done to the workshops and experimental stations, the greatest part of the bombs that did not fall harmlessly fell onto the adjacent concentration camp. Seven hundred of the "foreign workers" died within a few minutes; German researchers killed by the bombs of HYDRA numbered two. Afterward both Allied and German damage assessments agreed that the raid—which also cost the lives of two hundred

---

* And still, over four decades after flying its last mission, the only vehicle ever built capable of carrying human beings beyond a low earth orbit.

British airmen—had set the rocket program back by eight weeks at most.

If HYDRA had been ineffective, it was not without result. The V-2 program was now demonstrably vulnerable, and Heinrich Himmler seized on that vulnerability to bring it under control of his SS (in which Wernher von Braun had risen to the rank of *Sturmbann-führer*). Clearly, the projected factory was at grave risk. It could not be built on an expanse of open seacoast at coordinates well known to the enemy. It must be moved and protected against further attack. It would be kept secret, as Peenemünde had been, but that was insufficient; the factory must be hidden as well.

A new site, the Mittelwerk, was commissioned and constructed in the Harz Mountains, just outside the town of Nordhausen. In a display of the kind of inventive audacity that characterized German military research, the new rocket factory was constructed inside of a minor mountain.* Fresh gangs of Poles, along with Frenchmen, Russians, Czechs, and Ukrainians—prisoners of war, political prisoners—were conscripted from KZ Buchenwald fifty miles away and detailed to excavate and expand a tunnel system under the Kohnstein, site of a disused gypsum mine. The Mittelwerk's lattice of tunnels served as factory floor, administrative offices, staff dormitory, and at first as a subterranean concentration camp for the laborers who worked, ate, slept, and died in them. When they died, their bodies were shipped back to Buchenwald for cremation.

A steadily increasing rate of V-2 production demanded more inmates than the Mittelwerk could accommodate. The SS forced the prisoners to build a camp for themselves outside the south entrance to the tunnels, code-named Dora, which in time spawned further

---

* All the secret headquarters of evil scientists, hidden in volcanoes or disguised as islands, accessible by subterranean railways or retractable sphincters disguised as lakes, which afterward featured in James Bond movies and their imitators— not to mention the real-life Cheyenne Mountain facility, home of NORAD and the presidential nuclear bunker—descend from the Mittelwerk at Nordhausen.

subcamps, centered around the Mittelwerk and known collectively as Mittelbau. A subcamp in the town of Nordhausen, called the Boelcke-Kaserne, was used as a dumping ground for inmates too enfeebled or sick to work. From the start of excavation and the first shipments of Buchenwald prisoners in September 1943 until the capture of the Mittelwerk and the liberation of Dora-Mittelbau in April 1945, an estimated sixty thousand prisoners were put to work building the seven thousand V-2s that eventually rolled off the line.

The men who built the rockets lived in filth, underfed, malnourished, and brutalized. Packed into the barracks of Dora in their striped uniforms, in bunks stacked four high, the workers froze in the winter, roasted in the summer, and died by the tens of thousands all year round. They were worked beyond their capacity to endure, in primitive and dangerous conditions. The tunnels were hot, dark, cramped, crowded. They were filled with fumes, smoke, and the racket of machinery. Discipline was severe and the guards bestial. Minor infractions were punished by kicking, beating, torture, mutilation; fear of insurrection resulted in regular mass executions. The condemned would be hanged six at a time from a massive crane used to transport rocket assemblies from one part of the line to the next, in full view of the workers on the factory floor and of the project's scientists and engineers from von Braun on down the line. Bodies were left to dangle instructively overhead. Sabotage, though subject to swift and savage retribution, was rife and, along with the abysmal conditions and demoralized work force, may have led directly to the relatively high rate of failure experienced by the V-2.[*] In time a crematorium was built at Dora to save the trouble and expense of sending dead inmates all the way to Buchenwald.

---

[*] Throughout the entire period of their deployment, with nagging frequency, the rockets would crash immediately after launch, explode in midflight or before impact, go veering and yawing and pinwheeling wildly out of control, or vanish, leaving no trace and having caused no damage, into thin air or the sea. Sometimes, as my grandfather had learned, a rocket never even made it off the launch pad.

The 104th Infantry (Timberwolf) and the 3rd Armored (Spearhead) divisions rolled into Nordhausen on April 11, 1945, and found it abandoned by the enemy. They stumbled first across the subcamp in the town itself. Ravaged by an untreated outbreak of typhus, the Boelcke-Kaserne had also borne the brunt of an Allied air raid the week before that killed fifteen hundred inmates and wounded hundreds more. The death marches, forced transports, mass burials, and other attempts by the evacuating Germans to conceal the enormity of Nordhausen had left only the most enfeebled and grievously maimed in the Boelcke-Kaserne. The liberators had not even begun to grasp what they were seeing when they came upon Dora—these were among the first U.S. troops to enter a concentration camp. Photographs and film footage they took there featured in newsreels and on front pages all over the world. Even after the name and the business of Nordhausen had been carefully mislaid by history (at least in the adopted homeland of Wernher von Braun), the imagery of its horror endured: The dead ranged in corduroy roads to the vanishing point, bone-men slumped and staring. In the tunnels under Kohnstein Mountain, among incomplete rocket assemblies and machines left running, the liberators found the men of the Mittelwerk's final shift, abandoned by their captors, too weak to move, let alone try to escape. Heaps of sticks atop which solemn heads stood regarding them like owls. In the infirmary the bodies of the Mittelwerk's last on-the-job fatalities lay naked on tile slabs, drained of blood and awaiting transport to the crematorium.

Having come six hundred miles through some of the most brutal combat and one of the bitterest European winters of the twentieth century, the liberators were as inured to the routine of battlefield horror as any men have ever been obliged to become. When they saw what there was to see in the camps and under Kohnstein Mountain, according to their own subsequent accounts—accounts followed closely by Pynchon when he had his engineer Pökler tour KZ Dora—a considerable number of these men with their thousand-yard stares broke down in tears or turned away to vomit.

The liberators could not have endured so long and so much, however, without having learned the knack of repressing futile emotion. They soon moved on to anger and a desire to impose some measure of justice or, failing that, retribution, if clear distinction could be made between the two. They looked around for someone to lay their hands on. The SS guards and functionaries had all fled the area, along with the Mittelwerk's personnel. I couldn't find anything to suggest that the liberators contemplated trying to punish or even gave much thought to the brains of the operation, the men with slide rules and soldering irons whose great invention, only incidentally the first long-range ballistic missile, was a process by which horror could be converted into terror by dint of cruelty.* At any rate, had the liberators of Dora made this imaginative leap, there would have been no way to act upon it. Von Braun's rocketeers were miles away, scattered across southern Germany and Austria. In the end the townsmen paid the debt of horror. The liberators returned to Nordhausen from Dora and the Mittelwerk, rousted the men from their houses, and ordered them at gunpoint to fetch shovels and start digging until all the dead of KZ Dora-Mittelbau were buried.

That is what I found in the public record that night at the Montclair Public Library when I went to look up Nordhausen. Between the impressment of the local citizens as gravediggers and the beginning of the end of my grandfather's war, I can offer only informed speculation, combined with a few little facts that he inadvertently dropped over the course of the next few days.

I know that he arrived at Nordhausen the day after its liberation,

---

* With terrible inefficiency: Fatalities among the laborers at Nordhausen exceeded those on the ground in Antwerp and London by a ratio of nearly six to one.

along with the news that FDR was dead. He steered the Zündapp through the empty streets of the town. With every barrier lifted and every gateway open to him as a result of his "Eisenhower pass," he had no trouble entering the various subcamps or the factory under the mountain. Like the men of the Timberwolf and Spearhead Divisions, he had been hardened by prolonged exposure to violence. Like them, I imagine, what he saw around Dora-Mittelbau may have brought him to the point of tears or nausea. It was clear from what he told me afterward that, like the liberators, he looked around to find a fitting object of his rage when his tour of this particular hell and its environs was complete.

What he saw that day, and what he heard from the survivors he questioned, persuaded him that there was no way Wernher von Braun could have been technical director of the V-2 program while remaining unaware of how business was conducted in the Mittelwerk.* Von Braun could not be crowned with the glory of the rocket without shouldering the burden of its shame. All the suffering my grandfather saw had been amassed and all the cruelty deployed at the prompting and in the service of von Braun's dream. It turned out that the V-2 was not a means to liberate the human spirit from the chains of gravity; it was only a pretext for further enchainment. It was not an express bound for the stars but a mail rocket carrying one simple message, signed in high-explosive amatol with the name of Baron von Braun. Maybe the man's dream had begun as something beautiful and grand. For a time, maybe, its grandeur and its beauty had blinded von Braun to all the ways in which he

---

* Indeed, though the information was suppressed by von Braun and by the U.S. government nearly all his life, along with the memory of Nordhausen itself, von Braun made many visits to Kohnstein Mountain after September '43, and he appears to have been directly involved in the selection of inmates possessing technical aptitude (primarily Frenchmen) for transfer to the Mittelwerk from Buchenwald. See Michael Neufeld's *Von Braun: Dreamer of Space, Engineer of War* (Vintage, 2008).

was busily betraying it. That was only human, the common lot. But once your dream revealed itself, like most dreams, to be nothing but a current of raw compulsion flowing through a circuitry of delusion and lies, then that was the time to give it up. That was the time to damn your dream and trust your eyes. And maybe cock your revolver.

Over the course of that long day in Nordhausen my grandfather trusted his eyes and gave up the dream he had shared with the Wernher von Braun of his imaginings. Along with it, he surrendered the memory of a rocket in a clearing, a half hour of something that had felt like peace, a midnight conversation with the rector of Our Lady of the Moon. When those things were gone, there was a bad moment as my grandfather found himself confronted once more with the void that surrounded the planet of his heart for a thousand parsecs in every direction. After that, as with the liberators of Nordhausen putting away their disgust and useless anguish, there was only the matter of his anger and where to point it.

◗　　　◑　　　◑

"I went to track him down," my grandfather said. "Like I was supposed to. More or less."

"More or less?"

"Well, I wasn't supposed to go solo. But that didn't make any sense to me under the circumstances."

I wasn't sure whether he was talking about a specific, local set of circumstances or the general ones under which, like some gumshoe, he always preferred to work alone. He had made an exception in the case of Aughenbaugh; he would never entirely recover from the lapse. I nodded, but I must have looked confused.

"The circumstances being that when I found him, I was planning to, y'know," he said.

"Kill the guy."

"Right. On the other hand, I did have a fair amount of latitude. I had an Eisenhower pass signed by Ike himself, all of us CIOS guys did. I had been given a degree of discretion," he said. "Which I totally abused."

XXIII

In the town of Nordhausen, an intelligence officer attached to the 3rd Armored Division told my grandfather of being approached by one of the locals, who had hinted that he might be persuaded to betray certain of his neighbors. This fellow did not know exactly what behaviors the Americans might be looking to punish or secrets they hoped to extract, but he was certain they would find something in his inventory to suit their needs. He kept a shop in town that, appropriately enough, sold hunting and fishing gear.

In the early morning of his second day in Nordhausen, my grandfather went to the shop with cigarettes, SPAM, chocolate, and, he recalled, a miraculous bunch of bananas, the hand of a golden Buddha ablaze against the gray morning. He found the shop on a street that bore signs of damage from the RAF raid the previous week, the one that had killed fifteen hundred inmates of the Boelcke-Kaserne. The shop had two display windows. One was covered over with a stained oilcloth tarpaulin. The other was intact, but its shade had been lowered to hide, or spare the passerby from having to see, that there was nothing to display. If you turned around, you could see a corner of the walls of the Boelcke-Kaserne rising down at the end of the street. No doubt it had carried sounds and odors to the doorstep when the wind was right.

My grandfather went around to the back door. He did not care if his visit endangered the shopkeeper's life, but he wanted it to seem as though he did. He rang the bell and showed his Eisenhower pass.

They spoke in riddles and allusions, and then the shopkeeper let him in.

The shopkeeper explained to my grandfather that he belonged to some minor Christian sect that had been first frowned on and then harassed by the Reich. Recently, his stock of excellent Mann-licher rifles had been requisitioned by the local *Volkssturm* during a short-lived moment of planned resistance, in exchange for worth-less promissory notes. He was garrulous and priggish, and it was a wonder his neighbors had not done away with him years ago.

He turned down the cigarettes and chocolate as immoral indul-gences. The bananas and SPAM were welcome enough but struck the shopkeeper as perhaps, on their own, inadequate payment. My grandfather said that if his question got a useful answer, he would try to come up with a few more cans of SPAM and maybe a tub or two of corn syrup. If that would not do, my grandfather proposed hanging the shopkeeper by the ears on a couple of fishhooks from his heaviest-gauge fishing line, giving him a push to get him swing-ing, and inviting those neighbors whom the shopkeeper was so eager to betray to come and test their marksmanship using whatever blunderbusses the Volkssturm had left on the shelves.

A breeze blew in through the smashed window. The tarpaulin rustled and snapped like a sail.

The shopkeeper suggested that my grandfather try the Herzog farm, on the road to Sondershausen. Herzog was an infantryman killed during the course of the long retreat from Italy. His widow had taken up with one Stolzmann, an engineer from the Mittelwerk who was now living at the farm and posing as Herzog.

My grandfather rode the Zündapp out to the Herzog farm. The sidecar rode empty beside him. He crossed a stream and, just before the road made a bend to the south, entered a birchwood. The birches congregated in the fog, wrapped in their bark with its cryptic inscrip-tions. They reminded my grandfather of monuments in a graveyard. He felt a premonitory shiver and, a second later, a sharp tug at the left elbow of his army coat. He heard a crack of rifle fire. Small-caliber, by the sound. Someone was shooting at him from the cover of the trees north of the road. My grandfather glanced back and to his left but saw only trees and a bright dot of daylight in the wool at the elbow of his coat.

My grandfather felt foolish, which bothered him, since he would prefer to die in the grip of any emotion, no matter how abject, than in the knowledge of his own stupidity. If the dealer in sporting goods would betray his own neighbors for some canned ham and bananas, then it was likely he would not hesitate to betray an American soldier for less. The bastard probably had arranged for an ad hoc ambush as soon as my grandfather left the shop. My grandfather opened the throttle and let the beautiful engine do what its designers had engineered it to do. There was another rifle crack, but this time the shot went wide. The road left the birchwood and made its bend to the south. There was no more shooting after that.

When he saw the promised farmhouse and its stand of poplars about a quarter mile ahead on the left, he slowed the motorcycle and killed its engine. The farm had the appearance of prosperity neither untouched nor entirely diminished by war. The stucco farmhouse was large and new, with a second story and signs of modern plumbing. The large ground-floor windows had leaded lozenges in their upper panes. There was half-timbering, a red tiled roof, and an overall air of ersatz medievalism that my grandfather supposed to be good Nazi style. The barn was capacious, with a metal roof in fine repair. The Alsatian bitch who came bounding and chesty across the meadow to give my grandfather a piece of her mind had a lustrous coat. It had been a long time since my grandfather had seen a civilian dog who did not slink around corners with the ribcage visible and the head lowered in shame or calculation. This bold specimen was frankly asking to be shot, but in addition to the headless officer's rifle and Walther, my grandfather had come armed with a small can of Vienna sausages. After a moment's quick work with the can opener of his folding knife, a truce was agreed to. My grandfather fed the sausages to the dog at one-minute intervals until he gained some measure of adoration. She followed him to the house but gave no warning of his approach until he was almost to the kitchen door.

In the spotless kitchen he found Frau Herzog trying to help a boy of nine or ten to adjust his artificial leg. She was a good-looking woman with a remarkable bosom who displayed mild anxiety at an American officer's sudden appearance in her dooryard but nothing that was not called for. She explained that the boy, her son, suffered from diabetes and regrettably would have to decline the proffered Hershey bars. The boy, fair and slender, stared at my grandfather, fear showing unbribed and plain on his face. The bulb of his stump reminded my grandfather of the nosecone of a V-2. The skin over it looked chafed and sore. The prosthesis was too big, too long. At one time it might have been the property of another, larger amputee child. My grandfather had planned on confronting the widow Herzog to cut the bullshit and just ask for Stolzmann, but he was derailed by something in the face or the gestalt of the wide-eyed silent boy with his legs dying out from under him.

"Herr Herzog?" my grandfather inquired.

Alarm deepened the groove between Frau Herzog's eyebrows. She apologized. She said that she hoped there was nothing amiss. She said that her husband was an infantryman and that he had stepped on a mine—a German mine—in a place called San Gimignano. Now he was out of combat and of no danger to anyone. In the midst of making this statement, she glanced at the boy. My grandfather did not hear a lie in her voice but noted the ambiguous phrasing. If her husband was dead and she was covering up for this Stolzmann, my grandfather could not help but admire her apparent reluctance to tell an out-and-out lie in front of her child.

"My business is not with your husband," he said, answering her ambiguity with his own. "I'm in a hurry and would like nothing better than to leave all of you in peace as soon as I have the answer I need."

The bitch came in through the open door and, with a loving tongue, addressed herself to the fingers my grandfather had used to serve the Vienna sausages. She sat down at my grandfather's side and yawned. Frau Herzog stood with her arms folded under her bosom, which my grandfather could not help but admire, too. He could see that although it was likely she had never wanted anything more than she wanted him to leave them in peace, that would still be insufficient payment, in her view, for what he was asking in return. Then he thought of something she might want even more.

"I can get you insulin," he said. "Say three months' supply. If the man of the house answers my question."

Frau Herzog carried the boy to the bench of a refectory table and posed him there with the leg beside him. "Six months," she said.

She led him out to the barn, where a man dressed in duck overalls was busy delivering a pair of calves, so persuasively that my grandfather began to doubt the information he had been given by the shopkeeper. The overalls fit and so did the face, lean and raw-boned with patient blue eyes. Before Frau Herzog called out to him and interrupted his work, the man's face wore an expression of blissful absorption in the procedure and its proper execution, usual enough with engineers but presumably not unknown among farmers.

The man in the overalls inquired as to the nature of my grandfather's business. My grandfather turned to Frau Herzog. Speaking in the most formal German he could muster, he made the polite suggestion that her son was no doubt wondering when she would be returning to the kitchen. He made the deliberate mistake of addressing her as "Frau Stolzmann." A blush filled in the pale skin between her freckles and spread to the hollow of her throat. My grandfather took it for embarrassment, but it might just as well have been rage.

"Go," Stolzmann told her.

She seemed to be about to try to remonstrate or make some case, but in the end she kept silent and left the barn. Stolzmann turned back to the parturient animal in the stall. It was working over its pale pink firstborn with its tongue, raising moist spikes and whorls in the dappled tan coat. The cow lifted its head as if hearing a sound that alarmed it. It made an oddly human sound of uncertainty. It clunked drunkenly two steps to the side. A smell of iron filled the barn. Veiled in its pearly amnion, the second calf squirted out of its mother. The sound was like a boot being pulled from the mud.

"She had twins," my grandfather said. "Is that common?"

"Not very common, no," Stolzmann said.

He tended to the newborn, squatting beside it. He moved with deliberation and apparent calm, but my grandfather could see that he was stalling for time, going over his story, his head twitching a little from side to side as he aired it to himself. My grandfather waited him out. At last the cow seemed to lose patience with Stolzmann and brought the charade to an end by interposing itself between him and the calves. Stolzmann tumbled backward and sat down hard. My grandfather almost laughed.

When Stolzmann stood up and turned to my grandfather, he had his face arranged to represent what he must have hoped would pass for rustic matter-of-factness, calves safely delivered, another chore done out of the day's long schedule. He saw the Walther in my grandfather's hand. He sighed. He wiped his hands on the coveralls. They left long bloody streaks.

"I'm looking for a colleague of yours," my grandfather said, lowering the gun. "At the Mittelwerk."

"The Mittelwerk," Stolzmann repeated. His tone committed him to nothing. He might have heard of the Mittelwerk once or twice. He might just have been trying the word for the sound of it. He might have been trying to imagine what type of *mittel* was manufactured in this peculiar-sounding *werk*.

"We know you were employed there. You have been identified by witnesses." By trial and error my grandfather had learned that when he needed to tell a lie in the course of an interrogation, the technique that worked best was to sound like what he was saying bored him to tears. "We have the paymaster's ledgers and your name appears there." He fished a pack of cigarettes from his pocket and put one to his lips.

"If you please," Stolzmann said, sounding considerably less non-committal. "No fire." He gestured to the hay bales stacked man-high in the stall behind my grandfather, in the stalls to either side of him, in the loft.

My grandfather lit a match, held it to his cigarette, then gave it a shake. He tossed the match over his shoulder without looking to make sure it had gone out. "I want you to understand," he said. "I would gladly burn down this barn and everything in it if doing that would bring me one step closer to Freiherr von Braun."

A muscle twitched at the hinge of Stolzmann's jaw. Understanding leaked into his eyes, along with a hint of contempt. At the time my grandfather was not sure how to read that contempt but later thought he understood. Stolzmann had been looking down on him, a filthy and haggard American dogface, and on the backward empire whose army he served in, bent on stealing the stars they could not attain on their own.

"Tell me where he is hiding," my grandfather said. "I urge you to cooperate, or I will be obliged to see that you are arrested and imprisoned."

"If you must," Stolzmann said, working hard in his own right to sound dreadfully bored. "Do your duty, Lieutenant. Obviously, I am at the mercy of you and your country now. And its prisons."

"Oh, not *our* prison," my grandfather said in his sleepiest tone. "I'm going to have to hand you over to the Russians."

Stolzmann blinked. He gestured to my grandfather's cigarette and put out a hand. My grandfather handed him the pack and said he could keep what was left. Stolzmann lit a Lucky with the careful flame of his lighter. He cupped a hand under the end of the cigarette to intercept any coals that might fall out. He inhaled without bothering to conceal his pleasure in the quality of the cigarette. "I've never heard of this von Braun. I'm sorry."

My grandfather made a rough and hasty estimation of Stolzmann's weight, his reach, his agility, preparing for violence, but Stolzmann's eyes flicked to his right and he looked abruptly irritated. There was a scrape. My grandfather turned around. Frau Herzog was carrying the boy, hugging him against her. The chunky brown shoe of the artificial leg protruded from the cuff of his trousers. My grandfather could not see either of her hands.

"Tell him," she said to Stolzmann. "Help him, he is going to help Martin."

"Go back to the house," Stolzmann said.

She set the boy down. She was holding my grandfather's M1911, which he had exchanged for the Walther. Her finger snaked around the Browning's trigger. She raised her arm and took aim. But it was Stolzmann she was pointing the gun at, not my grandfather. "Tell him," she said again.

"Yes," my grandfather said. "Tell me."

Stolzmann smoked attentively, watching the coal at the end of his cigarette. My grandfather could hear the lapping of the mother cow's tongue. The widow moved the gun a little down and to the right, aiming for Stolzmann's shoulder. She pulled the trigger. Stolzmann cried out and looked suitably surprised but suffered no other ill effects, since the magazine of my grandfather's gun was empty.

My grandfather did not like the smug smile that crept across Stolzmann's face. He asked Frau Herzog for the Browning and took an extra clip from a pocket of his coat. He gave her back the gun. He hoped she would not use it to shoot him. Frau Herzog raised the Browning and, having already demonstrated her willingness to put a bullet into her paramour, took aim at Stolzmann's shoulder again. Stolzmann's smile was retired for the evening.

"Wernher is not hiding," Stolzmann told my grandfather. "He is being hidden."

"By whom?" my grandfather said.

Stolzmann and Frau Herzog eyed each other and engaged in a telepathic exchange that ended when she racked the slide of the Browning.

"By the SS," Stolzmann said. "To ensure that you don't find him. They're afraid that von Braun will surrender as soon as the opportunity presents itself, and offer his services to the American government."

"Why would he do that?"

Even with the end of his dream of von Braun's company in a motorcycle's sidecar or the cold empty reaches of space, and even with his horror at what had been done to the workers of the Mittelbau in the name of rocketry, my grandfather could not believe that the man was prepared to betray his country as smoothly as the shopkeeper his Nordhausen neighbors.

"So he can get to the Moon," Stolzmann said. "The SS know it. Two years ago they arrested him because they thought he was trying to divert resources from weapon development to space flight. They don't trust him."

"And where are they holding him, please?"

"I haven't the slightest idea."

Frau Herzog raised the Browning again. Its eye maintained its lidless vigil. Her fingers looked admirably relaxed on the grip.

"In Bavaria, in the mountains, but I don't know precisely where! Why would I know? Anna!" he appealed to Frau Herzog. Frau Herzog nodded and lowered the gun, looking disappointed. My grandfather grabbed the gun away from her and then she looked afraid.

"I'm sorry," she said.

"Please, Frau Herzog. I will get you the insulin. A six months' supply."

The Bavarian Alps. It was not enough, but it was something. A long way from Nordhausen, three hundred miles or more. He would have to check his maps, but even without looking he knew he would have to cross territory not yet occupied by the Allies to reach mountains where—according to rumor and U.S. intelligence reports alike—teenage Nazi fanatics known as Werwolf, bred to kill, had been equipped and provisioned to hold out for five years in an impregnable fortress called the Alpenfestung.* To the tally of crimes reckoned against von Braun by my grandfather, he added the offense of making oneself a pain in the ass to find. In his current state— which today would likely be diagnosed as post-traumatic shock— this felt like the most unpardonable offense of all. He told himself that he was only going to apprehend von Braun and turn him over to the authorities to be hanged as a war criminal, but offered the slightest pretext, my grandfather knew, he planned in his heart to shoot the bastard.

"I would have brought you the insulin anyway," he told Frau Herzog and Martin. "Even if he had told me nothing at all."

He had just adjusted his chinstrap and was pulling on his right glove when he heard a loping tread in the mud and turned, expecting to see the dog. It was Martin, in his rough woollen trousers and patched jumper. He had a plain face and watery eyes that narrowed to a pair of blue slits.

"He has a buried treasure," Martin said.

"That sounds exciting."

My grandfather pulled on the left glove. He grabbed the handlebars, the throttle, kicked the engine to life. If he could get hold of the insulin promptly, he could be in Nuremburg by dark.

The boy was standing there, talking over the motorbike's rumble. My grandfather cut the engine. "What?"

---

* Largely a farrago of propaganda and desperation concocted and served up by Joseph Goebbels.

". . . because of the tall blond man."

"A tall blond man."

"He came with two other men and told them to bury the treasure. And Herr Stolzmann said maybe there was a cave where they could bury it."

Stolzmann didn't want to tell my grandfather about the buried treasure in the cave. When my grandfather and Martin went back into the barn, interrupting a quarrel between Stolzmann and Frau Herzog, Stolzmann tried to persuade my grandfather, Frau Herzog, and Martin himself that the boy was prattling and, he suggested, mentally defective.

"But I heard you talking to the tall blond man," Martin said. "He told you to put it in a cave and bury it."

"Nonsense."

Frau Herzog went to a nearby stall, picked up a pitchfork and plunged it into Stolzmann's thigh. It was done with grace in a single continuous motion. Three of the four tines found meat. She jerked them out, and holes in the fabric of Herzog's coverall bloomed purple. Herzog grabbed at his leg and fell down.

"You are not mentally defective, Martin," Frau Herzog said.

"I know," said Martin.

In the kitchen my grandfather treated Stolzmann's wounds. He found a bottle of apple brandy and poured a glass for Stolzmann, who drained it in one draft. My grandfather poured him a second one.

"There is no treasure," Stolzmann said. "Just papers. Miles of them. Thousands of kilos. Enough to fill twenty file cabinets. All the documentation from the V-2 program. Every diagram, every report on research and testing. He asked me and two colleagues to hide it all just before he was evacuated to the south. I helped them load the documents, and then one of my colleagues found an old salt mine and they put them in there. They used some of the miners' dynamite to seal the opening of the cave."

"Did the SS know about this?"

"Of course not. Von Braun wanted something to bargain with. I imagine the United States of America would very much like to put their hands on these files."

"I imagine you're right," my grandfather said bitterly.

He got out his map and had Stolzmann show him the location of the salt mine, but Stolzmann had not been there when the documents were buried and could give him only a vague location "around Bleicherode."

My grandfather went out into the yard and lit a cigarette. He had to make a choice. The intelligence man with the 3rd Armored had told him that after the war, Nordhausen was due to be handed over to the Russians along with this whole chunk of Germany. The Russian Army was already on its way. If he went after von Braun, as his heart and his desire to punish von Braun urged him to do, then the documents—a virtual recipe for building a V-2 rocket— might fall into Russian hands before he could return. If he stayed to pursue the documents, then von Braun might elude capture, fall into Russian hands, or surrender to the Allies, but my grandfather would have had nothing to do with it, and there would be no chance for von Braun to give my grandfather the pretext he was hoping for. If von Braun surrendered to the Allies before my grandfather had managed to locate the documents, then the German would be able to negotiate the terms of his surrender and maybe avoid punish- ment entirely, and if the Russian Army overtook my grandfather in his efforts to find the salt mine, then there was a strong possibility that all would be lost. He could not report Stolzmann's informa- tion and then take off after von Braun; people would want to know just where he thought he was going. When they heard, he would be ordered to stick around Bleicherode or sent after von Braun as part of a team. He did not want to hunt von Braun with a team.

When he finished his cigarette, he went back inside the farm- house. Stolzmann had passed out in the bedroom. Martin and the dog were sharing a can of Vienna sausages. Frau Herzog scanned my grandfather's face and picked up some bit of information that led her to reach for the bottle of applejack. She poured two fingers into the glass and handed it to my grandfather. It burned with a harsh and clarifying fire all the way.

"What will you do?" she asked him.

"My duty," my grandfather said, and then added in English, "God fucking damn it."

On May 2, 1945, high above the Adolf Hitler Pass in the Austrian Tyrol, Wernher von Braun convened his inner circle on a sunny terrace of the Haus Ingeborg hotel. Hitler was dead. The war, as they were all aware, was lost. The fall of Berlin was imminent. Regrettably, then, the time had come to surrender. Forward elements of the U.S. 6th Army were already at the foot of the mountain on the Austrian side. The Russian Army was mere miles to the east and moving fast. If they did not act now, von Braun told his companions—among them his brother Magnus, General Walter Dornberger, the former commandant of the rocket research facility at Peenemünde, and Huzel and Tessman, the two men whom Stolzmann had helped to conceal the Mittelwerk files—they would lose their freedom to decide. It was a strange kind of freedom, to choose one's captor, but preferable to being the prisoner of chance. Von Braun had long since brought his companions around to the view that America was a fitter repository for his gifts than the Soviet Union. The decision was made. The next morning, equipped with a bicycle and a basic grasp of the English language, Magnus was sent down the mountain to bring the Americans the excellent news.

Halfway down, the younger von Braun brother was challenged by a sentry, Private Fred Schneikert of Sheboygan, Wisconsin, who proved both ignorant of and unimpressed by the exalted nature of the prize he was being offered. There was some comedy of mistranslation and regimental head-scratching, but in time the name of von Braun found its way up the chain to an intelligence unit, where it landed with the proper éclat. A couple of weeks before, there had been a report, received through channels from an operative in Nordhausen, alerting them that von Braun might be hiding in the Bavarian Alps. A few hours later, Wernher Magnus Maximilian Freiherr von Braun became a prisoner of the 44th Infantry Division. In less than a quarter century, this uncharacteristic act of submission would lead—as von Braun alone had always known that it must—to the imprinting of a human footprint in the soft dark dust of the Moon.

Von Braun was thirty-three. Tall, fair, gregarious, and goodlooking, with his left arm and shoulder bandaged in a cast as the result of a recent automobile accident, von Braun posed with his GI captors for an odd photograph that ran the next day on the front pages of newspapers across the United States. In the photograph von Braun looks startlingly dapper for a prisoner of war, in a double-breasted suit and a long coat, but the first thing you notice is the cast, a monstrosity of plaster that forces von Braun's arm to jut out at a bizarre angle, buttressed by a metal rod. It looks like a comedy prop, something you would see on Moe Howard when you cut from a scene of him challenging an old lady to an arm-wrestling contest. The second remarkable element of the photograph is von Braun's expression, a smile variously interpreted over the years as one of relief, high spirits, or a remarkable, even defiant smugness.

It was probably the latter; as far as von Braun knew at the moment of his capture, he was sitting on the secret to the location of twenty-four thousand pounds of documents of incomparable scientific and strategic value. As my grandfather had assumed, von Braun planned to use this secret to negotiate the most favorable terms imaginable for his surrender and postwar career. There is no photographic record of the expression on von Braun's face when he learned subsequently that the documents had been located and successfully disinterred from the salt mine near Bleicherode where Tessman and Huzel had buried them.

As for the U.S. intelligence officer who, just ahead of the Russian takeover of Nordhausen, had located and supervised the excavation of the Mittelwerk files, there is likewise no photographic record of the look on *his* face when, in the lobby of a Baltimore television station, he learned about the postwar clover in which, even without the cache of documents, Wernher von Braun had landed. But there was a testimony, and my grandfather made it to me.

XXIV

Two days before my grandfather surrendered to the New York State Department of Corrections, he drove my mother from New Jersey to Baltimore to entrust her to his brother's care. It was by no means the ideal situation, but nothing ever was, and he felt he had no choice. His mother and father had died of cancer within a couple of months of each other in the winter of 1954.

"Keep your eyes peeled," my grandfather told my mother. "It's going to be on your side of the street."

My mother had not seen Baltimore in five years, and it looked strange to her. The row houses had two stories clad in white siding upstairs, redbrick down. They made my mother think of gums crowded with teeth. Most of them had flat roofs, but every so often one had a peaked attic. Those were the eyeteeth. The houses had shallow porches held up by white pillars. They ran on for blocks unvaryingly, like a vista you might drive past in a dream.

"I forgot the number," my mother said.

My grandfather sighed. He took his right hand off the wheel to fish his wallet from the breast pocket of his jacket. A matchbook from Howard Johnson's fell out of the wallet into the area by his feet. He swore. He returned the wallet to its pocket. His tone was calm, but that meant nothing. "Find it," he said.

My mother leaned across the seat and felt around on the floor among the pedals and her father's black wing tips until her fingers kicked against the match cover. "Found it."

The comb of matches had been torn away cleanly along with the strip where you struck a light. She turned the match cover over to the side on which my grandfather had jotted down an address. My mother read the numbers aloud, but they failed to register. She was remembering the Howard Johnson's restaurant where my grandfather had taken her one particularly fine Saturday not long before. Their nearest neighbor, Mrs. Lopes, had unexpectedly dropped by the house that day, bringing along two albums of photos from a recent visit to her sister in Altoona. My grandmother had shown what struck my mother at the time as remarkable if not excessive interest in the Pennsylvanian travels of Mrs. Lopes. My mother was thrilled when my grandfather, who harbored little patience for their neighbor, abruptly proposed a father-daughter outing.

He drove my mother out to visit a petting zoo with goats, sheep, and an irritable alpaca named for Yma Sumac. My mother knew that at fourteen she was too old to enjoy a petting zoo. She had enjoyed it nonetheless. There were no other visitors, and the animals seemed eager for company. They rushed to greet my mother and never let her out of their sight. In the enormous barn there had been a tire swing lashed to the highest rafter, and at the end of the visit the farmer had set up empty soup cans along a fence. My mother, always a bit of a deadeye, had shot all but one of them off with a .22 rifle. On the way back from the petting zoo, they stopped at Howard Johnson's, where my grandfather had consented to my mother ordering a lunch of french fries with a side of peppermint ice cream.

The day was hot, but inside the Howard Johnson's her bare arms and legs had prickled as her sweat cooled in the air-conditioning. There was frost on the scalloped metal ice cream dish. My grandfather had made a comic show of disgust as he watched my mother languidly dip each fry into the pink mound of ice cream before eating it. But she could see something else moving behind his face, some deeper pain or preoccupation. After a while he got up to go to the men's room. He came back with a pack of Pall Mall cigarettes. He was not a habitual smoker, but there were months when he would go through two packs a day.

The lighter engraved with a molecular diagram was out of fuel, an oversight she could not remember ever having seen him commit. Their waitress had brought the book of matches in their aqua, white, and orange cover. My grandfather lit a cigarette and settled back in the booth. The look in his eyes of painful assessment appeared to have departed. He complimented my mother on her marksmanship and then, unusually, told her a story from his boyhood. It was a brief tale but a good one. It concerned a friend of my grandfather's, a boy called Moish, who had been shot by another boy with a .22 rifle. The tale concluded satisfyingly with a bloody fingertip wrapped in a sheet of newspaper and carried home in the victim's pocket.[*]

When they got home that afternoon from their outing, the radio in the living room was playing big-band rhumba music, but the house was empty. There was an envelope on the kitchen table, propped against a candlewick vase that held white peonies cut from the back garden. My grandmother had written my mother's name on the outside of the envelope. Her penmanship, improved by nuns, made every word look like notes to be played on a celesta. In the envelope my mother found a red feather wrapped inside a letter informing her that her mother had decided, for the good of the family, to return herself for treatment at Greystone. The meaning or origin of the red feather was information my mother never ascertained.

My grandfather swore again and stepped on the brake. "You were supposed to be looking," he said.

"I was looking."

When you drove it in reverse, the car made a sound that my mother imagined to be the whirring of her father's displeasure. My grandfather craned his head around and backed them past three houses

---

[*] My grandfather never told my mother what he confessed to me thirty-two years later: that he had been the shooter.

with his right arm slung across the top of the seat back. He stopped in front of a house with an attic story. Its porch was hedged with bare azalea bushes. Instead of brick and siding, it appeared to have been clad in a grid made of hundreds of cut stones, brown, purple-brown, and gray. Its porch had lost or been deprived of its pillars. In their place someone had installed trellises of wrought iron, entwined by wrought-iron vines. In one of the two windows that looked onto the porch my mother saw a woman's wide face before a muslin curtain fell across it.

My grandfather cut the engine. My mother grabbed handfuls of the skirt of her jumper and squeezed. Her eyes burned. Tears dripped from her chin to the Peter Pan collar of her blouse. It was so quiet in the car that she could hear the patter of the tears. My grandfather made a soft click with his tongue, irritation or pity. My mother pinned her scant hopes on pity.

"I have no choice in the matter," my grandfather said. "Forgive me."

"No," said my mother. Her daring surprised her. Her heart was thudding against her breastbone.

My grandfather opened the door on his side and got out of the car. "Fair enough," he said.

He put on his gray worsted suit jacket and shot his cuffs. He straightened the knot of his gray and black tie. He studied the stone face of the house.* He came around the front of the car and opened my mother's door on his way back to the trunk. My mother wiped her face on her sleeve and climbed out. She followed him to the trunk of the Crosley, which held two suitcases of clothes, a train case with her toilet articles and her glass animal collection, her portable record player, and a box of 45 rpm records, among them "Wake Up Little Susie," new that week, and "Dark Moon" by Gale Storm.

---

* In all likelihood the house had been clad not in genuine stone but in a molded concrete simulacrum known as Formstone, then in vogue among Baltimore householders.

"Let me worry about this stuff," my grandfather said. "You go ring the bell."

My mother stood on the concrete checkerboard looking at the stone house. It had felt so good to say no. She contemplated saying it again, but Uncle Ray beat her to it.

"No!" He was standing on the topmost porch step. He was wearing a sky-blue suit piped in white, and a green necktie patterned with gold circles over a gold shirt. He was taking her in, making a show of it, his arms folded across his bony chest, looking her up and down. He shook his head, his mouth turned up at one corner as though ready, in a moment, to smile. "Unbelievable," he said. "Impossible."

My mother had not seen very much of Uncle Ray since the move from Baltimore in 1952. Since then he had grown more outrageous, and she loved him for it. The improbability of his cars, his clothes, and of the gifts he brought her—a brown-skinned doll wearing a hat of wooden fruit and a red dress embroidered with the word HAVANA, a canvas sack stamped GOLDEN NUGGET containing a vial filled with gold dust—scandalized my grandfather in a way that paradoxically also seemed to bring him pleasure. When Uncle Ray came around, he and my grandmother would do the talking. My grandfather would just sit listening at the table or, once, on a blanket spread under the hickory tree. Uncle Ray's stories of his life featured people with suggestive or humorous nicknames and towns or neighborhoods with questionable reputations. To narrate that life's incidents and activities required an impenetrable jargon. The talk went over my mother's head so completely that nobody bothered to shoo her away. When Uncle Ray got to the end of a story, my grandfather would sink his chin into his hand and say something like "I don't believe it" or "That's appalling" or simply "Oy, Reynard, why?" But sometimes he would be smiling.

"Hi, Uncle Ray," my mother said.

"Hello, dollface."

She went up the steps and put her arms around Ray's neck and kissed him on the cheek. It was smoother than her father's cheek. As always, he smelled of gardenia and tobacco ash. She did not have to go up on tiptoe to kiss him. Not yet fifteen, she was two inches taller than he was.

"Look at you! Nobody told me you were already done growing up," he said. "This is going to be a piece of cake. My work is done!"

My mother did not reply.

"Right?" Uncle Ray said. "I'm looking forward to this, aren't you?"

"I guess."

"Sure you are, baby. This is going to be fun."

There was a flat metal mailbox by the front door with a wire bracket to hold the evening paper. The name on the mailbox was EINSTEIN. My mother had been told that this was the name of Uncle Ray's landlady, but seeing it spelled out on the mailbox gave her an uneasy feeling. It was a name long since affixed to matters of crucial importance that she knew she was never going to understand.

"You said a girl."

The voice was pitched low, masculine. It belonged to the woman my mother had seen at the window. She seemed old to my mother at the time, but in retrospect my mother thought she must not have been sixty. Her black hair was grained with silver. It jutted out on either side of her head in two fins that curved upward at the tips, the toes of a pair of Persian slippers. She was wearing what appeared to be a lab coat over a blouse printed with chrysanthemums and a brown skirt. She drew a thread of some bitter odor along with her when she came out onto the porch.

"Mrs. Einstein," Uncle Ray told my mother. "This is a girl, Mrs. E. She's only . . . How old are you now, sweetheart?"

"Fourteen."

Mrs. Einstein looked my mother up and down, her hands folded across her chest. My mother decided that the odor was coming from Mrs. Einstein. Later my mother would learn that her uncle's landlady worked as a receptionist at a veterinary hospital out in Pikesville. A smell compounded from carbolic and the secretions of animals' fear glands followed Mrs. Einstein wherever she went.

"Fourteen," Mrs. Einstein said. "Nonsense." She turned to Ray. "What do you take me for?"

"I can produce her birth documents," Uncle Ray said with smoothness and assurance, worrying my mother, who was not sure she owned any birth documents. "If you really think it's necessary."

The summer before, as a hurricane was about to hit the Gulf Coast of Texas, my mother had seen a picture in the newspaper of people in its path nailing sheets of plywood over the windows of their houses. A similar procedure now seemed to be undertaken by Mrs. Einstein with the expression in her eyes.

"It's all necessary when you're involved," she said to Uncle Ray. "I have to take every precaution."

"Now, Mrs. E."

"When you're involved I read the fine print." She shook her head infinitesimally, as if a fuller expression of disapproval might implicate her in whatever mischief her boarder had gotten himself into. Then she went back into the house.

"What did she mean, 'You said a girl'?" my mother asked her uncle. "Does she think I'm a boy?"

Uncle Ray's teeth were veined with gold. When he smiled, you felt he was giving you a glimpse of the wares he planned to sell you.

"No, sweetheart," he said, "she thought you were a woman." He started to ruffle her hair, then changed his mind and settled for a pat on the shoulder. "Don't let her— Well, well."

He was looking past my mother at my grandfather, coming up the walk with one of my mother's suitcases under each arm, holding the record player with his left hand and the train case and box of records with his right.

"Shame on you, Mandrake," Uncle Ray said to my mother. "Making Lothar here carry all your bags."

"He wouldn't let me help."

"No, he wouldn't, would he," Uncle Ray said.

My grandfather kept his head down, his eyes hidden behind the brim of his hat. He tromped up the porch steps and tried to bull past my mother and Uncle Ray without saying a word.

"Hey, sourpuss," Uncle Ray said. He stepped into his brother's path. He waited until my grandfather looked up from under the brim of his fedora. "You can't even manage a hello?"

My grandfather paused. He nodded without meeting his brother's gaze. "Hello," he said.

"That's it? That's all I get?"

"Move it," my grandfather said softly.

Uncle Ray stepped aside with a show of mock alarm. My grandfather went through the door with the luggage.

"We're putting her in the attic," Uncle Ray called after him. "Good luck getting all that up the ladder. I'd help you if you weren't such a jerk."

My grandfather reminded his brother that he didn't need help. Uncle Ray rolled his eyes at my mother. She wanted to smile but could not manage it. She was already apprehensive about having to sleep in an attic. She had not been told that the attic was reached by a ladder. This worried her, too. What if she had to go to the bathroom in the middle of the night?

"Good thing he's not sticking around," Uncle Ray said. "Himself and Mrs. Einstein under the same roof? Marciano versus Moore, duking it out for the heavyweight sourpuss title."

"He's going to prison," my mother said, remembering now that in spite of the affection and sense of mild wonder Uncle Ray inspired in her, there had always been something about him that got on her nerves. He was not a serious person. "If he weren't going to prison, neither of us would have to be here at all."

Uncle Ray looked as if she had slapped him. My mother felt instantly sorry. She forced herself to smile. "Anyway," she said. "I'd put my money on Daddy."

"For the sourpuss title?"

"Definitely."

"How much?"

"Five dollars?"

"You're on," Uncle Ray said. They shook on it.

Mrs. Einstein fed them. The fifteen dollars a week she charged Uncle Ray for a room with its own bathroom on the second floor of her house did not include meals. Mrs. Einstein took no interest in food. On the rare occasions when she cooked, the results were nothing anybody would pay money to eat. Though not observant, she shopped at a kosher butcher. She would buy the cheapest cuts, all string and gristle, sear them, then submerge them in a signature brown gravy that reminded my mother of Jell-O, only salty and hot. The vegetables were boiled until safely gray. Once a week Mrs. Einstein forced herself to sit down and eat a piece of fried beef liver with grilled onions, and if Uncle Ray and my mother were around, she forced them to eat it, too. Her husband and son had always refused to touch liver, and they were dead, and she was alive.

On that first night, however, she served an excellent dairy supper. She had stopped at an appetizing store and brought home smoked whitefish, pickled herring, a dozen deviled eggs. She put out cottage cheese and some sliced celery and carrots. For dessert there was a marvel of a cake, a slender block frosted with chocolate that revealed, when Mrs. Einstein sliced it open, gaudy layers of pink, green, and yellow separated by ribbons of raspberry jam. Mrs. Einstein had no illusions about her table—she had no illusions about anything except maybe the tonic properties of beef liver. But she knew where my grandfather would be headed after he departed her house. She felt that his last free meal ought to be edible, at least.

"You're very kind," my grandfather said, pushing away his plate.

"Not really," Mrs. Einstein said. She looked at my mother, who was just then contemplating asking for a second slice of ribbon cake. "One is enough," Mrs. Einstein said.

My mother nodded. She put her fork down.

"Maybe your brother told you, I have doubts about this arrangement," Mrs. Einstein said. "I have a hard time picturing Reynard looking after a child, and I worry that the burden is going to fall on me. I don't much care for children. I had one of my own. That was more than sufficient."

My grandfather turned on his brother. "You said it was fine with her."

"*Fine* is a relative term," Uncle Ray observed. "Maybe I ought to have said, as fine as anything ever gets with this one."

My mother told me that she still remembered the heat spreading across her cheeks as she listened to this exchange. A spasm of restlessness took hold in her legs, a kind of panic of the muscles. She ran through a handful of smart or angry or cold remarks she might toss at Mrs. Einstein on the subject of children and their feelings toward Mrs. Einstein. She reconfirmed with herself the certainty that she had nowhere else to go.

"I don't need it to be fine," Mrs. Einstein said. "Obviously, the girl needs a home."

It was not yet eight o'clock when my grandfather took his hat from a peg in the front hall. My mother tried to stay put on Mrs. Einstein's sofa. The sofa was upholstered in pale pink chenille sealed in a layer of clear vinyl. Under her circle skirt, my mother could feel her bare thighs sticking to the vinyl slipcover, and she pretended that the adhesion would be sufficient. But in the end she tore loose and ran to her father. He suffered her to put her arms around his waist and her cheek against his shirtfront. When he saw that she was not going to make a scene, he took hold of her head with both hands and raised her face to his.

"If I thought you were not up to this, I would not ask you to do it," he said. "Do you understand?"

My mother nodded. A tear spilled from her left eye, streaked down her temple, and chimed inside her right ear.

"You're tough," he said. "Like me."

He lowered his lips to her forehead and left the scratch of his whiskers on it. Hours afterward, lying on a folding cot in Mrs. Einstein's attic, trying to fall asleep, she could feel the abrasion of his kiss radiating heat across her forehead like a sunburn. It was only then, in the dark and the smell of old luggage and galoshes, that it occurred to my mother she should have asked my grandfather what he would have done if he'd thought she wasn't up to the ordeal. She lay there in the dark, picturing to herself all the bright forms his mercy might have taken if only she had not been so tough.

XXV

On the original charge of aggravated assault, my grandfather might have been looking at five years. But by 1957 New York was already struggling with the judicial backlog that, at the end of the sixties, brought its court system to the point of collapse. As a veteran and a family man with no criminal record, my grandfather was persuaded to waive his right to a trial and plead guilty to a lesser charge of simple assault. He was sentenced to twenty months in Wallkill Prison.

Wallkill had been built in a spirit of experiment, when FDR was governor of New York. Its perimeter was not enclosed by a wall or a fence. Its tree-lined walkways and gray Gothic stonework reminded visitors of a small men's college or seminary. It had a library, a gymnasium, a swimming pool, a profitable dairy farm, a horse barn, machine and craft shops, greenhouses and vegetable gardens, an orchard, livestock, and bees. Under qualified instructors, inmates were required to learn and paid to work at manual or agricultural trades, or to put in a daily shift for making eyeglasses or plastic novelties in one of Wallkill's two manufactories. The warden recruited the prison guards personally to ensure that they were in sympathy with Wallkill's philosophy and methods. The guards dressed like park rangers. They carried handcuffs but no guns or batons. You had your own cell with a small outdoor terrace on which you were free to grow vegetables or flowers. You carried a key to your cell. Between lights-out and reveille you were confined to quarters, but once you had proved trustworthy you were given a fair amount of liberty to come and go. As long as you reported promptly for work, chow, exercise, chapel, and other mandatory activities, your spare time was your own.

The first night in his cell my grandfather had trouble sleeping. Outside the window the prison yard was flooded with light. The cell door was inset with a large peephole that let in light and noise from the gallery. The mattress crinkled. The air felt close and heavy. Sleeping inmates made a racket out of a cartoon, a barn at night transformed into a calliope of cows, pigs, and chickens playing a wheezy polka. At intervals too random to anticipate or adjust to, the prisoner in the next cell would break into spasmodic coughing. It sounded like a drum falling down a flight of stairs. It sounded painful.

My grandfather lay for hours with his arms folded under his head, bothered by thoughts of his wife and daughter. He pictured my mother jostled in the grandstand of a racetrack, losing tickets snowing down around her as a crowd rose to its feet and roared. He pictured her alone at a table in the back of a poolhall in some godforsaken place like Hagerstown, hair falling across a page of algebra or *Modern Screen,* while Uncle Ray sandbagged some dumb bastard who afterward beat him to death in an alley before raping my mother. My grandmother, he envisioned shorn and strapped to a table in a harsh-lit operating theater, plunged into tubs of ice, wound into a straightjacket, and force-fed medicated pap. He sat up, shuddering.

My grandfather went to the window to look at the night sky, but it turned out that the floodlights of Wallkill abolished the stars. Returning to the cot, my grandfather determined to map the ceiling of his cell with the stars he knew to be overhead. He pretended that the ceiling could be rolled away like the roof of an observatory dome. With a clear view of the heavens he contemplated the Dolphin, the Indian, the Microscope. He found the Ring Nebula in Lyra. Cassiopeia and Andromeda ascended the inner surface of his skull with their uncomfortable mythology. He saw the mother crooked as an *M*

with torment, the oblique angle of the daughter chained and waiting for something monstrous to arrive. It was nothing he wanted to
think about. He switched off the Zeiss of his imagination. The stars
winked out.

He rolled onto his side, and in time my grandmother returned to
his thoughts. She lay naked across their marriage bed on her belly,
with her legs pressed together and my grandfather standing by her
feet. His gaze traveled up an arrow of shadow that pointed to the cleft
in her ass. Her ass, that ripe and downy apricot. He took hold of her
feet by the ankles and opened her legs.

He fell asleep and was roused from a dream of a girl he'd been
sweet on in high school by the blare of the bell that must have pro-
voked it. When he opened his eyes, he was in prison. In twenty
months it would be 1959.

He put on the dark blue workshirt and gray poplin trousers of the
Wallkill uniform and sat down on the cot to lace up his boots. As he
sat down, he happened to look out the window at the sky. Mysteriously, that turned out to be a mistake.

As I no doubt have made clear by now, my grandfather was not
a man for tears, and when tears did come he fought them. The last
time he had allowed himself to weep freely, he'd been in short pants
and Herbert Hoover had been the president. Like blood, tears had a
function. They served to indicate the severity and depth of the blow
you had absorbed. When your friend died in your arms, your wife
had lost her sanity, or you were saying goodbye to your daughter
in Mrs. Einstein's front hall, tears flowed, and as with blood, you
stanched them. So what the fuck was this? A blue sky on a clear
morning at the end of a Catskills summer. Big deal. A matter of
wavelength and refraction. An agitation of the rods and cones.

Meanwhile, breakfast was at seven o'clock sharp. If you showed
up at 7:01, he had been informed, you would be shut out of the mess
hall and then go hungry until lunch. The bathroom was all the way
down at the end of the gallery. There might be a wait for the toilet, for

the sink, for a place in front of the mirror. What was more, he needed to take a piss. Any second now he was going to stop looking at the sky and tie his boots and go. It was time to get moving.

There was a knock on the door. My grandfather jumped. "Yes?" he called. He cleared his throat. "Yes, what is it?"

"Excuse me. I don't mean to intrude." There was something arch about the intonation—*mannered* was the right word. "I'm— It's Dr. Alfred Storch."

On arrival yesterday my grandfather had been examined by an internist and interviewed by a psychiatrist. Neither of them had been named Alfred Storch. The name of the warden was Dr. Wallack.

"Just a minute." My grandfather knotted his bootlaces and got up off the cot. When he opened the door, he was surprised to find another prisoner standing there. He had noticed this man in the mess hall the night before. Well over six feet tall, gaunt, silver in his black brush mustache. An apologetic stoop from a lifetime of ducking through doorways. He wore heavy-rimmed black glasses, and his eyes were a mess. The left one turned outward. It was hyperopic and swam huge behind its lens. The right eye was nearsighted, and its correction left it looking shrunken by comparison. He appeared to be wearing not ordinary spectacles but some kind of crude device of his own manufacture that would let him see around corners or in opposite directions. Dr. Storch held out his right hand, large and long-fingered. On a piano keyboard it would have spanned an octave and a half without stretching.

"I'm just next door," Dr. Storch said. *I'm chust next door.* It was a German accent, tinged with British instruction. It sounded pretty classy, Leslie Howard playing a Prussian count. "I wanted to make sure you, ah—" He broke off and averted his face from my grandfather's, though the left eye maintained its vigil. "Terribly sorry. I see I'm disturbing you."

My grandfather wiped his cheeks savagely on the sleeve of his workshirt. "Not at all," he said. "I was just going to wash up before breakfast."

"Right," said Dr. Storch. "You know I, I saw your door was closed, you see, and you're new here, so I wasn't sure if you knew—"

"I know," my grandfather said. "Seven sharp or they lock you out."

"Oh, they really do," Dr. Storch said. "They are sticklers."

It was worded like a complaint, but to my grandfather it sounded more like boasting. You would have thought Dr. Storch himself had formulated the policy on promptness at mealtime.

My grandfather followed into the gallery and closed the door of his cell behind him. He took the key from his pocket.

"Oh, nobody locks them," Dr. Storch said. "Of course, you do as you think best. But the locks are so flimsy. There's really no point." My grandfather detected a note of bitterness, as though Dr. Storch had fallen prey to pilfering more than once. "You can pick them with a playing card." My grandfather locked his door and Dr. Storch shrugged graciously. "There's no harm in it, certainly," he said.

They went past the door of Dr. Storch's cell and he pushed open the door. "Same as yours, in every drab particular."

Again there was the note of sham complaint, as if the uniformity of prisoners' cells obeyed some principle that Dr. Storch endorsed. Anyway, it was true: same cot, lamp, chair, table, same small chest of drawers. Same boxed ration of blue sky. No photographs. A few pocket books piled on the table with typed library labels taped to their spines. The topmost book was *Mission of Gravity* by Hal Clement. My grandfather had adored this classic of "hard" science fiction when it was first serialized in *Astounding*, enough to drop three dollars when Doubleday brought out a hardcover edition a year later. In 1974, when he pressed a fresh copy on me, it remained one of his all-time favorite books.

My grandfather did not acknowledge to Dr. Storch this evidence of a shared interest that might form the basis of a friendship. It was like when you dropped by the neighbors' at suppertime with a piece of misdelivered mail, and their house had a warm smell of carrots and bay leaf, and before they had a chance to ask you to sit down, have a glass of water, try a little of the soup, at least take off your coat, you shook your head and said, *Don't worry, I'm not staying.*

"Very nice," he said.

They went along the gallery toward the bathroom. Most of the other prisoners had already gone down to the mess hall, leaving their cell doors unlocked or ajar. Calendar girls, some photographs of children. Prisoner watercolors of fruit, Ava Gardner, the green Shawangunks. A porcelain Virgin with a halo of gold wire.

"I think you'll find the food quite palatable," Dr. Storch said.

"Dinner was all right. Beef and macaroni. Hard to ruin."

"We do get a lot of macaroni."

"It's filling."

"And cheap. I'm a dentist, by the way," Dr. Storch said. "Not an MD. If you were wondering. And I would like to tell you the truth about why I'm here before you encounter the remarkable mythology my accent has engendered—every day a fresh outrage seems to have been added to the catalog of my mythical crimes! I feel it's imperative I tell you the truth, you see, because I think . . . Do I perceive that you are a Jew? Yes. Well, here it is: Rest assured, I am not a Nazi. I am a German, yes, of course. But I detested Hitler, and I was never a member of the Nazi Party. I left Germany just before the invasion of Poland, and lived through the Blitz in London, where I was nearly killed on three occasions by German ordnance, including a V-2 rocket. It was never my job to extract the gold teeth from mouths of deportees when they arrived at Auschwitz or Belsen. I lived my whole life in Hamburg and was never near any of those places. I never conducted hideous dental experiments or operated on patients without anesthesia. I never gave anyone a forked tongue or implanted a whore's jaw with shark's teeth. After the war I emigrated to Buffalo, where in 1953 I was arrested for practicing dentistry without a license, a felony in the state of New York, alas. And that's why you find me living in the cell next to yours."

It all came out in a burst, as though Wallkill regulations required that confession be done promptly, before one reached the bathroom door. There was a lot to digest in Dr. Storch's confession. It was hard to know what to say in reply.

"I'm a salesman," my grandfather said.

As they walked into the bathroom, Dr. Storch stiffened. He sidled around my grandfather and ducked into one of the stalls. At the trough-style sink a prisoner with a cauliflower ear and a barrel chest stood washing his hands. His forearms were blotched with dull tattoos. He closed the tap and went over to one of the continuous loops of linen towel that were mounted in white boxes on the wall. Patiently, he dried the blocks of pink marble that served him for hands. He smiled at my grandfather and said, "Hiya." Preceded by a half-second of cool appraisal, it was a friendly smile. Ex-marine, my grandfather guessed. Middleweight to light heavyweight. Good reach. Bad knees.

"Morning," my grandfather said.

"Name's Hub. Hub Gorman." He winked at my grandfather and called out, "See ya at breakfast, Al." He had a lazy midwestern drawl that reminded my grandfather of Dean Martin's.

If Dr. Storch had a reply, my grandfather didn't catch it. Hub angled his head at the stalls and rolled his eyes in that direction. "Want to watch yourself around that shitbird," he said cheerfully.

My grandfather didn't reply. He had an aversion to people who winked at him. The jury was out on Dr. Storch, but he was reasonably sure he would still hate Hub Gorman a week from now. There was nothing to be done or said about it. Bad blood, pissing contests, ongoing feuds, that would all constitute a surrender to Wallkill, every bit as much as would making a friend. Even if he had to serve the full twenty months, my grandfather's plan was to be always just dropping by.

Gorman stepped toward my grandfather, using the lurch imparted by bad knees as a pretext to push his face in much too close. His breath smelled like a cast-iron skillet.

"Word of advice," he said, arranging his ugly and genial features into a solemn mask. A pregnant pause followed. My grandfather endured it. "Never let a dentist put you under."

He shambled out, whistling a few aimless notes. My grandfather went to one of the urinals. The relief of urination helped to mitigate a feeling of foreboding brought on by the interaction of Dr. Storch and Hub Gorman. Dr. Storch came bustling out of the stall.

"There you are!" he said, as if he and my grandfather had become separated while hiking through the woods. "Ready for breakfast?"

They got to the mess hall one minute past seven. Since it was my grandfather's first breakfast at Wallkill, the guard at the door cut him a break. "Go on, then, you, and get your pancakes," he said, shoving with his shoulder against one of the swinging doors to let my grandfather in. "Don't let it happen again, all right?"

After my grandfather went through, the guard stepped into the doorway. The warmth went out of his voice. "You can just go hungry this morning, Doc," he said.

◑　　◐　　◑

"That's why you always say that?"

"Say what?"

"'Never let a dentist put you under,'" I quoted. "That's what you always say."

"I do?"

"It's one of your major pieces of advice."

"It's just common sense," my grandfather said. "I don't give advice."

I searched my memory to see if I could contradict him. I found statements on the order of *Get the hair dryer away from the bathtub* and *It will heal faster without a Band-Aid* and, of an approaching Doberman, *He can smell that you're afraid.*

"So you're anti-advice," I said.

"I'm not anti-advice, just there's no point to it."

"Okay."

"They wring their hands, should I do this, should I do that. They get seventeen different opinions. Then they do what they planned to do all along. If you give advice, they only blame you when it turns out bad."

I was not entirely certain, and thought of asking him, who this *they* were, pointlessly wasting his time. I decided he was in all likelihood talking about the human race.

"So next time a dentist wants to give me gas, I should just say, 'Go for it.'"

"Feel free. People die every day in dentist's chairs."

"Poor Dr. Storch," I said. "Did you get a little nicer to him later on?"

"I wasn't unkind to him. I just didn't talk to him. I didn't talk to anybody, and I didn't want anybody talking to me. That was the plan."

This did not strike me as necessarily marking a radical change in approach.

"Yeah, but, I mean, that guy Hub was tormenting him for months . . ."

"A year."

"And then you move in right next door. And you haven't been there for the whole history of Dr. Storch getting picked on and called a Nazi and treated like shit, even by the guards, who it sounds like were basically decent to the other prisoners."

"They were more than decent."

"And you're, you know, all muscley and tough-looking and whatever. He couldn't've known what a total, like, badass you were. But I bet he was maybe hoping you might want to stick up for him."

"'Badass.'" My grandfather sampled the flavor of the word. It did not seem to revolt him, but it was nothing he needed ever to sample again.

"I bet he was hoping you'd be his friend. It sounds like he needed one."

"He was," my grandfather said. "He did."

He closed his eyes and appeared to drift for a little while, and I thought the afternoon's conversation might have come to an end. It was nearing four. The palliative care nurse was due at four-thirty. But then his color deepened and he opened his eyes. They had the clarity of pain. The meds were wearing off.

"Every infraction at Wallkill, you got time added to your sentence. Fighting, getting into a dustup with another inmate, they would add a lot of time. Months. *Months* for one fight. The only thing worse was if you tried to escape, 'going over the hill,' they called it. And then? If you got into another fight after that? The way you probably would, if you started something serious with a hard-on like Hub Gorman? They shipped you off to Green Haven. Or Auburn. Maximum security. Where they put the bad guys, *prison* prison. Your mother was fourteen when I went in, Mike. Stuck in Baltimore, where she didn't know a soul. Living with a pool hustler and a grumpy old lady. Stuck there till the day I come get her. And your grandmother . . ."

"I know," I said. "I'm sorry. I'm not reproaching you. Hey, I'm sorry, Grandpa." He was looking out the window. The momzer sat on the top of the fence, facing the ivy-tangled slope, its back to the birdfeeder. Making a show of indifference or surrender. "It's time for your pill."

"I don't want it."

"Come on. I'm really sorry, okay? Come on, you need it. Grandpa." I said *Grandpa* again, but in an Eeyore voice. Then I said it in the voice of Darth Vader. He kept looking out the window at the squirrel, who was so much less trying company than his grandson. "What do you want to take it with?" I said.

He rolled his head in my direction. "Cold beer."

"Seriously? Is that okay?"

He lifted an eyebrow no more than a quarter of an inch. Just high enough to say, *What the fuck difference could it possibly make?*

I went to the kitchen, opened a bottle of Dos Equis, and poured some into a plastic cup. I was fairly new to California at the time, and Mexican beer still held considerable allure. On further reflection, I transferred the beer from the plastic cup into a tall glass and topped it off from the bottle, tilting it so he could swallow his pill without getting a mouthful of foam. I carried the glass of beer into the guest bedroom with a certain ceremoniousness. For some reason I was really looking forward to seeing him drink a little beer.

He put the Dilaudid onto his sueded tongue and washed it down with a healthy swallow of Dos Equis.

"Rock and roll," I said.

He closed his eyes. In his contentment he looked handsome and severe. "Mmm," he said.

"Good, right?"

"Good."

"Have a little more."

I passed the glass to him again and he took another long pull. He handed me back the glass. "Enough," he said. "Thank you. Go ahead, honey, you finish it."

I sat down in the chair and had a sip of beer and watched him smack his lips. The complicated bitterness seemed to linger and resonate on his tongue.

"Storch, what a nudnik," he said. "I must have been nuts."

XXVI

At Wallkill in the evenings your time, for the most part, was your own. The recreation room had table tennis, board games, and a monstrous console with a record player and a radio. Partway through my grandfather's stretch, Dr. Wallack, the warden, had a new Philco television brought in at his own expense and installed beside the radio, so the men could watch the fights on Friday night. The casualty rate for Ping-Pong balls exceeded the rate of resupply, and the records for some reason were devoted primarily to polka music or instruction in Portuguese. Many of the board games were on their fourth or fifth set of tokens, counters, and dice, improvised or crafted by inmates from spools, bottle caps, corks, modeling clay. In the case of Monopoly, the entire board had been redrafted onto a sheet of pine by some wistful or ironic cartographer who substituted the streets of Albany, New York, for those of Atlantic City, discounting all the properties by fifty percent. Reception on the television was dreadful, but many of the men would watch anything that passed across the screen of the Philco, furious blizzards of static, prizefighting ghosts.

Some of the prisoners, having exhausted the recreation room's store of wonders, simply retired to their cells every night. Many joined a prayer circle or weekly Bible study. Most of them took up a hobby sooner or later. They painted in watercolors and oils. They carved duck decoys, built birdhouses, bent sheets of metal into napkin holders. They turned table legs on lathes and then affixed them to tabletops they had coped and mortised. They put in extra time caring for the livestock, in particular the horses. My grandfather naturally found his way to the so-called Hut, where in addition to a Hallicrafters shortwave radio and a darkroom there was a radio repair workbench.

People from the towns and villages around Wallkill would bring their radios to the prison to be repaired for the price of parts. Radios went on the fritz in interesting ways and could be repaired in ways that were satisfying. It was a matter of having the right parts and the proper tools and then ruling out the possibilities one by one. To my grandfather that was more or less a recipe for solace. When he lay awake in his bunk at night, his own problems felt so amorphous; in his dreams they were as infinite as mirrors reflecting one another. But in the radio repair shop, in the innards of a Magnavox, problems could be picked off, hunted down, cornered. They could be eliminated with a cotton swab, a piece of copper braid, or a drop of solder. And he had always loved the sugary tang of solder smoke, hot off the tip of the iron.

Even on those nights when Dr. Storch showed up in the Hut, he was easier for my grandfather to handle or to ignore. Storch would put on a headset and sit for hours in front of the Hallicrafters in the corner. He took in the news from Rádio Nacional in Brazil, from Radio Moscow, from Deutsche Welle. He monitored the chatter and technical rundowns broadcast by stargazers and weather watchers around the world who had been recruited to record and transmit their observations during this International Geophysical Year. He lost himself amid the interlacing transmissions of a million solitary amateurs reaching out to one another in the night.

On the first Friday evening of my grandfather's first October at Wallkill, Hub Gorman wandered into the Hut. It was not a customary haunt of Gorman's, and my grandfather saw at once that he was looking to make trouble. Gorman stood for a moment just inside the doorway. He nodded to my grandfather. His close-cropped skull was indented on one side as by the corner of a two-by-four. In the crevice formed by his brow and cheekbones, his eyes glinted like dimes lost between sofa cushions. He had spotted Dr. Storch in the corner, his back to the door and the trouble that had just shambled through it.

Gorman started across the lab with practiced slowness. The man took his time to do almost anything: roll a cigarette, get out of a chair, finish a bowl of chile con carne, lick the spoon. When a guard gave him an order, he pondered it. His languor was partly a kind of insubordination through indifference. It was also a manner of predation. He was an alligator sunning himself on a rock.

"Gorman," my grandfather said. "C'mere, look at this."

Gorman stopped. He was only two or three feet from Dr. Storch. He cracked his knuckles. It sounded like a string of squibs going off. He turned with the usual show of hastelessness.

My grandfather held up a gaudy gold and red box that once held two dozen Romeo y Julietas.

"Don't smoke," Gorman said. He pointed at his mouth with a knobby finger. "Chew gum."

"Not cigars."

The cleft between Gorman's cheeks and brows diminished. He made his way over to the electronics workbench.

"Don't bring him over here, dumbass," said another prisoner, who had served as a radioman on the *Abraham Lincoln* during the war. "What do you care if he wants to fuck with the Nazi?"

"What is it?" Gorman said. Across the hemisphere of his left arm, some jarhead tattooist had mapped, island by greenish-black island, month by month, year by year, the bloody advance of the 10th Marines on the empire of Japan. The shoulder featured a mushroom cloud labeled NAGASAKI, where the 10th had patrolled the cinders postwar.

"It's a radio. Made out of a cigar box."

It was the work of a night, completed just five minutes or so before Gorman's appearance in the Hut. My grandfather had intended to present it as a gift for the warden's grandson, Theodore, the next time the boy visited; Theodore took an interest in science. He was bright and forthright and not in awe of the prison, its inmates, or his grandfather. Among inmates who pined for their own children, Theodore was a great favorite. They showered him with matchstick Eiffel Towers and tin can roadsters.

My grandfather handed the cigar box to Gorman, who hefted it. "Heavy."

"It runs on a flashlight battery."

My grandfather opened the lid to show Gorman the battery amid the capacitors and wires. He took out the little gray earphone on its braided gray wire, and Gorman poked it into the pleats and convolutions of his deformed right ear. My grandfather showed Gorman how to turn on and tune the radio. Gorman asked him to find the "church station" and my grandfather did. Gorman grinned. "Hey," he said. "A radio in a cigar box. That's pretty neat."

But Gorman did not leave to go play with his new toy, as my grandfather had hoped. He found a stool and sat, listening to a radio preacher. He stared at the back of Dr. Storch's head while the cricket in his cauliflower ear preached damnation. Then, without any apparent stimulus or cue, he stood up, tugged the earphone loose, wrapped the thin wire around three fingers, put the coil of wire inside the cigar box, and laid the box on the stool. The animal inside him was ready to dine.

Gorman sidled over to the radio corner. My grandfather opened his mouth to warn Dr. Storch, but just at that moment the dentist's shoulders tensed, and he turned to face his looming tormentor, eyes level with Guadalcanal on the back of Gorman's wrist. Gorman crouched beside Storch and laid his arm across the man's bony shoulders. He put his mouth to Storch's ear. His lips moved. He spoke into Storch's ear for a long time, renewing his grip on Storch's shoulders every few minutes. His voice was low, and the precise text of his sermon remained a mystery to my grandfather thirty years later. When he was through delivering it, he let Storch shed the yoke of his arm. He unbent himself and looked down at Storch with a pastoral smile. "Okay?" he said, audibly now. "That going to be all right with you?"

Storch was crying. The howls of the ionosphere leaked from the earpiece of the Hallicrafters' headset.

"Alfred? I can't hear you."

"How about you leave the poor bastard alone for a change?" said my grandfather.

Gorman's chin, followed by his lips, was on its way back down to the neighborhood of Storch's left ear. It took a long moment for my grandfather's words to have their effect. Gorman turned to my grandfather, raising himself to his full height. He had three, call it four, inches on my grandfather. In the hollow of his face, his pocket-change eyes flickered. With practiced care, he reviewed the stats he had amassed and recorded so far on my grandfather. The smile that he had pasted to his face fell off. My grandfather never saw it again. Gorman raised his hands to just below his chin, getting his guard up. He agitated the thumbs. "How about I stick these things right into your fucking eyeballs, okay? And then get Alfred here to lick the jelly off them?" he said. The notion genuinely seemed to appeal to him. "Then I can fuck both bloody holes in your skull."

Against his better judgment, my grandfather glanced at Storch, who had stopped crying but whose cheeks were fiery red. The lenses of his eyeglasses were fogged, but my grandfather could see through the fog that Storch expected him—needed him—to do something, to stand up for him, to fight. He needed my grandfather to be his friend.

My grandfather stared at the gaudy labels of radio tubes in their boxes ranged on a shelf against the wall and serially counted to ten, first in English, then in German, and finally in Yiddish. Even if he could survive a fight with Hub Gorman, which was far from certain, months or years might be added to his bid as a result. He might be transferred to someplace far worse than Wallkill, someplace where the fights were butchery and the sentences long. And in the end

Storch would still be a hapless nudnik of an ex-dentist, and my mother and grandmother would be obliged to stumble onward, lost and alone.

Gorman picked up the cigar box, took out the earphone, and poked it back into his ear. He turned the knob that controlled tuning and stopped at something that sounded like it might be jump blues, a 4/4 scratch of drums. Gorman bobbed his head in time, then winked at my grandfather. "A radio in a cigar box," he said. "That is just neat."

That night the shortwave frequencies lit up with the news that the Soviet Union had used a rocket to deploy Sputnik, the first artificial satellite, into orbit around the earth. The satellite transmitted a signal every three tenths of a second on a frequency of twenty megahertz, and between those pulses another signal on forty megahertz. Radio amateurs and shortwave listeners all over the world were able to tune in and listen to what struck many of them as the voice of the future itself.

Dr. Storch did not hear the signals, and my grandfather did not learn about Sputnik's deployment until the next day. As soon as Gorman was gone, Dr. Storch hung the radio headset from its peg on the wall, got up from the swivel chair, and walked out of the Hut without looking at my grandfather. When he got back to his cell, he swallowed fifty-two aspirin tablets he had painstakingly accumulated over a period of years by pretending to suffer from chronic headaches.

That night a grinding sound woke my grandfather, like a key being turned in the ignition of an engine that was already running. It was the sound of Dr. Storch vomiting. My grandfather ignored it for as long as he could, which was not very long, although it felt like forever. He got up and went into Dr. Storch's cell, reeling at the rancid smell of undigested aspirin. Dr. Storch lay conscious and making a sound that was somewhere between a low rhythmic moan of pain that would not stop throbbing and a sigh of unbearable regret.

"Never mind," he said to my grandfather, though he was confused and did not seem to know it was my grandfather grabbing him, dragging him out into the corridor, raising an alarm. "Never mind, never mind."

After the medical staff had come with a stretcher and carried Dr. Storch off to the prison's ambulance, my grandfather got hold of a bucket and mop and did what he could about the mess in Storch's cell so that it would be all right when they returned him. They would keep him a few days, then bring him back, and it would all start over again for him with Gorman, only now it would be worse. Gorman would be encouraged by his near-miss, and Storch would be more vulnerable than ever.

My grandfather cleaned himself up and returned to his own cell. He lay on his cot for hours, trying to focus his thoughts on his family and on the time remaining until the day they would be reunited, which diminished every day by a greater percentage than the one before. He powered up the Zeiss projector in his skull and eagerly sought Cassiopeia and Andromeda in their courses—and Cepheus, the husband and father. *That's you*, he told himself. *You are Cepheus. You are not Perseus. You are not a hero. It's not your job to rescue anybody.* But he could not sustain the planetarium show tonight. There was too much light pouring in from the stanchion outside his window. There was still a tang of vomit in the air.

Storch was going to be kept under observation at the county hospital for four days. On the first day of his absence my grandfather told the guard in charge of the grounds crew that he needed fence wire to repair the antenna of a "lousy made-in-Japan" radio set that had come into the shop. For a purpose directly opposed to his present one, my grandfather had earned the guards' trust. He was believed. Once inside the potting shed, my grandfather filled the rolled cuffs of his trousers with Hi-Yield. He had noticed the grounds crew mixing this crystalline white powder with water and applying it to tree stumps at the edge of the meadow. The crew called it *stump killer*; it acted to soften the stumps so that rain was enough to dissolve them. The active ingredient was basically chemical fertilizer: potassium nitrate.

The second day and third day of Storch's absence, my grandfather devoted to obtaining a quantity of sugar. This was trickier; the kitchen kept an eye on sugar because it could be used to make hooch. The cubes were counted and doled out with tongs, two to a prisoner per meal. My grandfather would have to stockpile for weeks. He thought of another approach. It was foolish, dangerous, and shameless but it would be efficient, and anyway, shamelessness was often the missing piece of many otherwise brilliant schemes.

A word that often cropped up when people talked or wrote about the warden of the Wallkill prison, Dr. Walter M. Wallack, was *tireless*. For every problem that arose in the life and administration of the prison, he came up with three possible solutions. He was always on the move. You never saw him sitting down. He arrived early and went home late. Part of this tirelessness was no doubt constitutional or even moral (he was a good man), but you could not discount the fact that he consumed—the legend varied—between fifteen and twenty cups of coffee a day, black and sweet. He kept a percolator in his office, on top of a low bookshelf by the door, and an ample supply of sugar.

After breakfast on the second day my grandfather begged one of the cooks for an empty drum of Quaker oats. That evening he went to the Hut and built a radio inside the cardboard drum. He sank a tuning knob through the *Q* of *Quaker* and a volume pot through the *O* of *Oats*. He cannibalized a speaker cone from a junked unit and cut a grille for it out of the drum's paper lid. The next day he got permission to deliver the radio to Wallack in his office.

He found Wallack behind his desk—standing up, as usual. There was a nice leather swivel chair, but Wallack almost never sat down in it. He stood, and he leaned on the top of a filing cabinet when he needed to jot something in his legal pad. The desk was bare except for a telephone, a calendar blotter, and a crude paper rocket, a foot high, clearly if unconsciously modeled on the V-2.

"Very kind of you," Wallack said, taking the radio from my grandfather. "Very clever. Theo will love it, I'm sure."

My grandfather showed Wallack how to operate the radio, suggesting that the warden move closer to the window to get better reception. He moved closer to the door and the shelf with the coffee percolator. Dr. Wallack turned to face the window and twiddled the knobs. He found Mozart. He found Eddie Fisher. While his back was to the room, my grandfather leaned over and grabbed one of a dozen unopened boxes of sugar cubes on the shelf below the percolator. He reached around to grab hold of his own shirt collar, jerked it away from his neck, and dropped the box of sugar cubes down the back of his shirt.

Dr. Wallack turned back and my grandfather had to put his eyes somewhere, so he put them on the rocket. A loving but clumsy hand had shaped the fins, nosecone, and sweep of the fuselage from strips of thin card around a tube left over from a roll of paper towels. The paper was crusted with dried mucilage and blotched with red, white, and blue paint, but the rocket's proportions were pretty good. There were stars and stripes and the legend u.s.a. written twenty times all up and down the thing in execrable handwriting.

"Theo's work," Dr. Wallack said.

"I figured."

"Gone space-mad, like all the other boys since Sputnik went up. Building rockets. Rockets to the Moon! Trying to figure out how to make them really fly."

"Interesting problem," my grandfather said. "I'll think about it." *All you would need*, he idly thought, *is a little bit of sugar.*

He backed out of the room, scuttled past the warden's secretary, and then hurried to his cell to hide the sugar cubes.

On the third night after lights-out, my grandfather sat on his cot with some tape, wire, a flashlight battery, and the guts of an old clock from the scrap heap in the Hut. Working by the blare of light through the window, he ground the cubes to powder in the box and then mixed in KNO3, packing the sugar box as tightly as he could with the "candy," as it was known. After an hour's patient work he had a configuration of wire, battery, candy, and time that was both plausible and strictly NUR ZU DEMONSTRATIONSZWECKEN. He was not sure how plausible it was that Hub Gorman would know how to construct even a rudimentary explosive device like this one, but he also wasn't sure it really mattered. The mere presence of it in Gorman's cell, once my grandfather had tipped off the guards, would likely be enough to get Gorman transferred out of Wallkill to Green Haven or Auburn or someplace where he really belonged. Hub Gorman did not belong in a prison that had beehives, a creamery, a complete *Encyclopaedia Britannica,* and a photo enlarger.

XXVII

Dr. Storch was returned to the prison in the ambulance on the tenth of October, a Tuesday. When my grandfather heard about it after chow he went to the Hut and looked in through the door. Dr. Storch was at the S-38, lenses glinting, face gaunt and livid as an El Greco Christ's in the glow of the radio's half-moons. He had the headset on and his movements on the dial were exceedingly fine, as if homing in on a single voice in the great megahertz chorale. My grandfather felt his eyes burn, and the muscles of his chest seemed to curl like a fist around his heart. When he first learned that the dentist would survive his suicide attempt, he had felt powerful relief; the news about Hub Gorman had added a disturbing wrinkle. On seeing Dr. Storch's gaunt suffering face again, however, all he felt was shame. He ought to have stood up for the poor bastard in the first place. He left the Hut, went to his cell, and waited for the lights to be put out.

He woke to a chill touch, long dry fingers pulling at his wrist.

"Shh."

He sat up and looked out the window of his cell. It was never easy to judge the time of night with the floodlights spilling in the yard outside. Call it about an hour before dawn. Dr. Storch winced, to show that he was sorry for waking my grandfather. He held up both hands and made a pushing motion that said, *I know, I know, but trust me.* He gestured to the doorway of the cell and then to the ceiling. He wanted my grandfather to follow him up to the roof.

A visit to the roof of this particular cell block was an exploit often discussed among the Wallkill population. It was a subject of debate.

Generally, it was agreed to be possible, but no one among the current crop of inmates would, or could, acknowledge having done it. A solid minority believed that the roof passage was a legend that had originated as deliberate misinformation, a trap laid by some unscrupulous guard to lure unwary prisoners into infraction. These men claimed that a guard was paid a bounty every time he caught an inmate in the act of trying to escape.

My grandfather pulled on a shirt and trousers and started to put on his shoes. Storch shook his head. They went out into the corridor. They stepped softly, and kept their thighs apart so that a whisper of twill would not betray them. They turned onto another corridor and went along past the doors of other men's cells to the end. There was a blank brick wall about five feet wide.

Dr. Storch crouched down by the base of the wall. He reached into the waistband of his trousers. It was too dark for my grandfather to see what he had in the waistband, but later he found out that it was two heavy-duty paperclips, unbent up to the last involution so that they made a pair of hooks. Dr. Storch slid these hooks under the bottom edge of the wall about three feet apart. He held his breath and let it out and lifted the bottom of the wall up and outward. It was a hinged wooden panel covered with a layer of bricks cut very thin and applied in a way that matched the course of the genuine wall. Behind it, a rectangular opening of the same dimensions as the panel led into an air duct. My grandfather afterward theorized that at one time there had been a grille over the opening and that some clever prisoner had replaced it with the panel, camouflaged so well that, when installed, it looked as if it belonged.

Dr. Storch sat down and slid his legs through, then poured the rest of himself into the hole. My grandfather heard a creak of metal, a pause, then another creak. Pause, creak, pause: The sound took on the familiar cadence of a man climbing a ladder. My grandfather hesitated. He had already taken too many crazy chances in the past week. He knew that following Storch would be tempting fate. If this exploit went wrong, it would be hard not to look back and say that he was asking to get caught. God knew he had enough on his conscience to justify that view of the matter.

Inside the airduct was a smell like the taste of a new filling. My grandfather grasped the first of the rungs and pulled himself up through the darkness. The rungs had been crafted, no doubt by the same gifted engineer, from the springs of shock absorbers, likely pilfered from the prison motor pool. Whoever the guy was, he had compressed each spring between two heavy blocks of wood, clad with pieces of tire, and then allowed the spring to expand across the duct. Pressure and rubber tread held the rungs in place at the back of the duct, leaving barely enough room for the vertical passage of a man. A little under three minutes after they began the climb, they were standing on the roof. It was a clear night full of stars. A poignant smell of leaf smoke blew in from the backyard of some fortunate free man.

"Which way?" my grandfather said in just above a whisper, having deduced what Dr. Storch had brought him to see.

"Northeast," Dr. Storch whispered back. "And it ought to be soon. I've been listening all night as the reports came in."

Anticipating that someone—the U.S. or Russia—would manage sooner or later to loft a satellite into orbit, a Harvard astronomer and well-known science fiction fan named Fred Whipple had taken advantage of the publicity around the International Geophysical Year to organize a network of amateurs connected by shortwave radio. Upon news of Sputnik's launch they had mobilized themselves all over the country, going out every night to watch the sky and report details of time and orientation.

They stood in the cold and the dark. Far away the lights of some town glittered. My grandfather inclined his face to the vast heavens until his neck began to ache.

"I was told there was an explosion," Storch said.

"Hell of a thing."

"He was making moonshine?"

"So goes the theory."

There had been nothing left of the candy bomb in Gorman's cell, and very little left of the cell and Gorman. There was an attempt at investigation, but the scene had been so heavily contaminated by the first guards to respond to the sound of the blast that no firm conclusions were ever drawn. My grandfather couldn't figure it out, either, but he was inclined to blame the detonation on some unforeseen interaction between the clockworks in the oatmeal box and the radio in the cigar box.

"My friend," said the German, his voice thickened by emotion, "was it you?"

"Only very indirectly," my grandfather said. He told Dr. Storch about the sugar and the KNO3 and explained his theory of the radio's detonation, which was really not much of a theory, as Dr. Storch pointed out.

"I would be more inclined to blame a discharge of static electricity," Dr. Storch said. "Perhaps from Gorman's wool blanket. At this time of the year, the air is so dry. I'm sure you've noticed the sparks when your hands pass across the bedclothes in the dark."

"Interesting," my grandfather said.

"Here's something else you may find interesting: I feel I'd like to inform you that I'm not here for practicing dentistry without a license," Dr. Storch said. "I thought you should know that. I've never told anybody else. I certainly never told Hub Gorman."

My grandfather waited.

"The reason I'm here is that one day I had a little boy in my chair, a very nice, well-mannered twelve-year-old boy named Walter Onderdonk. And for reasons that remain beyond my understanding, I made a mistake with the gas. A big mistake. A terrible mistake." Dr. Storch started to cry softly. And even though he was a German, and a nudnik, and a pain in the ass, my grandfather put his arm around the poor bastard.

"Oh," Dr. Storch said.

He pointed to the northeast. My grandfather felt his heart leap. A star had popped loose from its constellation and gone rolling down the sky. It was falling, but it was not a falling star. It did not flare up and wink out and leave a glowing ghost mark on the retinas. It just kept falling, and falling, and falling, until it disappeared behind the curvature of the earth. It was a prisoner of gravity like everything in the universe. Its orbit would degrade. It would spiral inward until it hit the air and then burn up and break apart and leave nothing but vapor and a memory. And then in time the memory itself would fade like vapor. But to my grandfather, watching secretly from the roof of the Wallkill prison, the passage of that chunk of radiant metal seemed to describe an everlasting arc of freedom. "Wow," he said. "Look at that."

"Sputnik!" Dr. Storch said with a childish glee.

My grandfather thought about correcting Dr. Storch. It was not Sputnik itself, which was far too small to be seen by the naked human eye. What they had seen was a section of the rocket that had boosted the satellite into orbit, burnished by the rays of the imminent sun. He decided that for now he would let it pass. "Thanks," he said instead. "Thank you, Storch, for bringing me to see it."

"Please," Dr. Storch said. "It's the least I could do."

A feather of blue brushed the bottom of the sky like breath on a mirror. It was time to get back to their cells. Neither of them moved. They stood there on the roof in the darkness. *I want to see it again,* my grandfather thought.

"Well," Dr. Storch said. "Shall we . . . What shall we do?"

My grandfather was surprised to find that he had an answer ready for this question, and surprised by the answer itself, though he saw now that it had been percolating inside him since the day of the sugar heist in Dr. Wallack's office.

"How about we make ourselves a rocket?" said my grandfather.

XXVIII

I never knew my other grandfather. One afternoon about a month before I was born, he sat down with his brother—Sam Chabon, my Uncle Sammy—for their weekly lunch at a midtown deli where, on every table in the place of butter, they put out a pot of schmaltz. When they had finished their pastrami sandwiches, my other grandfather walked Sammy back to the latter's offices, on the fourth floor of the Lincoln Building, a couple of blocks away. One of Sammy's suppliers had just delivered a sample, a working model of the nuclear submarine *Nautilus*, which they were planning to bring out in time for Christmas. It was, Sammy said, a marvel. It had functional ballast tanks that operated by means of a pocket-size circular bellows and a length of plastic tubing. A large washtub had been brought in to the office and filled with water. The salesmen had been playing with it all morning. My other grandfather was eager to get a crack at it.

The elevators that served the Lincoln Building's lower floors were undergoing maintenance that day. Neither brother was a patient man. They took the stairs. As he rounded the third-floor landing, Sammy heard his brother, a flight of stairs below him, cluck his tongue and sigh as if experiencing a moment of regret. An ambulance was sent for, but my other grandfather died on the way to the hospital.

Three weeks later my mother went into labor. She was twenty and made quick work of the job. Eight days after that I exchanged my foreskin for the dead man's Hebrew name. In my non-memory of my other grandfather, he is a human spaldeen, round and pink. His cheeks and pate shine as if smeared with rich fat.

My other grandfather had made a living all his life as a printer and typesetter. During the thirties he worked for a firm that printed movie posters. In the same West Side loft building as the print shop, there was a company that dealt in cheap novelties and tools for practical jokers. One day he happened to hear that the novelty company had an opening for a salesman. He passed the word to his kid brother, who got the job.

Sam Chabon went on the road selling onion gum, black soap, ink-squirting boutonnieres. He had an affable nature threaded with a strand of cruelty, and like a fat chef he took pleasure in his stock in trade. But by the early fifties his career had stalled. Raises came less frequently. Promotions passed him by. His ideas were ignored or misappropriated. He went through life trying doorknobs on locked doors. One day he found a knob that turned.

On a wet Friday afternoon at Jack Dempsey's in 1954, he struck up a conversation with his neighbor at the bar. The man, like Uncle Sammy, was nursing a Tom Collins. At his feet in a pool of rain stood a wooden sample case that might hold scientific instruments or specialty glassware. The man turned out to be a chemist for Corning. In his spare time he had designed a process for manufacturing imitation bone from one of the new synthetic plastics that were revolutionizing every field, including cheap novelties, where they made possible gags of great realism like Fake Vomit and Fly in Ice Cube. The chemist showed my uncle what was in the sample case. He stood it upright on the bar and opened it like a book. Nestled in flocked notches on the left side were a human mandible, a femur, two ribs, five vertebrae, and a patella, molded from plastic, all life-size. On the right was a 1:4-scale plastic model of a full human skeleton and a wire stand for displaying it.

Sammy was enchanted by the model skeleton dangling by its three-inch skull from the hook of the wire stand. He shook its little hand. He made it kick a maraschino cherry across the tabletop. He articulated its jaw while talking in the voice of Señor Wences.

"How much do you get for these?" he asked the imitation-bones man. "I love it."

The imitation-bones man was taken aback and a little offended. His product had serious purpose. It was intended as an educational aid for medical students, biology classrooms. It was a realistic and accurate scientific tool. "I don't think you understand," he said. "That's just a demonstration model. I made it small so it would be portable, fit in a sample case."

"I don't think *you* understand," Sammy said, knowing a novelty when he saw one. "Make it two inches smaller, I'll place an order for five thousand of them."

Two years later he was headquartered in the Lincoln Building and clearing two million dollars a year. His angle was science and educational value. The novelties he sold purported, at least implicitly, to prepare America's youth for the challenges of a Cold War future. His product list included a Paper Airplane Wind Tunnel and a Pocket Periscope, but the sales leader had remained the Exact Skeleton Model, advertised in national magazines ("Obviously a must for everyone's closet"), shipped in the hundreds of thousands to purchasers all over the world.

By 1957, however, business had begun to flag. There was competition from Japan, as accurate but cheaply made mini-skeletons flooded the market. Uncle Sammy looked for ways to lower his production costs. He ran into labor trouble, union activity. One day a pinochle crony happened to mention that he played golf with the fellow in charge of a state program that provided prisoner labor to private manufacturers in return for vocational training. That was how the so-called Bone Factory had come to occupy a production floor at the prison where my grandfather served his sentence.

Sammy paid regular visits to Wallkill, keeping an eye on operations. At first he stayed at an inn in the village nearby, but there was a guest room in the warden's house on the grounds, and after Sammy showed up two or three times bearing a bottle of the warden's brand of rye, he received a standing invitation to sleep there whenever he visited. He could have let his production manager handle the chore, but, like many visitors, he found something soothing in the ambience of the prison with its dairying and forestry, its choral group singing chanteys and spirituals, its population making themselves useful, sweeping the winding paths between ivy-clad buildings. He had come to see himself as harried by work and hectored by his family, and when he visited the prison, he would fantasize that he, too, had been relieved of his burdens along with his liberty. He slept well in the warden's guest room, waking refreshed, and would return to the city ready to contend with the latest importunements.

He was standing at the window of the guest bedroom early one morning, still in his pajamas, when he noticed a group of men walking across the oval of the running track. Two of the men were uniformed guards, two were prisoners in gray, and one appeared to be the warden, in a plaid hunting jacket and galoshes, walking beside a boy of twelve or so, the grandson. Theodore. One of the prisoners was a fireplug, chesty and bowlegged, humping a large packing crate. The other prisoner was tall and thin and walking backward in front of the prisoner with the big box. He was talking with his hands. Every so often he stumbled, and once he bumped into a guard, but he never stopped walking backward or talking. Even at a distance of a hundred yards, Sammy pegged the guy for a nudnik.

When the five men came to the wire fence that enclosed the dairy pasture, the guards and the warden struggled over it. The nudnik folded himself like a note and slid his body into the slot between the wires. The fireplug hoisted the crate over the fence, consigned it to the guards—it took both of them to hold it—and leapfrogged a fence post with both hands. The guards gave him back the packing crate. The nudnik hung back a moment and then followed the fireplug out into the pasture. It was just past sunrise and there was not a cow to be seen.

Sammy went to his overnight bag and took out his own personal pair of Powerful Pocket Binoculars. He saw the warden holding the boy back, the guards keeping their distance, not going much beyond the fence. The fireplug carried the box deeper into the pasture, coming right into line with the window of the warden's guest bedroom. He moved fast and the nudnik struggled to keep up.

The two prisoners began to empty and assemble the crate's contents into a configuration that left Sammy puzzled. As far as he could tell, they had stood a long slender cage of latticework on end in the middle of the field. It reached nearly to the fireplug's waist and seemed to have been made out of some kind of wire or narrow-gauge pipe. The two men anchored it to the turf with wire cleats. The fireplug removed what appeared to be a length of pipe from the box, fitted at one end with vanes. Some kind of turbine, maybe, or an anemometer. It was lowered into the latticed cage. The prisoners knelt down on either side of the thing, making adjustments. The fireplug had his back to Sammy, and his body blocked the view of whatever they were up to for a good two or three minutes. The warden fit a cigarette to his face and one of the guards lit it for him.

At last the nudnik clambered back, stumbling, in a hurry—afraid, Uncle Sammy almost would have said. The fireplug rose and took ten slow steps backward, then counted another ten. He stopped. The warden and the guards came away from the fence and crowded in behind the fireplug, who seemed to be in charge of the operation.

Toward the bottom of the latticed cage, a light kindled, intense and blue. It was like the powder burst of a camera, but it was not a flash. Its light held as it grew downward toward the ground. Presently, my great-uncle caught the sound of it, even through the window glass. It reminded him of the sound of water spraying from a fire hydrant tapped by street kids on an August afternoon. It was a sound that filled him with a pleasant anticipation of mischief.

With a shimmy and a hesitation, the finned tube that Sammy had taken for a wind gauge peeped its head out from the top of the latticework cage. It took one slow second to climb twenty feet into the air and then two more seconds to streak, an arcing shimmer, into the heavens, canted two degrees off the perpendicular. Sammy lost sight of the thing against some clouds and then, a moment later, in a patch of blue five hundred feet higher, found it again. His heart slipped its accustomed bonds.

"A rocket," he said to the guest bedroom of the warden's house.

It burst like a kernel of popcorn, sprouting a sudden white blossom that turned out to be a parachute.[*]

Thin and high, the boy's voice carried to Sammy's ear: *Wow!* The kid was literally jumping up and down with excitement as the rocket—a rocket!—floated, broken-necked, down from heaven. The nudnik waited for it, drifting now this way, now that way, head tilted back, a center fielder getting under a lazy can of corn. As the rocket slanted past him, he leaped up and snatched at it, and missed it, and fell over, and lost his glasses. The rocket lay down on the grass. The parachute draped itself over the rocket. The nudnik found his glasses. He picked up the rocket and the chute and carried them back to the fireplug. The two prisoners shook hands, without letting go, for as long as it took the warden and the guards to reach them. Pats on the back, more shaking of hands all around.

Sam tried to express, in that moment, the spasm of joy passing through him as he watched the launch of my grandfather's first model rocket.

"I could sell a ton of those things," he said, fogging the windowpane, wiping it clean with the cuff of his pajamas.

---

[*] Crafted, according to my grandfather, from a silk slip donated by the warden's wife.

XXIX

I was stretched out on the sofa in my mother's living room, reading *Nine Stories*. It was a sofa of the seventies, covered in synthetic wool of lunar gray, poufy yet severe. Beyond my bare feet, a set of sliding glass doors gave onto a redwood deck. At the back of the house the hillside fell away with alarming verticality. The trees here had been topped to permit constant monitoring, as by some fairy-tale miser, of the two-bridge view in which a puzzling percentage of the house's value was felt to lie. Down below at the western verge of Oakland, car lights scrolled along the interchanges like cryptic headlines on a zipper. San Francisco was an amber radiance of fog.

I can't say for sure which of the nine I was reading when my mother came in that night, but my favorite has always been "For Esmé—with Love and Squalor." From the first time I read it, in high school, this story and its protagonist had reminded me of my grandfather. The scant details I'd been provided at the time about his army career—ETO, a brief stay in London before being shipped over to France, some kind of intelligence work portrayed variously as "clerical in nature" or "nothing too exciting"—seemed to coincide with the situation of Salinger's autobiographical Sergeant X.* Nobody had ever used the phrase "nervous breakdown" or suggested

---

* There was a physical similarity, too, judging from the one photograph of Salinger I knew: thick black hair, pockmarked cheeks, long nose, eyebrow skeptically arched. My grandfather, for his part, always seemed to enjoy it when people told him he looked like the actor Robert Alda.

that my grandfather had not returned from the war with his "faculties intact," as Esmé puts it in the story. I had never thought of my grandfather as a man suffering from lingering effects of the condition his generation called "combat fatigue." And yet Salinger's story seemed to offer an explanation for something about my grandfather that must have felt to me, always, like it needed to be explained.

My mother came in holding a glass of Scotch, which she took poured over a handful of ice. She had on an old pink nightgown, wrapped in a brown chenille robe. It was late. The night nurse had been on the job for a couple of hours, time my mother had spent combing out tangles in my grandfather's taxes. Apparently, she had found an error in my grandfather's favor that would save him nearly a thousand dollars. That explained the tumbler of Johnnie Walker. She was holding an old photo album, bound in black cardboard impressed to resemble grained leather. The spine at top and bottom had split and frayed.

"Hey, I wanted to show you this," she said.

She sat down beside me. Her hair was damp and she smelled of Prell shampoo. It was her essential odor, cool as mint and somehow impervious. The actual fragrance of Prell was not at all minty, but it had a mentholated color and in the old TV commercials, a pearl would be shown descending languid and impervious through the green depths of a bottle of Prell. I never figured out what the ability of Prell to retard a pearl's descent implied about its hair-cleaning power, but the sight of that descent, like my mother, was always quietly impressive. As she sat down beside me on the Herculon sofa, the photo album snowed gray feathers of rotted paper.

"This was your grandmother's."

Across the album's cover in a slab-serif type, the word SOUVENIRS was stamped in gilt that had flaked away. There was a kind of fake-leather strap that wrapped around the album's front edge from back to front, where it snapped into a clasp, like a diary with no lock. I was pretty sure I had never seen the thing before.

"I don't know what all he's been telling you," my mother said.

I thought her tone held something accusatory, of my grandfather or of me for my narrative appetite. But I might have been wrong about that.

"He's not telling me anything."

"I heard him telling you about my mother."

"Well, yeah."

"And how I had to go live with Uncle Ray while he was serving time."

"Yeah, he told me that."

She had a certain eyebrow arch of her own that she could wield. I acknowledged that my grandfather, come to think of it, might have been telling me some things.

"Well, I just thought you might like to see this. It was one of the two belongings my mother brought over with her."

"What was the other thing?"

"Me."

"Oh, right, duh."

"I took it with me to Baltimore," she said. "When I went to live with Uncle Ray. I found it in the attic right before we moved."

"In the house in Ho-Ho-Kus?"

"We were packing to leave. Your grandmother had already gone into the hospital. I found this and just kind of grabbed it. I don't know why. I'd never seen it before." She ran a finger across the flaking gilt legend on the cover. "Souvenirs, as in *memories* in French." She drank a little of the Scotch. Her eyes widened and she let out a gasp. "Whoa."

"Easy, there."

"All right," she said. "Okay." But she just sat there, looking down at the album in her lap.

"Want to do this another time?"

"No, it's fine. I just haven't, you know, it's been a while. Since I looked." She took another, longer pull. This time it seemed to go down more easily. "The funny thing is, she didn't really have any photos. To put in the album. I mean, she had four. That was page one."

I tried to imagine how I would feel about the only four pictures to survive from the entire photographic record of my life to date—more or less the age of my grandmother when she arrived in the U.S. They might be four that I had chosen for their personal value, true likenesses, moments I could not bear to lose. They might be random shots: a portrait of my acne and my orthodontia, a grinning blur that was my father's face as he turned to laugh at something out of the frame. I knew that either way they would be precious to me, but having endured what my grandmother had endured did not mean I would be able to bring myself to look at them.

"At first I didn't understand. If you only have four pictures, why buy a whole album? Then I thought, *Well, probably she meant to fill it with pictures of her new life here.* And then maybe she forgot. Or got another album, I don't know. We had plenty of other albums, you've seen them."

"Sure."

"So I decided I would take it. Fill in the rest of the pages myself."

"The rest of it was blank when you found it?"

She nodded and let out a long breath. Its turbulence wove a paisley of dust motes in the slant of lamplight.

"We can skip that page."

"No." She undid the clasp and opened the old-fashioned album to its first black page. It was the kind of album where the photos had to be fixed to the pages by means of self-adhesive mounts like little corners of black crown molding. There were sixteen corners pasted to the page, neat and true. Four labels, tan rectangles with indented corners, each bearing a legend written with a fountain pen in the continental hand I remembered from birthday cards enclosing twenty-dollar checks. *Mère, vingt ans. Père. Toi. Toi et moi.* Above each label, inside a rectangular space delimited by the photo corners, was a region of black paper. The pictures themselves were all missing.

"What?" my mother said to the photo album. She lifted it from her lap to look pointlessly underneath. She set it back down. "Oh no," she said.

She started flipping pages, and we flashed through the world in which her childhood had come to an end, recorded in grids of black-and-white squares, pictures unmistakably taken with a Kodak Brownie. She flipped them faster and as she went, she was breathing through her nostrils like someone trying to hold her temper or her worst fears in check. The pages creaked as she turned them. I glimpsed a row of motel cabins, a motel swimming pool shaped like an arrowhead, a motel sign with a neon thunderbird. A beach at low tide, a beach awash in umbrellas, my mother with a bare-chested lifeguard. My mother in a poodle skirt nervously passing a hot dog on a bun to a bear on a chain. Uncle Ray looking sporting in a double-breasted suit and an open-shirt collar with a clocked foulard. My mother in short shorts and a halter top, posing beside the wooden Indian of a cigar shop. My mother, too young to drive, behind the wheel of a parked Alfa convertible. Another print of the picture my grandfather had brought with him from Florida, the one that showed my mother riding bareback in a bathing suit, holding a bow and arrow. A jockey in silks posing with a glossy thorough-bred, squinting at a man in a snap-brim hat. Other shots of horses and the fences and grandstands of racetracks. Shots that featured my mother or Uncle Ray with a zaftig little woman who had smoldering, even angry, eyes. Shots of my mother or her uncle posed beside other women with lipstick-dark mouths. My mother and Uncle Ray in front of a billiard parlor. My mother in front of the Lincoln Memorial, the gates of Pimlico racetrack, some historical palisaded fort. My mother astride an artillery cannon, like Kipling's Kim.

The world before my birth, a world of infinite degrees of gray. Gray ocean, gray blondes, gray ketchup, gray pines. Apart from the horseback shot, I had never seen any of these pictures. I had heard only the dimmest rumors of the period they recorded. I wanted to stop her hand from turning the pages and sink, like the pearl in the shampoo bottle, into this gray prehistory, this evidence of the years my mother had spent running wild. The pictures flicked past. The pages flapped.

On the last page there was no photograph. A sheet of paper had been glued in with a streak of mucilage. The mucilage had crystalized into sugary brown grains. The paper had been turned on its side and glued horizontally to fit it in the album. It was a mimeographed page torn from some kind of typed newsletter, yellow as the filter cotton of a cigarette butt. Rusty vampire bite of a stapler. Ink deepened to a bruise-black shade of purple. Before my mother slammed the album shut, I had time to glimpse the words *Lunch Menu, crabapple garnish, Poet's Corner,* and my grandmother's name, all typed in the refined-looking twelve-pitch size they used to call elite.

"Well, shit," said my mother.

"Did they fall out?"

"I don't know."

"Were they in there before? When did you see them last?"

"I don't know."

My mother clutched the album to her chest. I could see that she was running through the recent history of the album's whereabouts and movements, trying to work her way back to the last time she had seen it intact. She looked stricken. I was surprised. Anyone would have been upset by such a loss, naturally. I just would have expected my mother to try to hide her distress.

"I don't know," she repeated. She put down the album, got up from the couch, and went downstairs to the sewing room, where I was staying. In the closet by the daybed where I slept, she kept the few old things—souvenirs—that she had held on to. She had always been the kind of woman who kept her balloon aloft and sailing by cutting away sandbags and throwing nonessentials over the side. Her years spent among the karmic adventurers of the East Bay lent an aura of liberation from the chains of maya to her habit of discarding the evidence of her passage through the world. But it was not that. Sometimes, if she had an extra glass of wine, she might tell her current boyfriend or whomever she was living with that during her years "on the loose" with Uncle Ray, she had learned to travel light, so that when it was time to make a dash for it, there would be nothing to trip you up or hold you down. At this point the current boyfriend was likely to sense a metaphorical drift in the conversation and consider himself warned. But it was not that, either. My mother's lack of attachment to the past and its material embodiments went deeper than principle, training, or metaphor. It was an unbreakable habit of loss.

"Nope," she said. "God damn it."

She had been crouching in the closet's doorway, searching the shelves of a wire rack that also held her box of 45s and an old Carmen Miranda doll whose fruit hat said HAVANA. She had searched the floor underneath the rack, lifted the lids on her boxes of buttons and rick-rack, rifled the banker's box that held all her patterns from Butterick and Simplicity. Now she sank down and sat on the floor. She pulled her knees to her chest. She covered her face with her hands.

"I guess they're still at Daddy's," she theorized in a calm tone of voice from behind her hands. "In the storage space. The album was just in a box, the pictures were probably at the bottom. I should have checked. I should have dug around."

"I'm sure they're there," I said. "You can get them next time."

Now I understood why I had never seen the album. It must have been buried in my grandparents' storage space at the Skyview, then followed my grandfather, along with a whole lot of other crap, to Florida. When she'd gone to collect her father at Fontana Village, my mother had brought the album back to Oakland. I wondered why she had wanted it and if, were I to ask her, she would be able to tell me.

"But Mike, I mean, God knows when they fell out," she said. "It could have been years ago. Oh." She was still hiding her face behind the screen of her fingers. "I just feel sick."

"Mom, it's okay."

"I'm so sorry."

"They're just pictures. Pictures get lost."

It was the kind of thing she would have said, and I knew it would not strike her as callous or unsympathetic, but I did not believe it myself. It made my heart ache to think that the only known pictures of my grandmother's life before the war had been lost. But I wasn't going to tell her anything like that.

"You're right," she said. "Obviously, I haven't missed them before. Why should I care now?" She lowered her hands and sat up straight, as if she had recovered from the shock. "I just really wanted to show you," she said. She started, tentatively, to cry.

"Aw, Mom," I said. I waited. I had not seen my mother cry since the days when my father was busy setting fire to our lives. I didn't know how to console her or if she even wanted to be, or could be, consoled. She had given very few clues over the years to help me understand how she felt about the things that she had lost in her lifetime.

"How about some tea," I said.

"That might be nice. But I don't want to have trouble sleeping."

"I got some decaf Earl Grey at the Lucky."

"All right." She wiped her eyes with the cuff of a nightgown sleeve. "I'll have some decaf Earl Grey."

I went to the kitchen to put a kettle on. On the way I passed the guest room and heard the click of knitting needles. Lola, the night nurse, was a big knitter. She was knitting me a remarkably hideous pair of argyle socks in the colors of the Philippine flag, which for years afterward I considered to be my lucky socks, right up to the day they disappeared.

I made a pot of tea. My mother came in and sat down at the kitchen table, carrying the glass of Scotch. She poured the whiskey into a teacup and then topped it off with tea from the pot. The photo album lay between us. I opened it to its first page, the four empty frames with their French inscriptions. "Show me anyway," I said.

"What do you mean?"

"Describe them."

"I can't describe things," she said. "I don't have that."

"Please?" I said. "Just tell me what used to be there."

She closed her eyes and then reopened them, angling her head to one side, eyeing the page with a sidelong gaze of reminiscence. She pointed to the first empty space, over the label that said *Mère*. "This one was my grandmother," she said. "Her name was Sarah, they called her Sally. Sa*lee*. She was standing on a street. There was a car behind her, part of a car, an old-fashioned, I don't know . . . The fender kind of went like this." She drew a swooping sine wave in the air.

"A roadster?" I had recently been reading *A Sport and a Pastime*, set in postwar France, and could not help anachronistically picturing its hero's low-slung 1952 Delage. "A convertible?"

"You couldn't see the roof. Maybe. You could see a big brick building behind her, with no windows, or not many. Maybe that was the tannery, I don't know. My grandmother had on a knee-length wool skirt and a fitted jacket, tapered at the waist, with wide lapels and epaulettes." Clothes, she could describe; she had sewn her own for years, until overseas manufacture made doing so more expensive than buying ready-made. "Harris tweeds, maybe. Very English-looking. And a hat with a broad brim and a little ornamental bird on it." She touched the side of her head where the bird on a broad-brimmed hat would have perched.

"You mean like a stuffed bird? A real bird?"

"I always assumed it was real."

"Why would anyone want to have a dead bird on their hat?"

"You walk around all the time with a dead cow on your feet."

The spiked tea or the exercise of memory seemed to be helping. My mother jabbed the empty space above the label that said *Père*. "This was my grandfather Maurice. He was dark. Heavy. He had a, I think he had a mustache. And glasses, little round ones. The picture was posed, taken indoors. Not a snapshot. It was taken in a studio. The photographer's name was on the picture, here. Dumaurier, like the writer."

"In Lille?"

"Yes." She moved her finger down to the bottom right corner of the empty space. "He was wearing a pin-striped suit and a tiepin with a little chain. I remember thinking that he didn't look like a very nice man. Neither of them looked very nice or very warm. Actually? They scared me. But I was ashamed to feel that, because they had been killed by Hitler. It seemed . . ."

"Disloyal?"

"Yes."

"I get that."

It was rare for my mother to play a hand of memory with cards that the war and its brutalities had dealt her, but when she did, regardless of what was lying faceup on the table, the hole card always seemed to be guilt.

"It was like if I didn't love them, or even feel like I wished I had known them . . . if I didn't feel like I missed them even though I never met them . . . then somehow that had something to do with why they died. Like it was my fault. Like I thought what I did now, I mean when I was a kid, could have an effect on what happened then."

I recalled that Benjamin, in his "Theses on the Philosophy of History," had a good deal to say about the past and the dead and their redemption in the present by the living. I let it go. My mother probably knew as much about the subject as Walter Benjamin.

"I always thought it must have something to do with the tannery," my mother said. "How angry and unhappy they looked. Living in the midst of all that awfulness all the time. The blood. The carcasses. The stench." She shuddered. "Can you imagine?"

"I don't know. I've never been to a tannery."

"Neither have I," my mother said. "I can imagine it anyway."

"I know your mom hated it," I said. "I mean, according to Grandpa. He said that was part of the thing with the Skinless Horse."

"Huh." My mother closed her eyes again, and this time when she reopened them, the candle of remembrance seemed to have been snuffed. "He told you about that."

It was less a question than a realization of how far out of his accustomed sea roads my grandfather had elected to sail. I admitted that he had said a fair amount about the Skinless Horse, particularly in describing events leading up to the burning of the tree.

"That's something I don't think about," she said. She was not making an observation; she was stating a rule.

I pointed to the third empty rectangle on the page. "Tell me about this one."

"This? Was a picture of me. Sitting on a stone bench. At the convent. I was two, but I still had no hair, just a little baby hair. It hadn't come in. Somebody, I guess my mother, had put me in some kind of dirndl thing over a blouse with a Peter Pan collar. It was a terrible picture. I looked upset and uncomfortable. And ugly."

"The three *Us*."

"I looked like this."

She furrowed her brow and pursed her lips. Her whole face seemed to collapse angrily around her nose. I laughed out loud.

"I was the ugliest baby in the world."

"No."

"That picture I don't mind losing. Now this one . . . This was . . ." Her voice slowed and thickened as she pointed to the remaining empty space on the page. ". . . a picture of my mother and me. Obviously. I was littler in this one. Only an infant, in a little white sleeper. She was holding me on her lap. In a wooden chair, in a garden. A vegetable garden, things growing on stakes. Tomatoes, raspberries, I don't know. Peas. It was a, you know, a bentwood chair." She traced the bell curve of a chair back. "She was looking into the camera and pointing at it. Pointing it out to me. Telling me to look at the camera.

Smiling." My mother was smiling at the memory. "She had a real light in her eyes."

"She was beautiful."

"She was." Her tone shifted. She sounded almost disappointed in me. "But I think she let it define her a little too much. It was the only thing she really liked about herself."

My mother was beautiful, too, though not in the same way as her mother. She was dark where my grandmother had been fair and freckled, her nose long and straight where my grandmother's had been upturned, long-legged where my grandmother had been petite. I knew my mother regarded her own good looks and the social benefit they had afforded over the years as a kind of cheat or ambiguous grace. They often came in handy, but they were a source of recurrent trouble. They were nothing of which she could be proud.

"Well," I said. I had never heard my mother criticize her mother, even in such tempered terms. I knew she felt there were grounds for criticism, but I did not know how I knew it, since she had never said anything about it. It was just a kind of weather in the house from time to time. "I mean, there are worse things to like about yourself."

"I guess. I don't know. She was . . . She was overly concerned with appearances. With how things looked, how they seemed, what people would think and say about her. She heard, I mean, you know that she heard voices, and they used to say awful, just horrible, things about her. On the outside she was beautiful, but on the inside she felt ugly. She felt ruined. And she was so afraid of having that come out."

I was near breaking the rule about mentioning the Skinless Horse but caught myself in time. I turned the page. There was a picture of Uncle Ray and the zaftig woman with the hard eyes. "Mrs. Einstein?"

"Mrs. E."

A picnic table in some forgotten park outside Baltimore. Sandwiches wrapped in paper. Bottles of White Rock and National Bohemian on the picnic table. Uncle Ray sitting down with his legs crossed at the knee, wearing slacks, a knit polo shirt, two-tone loafers without socks. Mrs. Einstein stationed behind him, standing, in a sleeveless summer dress that clung to the ample splendor she retained. Uncle Ray smiling, Mrs. E. almost smiling. The fingers of her right hand rested all but imperceptibly on his right shoulder.

"Hey, were they—?"

My mother pursed her lips. She looked innocently at the ceiling.

"Oh my God," I said, "I so knew it."

"She was really in love with him."

"Uh-oh. Your voice got all filled with doom."

"Well, he broke her heart." She shook her head. "Fucking Reynard." Her tone was not entirely lacking in affection. "He was charming and fun, but he was a liar and a cheater and a dog. He was as bad as your father. Better in some ways, worse in others. Don't you be like him."

"Okay," I said. I knew that I could not have been that kind of man if I had devoted half of every day to the effort. Part of me never wanted to be anything else.

"He broke my heart, too." She might have been talking to herself.

"What?" I said.

I felt myself sinking into the lunar sofa that was the last thing my parents had purchased together before my father's disappearance. As a boy of the 1970s I had stood by and watched as my mother, like some patriotic young hothead after Fort Sumter or Pearl Harbor, had enlisted in the corps of liberated women. Among those who served under that banner, openness was held to be the consequence and not just the precondition of adventure. I had heard a thing or two during those years that shocked me. In time I grew used to and even began to look forward to, I suppose, being shocked. Around the time of Reagan's election, however, my mother had settled down. I was out of practice. She sat there pie-eyed with her mouth hanging open. After a minute I realized that she was imitating me. I closed my mouth.

"You didn't, you know, *sleep* with Uncle Ray, right?" I said.

"He wasn't *that* much older than me. Or it never seemed like he was." She tipped the teacup of Scotch to drain whatever was left in it. "Anyway, he wasn't really my uncle."

"Still," I said. "I mean, Mom, you were a minor. You were a *kid*."

"True," my mother said, refastening the clasp that sealed up the black-and-white planet of her girlhood and other lost things. "It was a crime." Her voice held bitterness and affection. "The man was definitely a criminal."

"Did he . . . ?"

"There was alcohol involved. To be honest, I don't really remember much. But I guess I must not have been too happy about it, because the next day I shot him in the eye."

"You what?"

"With a bow and arrow."

"Were you sitting on a horse at the time?"

"I told him I didn't want that photographer taking my picture," she said.

"Damn, Mom." I pictured Uncle Ray in a pair of Bermudas and a guayabera shirt, reeling across a hotel lawn with his hands cupped around the shaft of the arrow that was sticking out of his face.

"I guess I was angry. I guess at that point I was angry about everything."

I felt the cold bite of the arrowhead, a burst of red in my left eye. I shuddered.

"I know," said my mother.

"Well," I said, in a more philosophical tone. I was over the shock of it now and the more I thought about her act of retaliation, the less it surprised me. Uncle Ray had a reputation for shrewdness but he must not have understood my mother very well or he would never have let her anywhere near a bow and arrow. "I mean, you kind of got seriously fucked over."

"I got a head start on fucked over," my mother said. "Then your dad kind of finished me off."

"Same here." I held up my hand palm outward and after a moment she gave me a soft high-five.

"But I can't have been that angry at your grandpa," she said. "Or I would have told him about me and Ray. And I never did."

"Maybe you didn't need to."

"You think he knows?"

"There's five things he brings with him from Florida, that picture is one of them?"

"I thought that was a little weird. Maybe Ray confessed at some point."

"Maybe knowing you shot Uncle Ray with an arrow made Grandpa feel a little better about, his word, *abandoning* you with him."

"That is the correct word."

"I guess it kind of showed that you knew how to, like, handle yourself."

"Hmm," she said. She put a hand on my arm. "Still. Just in case. Don't tell him, okay? Maybe that was the only picture he could find, we didn't have much time to pack."

"Okay," I said. "I won't tell him that I know that you know that he knows what nobody wants to talk about."

"What's the point of talking about it?" my mother said. "Everybody already knows."

They arrived too late for lunch and whatever part of it had been garnished with slices of crabapple. It was early September 1958. The afternoon lay gray and heavy over Morristown. The east was a lustrous pile of thunderheads; to the west loomed Greystone Park, another thunderhead massed against the sky. Lightning flickered in the periphery of my grandfather's vision, but when he looked straight on at the clouds, it was never there. He wondered if this furtive lightning might be happening inside him and not over downtown Newark. He had not seen, held, or fucked my grandmother in fourteen months, and despite the sullen presence of their teenage daughter beside him in the car, his thoughts for the past hour or more had been of the plum of my grandmother's lower lip between his teeth, of the down on her ass, of reaching around to cup her breasts as he entered her from behind, of burying his nose in the cool salt parting of her hair as she lay with her head on his chest and a leg jackknifed across his abdomen.

He was at the wheel of a 1958 Buick Riviera purchased on Broadway three days before for a little over three thousand dollars cash. Its engine boomed up the green tunnel of elms that lined the road into Morristown. In the hip pocket of his new slacks were five hundred-dollar bills, nine fifties, two twenties, and change of a ten. My grandfather's underwear, shirts, socks, shoes, belt, wristwatch, and money clip were as new as the slacks. He had considered buying a suit but had opted instead for two pair of slacks, chocolate and dark navy, and a tropical-weight worsted sport coat in a muted gold windowpane plaid. Pale peach shirt worn without a tie, collar open. He was a free man with money in his pocket and a new hardtop coupe. He was the new-minted managing partner of MRX, Inc., with Sam Chabon for a partner and principal investor and a contract to supply Chabon Scientific with five thousand 1:20-scale solid-fueled Aerobee-Hi rockets. Even the bottled voltage of desire for my grandmother was a source of pleasure as it lit up his brain. He had never come closer in his life to something he was prepared to call happiness. But at the moment there was one set of y coordinates keeping my grandfather asymptotically from intersecting with that untouchable x axis.

"Could you please just attempt to drive normally?" my mother said.

"I'm going the speed limit."

"You might be *averaging* the speed limit. But you keep doing that thing where you tap the gas, take your foot off. Fast. Slow. Fast. Slow. Fast." My mother made a fist of her right hand and pushed it forward, pulled it back. There was an unsettling likeness in this gesture to the recent trend of his thoughts. He felt apprehended. "It's like you are *trying* to make me vomit."

"I'm sorry," he said. "I won't do it anymore."

Her head was tilted back against the headrest and she had her eyes closed. She sat wedged against the passenger door, hugging her knees in their stiff dungarees to her chest, her ankles under rolled cuffs a tale of summer written by sticker bushes, mosquitoes, and fingernails. The soles of her blue Sperry boat shoes had printed a moire of wavelets in white dust on the oxblood leather seat. Back in the new apartment he'd rented in Parkchester, on the new bed with a pink chenille spread, a sleeveless gingham sundress guaranteed by a Macy's salesclerk to be universally desirable to girls of sixteen lay untried beside a pair of open-toed flats still in their box. She had not even taken the dress off its hanger. Like everything he said and did, it appeared to revolt her. The first thing she had said to him after they'd gotten the preliminary inanities out of the way was:

"I thought you were supposed to be there longer."

He had explained that because of his spotless record (bearing only the invisible spots of an accidental homicide and violating curfew with an exploit in the walls), his new partner, who did business with the Department of Corrections, had been able to put in a good word for him and help win him early release. Later that day my grandfather had taken my mother to see the new offices of MRX. He had leased half a floor in a ten-year-old building on Cortlandt Street, downtown, a couple of blocks from the Arrow Radio shop he had managed in the mid-fifties. When they got there, Uncle Sammy was just giving a tour of the premises to his brother and his nephew, a dark-eyed good-looking kid, crown prince of his family, not yet twenty and already in medical school. His small stature, smart clothes, lustrous fingernails, and something indefinable ("maybe he just looked like a hustler") reminded my grandfather of Ray—before the mysterious eye patch, of course. What was the story there? The Chabon kid had that Reynardian way of looking inattentive when he was measuring someone—in this case, my mother—to the millimeter. My mother returned my father's attentive inattention with a display of her skill at striking unposed poses. After five minutes they had slipped out without anyone noticing. My grandfather found them out on a fire escape, smoking and "just talking."

Despite rulings handed down over the centuries by our sages concurring that handsome young medical students be given the benefit of the doubt, my grandfather could not help being annoyed. "You didn't even see the testing room," he had complained afterward. "You didn't see the wind tunnel."

"It smelled like old peanuts in there," my mother had replied.

He had deposited with his brother for safekeeping a girl who smelled of Lifebuoy and library paste and retrieved a young woman who smelled of cigarettes and Ban. He did not blame Ray for this alteration, however, for this strange and gawky changeling with her big bust and her eyes passing merciless judgment on everything they settled upon apart from lapdogs and babies. He did not simply attribute the change in my mother to the glandular inevitability of adolescent rebellion. He knew that he was responsible. His failure to control his own anger on that day in the offices of Feathercombs, Inc., was the source of the anger that seeped out of her every time she spoke to him or looked at him. In the thirty-seven hours they had spent together since their reunion, at the Schrafft's on Fordham Road, he had managed to keep them out of an outright argument. But there had been these regular low-level discharges, a plasma of anger that seemed to cling to her like St. Elmo's fire. Maybe that, he thought, was the flickering at the corner of his eye.

"Why did you make me eat all that food?"

"You have to eat."

"I do eat, just not breakfast. Uncle Ray never eats breakfast, either."

"Most important meal of the day."

"I told you, my stomach can't handle food in the morning."

He had attempted to surprise her, on their way down from the Bronx, with breakfast at the Howard Johnson's he remembered her having loved so much a couple of years before. It had not been his intention to cajole and then effectively coerce her into eating a short stack of chocolate-chip pancakes, but that was the way it had worked out.

"I know, honey. You did. I'm sorry."

"I said I only wanted coffee."

"And a cigarette."

"Oh, the horror," said my mother. "Oh, the everlasting shame."

My grandfather was still compiling an inventory of all the unwelcome changes in his daughter wrought during her thirteen months under his brother's careless care. Sarcasm and smoking headed the list so far.

As they turned in to the hospital's parking lot, the sun broke through the clouds and lent a confectionery splendor to the heaped-up arches and swags of Greystone Park. It was not a regular visiting day, and he found a spot close to the grand steps of the central building. He cut the engine. The clack of sprinklers filled the car. The wide empty lawns were veiled in shifting iridescence. One of the rivulets in the flow of his imaginings that morning had been the sight of my grandmother rising to her feet on the topmost step of the main building, in the belted navy blue dress she had been wearing the last time he'd seen her. She had lifted a tentative hand, then dropped it and come tearing down the steps toward him. He would burst from the Buick, leaving the engine running and the door open, and go to her. She would leap into his arms and scissor her legs around his waist. The contact of their mouths would be the fixed point around which the world, the day, and the state hospital would rotate.

The steps were empty. My mother lowered her chin and opened her eyes. She took a pack of Marlboro cigarettes from her handbag and put one between her lips. They were tipped with red paper to hide the print of a lady's lipstick, but my grandfather had succeeded, by dint of pleading that rapidly turned abject, in persuading my mother to leave her face unpainted, just for today, until they had all had a chance to adjust. "I already adjusted," she had said flatly.

Automatically, he took Aughenbaugh's lighter from his pocket and lit my mother's cigarette, then averted his face so he would not have to see how adeptly she handled the business of smoking it. She made a virtuous show of directing her smoke out the window of the Riviera. My grandfather saw that the cigarette was trembling in her fingers.

"How is she really?" my mother said. "Please don't say, 'We'll have to see.'"

As repeated by my mother, the words hung from the hooks of ironizing quotation marks, but my grandfather could find no weak points in the assessment.

"Did they shock her?"

"Who told you that? Ray?"

She nodded. She was crying. He reached for her, but she pushed him away. She jabbed at the cigarette lighter, pulled it out, and before he could stop her, touched the heating element with the tip of her index finger.

"Real nice," she said. She poked the lighter back into its slot. "They sold you a broken car."

"They did not shock her," he said. He was reasonably certain that this was the case. "As far as I can tell, the only thing they did is give her some hormones."

Over the phone the doctor had said that a year ago my grandmother had gone into early menopause, with a consequent intensification of her symptoms. They had tried a new treatment, a drug just on the market called Premarin.

"I don't know," my mother said. "I mean, if she's how she is because of the things that happened to her in her life, it seems like you would have to shock it out of her somehow."

My grandfather said that he didn't know much about electroshock therapy, but he didn't really think that was how it worked.

"Look at that place," my mother said, staring up through the windows at the battlements of Greystone. "Ugh. I can't go in. I don't want to see her in there. You go in, okay, and get her? And I'll wait in the car? Please? Dad, I'm sorry I've been such a pill. I want to see Mama, but I don't want to go in there."

My grandfather reached for the dashboard lighter. He did not want to force my mother to have to see her mother in a madhouse, and he did not want my grandmother to walk out of the madhouse after eleven months and see him standing there alone. He could not decide which of the two would represent the bigger failure on his part. He brought his fingertip near the element and felt the heat of it well before he let it touch his skin. There was a hiss, and the car filled with a nauseous odor like the smell of a tooth under the drill.

"Fixed," he said.

He moved the car to a shaded parking space and rolled the windows down. He got out of the car and slammed the door. He was almost to the steps leading up to the front doors of Greystone when he heard the scrape of her Topsiders against the pavement behind him. At the bottommost step, he turned and she was standing there. They looked up at the high oak doors entangled in vines of wrought iron and shared a moment of awe or dread or at the very least hesitation. He felt like he ought to take her hand—he felt that he wanted to—but he was afraid that when he reached for her, as on the day they first met, she would turn him down and leave him with his hand stuck out. He was still trying to decide if he could risk the disappointment when he felt the butterfly flutter of her fingers against his palm.

o   o   o

A woman wearing a white cardigan and white tennis shoes came out of the reception office on the far side of a sliding pane of glass. The glass was veined with wire mesh. She was not a nurse, but her short white hair had the upswept wings of a nurse's hat. She asked my grandfather to wait in the lobby for the doctor, Medved, who had been treating my grandmother. Everything was fine in the way of my grandmother's recovery, and not to worry; there was some aspect of her care that the doctor wanted to discuss.

"Come, dear," she said to my mother. "I'll take you along to the theater."

Her kindly manner was lost on my mother, who, on entering the lobby of the hospital, had awakened like a sleepwalker on a roof to find herself one step shy of an abyss. She was afraid to move. She remembered a scene from a movie she had seen in which a soldier trod on a land mine that would detonate only if he lifted his foot. She was afraid to speak, listen, or breathe. The lobby was very grand. It was framed by a double stairway rising to a colonnaded mezzanine. It had a crystal chandelier, a chessboard of marble for a floor, and, masked by Pine-Sol and narcissi in pots, a bloom of human feces in the air.

"I don't want to go to the theater. I'm just here to get my mom."

"Your mother is in the theater, sweetie," the woman said. "It's dress rehearsal for the play. She has been very involved."

"But we're taking her home today," my grandfather said.

"Oh yes. She knows that."

My grandfather was hurt, and his face must have shown it; the pity on the woman's face was plain to see.

"She only learned you were coming the other day, isn't that right? Did she know what time you two would be arriving today?"

"I must have forgotten to tell her," my grandfather said. He had sent a telegram, which might have gone astray, but he did not want this woman feeling sorry for him. He looked at his watch. The doctor had been promised in five and no more than ten minutes hence. He gave my mother a curt nod. "Go ahead."

My mother failed to take the cue. She was staring at something with an expression of uneasiness. My grandfather put a hand on her shoulder and followed her gaze. Expecting some ruin of a patient, shuffling, head-down, fingernails like guitar picks. He knew one instant of raw panic that the thing she was staring at, frozen in place, eyebrows furrowed, was my grandmother. But when he turned, he saw that my mother appeared simply to be staring at the wall.

"What's wrong?"

"Nothing," my mother said unconvincingly.

"Come, dear," the woman in the white cardigan said again. This time she took hold of my mother's elbow and pulled her gently toward a wide doorway between the stairways. She told my grandfather, "Please, have a seat. Dr. Medved won't be long."

My grandfather sat down in a Harvard chair by the front door, watching as my mother was led away. He stood up again and called out, "Excuse me?"

The woman in the white cardigan stopped and looked back at him. "Yes?"

"What is the play?"

"I really couldn't tell you that," said the woman. "I can't make head or tail out of any of it."

❍   ❍   ❍

The woman introduced herself as Mrs. Outcault. Between the entry hall and the theater, at the far end of a long series of alternating left and right turns through one of the hospital's lightning bolt–shaped wings, she punctuated the void of my mother's silence with bursts of hospital history and lore. She had a sixteen-year-old daughter of her own, she said. She knew the type of thing a girl my mother's age most wanted to hear about. If they passed a patient with an interesting biography or symptomology—narcolepsy, a pathological fear of hats, an inability to recognize danger, the folksinger Mr. Guthrie— she divulged it.

She told my mother that the hospital had a theater because of the opinions of a wealthy man named Adolf Hill, a manufacturer of necktie silk from Paterson. It was Mr. Hill's belief that the ancient Greeks had been the sanest men who ever lived. This was due, Hill further believed, to the greatness of Greek drama, which allowed audiences and actors alike to face the frightful things inside and outside their skulls. When, in time, Hill's wife was committed to Greystone, Hill had endowed construction of the Adolf and Millicent Hill Theater. It was not true, Mrs. Outcault said, that Hill deliberately arranged to have his wife committed in order to put his theories about drama therapy to the test, but it was possible that Mr. Hill's theorizing was the thing that had driven poor Millicent insane. Around 1927 she had hanged herself in her room—not in the theater, thank goodness—by stringing together three neckties made from Empire Silk Company's finest stock.

Outside the theater doors on a settee of tufted leather sat an old man in a green three-piece suit cut from a coarse-textured fabric the color of lederhosen and piped at the lapels and buttonholes in a paler shade of artichoke heart. He was sitting very erect with his hands on his knees. The lily of a pocket square peeped from the breast pocket of his jacket. He seemed to be studying the opposite wall with surprising intensity, given the fact that it was a blank expanse of beige. He did not look over or break off his study of the blank wall until Mrs. Outcault reached out to touch his shoulder. "Author! Author!"

He started, flinched, and cried out in a voice like a rusty pump.

"Oh, I *always* spook him," Mrs. Outcault said. "I'm *sorry*, Mr. Casamonaca." She clasped her hands together at her breast and looked deeply sorry. "Mr. Casamonaca wrote the play."

Mr. Casamonaca lurched to his feet and made another sound that did not form itself into a word or words. He smiled. He was long-shanked and, before gravity had bent him to its purpose, might have been tall once. Inside the green suit he was mostly skeleton. His palm against my mother's was powdery and cool.

"How are you?" Mrs. Outcault said very loudly.

Mr. Casamonaca nodded genially and made a looping benedictory gesture in the air, just in front of his face, more ornate than a cross, as if he were a priest in a sect whose symbol was the holy coat hanger of God.

"Sign language," Mrs. Outcault explained. "Poor thing's deaf as a boot. I heard he was struck by lightning, though I can't say for sure."

With his long pallid fingers and his nails manicured to a moon-like luster, Mr. Casamonaca continued to draw things across the space between him and my mother. The regular rippling of a corrugated roof. The outline of a jellyfish. The downward spiral of water in a toilet bowl.

Mrs. Outcault nodded emphatically. "Oh yes," she said. "I know. You're *so* right."

"What's he saying?"

"I have no idea," Mrs. Outcault said through a tight smile. She kept on nodding. "It isn't real sign language at all. Just something he made up. He never learned to speak English very well, and in the past few years he's lost the ability to read and write in Italian."

"He— Then how did he write a play?"

"He dictated it to your mother, which is why she has been so involved in all this. Using those crazy signs of his."

"My mom doesn't know any sign language."

"Apparently, she is fluent in Mr. Casamonaca's."

My mother watched Mr. Casamonaca's hands and fingers explain the behavior of skyrockets, the opening of a can of beer, and the proper means for setting a golf ball on a tee.

"It looks like he's just making it up as he goes along," she said.

"That is a popular theory," said Mrs. Outcault.

◑   ◑   ◑

Dr. Medved's head was a thumb upthrust from his shirt collar. Blue ink stain of chin stubble, white lab coat worn open over a summer suit the color of a manila folder. Purple bow tie. Barrel-chested with a heavy gut, the body of a dockworker belied or redeemed by framed diplomas from NYU and the Tulane School of Medicine. He winced as he belayed himself into the swivel chair behind his desk. His face suggested gas pain, a hemorrhoid, maybe both. The chair's steel joints creaked. Its spring uncoiled with a clang of metal fatigue.

"As I told you, there has been marked improvement," Dr. Medved said.

As in the course of their brief phone conversation, there was something off in the doctor's tone, a hint of hedging or doubt. Or maybe it was only chronic heartburn. Medved set down the paper cup of water he had stopped to fill from the cooler outside his office. He yanked open a drawer in his desk and found a bottle of Bromo-Seltzer. He unscrewed the bottle, dropped two tablets into the cup of water, and unbent a paperclip before he seemed to notice that my grandfather had yet to reply. He stirred the cup with the paperclip, looking up at my grandfather from under his wide-nib eyebrows. "Anything you want to say to that?"

Ordinarily, my grandfather distrusted Jews who wore bow ties, but something about Medved—probably the paperclip—inclined him to make an exception. "Naturally, I'm relieved to hear it," my grandfather said.

"But you've been relieved before. Of course. I understand. I have to tell you, though. A future setback. A relapse, should one occur. It won't in any way invalidate your present feelings of relief."

"In my experience, Doc, with all due respect, I beg to differ."

Dr. Medved nodded. The tablets hissed and chuckled in the cup. He picked it up and glugged it down. He held up a finger, begging my grandfather's indulgence for one minute, then curled the hand into a fist that he pressed against his abdomen under the rib cage. His expression grew thoughtful, searching. He let out a belch that was low and resonant, a sustained note drawn across the strings of a cello. He ducked his head shyly and smiled an embarrassed little smile. "Hoo boy."

"Mazel tov."

"Forgive me," he said. "Lunch was rather heavy. Now, listen. You hear me say *improvement*, I understand you may have some reason to be skeptical. Improvement is measured at a scale so much finer, more incremental, than calamity, isn't it? And it's perfectly normal to feel apprehension about a loved one's return to so-called civilization. As a general rule, when it comes to the families, I encourage efforts to keep expectations low, to minimize the impact of the inevitable disappointment."

This was more or less a précis of my grandfather's approach to existence itself. Hearing Medved formulate it, and in this particular context, undid a string long knotted inside him.

"I think I can do that," he said.

XXX!

She hangs back in the dark of the little theater. The bright stage under the proscenium reminds her of something she saw once in a Stewart Granger movie, a bonfire blazing in the maw of a stone god. She seems to be seeing faces everywhere today. Maybe she ought to take her mother's place here in this creepy joint. Above the proscenium, two more faces: masks representing the poles of mania. A woman in a gold-and-black-striped leotard looks out from the wings, her painted face as hectic as a ballerina's. A fat man in a bathrobe plays glassy ostinatos on a Wurlitzer organ, shards of waltz from some half-familiar whole. Rocking back and forth on the bench, wildly out of tempo with his music. Later, she will learn that the fat man was really a fat woman.

There is something awful about this cave of make-believe with its smell of velvet and dust. It has the magic weirdness of the old amusement halls on Uncle Ray's nine-ball circuit, the back rooms beyond the pool tables and pinball machines. The penny catacombs of entertainment. Live chickens in glass music boxes that dance when subjected to mild electrocution through the feet. Coin-operated beheadings of tiny queens, lynchings of tiny clockwork Negroes. A lifesize Little Egypt automaton enacting a creaky seizure of a hoochie-koochie dance. A clockwork Lucifer with a clockwork leer who makes predictions about your love life in racy slang rendered incomprehensible by time.

She stands unnerved by the bright mouth of the stage as if it is about to render prophecy.

❍ ❍ ❍

"It's all right," the woman in the white cardigan says. "Do you see your mother, sweetheart?"

"No."

Here and there among the seats she sees the outlined heads of other people in the audience, but none of them is right. She cannot imagine and will never discover the nature or identities of these other people. Doctors. Attendants. Napoleons and mothers of Christ. She hears the *clunk* of a switch. In the sudden total dark, a ghostly half-moon slews across her retinae.

The lights come up again on a field of clover. Trefoil hands, faces uplifted toward a shiny sun that hangs above their spiky pink and white heads. A swarm of fat-bottomed bees careen in and out among the flowers. Wordlessly, they quarrel with the flowers. They dip into the flowers' faces with the bowls of big wooden spoons.

George Washington appears, dressed in knee britches, a powdered wig, a greatcoat, hatchet slung from his belt. He stomps around abusing the flowers and exhorting the bees to molest them for their nectar. This is not George Washington, it turns out, but a herdsman of bees. The purpose or significance of the hatchet, apparently not intended for the chopping down of a cherry tree, remains unclear. The bee herder watches contentedly as his bees fly back and forth with their ladles full of nectar from the looted flowers to their unseen hive. All of this is routine for the bee herder. He lounges on a hummock and fights to stay awake. The sun with its metallic glow goes down. Evening hoists a silvery moon into the heavens.

A pair of bears, unseen by the bee herder, shamble on from stage left. They swing their heads in unison from side to side as they advance. They are shabby-looking bears, a couple of ruffians with patchy coats. They observe the traffic in nectar. When the bee herder's back is turned, they accost the plumpest of his bees. They threaten it with violence and confiscate its wooden spoon. With bearish ardor, they guzzle up every drop. At last the cries of the assaulted bee attract the attention of the drowsing bee herder. He leaps to his feet and throws his silver hatchet at the bears. But instead of striking them, it just keeps rising, all the way to the Moon overhead, where it lodges with a soft thump like a dictionary falling onto a pillow.

The bee herder studies the problem. He fidgets with his wig. Then he remembers his rope. He makes a lariat, swings it over his head with an audible whirr, and then launches the loop toward the hatchet with its handle protruding from the Moon. The loop misses the handle and the rope falls back to earth. He windmills it and launches it moonward again. This time the eye of the rope snags the wooden handle. He gives it a tug and then starts to pull himself up the rope hand over hand. Bees, bears, and flowers raise their heads and gawp in amazement. The bee herder climbs unamazed.

Darkness falls over the field of clover, dawn breaks on the Moon. Jagged moon mountains glow cool and silvery blue in the background as the bee herder, hatchet restored, strolls along unfazed by his new surroundings. He passes silver moon trees like the skeletons of cacti. He picks a bouquet of silver moonflowers. As he turns, he notices a small silver ball rolling toward his feet. A woman comes running in after it but stops when she sees him. She wears a silver gown and a silver crown. A large pair of silver wings rise up behind her, a moth's wings, billowing gently in a lunar breeze. He picks up the ball, and for a moment they regard each other. Then he tosses her the ball, and she catches it.

What befalls the bee herder and the Queen of the Moon after this first encounter—how the pantomime is meant to end—will remain forever unknown by my mother.*

---

* But not to a reader of the book by Rudolf Erich Raspe (1736–1794) whose proper title is *Gulliver Revived*, from which my grandmother (or, it is dimly possible, I suppose, Mr. Casamonaca) appears to have cribbed this lunar episode.

The mountains of the Moon glowing under the light of a blue gel at the back of the stage were tinfoil balls, massed and squashed into cake-frosting peaks. The moon trees were a couple of branching coat racks wrapped in more foil—"silver paper," my grandmother always called it. The moonflowers were clusters of eggbeaters, whisks, and serving spoons planted in cake pans. It was all so ridiculous and sad. It was pathetic. And yet the foil shone in the subaqueous light. The coat racks raising their jubilant arms and the bouquets of kitchen implements had the incongruous dignity of homely things.

Looking into the radiant mouth of the stage, my mother felt a strong sense of recognition, as if she had visited this world in a dream. As if, when she was a child, the fog of her mother's dreams had rolled through the house every night and left this sparkling residue on her memory. There was no way the baffling history of a spacefaring bee herder and his visit to the Moon had been dictated to her mother in some kind of bogus hand symbology by poor old lightning-addled Mr. Casamonaca. The Queen of the Moon entered, chasing the little ball of foil, in her tinfoil dress and crown, and her wobbling wings made from nylons stretched over coat hangers and glued with sequins. This was not the Moon at all. It was some other world—some other mother—uncharted and hitherto unknown.

It was just the most beautiful thing, my mother told me.

Then the bright glints seemed to startle from her the tinfoil crown and swarm the air between her mother and her, jigging and flittering, until they all flew away and left her in the dark.

She came to herself on the leather settee outside the theater door, sitting beside Mr. Casamonaca, her nose rife with the smell of mothballs oozing from his suit. Mrs. Outcault crouched in front of her, frowning as if watching a doubtful cake through the window of an oven. Behind Mrs. Outcault stood a bear, three clovers, two bees, and the fat pianist in his bathrobe and slippers. Behind them stretched an expanse of wall covered in the same wallpaper that was in the entry hall, which my grandfather had caught her staring at without understanding why. The thing was that if you looked at the wallpaper one way it was nothing special, a repeating pattern of carnation-pink escutcheons with white roundels, each shield supported by a pair of gold willow-leaf garlands. But if you looked at the wallpaper another way, you were confronted by a crowd of bloody-mouthed faces, ass-eared and staring.*

"Here she is!" Mrs. Outcault said. "You're fine, honey, aren't you?"

My mother nodded, though she was not entirely sure. She averted her eyes from the wallpaper and found Mr. Casamonaca beside her. He had his chin in the air and was looking down his long nose at her with an air of satisfaction and calm. *Don't worry*, said his eyes, *everything is unfolding just as I intended.*

"I enjoyed your play," my mother told him.

In reply, Mr. Casamonaca gravely unscrewed an invisible jar. My mother heard heels tapping, a rustling that was also a rattle. My grandmother came running into the small lobby minus her wings, with her crown askew, pressing it against her head with one hand. Mrs. Outcault stood up, and everyone stepped back and looked at my grandmother except Mr. Casamonaca, who seemed not to notice. My mother got up too fast. Her pulse drummed its fingers along the hinge of her jaw.

---

* In an unpublished memoir, "Greystone Notes" (1979), Dr. Medved records that this wallpaper with its protean gestalt was a source of anxiety and at times abject terror to many of Greystone Park's inmates. He and some of the other doctors on the hospital staff lobbied to have it removed or covered over, but the "devil masks" remained in place until 1972, when the walls were painted "a sebaceous shade of green called 'avocado,' which many of us found no less distressing."

"I'm sorry, Mom," my mother said. It was the first thing she could think of to say.

My mother went to her mother, who slid her cool bare arms alongside my mother's neck and scissored her between them. It was an awkward but sincere embrace. My mother's gaze strayed again to the wallpaper with its thousand gaping, long-eared faces, and my grandmother knew without following it what there was to see. "You don't have to look," she said.

My mother turned her face from the wallpaper for good.

●   ○   ○

"You have been in prison," Dr. Medved said.

"Wallkill," my grandfather said. "Thirteen months."

"For a violent crime."

My grandfather had anticipated that from time to time, over the course of his life to come, he would be expected to give some account of events between August 1957 and September 1958. He would do so, he had decided, only when asked directly by someone who had a reasonable right to know. Employers, inevitably; though in his present situation, since he'd been recruited by Sam Chabon—who was filled in by the warden—on the very grounds of the prison, nothing had needed to be said. He would tell my grandmother about his time served, provided she asked; the details were nothing he felt a need to volunteer. As for my mother, *What was it like in prison?* had been among the few spontaneous questions aimed his way during their drive down from New York City, and she had seemed content—or, according to her version, she had been obliged to content herself—with a one-word answer: *Interesting.* Beyond these moments, my grandfather had estimated that he was likely to be forced into, and had therefore budgeted, ballpark three to five discussions of his incarceration between now and the day he died. He decided to spend one of them now.

"I attacked a man. My employer. I tried to strangle him with a telephone cord."

"I see. And what had he done to deserve such treatment?"

"Nothing," my grandfather said. "As far as I know."

"Ha," the doctor said. "And to provoke it?"

"I got fired."

"Ah."

"It was the day after the first time she tried to burn the tree. I was, you know. I was agitated."

"Because she had set fire to this tree. After a period of more than a year—"

"Almost two years."

"—during which her illness appeared largely to have disappeared. The hallucinations abated."

"Yes. Only looking back, I could see . . . I realized they . . . It had been there all along. It was just that somehow we all managed to ignore it for a while."

"And then it came charging back that night. In a great fiery rush. That must have been terrifying."

"It definitely seemed to invalidate the sense of relief, I'll tell you that."

"And the next day. The attack. How much of the anger that led you to try to strangle your employer do you feel was really misdirected anger toward your—"

"All of it. I didn't even really know the man."

"Ah."

"It wasn't her, exactly, I was angry at. I didn't blame her, and I don't now. I knew she couldn't help it. I knew she had no way to stop herself."

"Which is why you felt you had to take your anger out on someone else."

"It's not impossible."

"I'd say it's quite likely."

"It has a certain logic."

"And what if—well. What if you had not been so clear in your own mind about her fundamental lack of culpability due to mental instability? What if you did feel that somehow she was to blame for her actions? Do you think your anger would have directed itself more, ah, more appropriately? In the sense that you would have tried to take it out on her and not a relative stranger."

"What are we talking about here? Is there something that I don't know about? How could she be to blame?" My grandfather caught himself before the next logical question slipped out: *Was the Skinless Horse real?* Then he saw a look in Medved's face that made his heart want to rephrase the unasked question, come at it from the opposite side: *Or had she been making the whole thing up?*

Medved sat without saying anything for an uncomfortably long time. He gripped the arms of his chair and pushed himself to his feet. He went to a large steel cabinet in the corner. Inside it on steel shelves were rows of thin cardboard boxes, lined up like books with their spines outward, five or six dozen. The spines of the boxes had blank white rectangles on each of which a patient's name had been written, along with some dates. Each patient had at least three boxes; my grandmother had seven. Medved pointed to a chunky gray machine sitting on a low steel typing table beside the cabinet. "Know what that is?"

"A tape recorder. Looks like a Wollensak."

"It is. I use it to record my sessions with patients." He pointed to the boxes in the cabinet that had my grandmother's name on them. "These are my sessions with your wife. I can't share them with you, of course. I am not really supposed to characterize or paraphrase or even discuss them with you at all."

He closed the cabinet and sat back down. He grabbed hold of his cheeks and pulled on them, worked them between his fingers. "At first there was not much of interest that she wanted to tell me. Her guard was up, not against me and my questions so much as against her tormentor. But once we began the Premarin treatment . . . Well, it has had a profound effect on her symptoms and behavior. On the pattern of her thoughts and the way she expresses them. The effect has been so considerable that I am forced to question the earlier diagnosis of trauma-induced schizophrenia and consider that all along your wife has been suffering from some kind of acute hormonal imbalance, some deficiency in the production of estradiol by her ovaries."

"Unless that is schizophrenia."

"Not out of the question, in females, at any rate. Clearly, it's possible that estradiol played some critical role. We really know nothing at all about it. At any rate, as soon as the voice began to recede . . . as soon as her guard could be let down . . . She began to talk, during our sessions, with a freedom she had never had or felt before. Naturally, I listened. And not only because that is what I am obligated and paid to do. The account she gave. Of her experiences. During the war. It was . . ." Medved settled his chin in his left palm, his left elbow resting on the desk. He looked out the window of his office at the sky turning black in the east. "I will be honest. I really don't know how to finish that sentence," he said.

"I've heard it," my grandfather said. "I know."

"You have heard something. Have you heard everything?"

"I would have no way of knowing that."

"True. But let me ask you. When she talked about her family, her experiences during the war. The circumstances of your daughter's birth. Or set that to one side. Generally speaking, in the course of your life with her, in her expressions of emotion and the patterns of her thought, would you say that there was a . . . *coherence* to her? What we might call her presentation of self—did it feel consistent?"

It was like when you climbed a stairway with the lights out, reached for the top step, and lurched into a hole in the dark. From that long-ago Sunday afternoon outside the doors of Ahavas Sholom synagogue when, from one day to the next, my grandmother seemed to have forgotten or switched off a supposedly acute aversion to the touch of animal skin, the answer to Dr. Medved's question had always been *No.*

"Here's what worries me," Medved said gently when my grandfather didn't say anything. "Because of the incident with the tree and your response to it. What if she were to tell you something or you learned something about her, her account of who she is, her history, that caused you to question everything she had told you before?"

"Sounds like I ought to tell her not to tell me," my grandfather said.

"Really." Dr. Medved looked surprised. Maybe he was even a little disappointed.

"If she's feeling better, that's all I care about."

"But as I suggested, I hope I made it clear—of course we'll continue her on the Premarin, but there's no history or precedent here. I've never seen a case like hers, and there's no way of knowing whether the effects we're seeing will be durable, let alone permanent.* If she should stop feeling better . . ."

"Whatever bad or ugly thing it is, Doc. Whatever's at the bottom of whatever's the matter with my wife? I've already seen and heard it. I know it's ugly and she hates herself for it—"

"I doubt it's quite as simple as that. It isn't something she did or didn't do but the action of her particular hormonal, ah, situation on a set of circumstances—"

"Doc, I'm an engineer, an electrical engineer. That's my training. Engineers spend a lot of time on what's called failure analysis. Whether you're designing, or testing, or building, you . . . because, you know, things break. They fail, they explode, collapse, burn out, there's stress, fatigue, fracture. And you want to find out why it failed, that's part of your job. You want to figure out what's wrong

---

* "The effects were fairly permanent," my mother observed bitterly when she read this memoir for the first time.

so you can fix it. Maybe I used to look at my wife in that regard. At the beginning, maybe for a long time. Wanting to know what went wrong. Thinking I could fix her. But I don't want to think of her like that anymore, you know, looking for the bad capacitor. I just want to, I mean . . . I accept her and I . . ." He was going to say that he loved my grandmother, but that didn't feel like something one man ought to bother another man with. "She's broken, I'm broken," he said. "Everybody's broken. If she's not in misery anymore, I'll take it."

Dr. Medved blinked. It looked like he was organizing an argument in his thoughts. "I— All right," he said. "You know yourself better than I do."

"Don't be too sure," my grandfather said.

There was a soft tap, and then the door swung open and my grandmother was there. Hair curled, looking into him from somewhere on the far side of those damaged eyes, blue as the Monte Carlo night. Her face, all the angles of beauty and torment he had fallen for then, in spite of combat fatigue and a blanket disdain for sentimental conventions, at first sight. She was wearing the navy dress, the one she'd been wearing on admission to Greystone Park. It had a wide belt that cinched her waist very much to the advantage of her breasts and hips. She had put on a little weight, and that also proved advantageous.

"Hello, darling," my grandfather said. He got up and went to put his arms around her. He kissed her. It was meant only to be a kiss hello, but it lasted a while and ended with her giving his lower lip the gentlest of bites. If the damn doctor were not there with his diplomas and his Bromo-Seltzer and his useless addiction to the truth, my grandfather would have laid my grandmother on her belly across the desk in a shower of pens and paperclips. Testing the connection that never seemed to fail. They parted. She looked at Dr. Medved. Hopeful, afraid, wanting to know: "It's okay?"

My grandfather glanced at the doctor. Dr. Medved, on his feet now, looked from my grandfather to my grandmother and then back.

He offered his final judgment on the situation, on the failure in her circuitry that my grandfather chose not to analyze. "If it works for you," he said. "I guess it's okay."

⠀⠀⠀⠀⠀❍⠀⠀⠀⠀⠀❍⠀⠀⠀⠀⠀❍

A widower like my grandfather, Dr. Leo Medved died of heart failure in 1979. His professional correspondence and the records, stored in marbleized cardboard boxes and still under seal of confidentiality, passed into the hands of his adult daughter and son. The Medved children tried to find an archive that might take their father's documents and tapes: at the New Jersey Psychiatric Association, at Tulane and NYU, at the library of his synagogue in Fair Lawn. But there were an awful lot of boxes: "at least two hundred and fifty," according to his eldest child, Lorraine Medved-Engel, a retired schoolteacher and holotropic breathwork facilitator in Mantoloking, New Jersey.

I tracked Lorraine down in early 2013. I had been thinking of writing a novel based on what I knew about my grandmother and her illness, and I was hoping I might find something useful in Dr. Medved's records. By the time I found my way to Lorraine Medved-Engel, the number of boxes had been reduced to twenty-seven by vicissitude, disaster, and Dr. Medved's son, Wayne. "Always sort of resentful-slash-worshipful about Dad," according to Lorraine, Wayne Medved consigned most of the boxes to a landfill shortly before taking his own life on the tenth anniversary of his father's death. Hurricane Sandy, on its way through Mantoloking and Lorraine's basement in September 2012, had done for most of the rest of the boxes.

Two of the remaining twenty-seven boxes contained tape reels of treatment sessions from the mid-1960s, after Medved had left Greystone Park and gone into private practice in New York City. A few more held a small fraction of what must have been hundreds of Fisher scientific notebooks—black covers, numbered gridded pages—in which

Medved set down treatment notes at the end of every workday. Unfortunately, none of these journals happened to coincide with my grandmother's time at Greystone Park. As far as I could determine over the course of two days' intrusion on Lorraine's hospitality, the sole trace of my grandmother in the surviving Medved records were two paragraphs in an entry that filled out the back pages of the lab notebook in which the doctor had completed the writing of his unpublished memoir, "Greystone Notes."

Dated *11 November 1979*—two days before his fatal heart attack—and headed NEXT PROJECT, the ten-page entry outlines a book that Medved intended to call either *The Bathyscaphe* or *Rapture of the Deep.* It was to be a series of extended case studies, modeled on Robert Lindner's *The Fifty-Minute Hour,* culled from the pages of all those other Fisher notebooks consigned by poor Wayne Medved to molder in the Meadowlands. Medved laid out the narrative contours for five of a proposed nine memorable "dives" he planned to revisit in his literary bathyscaphe. After these, running out of pages and—did he sense it?—time, Medved jotted down a few more paragraphs, sketching the four other cases he saw as likely candidates for inclusion. Among these last words of Dr. Leo Medved I found this:

The Skinless Horse: Case of "N—" Foundling, b ≈ 1923. P* (given name at birth: Liliane) was married woman of French/Belgian-Jewish ancestry, mother of adolescent female. Prior diag. SCZD.†
Experienced hallucinations after 1947, prim. auditory, some visual. Delusional persecutor: "Skinless Horse."

P told her mother was Jewish mistress of married "businessman from Ostend." Raised by Carmelite nuns outside Lille. Sporadic early hints of eventual symptomology, primarily aud.: "angry" or "critical" whispering voices. Reported having seen "burning angels

---

* Patient

† Schizophrenia

in the fireplace," "shadowy face" alongside her own in mirror, etc. Late 1941 experienced return of vivid early memory, sight of engorged "skinless" penis of stallion, flashed through her mind while P was engaged in sexual intercourse with a local SS captain, father of biological child (an act which P "only much later" came to recognize as non-consensual).

Prolonged, acute depression postpartum. Retrospective indic. persecution mania, paranoia at this time. However not marked (nor inappropriate to circumstances).

Recovery coincided with P forming close attachment to another Belgian Jewish girl, N—, slightly younger, taken into hiding late '42 by nuns. P claimed friendship with N— "saved my life" at time of suicidal ideation. N— was the daughter of wealthy tanners: "maroquinnerie," [sic] N— gave vivid accounts of slaughter, skinning, treatment of hides, stench, etc. Strong physical resemblance betw. girls led to elaborate fantasy of being sisters. N— betrayed, deported to Auschwitz. Presumed dead.

Convent destroyed Oct. 1944 by V-2 rocket. P forced into months of vagrancy, cold, near-starvation. Stealing, prostitution for food and money. Experienced amenorrhea, hair loss. (Regular menses never resumed, P conceived only once postwar, 1952, see below.) P's daughter spent part of time with Catholic family in Lille. War's end, P and daughter in DP camp, Wittenau, Germany. P observed HIAS agents with brief to bring Jewish ex-camp inmates to US. P managed to persuade agents that she was N—. Adopted N—'s name and identity. Started as impulse, seized opportunity. Fabricated narrative based on fellow inmates' accounts of internment at Auschwitz, liberation. US soldier w/ sewing needle and pen ink tattooed numbers on patient's arm in return for sex.

Arr. US July 1946. Met husband, ex-GI, Baltimore. From hunger to plenty, illness to health. Father for child. At this moment of apparent safety symptoms begin to recur, worsen through circa September 1952 when P becomes pregnant. Experiences near-total

remission of illness during pregnancy. First hospitalization trig-
gered by miscarriage ca. 10 wks.

After that Medved gave some details about the nature of the Skinless Horse. He planned to conclude the case history with his own
surprise when the routine administration of Premarin—"derived,"
he noted, "from the urine of horses"—appeared to cure her delusions
far more effectively than talk therapy had ever done. In the end, the
chapter was to be a record of dumb luck and success through failure.

This discovery—that my genetic grandfather had been a Nazi,
that my grandmother had been born to a life, with a biography, very
different than the one I had always been told, that she had perpetrated such a charged deception on everyone for so long—messed
me up for a long time. One by one I began to subject my memories
of my grandmother, of the things she had told me and the way she
had behaved, to a formal review, a kind of failure analysis, searching and testing them for their content of deceit, for the hidden presence in them of the truth. I kept what I had learned from my wife
until I returned from Mantoloking. I kept it from my mother and
the rest of the world until I began to research and write this memoir,
abandoning—repudiating—a novelistic approach to the material.
Sometimes even lovers of fiction can be satisfied only by the truth. I
felt like I needed to "get my story straight," so to speak, in my mind
and in my heart. I needed to work out, if I could, the relationship
between the things I had heard and learned about my family and
its history while growing up, and the things I now knew to be true.

"So what was it?" I asked my grandfather on an afternoon—it
turned out to be the next-to-last afternoon of his life—a little over
thirteen years before I found the answer in Dr. Medved's notes.
"What did Dr. Medved want to tell you about Mamie?"

"I don't know."

"You don't know. You never asked?"

"I didn't want to know. I still don't."

"Do you have any theories?"

"I did, probably, the first few years. It was nothing I enjoyed think-ing about. So eventually, I stopped thinking about it."

"But do you think . . . I mean, it seems like he was hinting that she was lying to you about something. Something from her past."

"She probably was. It's hardly unusual."

His tongue darted out, retreated. I handed him a cup of apple juice and spotted it while he took a sip.

"Everything you've been telling *me* is true, though, right?"

"It's all the way I remember it happening," he said. "Beyond that I make no guarantees."

I sat beside the bed with an uncomfortable sensation, a kind of premonition of shock, about whatever it was that my grandmother had told Dr. Medved. I had already made the disquieting connection between the play my mother had told me about the night before, in which my grandmother had featured as Queen of the Moon, and a story my grandmother had told me when I was little. I had long since rediscovered the source of that story of my grandmother's in the pages of *The Adventures of Baron Munchausen*, an edition with the Doré illustrations, which she had given to me as a gift.

"Look, Mike," my grandfather said, "it took your mom a long time to get over some of the things about Mamie that . . . that were hard on her. I mean, your grandmother always felt like she had been a bad mother, you know?"

"Yeah."

"I don't see it that way. The way I see it is she lived, she got your mother out of there, she loved her, so in my book that's mother enough. But I don't want to give Mom a reason to doubt. So do me a favor. Don't say anything to your mother about this."

"Don't say anything to me about what?" said my mother, entering the room. She looked at me, then at my grandfather, suspicious.

"Grandpa had a beer," I said. "I think he's a little bit drunk."

XXXII

When I was little and we still lived in Flushing, the Whip used to come shambling down our block, a hectic fanfare blowing from its loudspeaker horn. The Whip was a truck with a carnival ride in a wire cage mounted on its flatbed, painted red and yellow like a circus tent. The music that attended its migrations and advertised its arrival had a slapstick wooziness and in hindsight may have been a tarantella. It seemed as long and as looming as a tractor-trailer to me, but it was probably no bigger than a moving van. If you were already in the street playing when the Whip rolled up, you ran in to beg for a quarter. If you were indoors, you heard the drunken music and ran out to meet it with a quarter sweating against your palm.

The Whip Man was a beefy dark-skinned fellow in a billed cap who said little and smiled less, although he did not seem unfriendly. He would relieve you of your change and then help you up three steel stairs to the interior of the cage where the Whip's six cars waited, alternately red or yellow, arranged on a hidden track in an elongated oval. Sometimes the cars reminded me of tulips and sometimes of painted hands upturned to cup a pair of children. The cars wobbled around the oval, trundling along the straightaways, then picking up speed at each end in a burst that smashed you against the outside of the car or the person beside you. During the slow parts you recovered, and then you got smashed again, and when the ride was over you went back down the stairs. Just before you exited his cage, the Whip Man would reach up to take a piece of Bazooka bubble gum from a shelf over his head and press it into your hand with a murmured benediction.

One day as I came down the stairs from the back of the Whip truck, I was surprised to find my father waiting for me in his suit, tie, and white coat. The rubber-tipped antlers of a stethoscope protruded from a hip pocket. There was a fleck of red on his shirtfront that looked like blood but was more likely to be his lunch: tomato soup, ketchup. I knew that if I asked him, he would say it was blood. I had recently begun to understand that my father only rarely meant what he said and that usually he meant precisely the opposite. If he said it was a gorgeous day, that meant it was snowing or raining. If he said something couldn't have happened to a nicer guy, then something bad had happened to someone who deserved it. When he was imparting information of a factual nature, you could generally take what he said at face value, but even then you had to be careful. I had endured a painful day of teasing by the older kids on the block, after I cited my father's authority in claiming that the "crunch berries" in Cap'n Crunch's Crunch Berries cereal were made from actual dehydrated strawberries.

"Does Mommy have a stomach flu?" I said.

The only time I could remember my father having come home in the middle of a workday had been a few months earlier, when my mother fell ill and was too weak from vomiting to look after me. She had seemed fine at breakfast this morning, but I had been at my friend Roland's house since then, and in the meantime she must have succumbed.

"She had to go to the hospital," my father said. He unlocked the car on my mother's side and held open the rear door. I got in. "Mrs. Kartakis drove her."

"Does she have to have an operation?" I said.

"Yes, but you don't have to worry, Mike. She's going to be fine."

My father was wanting as a father, still less of a businessman, and as a crook he was grossly incompetent, but he seems to have been a very good doctor. Among the gifts he could bring to bear was a fine bedside manner; I don't think I've ever seen finer. Like his mother-in-law telling a story, my father became a different person when he wanted to comfort you. His voice grew deeper and more gentle, and he seemed—uniquely at such moments—to relax. He looked you right in the eye. He knew you had questions; he understood your concerns. In the years that he spent practicing medicine, his patients always loved him. No doubt this manner had its effect on creditors and investors, too. Up to a point.

"It isn't serious," he said. "A minor procedure." He crouched beside the car and buckled my seat belt, even though I had known how to buckle my own seat belt for some time. "Don't worry, honey."

"Okay."

He put his hand with its manicured nails on my shoulder. A clean smell between peppermint and leather escaped the cuff of his lab coat. His class ring with its gemstone and cryptic inscription radiated strength like the ring of Hercules in the cartoons; if you held it to the sky, it might call down lightning. I looked at the glittering stone and the moons of his fingernails. I felt like crying about my mother having to go to the hospital, but I arrested the feeling at the back of my throat and managed to work it down. I asked my father what kind of operation my mother would be having.

"What kind of operation do you think she might be having?" he said.

He closed the door and I was surprised to notice on the seat beside me a small suitcase, ivory leather, with spring-action brass clasps and hinges that creaked when you opened it. Scuffed as an old white oxford shoe, it had been my father's when he was a boy and was therefore always referred to as my valise, because that was what they had called a suitcase in my father's family. I took it be a Yiddish word. I was not sure why my father wanted me to guess what kind of operation my mother was having. I wondered if I would be judged on the quality of my answer. I remembered that one of my valise-toting relatives, his late mother's sister Dottie, had recently gone into the hospital for a foot operation.

"Maybe her feet?" I tried.

"You're right," he said. "Very good."

He switched on the radio, tuned as usual to WQXR. Someone was hitting the keys of a piano hard, in fitful handfuls. My father turned up the volume. We drove down the street, past the Whip. The angry piano tangled momentarily with the drunken trumpet pouring from the speaker horn over the Whip's cab. My friend Roland and his brother, Pierre, stood at the Whip's bottommost step, squinting hopefully up at the Whip Man. I realized that I was still holding the piece of bubble gum.

I unwrapped it and put my jaw to work on it. I puzzled over the gag in the Bazooka Joe comic strip, which I was newly capable of reading. I didn't ask my father about the valise. I assumed that I was going to stay with my mother in the hospital. I wondered if I would have a bed of my own or if I would be sharing a bed with her. I envisioned a room in New York Hospital, where my father had done his residency in orthopedics—the only hospital I really knew. After a while I understood that we were going the wrong way for NYH and must be headed to a different hospital. I knew, of course, that New York City was full of hospitals—Montefiore, Presbyterian, St. Luke's. Mrs. Kartakis must have taken my mother to one of those. There were Jewish and Catholic hospitals; maybe there were Greek hospitals. Maybe Mrs. Kartakis had taken my mother to the Public Health Service hospital on Staten Island, where my father was currently posted.

The piano was under heavy attack now—it must have been a Liszt waltz, maybe Rachmaninoff. It was so loud that I would almost have to shout to be heard over it, and my father didn't like it when I shouted over his music. It annoyed him, and sometimes if I did not shut up, annoyance slipped into anger. He would reach back and uncoil his right arm, slowly at first and then with a sudden snap. His Mighty Hercules ring would crack against my skull, making a sound that I could see, a thunderclap behind my eyeballs. Therefore I did not ask him if we would be riding the Staten Island Ferry to visit my mother. It was only when it became clear that we were headed across the Bronx to Riverdale that I opened my mouth. Even then I waited until the piece ended and a commercial came on before saying what I had to say. "I don't want to sleep over at Grandpa and Grandma's."

"Oh, come on, Mike!" It came out as irritable, halfway to yelling. He lowered his voice. "The puppets are not going to hurt you," he said, in a controlled tone. "They are toys. You know that."

"I know," I said. "I'm just afraid of them."

"Why?"

"I don't know."

"Mike . . ."

"I just am."

A new piece began to play on the radio. My father turned down the volume but drove on for a while without saying anything.

"Well, I don't know what to do about that," he said.

He sounded more sad than irritated; he sounded disappointed. I was very sorry to disappoint him, but it was hardly my fault that in a hatbox at the top of the closet in the guest bedroom of my grandparents' apartment, a dozen hand puppets (a rubicund King, a sour-faced Queen, a leering Shepherd, two white and one black Sheep, a sneaky-eyed Fishwife, four Musicians, and a masked Robber with a black beard made horribly from human hair) lay plotting in darkness to kill me while I slept. They had sewn bodies and painted wooden heads carved by a master craftsman in Lille, France. I knew that they had cost my grandparents "an arm and a leg," which intensified my shame and guilt over being terrified of them and of course merely helped the puppets' case against me. I tried to think of something I could say to mitigate my father's disappointment.

"I'm just afraid of them at night," I said. "In the daytime they don't bother me at all."

❍   ❍   ❍

The valise was heavy, and I struggled with it across the lobby of the building. The doorman, called Irish George to distinguish him from another doorman known as Tall George, offered me a hand. I declined. I wanted my father to see that in spite of an emotional weakness that made me fear hand puppets, I could at least carry my own valise.

"Big strong fella you got there, Doc," said Irish George.

My father pushed the up button and stood back appraising me for a moment before lowering his eyes to his Florsheim loafers. "He's a big boy," my father agreed.

He still sounded disappointed, I thought, but in a regretful way, as if mostly disappointed in himself. Mistaking incapacity for a philosophy of life, my father did not often apologize, but when he did, he would first look down at his shoes. It hurt my heart to see him hang his head that way. I couldn't handle it. I did not want him to apologize for whatever was making him feel sorry. I looked at the gondola instead.

There was a beauty salon on the ground floor of my grandparents' building. It had an Italian name and a Venetian theme and, in the lobby, a sign that was a miniature replica of a gondola. The gondola hung from the ceiling by the elevator. It was nearly two feet long, piano black with red and gold trim, its prow pointed at the hallway that led to the beauty salon. I had been enchanted by this model gondola for as long as I could remember and now—not for the first time—I sought refuge aboard it and began poling slowly in my imagination through waters untroubled by thoughts of the Robber with his veritable beard, or the bad thing happening to my mother that my father was so sorry about, or the chances that, once she and I were alone, my grandmother would find herself in a storytelling mood.

"Is Grandpa home?" I said.

"Of course not. He's at work."

"Okay."

"Why do you ask?"

I said that I had just been wondering. As soon as the elevator doors closed and we started to go up, I felt a djinn of expectancy or dread (there was no difference) flicker to life in my belly. I ran my eyes from the twelfth-floor button to the fourteenth and back. Recently, I had come across a laminated card, printed with the Mourner's Kaddish in two alphabets, inside a copy of Errol Flynn's *My Wicked, Wicked Ways* that had belonged to my other grandfather, my namesake. I wondered if, in spite of the effort made to protect the dummies of the world from their fear of bad luck, some residual thirteenth floor might not linger, hidden like that Kaddish between floors twelve and fourteen.

When we got off the elevator, I let my father carry the suitcase and took his right hand between both of my own. I lagged behind a little, steeling myself for my part in the coming ritual.

The doorbell was mounted under the peephole in a metal frame I could now reach without going up on tiptoe. The way it always worked was that I would ring and, wearing the same look of fresh mischief each time, my father would cover the peephole like a magician palming a coin. A moment later, in a worried voice, my grandmother would call out, "Who is it?" from the other side of the door, even though she knew it could only be us.

The joke was that she was pretending to be worried, but the real joke, at least to my father, was that she was only *pretending* to pretend. He covered the peephole because he had noticed that his mother-in-law never opened a letter without first holding the envelope to a light, or a door without first peeping through the spyhole. A deadbolt would roll back with a ratcheting sound, a chain would rattle, and my grandparents' door would swing slowly open—and there would be nobody there.

Here the joke was that it had been a ghost grandmother calling out "Who is it?" My role was to step up and declare in my firm-est tone, "There's no such thing as ghosts!" and my grandmother would then emerge from behind the door and affirm in a reassuring tone that I was absolutely right. Even though I had known for a long time that it was my grandmother hiding herself and not a ghost grandmother, when the invisible hand pulled open the door I often would catch hold of my father's or mother's arm or take an involuntary step away. My parents would chuckle or chide me. They failed to understand that it was not the ghost that spooked me, it was the hidden grandmother.

None of that happened this time. My father rang the doorbell. My grandmother opened the door. It was the middle of the afternoon, but she was still wearing her housecoat. This was a kind of slender tent with a Nehru collar that buttoned up the front and fell to her ankles, violently patterned with red and purple op-art oblongs. Today it would seem like the relic of an audacious moment in the history of midcentury design, but at the time I simply accepted it as routine loungewear for a grandmother.

"Go in." The bangles on her wrists clinked as she waved me into the apartment. "Put your things in the, the cabinet in the bedroom. In the chest of drawers."

My father handed me the valise. "It's just a couple of days," he said. "Grandma will take you to buy a Matchbox car." He pulled out his billfold and gave me five ones and a five, a considerable sum. He frowned and extracted an additional five-dollar bill from the billfold. This one was frayed, stained, and missing a chip at one corner. He was the son of a print jobber, and until his uncle's fateful encounter at Jack Dempsey's with a six-inch human skeleton, his family had clipped coupons, saved Green Stamps in tattered albums, and hoarded pennies in mayonnaise jars. I think there was something unbearable to my father, some imprisoning shame, in the saving of money. It never hung around his wallet very long. But while it was there, he liked it clean and new.

"Dirty," my grandmother said in mock sympathy as my father handed me the abominable five. "And torn, *pouah!*"

My father grabbed at the back of my head, ruffled my hair, and gave me a gentle shove toward the bedroom. I could feel them waiting until I was out of earshot to start talking about my mother. I took my time getting there. Across the living room windows the Palisades rippled like a stone flag banded with river, trees, and sky. A cast-metal Degas ballerina on a teak console leveled her contemptuous gaze at a balsa-wood model of a Vanguard rocket on a bookshelf by the hall.

When I went into the guest bedroom, my grandmother and my father started talking in low voices. I set the suitcase on the bed and stood in the doorway, trying to eavesdrop. I suspected that my mother was already dead, that the operation on her feet had been a failure or a fiction, and that everyone was conspiring to keep the information from me. Between the hushed tones, my grandmother's accent, and the elliptical nature of adult conversation, I could not catch the drift. I stared at the worn five-dollar bill in my hand, at the portrait of Abraham Lincoln, whose own mother had died when he was not much older than I was. I felt like I could see the loss in Abraham Lincoln's eyes.

My father called out a goodbye, and a moment later my grandmother came into the guest bedroom to check on my progress unpacking. I had made no progress. I had been too busy trying to eavesdrop, and anyway, I was confused by my father's packing technique. He had mistaken pajama tops for pullovers and bathing trunks for short pants. He had packed two handkerchiefs. *Handkerchiefs!* He had thought to equip me with the fake-ponyskin cowboy vest that had been part of my most recent Halloween costume. There were three pairs of underpants but four pairs of socks, one of them mismatched and one my mother's.

"Did Mommy die?"

"No, little mouse," my grandmother said. "You will see her very soon. Now let's put your things away."

She took a quick inventory of the contents of the valise. Just before she said it, I knew she was going to say *"Oh la la,"* an interjection I always enjoyed. She put everything but the buckaroo vest in the chest of drawers and said that we would get some things at Alexander's when we went to buy me a Matchbox car with all that dirty money.

I asked her what I should do about the vest. She told me I should put it on because she had a presentiment that we might need to be cowboys today, and if I wore the vest it would establish a mood.

"This will be our inspiration," she said, the first time I can remember having heard the word used. "I am *inspired.*"

She went into her bedroom, and when she came back she was wearing a Pierre Cardin shearling "cowboy coat" and a pair of Ferragamo "cowboy shoes" with chased-silver clasps on their stacked heels. She said that I should put the valise in the closet, but I ended up leaving it just outside the closet door. On the other side, in the hatbox, the masked Robber and his confederates bided their time.

❍   ❍   ❍

I was known (by me) as the Cheyenne Kid. My sidekick or (as she put it) "kickside" styled herself Tumblesweed Bill. Tumblesweed Bill had curious ideas about how cowboys talked, what they did, and the cowboy way of life. Her cowboy accent sounded like Buckwheat on *The Little Rascals.* Her cowboy walk looked like a sailor hornpipe performed in slow motion. She had assimilated the notion that *cowpoke* was another word for *cowboy,* and as we trotted to the bus from the Skyview to Fordham Road and Grand Concourse, she did a lot of poking among our imaginary herd with an invisible picador's lance (which she called an "arpoon").

The Cheyenne Kid and Tumblesweed Bill went to Alexander's and bought T-shirts, underpants and a pair of shorts, and a Matchbox car (a Land Rover like they drove on *Daktari,* brown plastic luggage packed on its roof). Then Cheyenne and his kickside came home and baked a *tarte tatin*. As always when she was in this kind of mood, the time passed swiftly. I forgot to worry about my mother for long stretches of the afternoon.*

The blue over New Jersey deepened and then faded. My grandfather was still at the office. Earlier there had been talk about what he might want for his supper when he got home, but when Bill and Cheyenne ate an entire *tarte tatin*, the question of the night's menu lost its urgency. Tumblesweed Bill, to my dismay, seemed to vanish along with the daylight and my grandmother's half of the pie. Her voice darkened. Her eyes went sad. A new mood was gathering the folds of its cloak around her. I had seen it happen before.

"Whatcha wanta do now, Bill?" I tried.

My grandmother didn't reply but at first seemed to be considering the possible responses. After a moment she began to pinch and press at a certain spot at the base of her skull. She got up from the table, and from the expression on her face you would have said that she had just delivered herself of an opinion in the matter of what we ought to do next, even though she had said nothing at all. I had seen that happen before, too. She stood in the middle of the kitchen frowning, as if she had forgotten why she stood up. She opened a drawer, then another. She started rooting around until she found a tin of her Wintermans cigarillos. She clasped the tin in both hands and made a grateful sound but then once again seemed to lose track of her intentions. She laid the tin of Wintermans against the place at the back of her neck.

---

* Clearly, this was the point of my grandmother's pantomime, but there was more to it than that. Of the four most important adults in my early childhood, she was the only one who seemed comfortable with my being a child. She fell easily and unself-consciously into make-believe without archness or condescension. Unlike my parents and my grandfather, she never tasked me with public displays of my learnedness, never demanded that I list the fifty states and their capitals or the U.S. presidents in order from Washington to LBJ. When she called me her "petit professeur," it meant I had been holding forth, lecturing her, correcting her grammar or her shaky grasp of fact. There was a gentle mockery in the pet name.

"Mamie?" I said.

I was surprised by how shaky and small my voice sounded. I was not afraid of my grandmother, exactly; I was never afraid of her except at those times when she was actively trying to scare me. I felt abandoned by her, or by my faithful kickside, and as the sky darkened outside the windows and night came down, I started to think about the puppets again. I did not want to think about the puppets or to be afraid of them, but before long it would be time for bed and already, in the imagined dark of their closet, I could see the shine on their lidless glass eyes. I could hear their voices whispering that my mother was dead. Before she had sent me out to play that morning, my mother had offered to tie my sneakers for me, even though she knew I could tie them myself. At the time I had rebuffed her, but now her offer struck me as ominous. Knowing that she was about to die, she had wanted only to tie her little boy's shoes for him one last time. And I had refused her!

"I want to hear a story," I said to my grandmother. I saw that I had surprised her; I had surprised myself. For my grandmother, enticing a story from the deck of fortune-telling cards was not like baking, going to the movies, or playing piquet. Her stories were like moods or fevers: They came over her.

"You want to hear a story," my grandmother said.

I nodded. In fact, I didn't want to hear a story at all. Between my mother's operation and the half-intelligible rustlings from the closet, I had plenty to unsettle me already. She looked doubtful, and I hoped fiercely that she was going to decline, but she just looked at me, rubbing the tin of Wintermans against her nape. I decided to issue a retraction, but it got stuck in my throat and I could not seem to dislodge it.

"Little mouse," my grandmother said. "Don't cry." She came to me, put a hand on top of my head, and tilted my face to hers. The hand slid down to caress my cheek. "I know you are worried, but don't worry. All right?"

"Yeah."

"Yes?"

"Yes."

"Go. Go and get the cards."

I went very slowly to find the tin of almond kisses and returned to the kitchen more slowly still. By the time I got back, I had managed to console myself with the idea that at least now my grandmother would not be abandoning me, which, of course, I now see, must have been the impulse behind my asking for a story in the first place. When she acted out the parts and did all the different voices, it would be like a continuation of her turn as Tumblesweed Bill. And for however long it lasted, the story would prolong the hours until I was sent to bed, and the voices she gave to her characters would drown out the whisperings and insinuations from the hatbox in the closet.

I gave the fortune-telling cards to my grandmother and sat down across the table from her. I watched her compose herself around the deck of cards, as if it held a quantity of something rare and important. Our eyes met, and then with a nod she broke open the deck and decanted its contents in a torrent from one hand to the other. The deck of cards became a wide elastic band that she stretched and snapped and stretched again. She riffled the cards with her thumbs and sprang them with a flourish. Then she set the deck on the table in front of me. I cut it. I cut it again. I reached for the topmost card.

Abruptly, she covered my hand with hers. Her wedding ring struck my knuckles and I cried out.

"No," she said. "Never mind."

I looked up, my fingers stinging, feeling reprimanded. Her cheeks were wet with tears. I could not remember having seen my grandmother cry. For some reason the sight displeased me. "Do you have a migraine?"

She shook her head. She opened her arms, and with a powerful reluctance I got up and took a step in her direction. She grabbed me and pulled me to her chest. My grandmother's embrace was something implacable and impersonal. It was like an undertow or the impact of a concrete sidewalk. Her amber miasma of Chanel was too much, a mouthful of honey.

"You're choking me!" I said.

"Oh!" She let go. "I'm sorry!"

She was smiling. There was something about her smile and the flush in her cheeks that made me feel I had done something unforgivable. Her hand went to the place on the back of her neck.

"Maybe I do feel the migraine coming, little mouse," she said. "I am going to go lie down. Grandpa, he is stopping to the hospital to see Mommy. Then he will come home and I can get up and make supper for us. It's okay?"

After she left I sat at the kitchen table awash in guilt and regret that seemed disproportionate to the crime of simply having, for the hundredth time, slipped free of her imprisoning arms. And she must have been crying, I understood now, because she was sad about whatever was happening or had happened to my mother. If only I had endured her embrace a moment or two longer, I might have been able to discover the truth.

I decided I would make her some tea and take it to her with a wet cloth for her forehead. I would sit on the edge of her bed and wait until she felt a little better, and then maybe, at last, someone would tell me what was really going on.

While I waited for the kettle to boil, I went to the deck of cards on the kitchen table and turned over the topmost card. It was the Lady, in her long skirts and hunting coat, standing by a stone bench in a garden. I turned over the second card: the Coffin, adrift on a gaudy bed of flowers, blazoned with an ornate cross.

My grandmother had explained to me that when you were telling fortunes, the Coffin did not necessarily stand for death or dying. It might stand for anything that was coming to an end, or even for something that was beginning. The Coffin had come up twice for me in the course of our time together. Once, in the story that resulted, my grandmother had transformed the Coffin into a little boat employed by the grandmother of Moses to paddle anxiously down the Nile after his basket *because she could not let him out of her sight.* The other time it came up, the Coffin had become a chest of iron into which a hapless escape artist named Paree Poudini had been foolish enough to have himself sealed and thrown into the Hudson River.

Nevertheless, I hated to see that card turn up.

I pushed my chair back from the table and stood up. I stared down at the deck, knowing that I now had to turn over the third card. I had to turn over the third card, a rough voice whispered in my head, because the first card had been the Lady and the second the Coffin, and if I did not turn over the third card then it would be true, for real and forever, that my mother was dead.*

I don't know how long I stood there trying to work up the courage to turn over the third card. I heard the creaking of the teakettle. The electricity inside the clock on the wall hummed its unending note— A#, my grandfather had told me. The tap dripped and the drops rang against the tart pan. When I turned the card over, it was going to be the Bouquet, I decided, because my mother was dead, and though I had yet to attend one I understood that for a funeral you needed a lot of flowers. On the other hand, said the whispering (which the clock, the kettle, and the tap could not drown out), if I failed to turn the card over, that would *kill* my mother. My thoughts circled this paradox like a bee I once saw chasing itself around a lamppost. I pressed my hands against the sides of my head in a vain attempt to slow them. Finally, I reached for the deck.

---

* I still hear that raucous voice; I hear a hatbox full of voices. They bubble up from a crack in my brain, dark mutterings, shouts, and low reproaches that fall just short of sense, intruding on my thoughts almost any time I'm alone in a quiet room, working on a task that requires a certain focus—when I'm drawing, cooking, soldering a circuit, assembling a toy. When I'm writing, I never hear the hatbox voices; I hear some other voice.

There was a chiming of keys on a key ring. My grandfather sighed. "Somebody want to come and take the chain off?"

I went to the door to let in my grandfather and his own enveloping smell: raincoat, cigarette smoke, the dusty and metallic innards of a typewriter. I had never been so relieved to see anyone in my life. He did not look like the father of a woman who was dead or even, for that matter, of a woman who no longer had any feet. I wanted to hug him, but I was not sure how he would respond, since from his point of view all he had done was walk through his front door. It was not that he never hugged me, but there needed to be an occasion. He dropped his coat, briefcase, and the jumble of an evening paper on a nearby chair. He asked for a brief summary of my day and I provided one. He was almost always in a cheerful mood in those days, when MRX and he were in their prime, but tonight his manner seemed a little wan. I told him that Mamie had a headache and also that she had been crying but I was not exactly sure why. I said that I was making her a cup of tea.

"That's nice," he said. "You're a good boy, aren't you?"

"Yes."

He loosened his tie and unbuttoned his collar. I followed him back into the kitchen. "What's dinner? What's all this?"

There were two dirty plates, two forks, and a tart pan in the sink, but he meant the cards. I could tell by his face that he knew what he was looking at and that seeing the cards made him upset. I decided not to answer either of his questions. I was afraid that he might throw the cards away. Before he could gather them up, I turned over the card that was now topmost on the deck.

It was the Child.

Was *I* the child? I had to be the child. The Coffin was *my* coffin, and the Lady was my mother, grieving over the news of my death. I wondered how I was going to die. I suspected strongly that a gang of French puppets would be involved. I saw the puppets inching themselves like worms across the carpet in the guest bedroom, crawling up the side of the bed, creeping across my body in the darkness like groping hands.

"Hey," my grandfather said, his tone gentle. He crouched down and turned me to face him. "Mike, look at me. Your mother's fine. Everything's going to be all right. Okay, she lost the baby, but that's a misnomer, because it wasn't really a baby yet at all."

That was how I learned that my mother had been pregnant, and that the pregnancy had miscarried, though I did not yet fully grasp that or the import in this context of a baby being *lost*. Someone had forgotten to tell my grandfather that I was not to be told.

"All right?" he said.

He needed me to say it was all right so that we could stop talking about the lost baby and get it over with. I didn't say anything. Naturally, I had a lot of questions about the loss of babies, but I refused to ask them. I was angry; there had been a brother or a sister, and nobody had said a thing to me about it. Now that brother or sister was dead and nobody had let me know that, either.

My grandfather sat down at the table in the chair my grandmother had been using. He picked up the deck of cards and riffled through them deliberately. "What nonsense," he said. "She was wasting your time with this?"

"We were playing piquet."

"I count thirty-six cards," he said. "What kind of piquet is that?"

I felt I ought to try to protect my grandmother. "Cowboy piquet," I ventured. It sounded plausible enough to me.

He looked at me. I looked back at him. He nodded. "How about I fry us some salami," he said.

While he was scrambling the eggs and chopping up three inches of a fat Hebrew National salami, I carried a cup of tea to my grandmother. She was sitting on the edge of the bed, talking softly into the bedroom extension. She sounded angry, with the particular sarcastic intonation that she reserved for my father. I don't remember, if I ever really caught, what she was saying to him. Hindsight, and a taste for melodrama, and some faint ghost of veritable memory incline me to feel that they were words to this effect: *You are not now free to leave them.** When she saw me come in, she gave her head one firm shake. She waved me and the cup of tea away. She mouthed the word *Go*. I turned and went back down along the hallway. The teacup jingled against the saucer with a sound like a ringing telephone.

I sat down at the kitchen table. My grandfather had turned on the radio and tuned it to the news. It was the usual obscurities of statistics and disaster. He was banging pans, rifling drawers, and slamming cabinets shut. Sometimes the news had that effect on him, in particular when it concerned Richard Nixon, but when the ads came on, this time he kept on banging and slamming. It occurred to me that, like my grandmother, he might be angry about the lost baby and my father's apparent role in its loss, but all of that was unclear to me. On the off chance that he was mad about the fortune-telling cards, however, I decided to throw him off the scent.

Sometimes after he had played a round of solitaire, my grandfather used the cards to build a tower (though he always called it a "house") of cards. There were two ways to do it, a good way and a bad way. Most people did it the bad way, which formed a part of the understanding of human behavior that my grandfather passed on to me along with his lessons in playing-card construction methods. With the bad way, you tilted pairs of cards against each other like precarious lean-tos and formed them into rows of triangles that you stacked, each story narrower by one lean-to than the one below it, to make one big triangle. This method was inherently unstable, and

---

* A few days after this my father informed me that, because so many people were sick, he would have to live at the hospital where he worked for a little while; he said they had a special bedroom for busy doctors. A week later he moved out. This was the first of three separations, a series that culminated in my parents' 1975 divorce. Nine months after my father came home for the first time—a year after the miscarriage—my brother was born.

even if you executed flawlessly, you could build only a few stories high before the thing collapsed under its own weight.

The good way was to stand four cards on their long edges, forming a pinwheel configuration that made a square cell where they came together. If you laid a card flat across the central square, you got a sturdy box that could support the weight of many stories. Each radiating vane of the pinwheel could in turn be interlocked with three fresh cards, and so by going outward and upward you could erect something of substance and loft. Some of the cards I used hid, and others revealed, their faces: the Mice, the Clover, the Scythe. I thought of the stories that my grandmother had built for me out of those cards when they had turned up in the past. I saw that my tower was made of stories in two senses of the word.

I experienced this not as a pun but as an enigmatic metaphor. I assumed there must be a reason that buildings were said to be made out of narratives or, conversely, that narratives were seen to be the stacked components of mysterious towers in some way I couldn't grasp. Maybe it had something to do, I thought, with the Tower of Babel. I wanted to ask my grandfather, but then I would have to explain to him exactly how my grandmother made use of the cards. I felt that he would approve of her telling stories, or at least the kind of stories she used to tell me, even less than he evidently approved of her telling fortunes.

"Look at that," he said, casting a critical eye up and down my tower. He was holding a couple of plates and forks.

"It's easy," I assured him. "These cards are *really* good for building with. That's why Mamie lets me use them."

"Oh, is that why?" He started to set two places at the opposite end of the Formica table.

"Yes. Be careful. You'll knock it down."

"It's going to have to come down sometime."

"No."

A counter furnished with a pair of barstools divided the kitchen from the dining room. He set two places there instead of on the table, where my tower aspired.

"That's what houses of cards do," my grandfather said, returning to the stove for the pan of salami and eggs. "It's proverbial."

"What's *proverbial* mean?"

"You know what *proverbial* means."

He held out the frying pan so I could see it. He did his salami and eggs pancake-style, pouring the scrambled eggs around the fried salami, letting it set and get brown on the bottom, then flipping the "pancake" to brown on the other side.

"How many degrees in a circle?" he asked me.

"Three hundred and sixty."

"Correct. How many degrees do you want?"

"A hundred and twenty."

He cut me a fat wedge and slid it onto my plate. We sat at the counter with our food. The radio erected its tower of accidents, crime, money, love, good and bad fortune, and war. I looked at my house of cards and reflected on the proverbial inevitability of its collapse.

"Why aren't you eating?" my grandfather said.

Having only lately consumed an entire *tarte tatin* was another secret I felt that my grandmother would prefer I didn't betray. I didn't answer.

"Your dad will be here tomorrow," my grandfather said, guessing at the reason for my unaccustomed pensiveness and silence. "To take you home. You'll see Mommy. She's really all right."

"Okay."

"What's wrong?"

"Nothing."

"So eat."

"Why didn't God want them to build the Tower of Babel?" I said. "Why did He make it so everybody couldn't understand each other?"

"You know I don't believe in God."

"I know."

"Probably there was just a ziggurat, you know what a ziggurat is? Over in Mesopotamia. Maybe it was in ruins. Maybe it was only half-way built, left unfinished. And they made up a story to explain what happened to it, why it looked incomplete."

"Oh."

"You understand what I'm saying?"

I understood: Everything got ruined and nothing was ever fin-ished. The world, like the Tower of Babel or my grandmother's deck of cards, was made out of stories, and it was always on the verge of collapse. That was proverbial.

"Maybe God doesn't want this tower," my grandmother theo-rized. She was standing in the middle of the living room, holding my grandfather's coat and briefcase and the crumpled mess of his newspaper. "Because from the top of it, people they can look inside of His house and see He is a big pork."

My grandfather smiled for the first time since walking in the door. He acknowledged that there might be something to her theory. He offered my grandmother some of the salami and eggs on his plate. She shook her head and made a face, but she came over and plucked a bit of salami from the plate and popped it into her mouth. She stood very close to my grandfather, leaning her hip against his shoulder. "Mmm," she said. She looked at me without looking at me. "Poor little one."

My grandfather got down off the stool and put his arms around my grandmother. They held on to each other for what seemed to me to be a very long time. She murmured something into his ear, too low for me to catch, and he nodded and said, "I know. Me, too."

Then she seemed to recover herself. She reached out to me for a second time that afternoon. I got down from my stool and went to my grandparents. I took her left hand in my right, and my grandfa-ther did the same with my left hand. With his left hand, he reached for my grandmother and we made a brief circle before letting go.

"He's fine," my grandfather said. "I told him everything's going to be fine."

"He isn't fine," my grandmother said. "He's terrified because of those puppets you bought! They are so *horrible*. He's the nervous wrecks all day long because he is so afraid to go to sleep in there."

I had said nothing to my grandmother, at any time since their arrival from Lille, France, about my fear of the puppets.

She frowned and let go of our hands. "Oh no." She had noticed the house of cards, and now she glanced from it to my grandfather. Their eyes locked and held, and I saw they were conducting some kind of discussion about the cards and me without saying anything at all. My grandmother looked at me, a little sadly, I thought. Then she went to the kitchen table and blew on the cards like the Big Bad Wolf. The tower collapsed and rattled to the tabletop.

"See?" said my grandfather.

My grandmother gathered up the cards and slid them into their box. I don't know what became of them; I never saw them again. After he finished his dinner, my grandfather went into the guest bedroom. He took the hatbox out of the closet and carried it in the elevator to the storage space in the basement of the building.

The next day my father came to retrieve me, and together we picked up my mother from the hospital. I told her I knew about the lost baby, and she said that it was so new it hadn't really been a baby at all.

The following year my father left the Public Health Service for the short-lived job with the Senators baseball club, and we left New York for good. I saw my grandmother much less frequently; when I did see her, she was fragile and ill. We never cooked or played cards. She sat wrapped in blankets and stared at the television or watched the sky outside the window. And then one day when I was eleven years old, she died and was buried in Montefiore Cemetery, leaving me her legacy of voices in the dark.

XXXIII

Toward the end of the mourning period my grandfather attended the Twelfth Space Congress, in Cocoa Beach, Florida.

On the opening Saturday the first panel discussion was held over coffee and Danish in the Egret Room of the Atlantis Beach Lodge. An engineer on the team developing the new space shuttle led off his session by denying that he had ever referred to NASA's astronaut corps as "a buncha flying truck drivers." His accent had been engineered in Flatbush. His necktie and lapels were as wide as tire sidewalls. He wore round granny glasses and his sandy hair in a puffball. Astronauts were heroes, he said, that was obvious. And they would remain heroes right up to the day the Space Transportation System (STS) became operational. After that, "flying truck drivers" would be a fair description. Everybody in the Egret Room cracked up.

My grandfather laughed, too. He was on his way out the door with hot coffee from the catering table in a Styrofoam cup, already running late for his weekly appointment with grief.

"Space travel is still an incredibly exciting adventure in 1975," the young engineer said. "But don't worry, because at NASA we're doing everything we can to change that."

My grandfather laughed again, lingering in the doorway. In his view, heroism (if there was such a thing) would always be the residue of training. If you had been well trained, then adventure was something you hoped to avoid.

At the sound of his laughter, a woman sitting in the last row of chairs turned around and smiled at him. She patted the seat of the empty chair beside her and lifted an eyebrow. She was fifty, but her hand was youthful, the nails painted geranium pink. She was a vice president of accounting at Walt Disney World and recording secretary of the committee that put on this annual aerospace congress. She lived in Orlando. She had a daughter at Duke and an ex-husband who had flown jets for the navy in Vietnam. She wore L'Air du Temps. She also wore panty hose, which, until the previous evening, my grandfather had never encountered at close range, my grandmother having stuck till the last—February 10, 1974, (probable) age fifty-two—with girdle and garter belt. A high school classmate of Tony Bennett. An amateur photographer. Owner of a late-model Mercury Cougar the color of a spoonful of sweetened condensed milk.

He riffled through this deck of facts, trying to force the ace of the woman's name. He was appalled to realize that he had forgotten it since the night before. The name of the first woman he had slept with since losing his wife, the first since 1944 who was not my grandmother! The woman gave the empty chair another pat, like she was attempting to lure a recalcitrant pussycat. My grandfather could feel his cheeks and the back of his neck prickling. He felt like he might have to be sick. He shook his head, hoping the look on his face came off wistful but fearing that it clearly read as nausea. He turned to go, using the cup of hot coffee as a focus of attention, of the will to refrain from vomiting. He escorted stomach and brimming cup along the carpeted corridor, a man in no kind of hurry. Past the Panther Room, past the Manatee Room, out into the lobby of the motor lodge.

She caught up to him by the registration table. It was stacked with bound copies of the proceedings from last year's congress, at which the guest speaker had been Gene Roddenberry. Their tryst had begun at the Friday-night cocktail reception, held in Ramon's Rainbow Room atop a space-age modernist bank in downtown Cocoa Beach, with a mutual confession of love for *Star Trek*. My grandfather had attended the annual space congress for ten straight years as co-owner and director of product development for MRX, Inc., and had skipped nine straight cocktail receptions until last night's. He could not entirely dismiss the possibility that even in the midst of mourning my grandmother, he had been on the prowl for female company that year. But an annual conference of professionals and amateurs of rocketry and space travel was a pretty stupid place to go prowling, even at Ramon's Rainbow Room.

"You okay, mister?" She had brought him a plastic lid for the coffee cup and a banana. She made a quick survey of his face, his hairline tingling with sweat, yesterday's knot reused for his necktie. "You look pretty green. Hold this."

She handed him the banana. She took a tissue from the hip pocket of the raw silk blazer, more or less the color of her fingernails, that she must have changed into that morning after slipping unnoticed out of his room. At seven o'clock his alarm had gone off, and when he reached for her in a place where for so many months there had been only cold linens, the trace of her warmth and lingering odor of L'Air du Temps made the bed feel emptier than usual; he had lived for eleven months with bereavement, but he had never felt so bereft.

"I know it's probably the last thing you feel like doing, but if you ate that banana, you would feel better." She dabbed at his clammy brow with the tissue. "Potassium. Electrolytes."

He peeled the banana, ate half of it. Almost immediately, he felt better. "Oh," he said, feeling like an idiot for not having realized sooner. "I have a hangover."

"Guess it's been a while."

It was not a question but a laminate of implication and sass. Last night he had in all probability consumed more alcohol than cumulatively in all the years since V-E Day. Clearly, she knew more about him and his life than he could remember having told her. He made a quick probe at his memory, and guessed that some portion of the previous evening was likely never to be fully accounted for. He hoped that he had not sexually disappointed this good woman. He hoped that he had not cried on her shoulder. He feared that he might have done both.

"You better go," she said. She looked at her wristwatch, a man's big Accutron Astronaut. The lady was a space nut all the way. "Melbourne is a good half hour, depending on the traffic."

Among the things he could not remember having told her, apparently, was that he would be missing that morning's session on "The Space Shuttle (STS): A Progress Report" to drive down to Melbourne, Florida, a place he had never been, to say *kaddish* for my grandmother. He had found Beth Isaac listed in the Yellow Pages.

"Here," she said. She took the cup of coffee from him and tenderly fitted it with the lid she had brought. A drop splashed the meat of her thumb and she said, "*Ow.*" She licked away the droplet and handed the cup back to him. "Aramaic, right?"

It seemed he had gone into a fair amount of detail about the nature of Jewish customs relating to death and mourning. "That's right," he said.

"And where do they speak Aramaic again?"

"Nowhere."*

She gave his right arm a squeeze just above the elbow. He was not pleased to detect a certain amount of pity in her eyes. She brushed his cheek with her lips. "Finish your banana," she said.

That afternoon, after he had returned from his errand in Melbourne, he would catch a glimpse of her as she was walking into the Atlantis Beach Lodge's banquet room to attend the award luncheon. She formed part of a crowd of admirers and well-wishers, including all four of the other female attendees, around the imposing silverhaired gentleman who had come to Cocoa Beach to collect the award in question. That glimpse would turn out to be, as far my grandfa-

---

* Syriac, a distinct dialect of Aramaic, is the holy language of Syrian rite Christianity; yet another Aramaic dialect, Assyrian, remains the mother tongue of two hundred thousand people scattered across West Asia.

ther could remember afterward, the last time he ever saw her. And yet she would turn out to have been a key figure in shaping the subsequent course of his life.

He finished the banana she had given him as he was walking out to his car, and that was when he suddenly remembered her name, though by the time he got around to telling me the story, he had forgotten it again.*

◖   ◖   ◖

"Every Saturday, for a year," my grandfather told me. "No matter where I was. And I was a lot of places. Your dad and Ray, let me tell you, they had really spread that mess of theirs around."

It was a warm afternoon. At his request I had helped him out onto the patio he liked to observe, through the window, from his rented hospital bed. The abutilon was in flower, hung with a thousand plump red lanterns. The birdfeeder had been getting a lot of action, and the pebbled concrete beneath it was scattered with seed. "They managed to get themselves sued in four states. New York, New Jersey, Maryland, and Pennsylvania."

"Delaware."

"That's right. Delaware. How did you know that?"

"I used to snoop."

It was the only way I ever reliably found out anything as a boy.

"You remember one time, or maybe you don't remember. The summer you and your brother stayed with us."

"Mom was studying for the bar."

"The two of you were playing outside. And he, I guess he must have stepped in some dog poop. Without knowing."

"Vaguely."

---

* It was Sandra Gladfelter. See Canaveral Council of Technical Societies, "1975 Twelfth Space Congress Program" (1975).

"After a while you and he come inside, you're done playing. He goes into the kitchen. He goes into the living room, the TV room. Up the stairs, down the stairs. The bathroom. The garage. He goes into the coat closet! Like he's giving a house tour. Every room, there's a stinky little brown footprint."

I laughed.

"See?" he said. "You're not the only one with the fancy metaphors."

"Uh-huh."

"I'm talking about the mess your father and my goddamn brother made."

"Yeah, I got that."

"I mean, your mother's just starting out with her law degree. Now her credit's going to be destroyed? She's going to lose her house? At first I went around, D.C., Baltimore. I was just trying to find out how much shit there was and how far they had tracked it. Then I started trying to get on top of it, negotiate with the IRS. Negotiate with the ones suing them. Sam Chabon was suing your father, did you know that?"

"Yeah."

"His own uncle, suing him."

"A proud moment."

"I'm sorry," my grandfather said. "He's your father, you should love him."

"I shouldn't," I said. "But I do."

"Anyway, no matter where I was, if it was a Saturday, I would go and say *kaddish*. Adath Jeshurun or maybe B'nai Abraham in Philly. Ahavas Sholom in Baltimore, of course. Rodef Sholom in Pittsburgh. Beth El in Silver Spring."

"You took me to Beth El."

"A couple of times."

The *momzer* appeared over the top of the roof and began to case the joint.

"I really don't know why I was doing it, to be honest. Week after week, shlepping out Reisterstown Road or wherever to say a prayer."

"You must have gotten something out of it."

"I must have wanted to get something out of it, anyway." He stuck out his tongue. "Moment of weakness."

The *momzer* inched his way down the roof.

"Look at this guy."

"I know. I kind of just want to give him some damn birdseed."

"He wouldn't know what to do if you did," my grandfather said. "He would think you put poison in it."

"You think he's that smart?"

"He's a *momzer.*"

We didn't say anything for a while, and he closed his eyes. He had already told me that he could feel the sun "in his bones" and that the warmth of it was "pleasant."

"We're good at death, I will say that," he said.

"Jews?"

"It's 'Do this, do that. Don't do that.' That's what you need, somebody just to tell you what to do. Tear a ribbon, cover the mirror. Sit around for a week. Grow your beard for a month. And then for eleven months, every week you go to a synagogue, you stand up, and you just . . . it's . . . I don't know."

He closed his eyes again. A faint breeze stirred his soft white forelock. "If your wife, your brother, or God forbid, your child dies. It leaves a big hole in your life. It's much better not to pretend there's no hole. Not to try to, what do they say nowadays, get over it."

I reflected that it seemed to be in the nature of human beings to spend the first part of their lives mocking the clichés and conventions of their elders and the final part mocking the clichés and conventions of the young.

"So you, you know, when it's time for the *kaddish*. You stand up in front of everybody, and you point to the hole, and you say, 'Look at this. This is what I'm living with, this hole. Eleven months, every week. It doesn't go away, you don't 'put it behind you.'"

"That's another one."

"And then after a while you get used to it. I mean, that's the theory. That's why I went every week, no matter where I was, so I would get used to it. It worked that way with my parents. I guess I thought it would work with your grandmother, too."

◗   ◗   ◗

Congregation Beth Isaac was housed in a midcentury modernist chalet whose A-frame gables of azure blue betrayed its original career as an International House of Pancakes. Indeed, the shul was known locally, my grandfather learned, as Beth IHOP. In a showcase on a wall just inside the front entrance, among some newspaper clippings eulogizing the generosity and community spirit of various congregants living and dead, my grandfather noticed a trophy topped by a gold shaygets with a racquet. Beside it was a photo of a beefy young Jew shaking hands with a lanky fellow, both men wearing white polo shirts and white shorts. The lean-faced athlete was said to be British Open champion Geoff Hunt. The strapping Jew on the other end of the handshake was identified as Rabbi Lance Teppler.

An elderly female congregant saw my grandfather looking at the showcase as she was entering the sanctuary. She told her male companion to wait a minute, hold on a minute. She was wearing shapeless knit pants, cheddar orange, and a shapeless knit pullover top, black-and-orange poppies on a white ground. Her glasses were orange, too.

"Rabbi Lance is the world's greatest Jewish squash champion," she informed my grandfather.

My grandfather laughed, louder and harder than he meant to. Louder and harder than he had laughed in months, in years, than he had laughed since taking my father to see Buddy Hackett* play

---

* "The funniest Jew who ever lived," in my grandfather's estimation, one of the

the Latin Palace in 1966. There was something absurd not just in the assertion but in the woman's solemn expression and old-country accent—*skvash tchempyin*—when she made it. It hurt to laugh; it made his heart ache. And he felt sorry when he saw that the old woman was understandably offended. His effort to disguise his laughter as an uncontrollable coughing spasm did not fool her. She turned her back on my grandfather.

"A crazy man," she said in Yiddish to her male companion, employing the audible whisper relied on by old Jewish ladies for millennia in their generous efforts to ensure that no one, in particular the target of their aspersions, ever be left in the dark about who was the target of their aspersions. My grandfather was just able to make out her companion's English reply: "Looked a little hungover to me."

Attendance was spotty that morning at Beth IHOP, and when he bounded onto the *bimah*, Rabbi Lance immediately picked out the new congregant with the poorly knotted necktie sitting in the back row. He nodded once, his expression hovering somewhere between smugness and reassurance: *You are in excellent hands.* He was blond and big-jawed, good-looking in the George Segal manner.

"I'd like to begin with a very simple, very heartfelt prayer," he said. "Thank God the air-conditioning is working again."

This prayer appeared to have been offered in earnest. It received a number of amens. Nine in the morning, it was already eighty-three degrees outside. My grandfather himself was an oenophile of air-conditioning and had already given top marks to the Beth Isaac vintage. From a wide grille on the back wall of the sanctuary, a cold blast blew down on his head, and maybe that had something to do with the fact that he did not attend so much as outlast the following service, preserved cryogenically by the air-conditioning until his tedium could be cured. He thought about the young physicist, with

---

few points on which he and my father ever agreed. "He just sits in a chair, you laugh."

his appealing irreverence, and the recording secretary's soft plump hand patting the empty place beside her. No sense of connection to his past, to the past of his ancestors, or to the scattering of congregants in the pews around him. They might have been strangers in a bus station, solo travelers bound for all points. They might have been separate parties at a pancake house, awash in the syrup emerging from a Wurlitzer organ, played by an old Jew with a Shinola-black pompadour, dressed in a curious tan coverall or jumpsuit and platform saddle shoes. As with pantyhose, though my grandfather had been aware for some time that Reform temples employed organists, this was his first direct experience of the phenomenon. He had always believed that the only real satisfaction offered by the experience of attending synagogue lay in the knowledge that church would be even worse. The presence and sound of the organ, he felt, went a long way to erasing that advantage.

When at last his moment came, he rose and stood, the only mourner at his end of the room, a solitary tower imprisoning an anonymous sorrow. First he wished for a Redeemer whose arrival he did not expect and a redemption he knew to be impossible. Then he told God all the nice things God seemed to need to hear about Himself. Finally, he wished for peace as it was conventionally understood, which he supposed was unobjectionable if no more likely than the coming of a messiah. At any rate, as Uncle Ray once explained to him, if you examined the language, the concluding lines of the kaddish might have been interpreted as a wish that God and everyone else would just, for once, leave the speaker and all his fellow Jews alone.

Rabbi Lance in turn wished that my grandfather and all the other mourning Jews around the world find comfort, and he gestured for people to sit down. My grandfather sat. It seemed to take a long time for his ass to hit the wooden pew again, and even when it did, the rest of him seemed to keep on going down, down.

Over the course of the past year he had trusted, in the absence of evidence, that in time, if he stuck to the formula prescribed by the kaddish, it would work in this instance as it had when his parents died, his mother shortly after his father. Since my grandmother's death, in the most hardened bunker buried deepest under the Cheyenne Mountain of his heart, he had clung, as though it were a nuclear briefcase handcuffed to his wrist, to a contingency plan: Sooner or later, when he was ready, a woman was going to come along and fuck him. When that happened, he would know that he had begun to recover at last. But sitting in his pew at the back of Beth Isaac, with the organ sounding like the incidental music of an old radio soap opera and the final set of platitudes and baseless claims washing over him, he was obliged to confront the possibility that he might never recover from the loss of my grandmother. Her death had left everything, not just the bed, half empty. A Sandra Gladfelter with her undoubted charms and her clean L'Air du Temps smell of carnations would only ever make the hole seem larger, like a human figure placed alongside a Titan rocket in a diagram to give a sense of the rocket's scale.

"Hi, there."

It was the organist, the little old man with the jumpsuit and the shoe-polish hair. A homosexual, my grandfather supposed. He looked around and was surprised to discover that in spite of the impatience verging on rage that had compelled him to leave Beth IHOP, he appeared to be the only person left sitting in the pews. He had no idea how long it had been since the service concluded.

"I just wanted to see if you were all right."

"I'm fine."

For the second time that morning, somebody handed him a tissue. My grandfather wiped his eyes.

"You don't want to go to the *oneg*?" the organist said. "You don't want to eat a little something?"

My grandfather shook his head.

"I noticed you stood for the *kaddish*," the organist said.

"My wife died last year."

"Cancer?"

"Yeah."

"Hey, that's too bad, sweetheart, I'm sorry. She was sick a long time?"

"The first diagnosis was, I guess it was 1968. They operated, you know, they did radiation. It went into remission, but then it came back."

"I had it, too," said the organist. "Cancer. Radiation. Believe you me, sweetheart, it's no fun."

"I believe you," my grandfather said.

"I'm going to the *oneg* now, all right?"

"Sure. Nice to meet you."

"You're all right?"

"I'm fine."

"You don't want to have a piece of cake?"

"No, thanks."

The old man patted my grandfather on the shoulder and walked out of the sanctuary. He moved with grace and remarkable dignity, given the platform shoes. My grandfather looked at his watch. He had volunteered to give a demonstration of model building in the Atlantis Beach Lodge's exhibition room that afternoon, and it was time to be getting back. He sat for a minute longer. He was maybe a little bit tired. He was tired of lawyers and their posturings and of the brutal politesse of taxmen. He was tired of shouldering the weight of other people's bad decisions along with his own. Most of all he was tired of mourning my grandmother. Even after intermittent full-blown madness had subsided to chronic nervousness and the limitless insecurity common to actors, she had been an exhausting woman to love. But he had loved her no less passionately for the hard work. If there were times when the weight of the secret she carried, whatever it had been, made it impossible for her to love herself and thus to return his love, the fierceness with which she had clung to him even at those moments was recompense enough. It had fed his various hungers. Now there was only the daily scutwork of missing her. He wanted to rest. He wanted, like all the mourners of Zion, to be left in peace.

The car had sat for two hours in the hot sun. It stank of scorched coffee. He leaned in to grab the cup. As he turned back toward the building to look for a waste bin, he stepped on something round that gave under his heel. His foot shot out in front of him and he sat down hard on the asphalt. He dropped the cup and the lid popped off. The remnant inch of coffee dispersed itself efficiently, spattering his shirtfront, necktie, and pants. That night he would find a brown stain on his right sock.

A black rubber ball huddled against the left front tire of his car, as if seeking protection against his wrath. It was smaller than a tennis ball, a Dunlop with a tiny yellow dot. My grandfather picked up the squash ball and heaved it back overhead, in the direction of the synagogue. "Fuck you, Rabbi Lance," he said.

He reached for the plastic cup lid (he never located the errant cup) and for the first time noticed the complexity, even intricacy, of its molded surface. Coffee served to go in a Styrofoam cup with a polystyrene lid was a relative novelty in 1975. At first the lids had been plain disks that you needed to remove completely to get at your drink. A couple of years back you started to see lids with a tabbed lip. You were meant to pull the tab, thus tearing a suitable opening into the frangible plastic. Since the lid was an otherwise featureless disk, however, with no perforations, what usually happened was that either you ended up with a jagged slit or else ripped the lid in half. By habit, when he got coffee to go, my grandfather had learned to ignore the treacherous tab and, as he had this morning, remove and then replace the entire lid every time he wanted to take a sip of coffee.

The lid on the coffee Sandra Gladfelter had given him was something new: It had grooved perforations to make tearing a spout easier. It had a notched slot that was clearly intended to hold the tab open and in place once you had peeled it back. The lid's surface was reinforced by a structure of four raised ribs, in an *X*, to further reduce the chance of misadventure while tearing. Thought and consideration had gone into the design, but even apart from its functional engineering, as an object it was beautiful. Its whiteness and the abstract geometry of its protuberances had something futuristic about them, as if it were a line cap or battery hatch that had fallen off a passing starship.

It reminded my grandfather of the surfaces fabricated by modeler Douglas Trumbull to render the spaceships, vehicles, and lunar buildings in *2001: A Space Odyssey*, covered in bumps, ridges, and raised grids meant to suggest machinery whose function was obscure and yet plausible. In fact, my grandfather thought, this lid might have been used to model an architectural element of the Clavius moon base in that film. He turned the lid this way, that way, ignoring the heat rising up from the pavement through the seat of his trousers. He remembered the promise he once made to my grandmother: that he would fly her to find refuge on the Moon. He pictured the two of them in colorful spacesuits like those worn by the astronauts in *2001*, an orange one for him, a blue one for her, out for a spin across the lunar surface in their rover. They approached a hatchway embedded in the lunar soil. His gloved hand reached for a control switch and slowly, along its parallel grooves, the automatic hatch panel rose into the black sky so that he could drive the rover into its sublunarian garage. The hatch closed behind them. The garage filled with breathable air. In just a little while, they would regain the peace of the sanctuary he had built for her on the Moon. Slung from the webbing of his rack, he would watch her cutting flowers in her hydroponic garden as the world hid its nightside and peace descended on their refuge in space.

○　　　○　　　○

An accordion wall of carpeted beige panels divided the Atlantis Beach Lodge's banquet room from its exhibition hall, where my grandfather sat at a table, behind a sign with his name printed below the word DEMONSTRATION and above the melancholy legend FORMER PRESIDENT AND TECHNICAL DIRECTOR, MRX, INC. The exhibition hall was divided into three areas by a series of movable partitions, also carpeted, but in orange. My grandfather sat in the area devoted to "Space Arts and Spacecrafts." He had the entire room to himself, so the question of what he was in the act of demonstrating remained open. Taking refuge, he supposed: his body behind a partition in the exhibition hall, his imagination in the main reactor unit of the first human settlement on the Moon. He had not been able to keep his promise to my grandmother—or to himself, really—during her lifetime, but maybe, he was thinking, there was a way to make it happen in his imagination, where my grandmother lived on.

From the other side of the accordion wall came muffled rumors of the proceedings taking place in the banquet room. Men delivered speeches that verged dreamlike on intelligibility. Submarine speeches, turbulent with laughter and applause; then one great swell of applause that took a long time to ebb. After that my grandfather heard a new voice, thin but strong, with a singsong intonation.

The autumn *Bulletin* of the space congress had trumpeted the inauguration of an annual Saturn Medal "for significant contribution by an individual who has helped mankind to aim for the stars."[*] It offered a slate of candidates chosen by the committee of which Sandra Gladfelter served as recording secretary, a ballot card, and a preaddressed return envelope. Voting was open to all subscribers who could afford the price of a stamp, with the results to be announced in the next issue.

---

[*] Underwritten by a charter airline called Saturn Airways, which ceased operations in 1976. Only one further Saturn Medal was awarded, to writer Arthur C. Clarke.

When my grandfather saw the final tally—a landslide—he considered coming forward with an account of the things he had witnessed at Nordhausen. He started writing an open letter to the *Bulletin*, thinking he might also send it to the editorial page of a newspaper, but he soon began to question the letter's value or point. It was hardly a secret that the "father of space flight" had some kind of Nazi past. Since the end of the war, historians, journalists, and former inmates of KZ Dora had made well-documented attempts to refute the Saturn medalist's lifelong position: that he was innocent not just of having committed war crimes at the Mittelbau but of having the faintest idea that war crimes were being committed there at all. None of the worst charges leveled against him ever seemed to stick, let alone register, in the public's mind. If they did register, they were dismissed as part of what seems to have been an actual Soviet campaign to discredit him.[*] To the extent that the Cold War was fought by means of symbols, Wernher von Braun had delivered the greatest blow ever struck by either side. Usually, you could rely on Americans to believe the worst about their heroes, but nobody wanted to hear that America's ascent to the Moon had been made with a ladder of bones.

It turned out that after thirty years of carrying the outrage in his pocket like Aughenbaugh's lighter, ready to strike its flint at any moment, my grandfather had lost or misplaced it. He couldn't bring himself to rail against the rehabilitation of SS-*Sturmbannführer* von Braun for as long as it would have taken to write a one-page letter. He didn't have the heart or the stomach for the implications:

1. Scientific inquiry and pursuit were inherently amoral or ultramoral.

2. The wonder of rockets was inextricable from their fitness as instruments of death.

---

[*] Whom the Soviets would have been only too happy to abduct into their own rocket research program, of course, had the U.S. not abducted him first.

3. The ideals of justice, of openness, of protecting the weak—of fundamental decency—for which he had fought, and Alvin Aughenbaugh and so many others had died, meant nothing to the country that espoused them. They were encumbrances to be circumvented in the exercise of power. They had not, in fact, survived the war. This last implied that:

4. In a fundamental way both proved and exemplified by the spectacular postwar ascent of Wernher von Braun, Nazi Germany had won the war.

It was the final point that my grandfather felt most reluctant to dwell on or ponder. He disdained patriotism. His illusions about American decency had not survived his reading of American history. In every presidential election from 1936 to 1948, he had voted for Norman Thomas, the Socialist candidate. But even skepticism, setting a limit to all belief, has its limits. That afternoon in the office of Dr. Leo Medved, he had chosen to continue to believe, not to question, what my grandmother had always told him about her wartime history. Under the circumstances, skepticism had felt like a kind of madness; to choose belief was the only way forward. It was the same with von Braun and the war itself. My grandfather chose the only way forward. He chose to believe that the bloodshed and destruction had not been in vain. It made a difference that Old Glory and not the *Nationalflagge* had been planted in the lunar dust. So he had put aside the letter, deciding just to try to keep out of von Braun's way during the congress, and hope they never crossed paths. That was the motive behind his volunteering to mind the exhibition room during the Saturn Medal luncheon.

At the fifty-minute mark the hectoring tone gave way to a hushed rasp; von Braun had become an avowed Christian on his conversion to all-American and it was not unusual for his public remarks to take a pious, indeed mystical, turn. A few moments later there was a second torrent of applause. The sound pressed against and rattled the accordion wall until, on a surge of applause so loud it made my grandfather jump, one of the carpeted panels seemed to give way.

My grandfather stood up and peered over the partition into the middle section of the exhibition, given over to displays by Bendix, Rockwell, and other corporations that sponsored the congress. He saw that the accordion wall in this section had a small doorway in one of its panels. The carpeted door was open, and through it applause rolled in to flood Wernher von Braun. He stood in the doorway with his back to the exhibition room. He bowed and nodded to the audience. He assured well-wishers and some nearby minder that, yes, he was perfectly fine. He shut the door, muting the sound of applause, and turned to face the corporate sponsors section of the exhibition room. His eyes appraised the exhibits as though he intended to loot them or have them demolished. His blond hair had turned to white with ivory stains, like nicotine on the teeth. It still grew thick and he wore it modishly long. Its pallor contrasted with the flush of his face. He looked like a man in the grip of some kind of bodily attack—stomach cramps, back spasms, cardiac arrest. My grandfather tried to remember what disease was rumored to be killing the man.

Von Braun's gaze lighted on a tall ficus in a pumpkin-shaped terra-cotta pot in the corner opposite him. He moved toward the potted plant with a hitch in his gait. He unzipped the fly of his brown suit trousers and took out his pallid old nozzle. There was a pattering, the first drops of rain hitting a dirt infield, then a fitful sloshing like somebody after a party pouring the dregs of beer bottles onto the lawn. Von Braun groaned and cursed softly to himself in the most scabrous German my grandfather had heard since the war. His own urinary vigor was no longer what it once was, and he felt an automatic pity for von Braun. The Conqueror of the Moon kept at it, and after a minute or two it was clear from the acoustics that he had himself a puddle. He coaxed out another laggard drop or two and then hunched his shoulders to zip himself up.

My grandfather forgot that he was supposed to be trying to keep out of von Braun's way. When von Braun turned from the ficus tree, he saw my grandfather looking at him over the partition. Von Braun looked more embarrassed, certainly more contrite, than my grandfather would have expected. He felt his long-nurtured hatred of the man begin to waver. After all, how was the case of von Braun different from that of any other man whose greatness was chiefly the fruit of his ambition, that reliable breeder of monsters? Ambitious men from Hercules to Napoleon had stood ankle-deep in slaughter as they reached for the heavens. Meanwhile, there was no getting away from the fact that, thanks to von Braun's unrelenting ambition, only one nation in the whole of human history had left its flag, not to mention a pair of golf balls, on the Moon.

"Congratulations on the prize," my grandfather said.

"Thank you," said von Braun. The wide-eyed look of culpability had already left his face, and now he squinted, studying my grandfather's face. He might have been wondering if he ought to know it. He might have been trying simply to infer my grandfather's opinion, in general or just in this instance, of a grown man who urinated into a motel flowerpot. My grandfather suspected that it was the former. "I very much appreciate the honor and support."

"Oh, I didn't vote for you," my grandfather said.

Von Braun blinked and bobbed his big white unkempt head. "Who did you vote for?"

"Myself."

Von Braun grinned and then asked my grandfather his name.

My grandfather felt his heart rate ascend steeply. Was it possible that von Braun had been told the name of the man who had uncovered the trove of V-2 documents that he'd ordered hidden, taking away one of his bargaining chips with the Allies upon capture? If von Braun should happen to recollect and recognize his name, would he call the police or have my grandfather thrown out of the congress? More to the point: Was this my grandfather's chance, at last, to finish the job he had laid aside that night in favor of doing his duty? He was fifty-nine years old, and if he was no longer as strong as he had been at twenty-nine or thirty-nine, he was also no longer anywhere near so prone to fury. Since the day of his release from prison, he had never once gone looking for trouble. This turned out to be surprisingly effective as a means of avoiding it.

He told Wernher von Braun his name. It did not appear to ring any bells. It certainly had not come up for discussion, as von Braun observed, nor had it appeared, as far as he could recall, on the ballot.

"I was a write-in candidate," my grandfather explained.

◑   ◑   ◑

The walls of the Space Arts and Spacecrafts section of the exhibition room were hung with large-format color photos taken by attendees of the congress: Rocketdyne engines slashing a bright rip across the blue banner of a Canaveral morning. A crowd of people dressed in gumball colors, all craning their necks in the same direction to gape at something overhead. A slow-shutter telephoto exposure of a full moon rising over Mount Erebus that had been taken, according to its label, by von Braun himself during his trip to Antarctica in 1966. Oil paintings and watercolors of spacewalks, moonscapes, and splashdowns were displayed on easels of gold-painted bamboo. A number of paintings depicted with painstaking realism the unbuilt spacecraft and unvisited worlds that were the stuff of space-fan dreams. A few had been painted by the great Chesley Bonestall, a hero to my grandfather. And there were three tables of models: rockets, space planes, capsules, lunar modules, and rovers, built to a variety of scales from a variety of materials. Von Braun came around a partition from the corporate sponsors area, past a large Bonestall of Earth as seen from the Martian surface, a glowing aquamarine dot against the starry black.

Passing the models table, von Braun took a moment to admire a pair of French rockets, a Véronique and a Centaure, that my grandfather had brought with him to the show. My grandfather was identified as their modeler on little cards in front of them, and he accepted von Braun's praise for their beauty. Von Braun came over to the demonstration table, where my grandfather was sitting behind the mess he had made. Fanciful bits of plastic in drab grays and whites were scattered across the tablecloth.

"What is all this?" von Braun said.

My grandfather noticed that when von Braun's eyes strayed across a three-fourths-complete model of the prototype STS, he averted his face with a slight jerk of the head, as if the sight of the space shuttle were painful or loathsome. Von Braun leaned over to take a closer look at the scattered bits of molded plastic. He reached down to pick up an elongated and *U*-shaped extrusion of gray PVC. There was another beside it, the curve of its *U* slightly flattened. He fitted the pieces together to form the tapered cylinder of a jet engine's housing.

"You use commercial model kits?" Von Braun looked back at the two French vehicles on the models table. Like all my grandfather's hobby work to this point, they had been made, with fine woodworking tools and a Dremel, generally from balsa and maple. Each vane, flap, and fairing was custom-built. "No, surely not."

"Normally, no," said my grandfather. "I'm just fooling around; they call it 'kit bashing.'"

On the way down to the space congress from New York, stopping for gas in Myrtle Beach, my grandfather had spotted a hobby shop. He had stopped to pick up some extra 0000 sandpaper for the STS model, which had been the intended demonstration object until the intervention of fate in the form of a one-night stand, a squash ball, and a coffee cup lid. He had begun the shuttle model shortly after the previous congress. But the turmoil of the past year had taken a toll on his time for model building, along with everything else.

The hobby shop in Myrtle Beach turned out to be having a sale on plastic model kits. Impulsively, thinking I might enjoy them—he was planning to stay at our house in Columbia on his way back to New York City after the congress—he had picked up several kits: a couple of panzers, a Zero, a French Mirage, a Bell Huey, an AMC Matador, and a model of the PT-73 from the old *McHale's Navy* television show. He also bought several tubes of Testors glue.

In the hour that had passed since he began his demonstration, he had cut the parts from the sprues of the latticed frames that held them and spread them out—axles, struts, rotors, turret guns, joysticks, the components needed to form the Matador's bucket seats—to get a sense of them. He had pulled out the pieces needed to build one of the panzers' hulls and, with the help of an X-Acto knife and glue, configured them into a flattened square structure about the size and shape of a coaster. It was wider by about half an inch than the plastic lid that, having dabbed it with Testors, he now settled onto its smooth upper surface.

"What is it? May I ask?"

My grandfather did not reply. He did not intend to reply. He was relieved to discover, on meeting Wernher von Braun, that his heart was no longer filled with homicide nor his brain with retribution. But he had no desire to converse with the man.

"Some sort of hatch? A launch pad?"

My grandfather heard and recognized—picked up like a beacon—the uncontrollable curiosity that was so often the vice of a solitary dreamer. He fought down the urge to explain his theories of lunar settlement, though the urge to explain was overwhelming in my grandfather, quasi-sexual, a kind of intellectual horniness. Anyway, what did he think his silence could accomplish? In 1945 Von Braun had eluded my grandfather's grasp and the grasp of justice. He had not simply managed to avoid the violent, sordid, or punitive fates that befell so many of his comrades and superiors—he had risen to a singular pinnacle of fame and lionization. He was, by any measure, the luckiest Nazi motherfucker who ever lived.

"A satellite!" von Braun guessed. "Some kind of solar cell?"

In the end, in classic Nazi style, Wernher von Braun had commit-ted suicide—or anyway his dream had killed itself, a victim of its own success. The Moon had been abandoned. The Apollo program was dead. Thanks to the relentless obsession of von Braun, in a span of five years a lunar voyage had gone, in public opinion, from won-drous and impossible odyssey to short-haul bus run, from national mandate to the greatest waste of dough that human improvidence had ever conceived. At NASA Braun himself had been first sidelined, along with the Saturn Vs, and then shown the door. All the grandi-ose mission plans that he'd been hawking for decades, in the books he cowrote with Willy Ley, on *The Wonderful World of Disney* and in the pages of *Collier's* and *Life*, with all those stunning Bonestall paintings of earthrises and Mars landers and farms rotating in low earth orbit, seemed to have been mislaid in some cultural bottom drawer. Nobody talked anymore about orbital wheels at the Lagrange points, about lunar He3 mines or human settlement of Mars. It was the age of the space shuttle, of flying truck drivers. Like the Saturn V, Von Braun was a dinosaur. My grandfather could not help feeling a certain amount of pity.

"Nuclear reactor," my grandfather said.

"Are you serious?"

"Just the upper portion. Rest of it will be buried."

"Buried in what?"

"Lunar surface."

"It's a moon base?"

"I just started."

Von Braun lowered himself, grimacing with pain, until he was at eye level with the table. "What is the scale?" he said. He seemed to have forgotten that only two minutes before, my grandfather had caught him pissing into a potted ficus. He was a past master, after all, in the art of expedient forgetting.

"Dunno, 1:66, maybe?"

"Not large, then."

"Forty kilowatts ought to be enough at first."

My grandfather picked through the model parts looking for tiny rectangular bits—mirrors, battery covers, gun-port covers—that he could use to complicate and give realistic texture to the model's surface. This was precisely the technique Trumbull had used for the models in 2001. The pieces were all the various colors of plastic used in the kits they'd been pillaged from, and none the same color as the plastic lid, but once you had spray-painted them the same matte shade of pale gray, the unit would take on a convincing texture.

"Rankine cycle?" von Braun said. "Like the SNAP-10."

This supposition was lamentably mistaken, and my grandfather was desperate to explain why the simpler mechanics and greater efficiency of a Stirling engine would be infinitely preferable to the turbine of the SNAP models that von Braun and NASA had been pushing a decade earlier. This time he managed to stick to his resolve, and this time von Braun seemed to get the message. Or maybe he was just tired of crouching. He gripped the edges of the table and pulled himself to his feet. He went back over to the models table and reached out with a finger to stroke the smooth-sanded surface of the Véronique, finished in a glossy shade of cream.

"She is really quite beautiful," he said. He waited to give my grandfather a chance to agree with or dispute this opinion. My grandfather refrained from observing that it wasn't too surprising the Véronique had caught von Braun's eye, since it had been engineered in large degree by France's own cadre of captured Peenemünders. "Still," von Braun continued, "Frenchmen in space." He smiled. "You have to admit, there's comedy in the notion."

"Yeah?" my grandfather could not prevent himself from saying. "How do you feel about Jews on the Moon?"

"Beg your pardon?"

"I did a little consulting work for the state of Israel," my grandfather lied wildly. "They're putting a lot of muscle and money and brainpower into a next-level system, Jericho 2. Lunar orbiters and landers. To build a Jewish settlement on the Moon."

Von Braun looked momentarily taken aback but recovered himself. Give him credit: Having generated so much of his own in his lifetime, the man knew bullshit when he heard it. "Perfect," he said. "Just the place for them."

But that was not the end of the story of magic coffee-cup lid. Later that afternoon the young shuttle engineer from Brooklyn came looking for my grandfather. His attention had been drawn to the Véronique and the Centaure models and he had to agree, the work was exquisite, just as Dr. von Braun had told him. He wondered if my grandfather might be amenable to or interested in building models for NASA, both as part of the research and development process and for purposes of education and display? The pay, he said, would be not half bad.

My grandfather said he would think about it. Then he changed his mind and decided to accept the young engineer's offer without thinking about it. He said he did too much thinking as it was, and if he got this decision out of the way it would free up his brain to think about something else. The young engineer asked for an example of the kind of thing my grandfather had in mind, thinking-wise. "Jews on the Moon?" my grandfather said.

"Oh yeah, I heard about that," said the young engineer. "I think the old Nazi motherfucker was totally freaked out."

My grandfather started to laugh.

"Score one for the Hebes," said the young engineer.

At that my grandfather laughed long and hard. When he could speak again he thanked the young engineer, wrote down his telephone number, and they agreed to be in touch soon. Over the next fourteen years my grandfather went on to build more than thirty-five models for NASA, of different types and functions, at a variety of scales. The reputation of his work for faithfulness and quality brought him commissions from private collectors all over the world. He had no doubt that the work Wernher von Braun indirectly brought his way had helped him emerge from mourning the loss of my grandmother and of the company and the success that meant so much to him.

XXXIV

My grandfather stood on his left foot to pull his jeans on over his right leg and lost his balance. He reached out to steady himself on the edge of her dresser. He missed the dresser and knocked into a floor lamp. The lamp had a chrome stand whose surface reflected just enough ambient light to be visible in the dark bedroom, and he could see that it was falling. It was not yet sunrise. He was trying to be quiet. Meanwhile he was falling, too. He had to choose between breaking his own fall or the lamp's. He opted for the former, making a second, successful try for the edge of the dresser. The lamp hit the terrazzo floor with a cowbell clang, and there was a blue burst in the dark, the soft pow! of a lightbulb losing its vacuum.

"So when you said you weren't going to sneak out at dawn anymore," Sally said. Her voice was coming from somewhere underneath a pillow. "You meant you would still leave, but you would make a lot of noise."

"I'm sorry."

"Broom's in the kitchen."

He went to fetch the dustpan broom, and when he got back she had gone into the bathroom. He heard the chord of her urine spray resonating against different curvatures of the toilet bowl. It was a sound he had always found comforting. It erased all midnight loneliness. He righted the lamp and swept up the glass, then went to the kitchen to dump the mess in the trash. The trash can was full, so he cinched the bag and carried it out to the bin alongside the house. It took him another minute to track down a sixty-watt bulb. By the time he returned to the bedroom, she was sitting on the made bed, lacing up a pair of duck boots.

"What's this?"

"You're going to spend all morning chasing after that fucking snake again?"

"I was just going back to my place."

"And then?"

"And then I was planning to spend all morning chasing after that fucking snake."

"So today I'm coming with you."

"I'm meeting Devaughn."

"Did Devaughn let you stick your thing in his bottom last night?"

He was shocked by the question, or the way she phrased it, or the startling image it rhetorically conveyed, but that was all right. He needed a woman who could deliver him a shock. He conceded that indeed Devaughn had granted him no such liberties.

"Is Devaughn going to make you waffles?"

"That seems unlikely."

She stopped tying her boot and looked up at him, her eyes saying, *I rest my case.*

"Fine," said my grandfather. "But could you please make them for me at my place, on my waffle iron?"

"All right." She looked surprised, not unpleasantly, and a bit puzzled.

As of this point in their relationship Sally had never been to his place. This was just becoming a bit odd. He knew that the longer he put it off, the more it would begin to seem like he had something to hide.

"What's so special about your waffle iron?"

"It works better than yours."

"Is that so?"

"Mine, the iron is better seasoned. The waffles never stick."

"I see. You've seasoned yours very thoroughly, haven't you?"

"Yes."

"I imagine there's an entire procedure."

"That's right."

"A right way and a wrong way."

"Oh, there's more than one wrong way."

"And only one right way."

"If that."

When they got to my grandfather's place, Devaughn was sitting on the front steps smoking a Tiparillo. My grandfather was seven minutes late. "Sally's going to drive me today," he said.

Devaughn looked genuinely confused for a few seconds and pretended to be confused for a few seconds more. Then he looked a little hurt. He had not said so, but my grandfather could tell that the guard had started to enjoy their expeditions into the ruins of Mandeville.

"She know how to kill a snake?"

"Why don't you ask her yourself?"

Devaughn looked at Sally.

"I know you aim for the legs," Sally said. "Right?"

Devaughn hauled himself to his feet. He stood on the doorstep, rocking back and forth, crunching the plastic tip of the cheroot between his teeth.

"Yes?" my grandfather said.

"Least you could do's pay me for all the time I done wasted."

"What am I, Warren Buffett, I don't have that kind of money."

"I mean today. This morning."

"I cost you an hour of Devaughn Time."

"'s right."

My grandfather gave him a ten. Devaughn folded it and folded it again, then slid it into the Tiparillo box that he carried in his shirt pocket. He nodded to my grandfather and touched the bill of his cap to Sally.

My grandfather unlocked the door to his condo and stood aside to let Sally in. There was a small foyer that opened onto the living room.

They were separated by a partition wall about waist-high. Along the top of this partition, posed like a row of duck decoys on display bases, six large-scale models re-created the history of the space shuttle program in order of construction, from *Enterprise* to *Endeavour.*

"Spaceships, huh?" Sally said.

"Shuttles."

"Uh-huh."

My grandfather went into the kitchen and got out the waffle iron. Then he told Sally he was going to change into his snake-hunting clothes. Sally didn't say anything, or if she did, neither of them recalled it to me afterward. She had gone on into the living room and was trying to get her head around it. There were, as she would later put it to me, rockets everywhere. On every available horizontal surface: the coffee table, the bookshelves, on top of the television set. French Arianes, Japanese Mus, Chinese CZs, an Argentine Gamma Centauro. The expanse of wall that carried from the living area to the dining area beyond, which in Sally's unit was taken up by a large hutch full of china, and in other units was often occupied by family photo galleries or earth-toned batik prints of Israeli and biblical scenes, was here taken up by four glass shelves mounted on metal brackets from just above the terrazzo floor to within fifteen inches of the ceiling. These held models of known Soviet launch vehicles, from the early R-7s that had put Sputniks aloft to the Proton. On another, relatively small shelf on the wall over the television was a collection of American rockets: the Atlas, the Aerobee, the Titan. Sally didn't fully grasp all of this, and even when she glanced at the plaques mounted on each base, the names and designations meant very little to her. She could see the incredible detail, the antennae and hatch hinges, the care that had been taken with paint and identifying markings and national symbols. It was all very impressive, but in her view it was not necessarily admirable.

In the dining room table during the first years of my grandfather's residency, there had been a proper dining set that was, to my knowledge, never used. At some point he had gotten rid of the chairs, shoved the table to one side, and put in a workbench. Sally looked at the orderly chaos of plastic and wire on the workbench, the rows and columns of little plastic drawers, each labeled with a bit of masking tape on which an enigmatic hand had scrawled something like *ailerons* or *rearview mirrors* or *bushings*.

"You made all these?" she called out. She was not able to keep the note of horror out of her voice. It was not that she had any particular objection to hobbies and hobbyists—they were hardly rare among her cohort or in the units of Fontana Village. But in the scope, depth, and singular-mindedness of my grandfather's focus on rocketry and in the degree of painstaking detail he brought to bear, there was such naked obsessiveness that she was appalled. Not, again, because she had any objection to obsessiveness—on the contrary. When it came to art, she thought, the more naked the better. In the execution of her own paintings, she relied on obsessiveness and the compulsion to keep going, dig deeper, push further.

("I guess it was just, well . . . Rockets?" she told me. "The whole Freudian aspect. I mean, the decor of this man's house is basically nothing but phallic symbols.")

But not quite. She lifted the sheet and looked at the model of LAV One that my grandfather had completed the day before they met. She knelt down to see it from eye level. She tried to imagine herself driving that tiny rover around the rim of the moon's northernmost crater. She couldn't manage it.

"How the waffles coming?" my grandfather said.

He came clomping out dressed in blue coveralls, black waders, and a pink-and-green madras bucket hat from the lost and found, courtesy of Devaughn.

"Oh no." Sally stood up and turned to see what was making all the noise. "No, dear. That is not at all what you wear to go on a snake hunt."

"It isn't?"

Sally shook her head. "Think you know everything," she said.

For a while she vanished into his walk-in closet. There was a pole on either side, but the left-hand pole was bare of clothes or hangers. The right-hand pole held scattered guayaberas and pairs of slacks and the charcoal suit he had worn to my grandmother's funeral and every funeral since. He heard a mock-bitter sigh that did not sound entirely mock. Then he heard her raucous seagull laugh. She came out holding the aloha shirt that I had given him as a joke, palm green with topless brown hula girls who varied by color of lei. She handed him the shirt on its hanger without comment, and a pair of chinos. While he took off his boots and coveralls and put on the clothes she wanted him to wear to the snake hunt, he heard her talking on the phone. When he came out of the bedroom a second time, she was holding a Sputnik in her left hand like the skull of Yorick and using its accurately mirrored surface—an effect painstakingly achieved—to check the state of her hair bun. She looked him over. "Much better. Much more effective," she said.

As she returned the Sputnik to its place, taking care with the four prongs of its long antennae, its identity seemed to register with her. "I was living in California then," she said. "First husband. I remember one night there was a party going on, if you looked up you could see it, this moving pinpoint like a star in a hurry. People were afraid it might have a bomb or be a weapon of some kind, remember? Some bozo tried to convince me to sleep with him because the death ray was going to come down and vaporize us all."

"And what happened?"

"He was right, we all got vaporized."

"It was the booster rocket that you could see," my grandfather said. "To be precise. You needed binoculars to see the satellite itself."

"Let's definitely be precise. What's this one?" She leaned in to read the plaque. "Sputnik 2. The one with the dog?"

"Laika."

"Laika! Right. And this one?" She pointed to a model of a satellite that looked something like a cruder version of the familiar space capsules of the manned era. "Lunik 3."

"It took the first pictures of the far side of the moon. No one had ever seen it before."

"Because it was so dark?"

"That's a misnomer."

"Oh, is it."

"It all depends on how you define *dark*."

"Indeed it does," Sally said. "Now let's go hunt that snake."

She drove them to the shopping center in her Mercedes. Daimler and all the rest had used more or less the same type of slave labor as the Mittelwerk, and my grandfather disapproved in particular of Jews driving German cars, but it was a beautiful thing, with its stacked headlights and its grille like a chrome jukebox. Its six cylinders bubbled like mountain water over rocks. Anyway, it was 1990, and he would soon be seventy-five, and there was no use and certainly no virtue in holding on to a grudge. The Jews had outlived Hitler and he had outlived von Braun.

He was not accustomed to being driven by a woman who was not his daughter. Even when my mother was around, he generally did the driving. He surrendered the role to Sally along with his qualms about German automobiles and his doubts about the soundness of her ideas when it came to hunting pythons.

She had placed an order at the Italian delicatessen next to the Piggly Wiggly. Bread, a salami, a container of olives, a container of artichoke hearts, a container of stuffed hot peppers, three kinds of cheese, hard, soft, and semi-soft.

"What, no semi-hard cheese?" my grandfather said.

"That's you," said Sally.

She had two folding beach chairs in the trunk of the car along with an old wool blanket. He stood while she hung the chairs from his shoulder and then led her to the padlocked gate.

"Now what?" Sally said.

He did something odd then. He set the chairs on the ground beside the grocery bag with the food. He knelt down in front of the lock, working hard not to grimace or grunt. He put his ear to the padlock and twirled the dial to the left a little ways. He put an air of concentration on his face.

"You can hear it?"

"Sh."

He stopped at the first number and then went on with the safe-cracker routine until the padlock sprang open.

"That is very impressive," Sally said gratifyingly. "I'm really impressed."

"Once you know how."

"So they change the lock every time you come, I guess? That's why you don't bother to just memorize it?"

"You," my grandfather said, "are a sharp cookie." He swung open the gate. "After you."

He led her onto the grounds. They walked up the road toward the old clubhouse drowning in kudzu, then bore to the left. The road stayed more or less clear until you reached what had been the clubhouse parking lot. They sat down in the folding chairs and spread napkins on their laps. He laid the salami and the cheeses on his lap and took out his pocketknife. He sliced off half a dozen roundels of French bread and passed them to her. She cupped them in her hands. He peeled the papery skin from the salami. She fed him a stuffed pepper while he worked, and then an olive.

My grandfather had finally gone to see the specialist his doctor had referred him to, and the news was not good. He knew he would have to tell Sally about it, but he was afraid that when he did, she would decide—and he would not blame her—that she was just not up to crawling down that road again.

"I'm going to make you a perfect bite," my grandfather said. "That's what my daughter used to call it."

"What's that?"

"A little bit of everything all together."

"That's exactly what I want. Make me a perfect bite."

He sliced a thin wedge of the semi-soft cheese and laid it on a slice of bread. The salami went on that, and the whole thing was topped with an artichoke heart and a sliver of hot pepper. He passed it to her.

"Perfect," she said.

He made one for himself. There was a strong breeze moving across the grass and through the leaves of the Australian pine and melaleuca trees. An airplane passed overhead, trailing a banner that reminded the public to go wild by consuming some product. It was seventy-two degrees.

"You see?" she told him. "This is the way to do it." She leaned over and planted a kiss on his cheek, and he took advantage of the opportunity to kiss her back, on the mouth. She slid her chair nearer to his to make it easier on her arthritic shoulder. He took hold of her by the waist and lifted her out of her chair and onto his lap. He heard a creak in his own shoulder, and the canvas seat of the beach chair groaned under their combined weight.

"Who was president the last time you just sat around necking with somebody?" Sally asked him.

"Gerald Ford."

"Richard Nixon."

Out on the road beyond the trees and the gates a car tore past, scattering Cuban trumpet by the fluttering handful. He kissed her at the salt cellar of her throat. The open collar of her shirt released a cloud of Opium perfume that literally dizzied him. He laid a cheek against the scrollwork of her clavicles and tried to collect his thoughts. He remembered having read that the temple of Delphi, home of the ancient oracle, was built over a geologic fault that released vapor from a seam of hydrocarbons far below the surface, that the sibyl's trances and prophecies were effects of ethylene intoxication. He hoped that he was not about to start talking some kindred type of nonsense. He closed his eyes and helplessly imbibed.

"I love you," he said.

He felt her tense and, when he lifted his face, found that she was looking at him with a puzzled, even doubtful expression, as if his words had been particularly oracular. It was the truth, though, so what could he do about it but surrender.

There was a rustle in the scrub about twenty feet from the clearing where they had lunched. A snap of branches. My grandfather got to his feet. He watched the brush where he thought the sound had come from. His nostrils flared, and he caught a whiff of rotten egg, or maybe it was more like the smell of flowers left to rot in a vase of water. He could feel each hair on the back of his neck standing erect. Something light-colored passed among the spaces in the tangle of brown branches and dark green leaves. He reached for the snake hammer.

"No," Sally said. "Let it go."

He gripped the handle and flexed his fingers restlessly along its lacquered surface. He had been thinking for a long time about how it would feel to bring the hunk of lead down onto that skull with all its needle teeth. Looking back from the rented hospital bed in my mother's guest room before he died, my grandfather conceded that he was probably looking forward to smashing the snake's skull. He had been repressing his anger from the day he entered the Wallkill prison, and there was no doubt that since then, right up to last week's diagnosis, life had afforded his anger ample fuel. But the truth was that anger required no trigger or pretext. It was sourceless, a part of him, like yearning, curiosity, or sadness. Anger was his birthright. It was hard for him to surrender that longed-for crunch of bone.

"It's very charming how you have sworn revenge on behalf of my late husband's cat and taken on this noble quest and so forth. But to be totally honest, it's sort of irritating, too. I don't need you to be my paladin. I don't need to be rescued. And I promise you, kiddo, I'm never going to love you back until I am absolutely persuaded that you are not the kind of person who would beat a snake to death with a sledgehammer."

"I see," my grandfather said. He put down the hammer. He went back to the chair and stood behind Sally with his hand on her shoulder.

The rustle and snap got very loud and resolved themselves into a padding kind of rhythm, paws moving in sequence, and then an animal broke into the clearing. At first my grandfather was uncertain in his identification. It came stepping out of the brush, gray fur streaked with brown and black. At first he thought that it might be a very large and well-fed raccoon, but it didn't have that flat-footed gait.

"Oh, good Lord," Sally said. The animal stood still. It made a sound like a bullfrog. "Ramon."

The cat's forehead and neck were caked with blackened blood. His socks were dyed pinkish brown. He appeared to have lost an ear, and his tail had a buttonhook kink. His belly hung nearly to the blacktop.

"You got fat, Ramon," Sally said.

The cat replied with another irascible croak. Sally got up and started toward him before my grandfather could prevent her. The cat bared his teeth and growled, warning her off. My grandfather wondered if the cat might be rabid, if he would have to use the hammer after all, and if, should he sky or brain Ramon, Sally would never be able to love him.

"You smell just awful," Sally told Ramon. "You're fat and you stink."

The cat paced a lopsided figure eight of indecision. There seemed to be something wrong with one of his legs. He moved stiffly and his leg turned out.

"He has holes in his face."

"Tooth marks."

"Oh my God. He got into a fight with the python."

"There hasn't been a missing pet in a month," my grandfather said. "I think Ramon might have won the fight."

"Ramon!" Sally said admiringly. "Oy, his poor ear," she called over her shoulder. "And his tail, do you see? He's a mess. You really think he killed it?"

"I think so."

"So much for that big *shtekn* you've been dragging around the swamps for weeks." She took another step toward Ramon, and the cat abruptly seemed to lose interest. He turned and hobbled back into the leafy darkness among the trees.

"Oops. That's it? He's gone."

"That is a tough fucking cat," my grandfather said.

Sally called after the cat once, then again in the loud South Philly holler she had used on the night they met. "I guess he's happy."

"I can't believe he beat me to it."

"Are you jealous?"

"I'm annoyed."

Sally came over and put her arms around my grandfather. "I'm sorry," she said. "You want to maybe kill Ramon instead?"

"Not today," my grandfather said.

Sally leaned his head on her shoulder. She didn't say that she loved him back, and he never told her about the shadow in his gut, then or on any of the few, happy days they subsequently spent together.

XXXV

A little over a year later I passed through Coral Gables to do a reading in support of my second book. At that time Books & Books was crammed into a few hundred square feet of pink stucco down the street from its present location. Lack of space was not an issue in my case, but it meant there was not a lot of room for folding chairs. If you drew more than a minyan of elderly Jews, combat for a place to sit down could be savage. The people who did show up for my readings in those days were often not entirely strangers to me, and among the combatants at Books & Books that night were a few who knew me as my grandparents' grandson: The dentist who had repaired my grandmother's teeth after her arrival in Baltimore. The neighbor lady at Fontana Village who had made such a strong play for my grandfather's attention—at least in my view—with her version of Horn & Hardart's macaroni and cheese. An old buddy of my grandfather's from Shunk Street days. The former sales director of MRX.

When I was in college, before a poetry reading at the old Gustine's bar on Forbes Avenue, some prankster had advised me to look up from the page now and then, to make "eye contact." It turned out there was no surer way to make you lose your place in the text, persuade the audience that you were some kind of freak, or crush your soul. If the turnout was light, your soul got crushed by the sight of empty chairs. If by chance or misprint there was a decent showing, then it was crushed by its own unerring instinct to contact only the eyes in a face that was busy frowning, yawning, or looking vaguely ill. As the interval ballooned since the last botched attempt, I would grow increasingly tense, and finally look up at an arbitrary moment, giving peculiar weight to a random *therefore* or, inevitably, a word like *snatch, nuts,* or *blown.* By the time I hit Coral Gables, I had learned to mark four or five appropriate words at different points in whatever text I was reading. I would look up on cue and pray that my gaze alighted on somebody who was having an okay time or was kind enough to fake it.

That night at Books & Books, when I looked up in observance of mark number two, I saw a beautiful woman standing by the door where Salzedo Street met Aragon Avenue. She was looking back at me in a friendly but appraising way. She had the eyes of a no-ticer, cool but not chilly, unsentimental but not hard. The eyes of a painter, I thought. Silver hair streaked with dark gray and swept up into an untidy bun, born with a suntan, and some bold archi-tecture in her nose and cheeks. My grandfather had said Katharine Hepburn because of the cheekbones, but I would have gone with Anjelica Huston. At mark number three, when I looked up again, she was gone. My soul and I alike experienced a certain degree of crushedness.

She didn't reappear during the reading or afterward, when I was signing a few books. I heard about the horror of my grandmother's dentition. I heard about how annoying my grandfather's attention to modeling detail was when all you were trying to make was basically a Roman candle that would go really high and not explode. I accepted a few belated condolences. Then I said goodbye to Mitch Kaplan and took off. I was staying at a hotel on Ponce de Leon Boulevard—more of a glorified motor lodge—and I figured I might as well walk. I hadn't gone even a block when I felt a touch on my arm, heard a woman calling me Mike.

"I thought that might have been you," I said.

We shook hands, but then she said, "No," so we hugged each other, standing out there on the sidewalk along the Miracle Mile. She had the hourglass shape that my grandfather always favored, but she felt much lighter than she looked. The bones of her shoulders flexed like clothespins under her blouse. I got a noseful of oranges and cloves. I remembered my grandfather saying that Sally had a heavy hand with the Opium spritz.

"I almost didn't have the nerve," she told me after she had let go of me. She took a Kleenex from a red knapsack-style leather purse and used it dry her eyes. I said maybe I would help myself to a Kleenex, too. "I would have just hated myself."

"Actually, I thought you left."

"I did. After I heard a little of what you were reading, I went and had a cup of coffee."

"Oh," I said.

"You were fine. I'm just visual. I can't take things in through the ear."

"Ah."

"Frankly, I might be getting a little bit deaf. Are you hungry? Could you eat?"

We found her car, a stately Mercedes 280 the color of a camel-hair coat. A Hewlett-Packard parking decal faded in a corner of the rear window. The interior was drenched in Opium, and under that a smell of sun-damaged leather, and under that an acrid whiff of vitamins. Sally drove us to a Cuban restaurant she said she liked, but when we got there she only picked at her fried fish. When I ordered the *lechón*, she had said what the hell, she would have the pork, too. But the waiter had not reached the kitchen before she called him back and said she would have the fish after all.

"I was raised kosher, but after I left home I ate pork for the next fifty years. Suddenly, I can't do it anymore. Even bacon! So what's that about?"

I said I didn't really have a theory to offer, but that was a lie. Something similar had happened to my grandfather at the end of his life, and I figured it had something to do with mortality. That didn't seem like the polite thing to say to an old lady I had only just met. In the end she went and said it herself.

"No atheists in foxholes, right?" She looked around at the fake brick walls, the red Formica, the wrought-iron chandeliers. "I must be in a foxhole."

"At least it's a foxhole where you can get *lechón*."

"Do you think God gives a shit what people eat?"

"I would hope He has better things to do with His time."

"Ha. You know who you sound like?"

She had cut up her fish into neat little squares. She loaded some black beans and rice onto her fork and added one of the squares of fish. Then, when she had it all ready to go, she put down the fork with a chink. The bite she had prepared sat uneaten for the rest of the meal.

"I wasn't in love with him," she said. "For the record."

"No?"

"Maybe I was getting there. We were going pretty hot and heavy for a couple of old people, I guess. But we only had six months."

"I know," I said. "That's not very long."

"When you're seventy-two? It's like six weeks when you're fifteen. Then he went and got cancer."

"You were making him too happy. He was having none of that."

"That would be funny if it weren't true. Do you smoke?"

"Trying to quit."

"Me, too."

She flagged the waiter, handed him a five, and asked him in serviceable Spanish to go next door to the liquor store and buy her a pack of Trues. In the end she settled for bumming one of his Winstons.

"*Muchas gracias, corazón.*"

"*A la orden, señora.*"

He patted his pockets for a light. I came out with Aughenbaugh's lighter, which my mother had passed on to me. Sally noticed it. She angled her face away from me and blew out a long turbulence of smoke.

"Also, I hope you don't mind my saying this, but he was not an easy man to love. I don't mean that he wasn't lovable."

"No?"

"He was very lovable. Intelligent. Nice-looking, had those big shoulders. Pretty fit for his age but not, you know, one of these geezers running around in the ninety-degree heat, with the headband and the heavy-hands. Also, the man could fix anything. I mean anything. I have this, you know, CD thingy. A 'boom box.' It kept skipping. He fixed that. Those things have lasers inside."

No one held my grandfather's technical knowledge and dexterity in higher esteem than I did, but I doubted they extended to the repair of lasers. I just nodded.

"He even had a sense of humor in there somewhere."

"Oh, yeah."

"A dark one."

"Very dark."

"It only came out once you knew him, though. Also, maybe the most lovable thing of all?"

I waited. It seemed to me that there were an awful lot of things she had loved about this man with whom she was not in love.

"He didn't mind that I made fun of him if he was being ridiculous. And he was so ridiculous with his little affectations. Using a, what do you call it, a graduated cylinder for a measuring cup."

"I always thought that was cool."

"Brewing his coffee in an Erlenmeyer flask."

"He made really good coffee that way."

"That lighter."

"There was a story behind it."

"I'm sure. All of his stories were stuck behind something. Do you know about the snake hunt?"

"A little."

"Like he was Captain Ahab. Like John Wayne in that movie."

"*The Searchers.*"

"Because of an old flatulent cat. And passing it off as gallantry to boot."

"He liked having a concrete goal."

"And the rockets. The models everywhere. The whole space thing. Driving two hundred miles with his binoculars to watch them shoot a metal can into orbit. That was funny to me."

"Not to him, it was very serious."

"That's what was funny about it." She helped herself to a forkful of my *lechón*. "Mm. Did your grandmother tease him?"

"Sometimes," I said. I couldn't really remember. "Definitely."

"He needed to fight. To wrestle. He needed to feel like he was working harder, carrying more weight on his shoulders, than anybody else. Everything had to be a wrestling match. Jacob with the angel. Even cancer, he was going to fight it on his own. He didn't say a word about it to me. Did you know?"

"We had no idea."

"To be honest, the man had a tendency to play the martyr."

"He was comfortable in the role," I said.

Sally called for the check. "It was hard to be your grandfather," she said. "But maybe I made it a little bit easier for him, I don't know." She got a little teary. "God forbid he could have made it a little easier on me."

When the waiter brought the check, she tried to pay it, but I told her I would just bill my publisher for the dinner.

"Oh ho," she said. "*You* got it easy, kid."

 XXXVI

At Oakland my mother put her father's body on a plane to be flown back to Philadelphia for the funeral and burial. The service was held at Montefiore Cemetery, where he was laid beside my grandmother and his parents and brother.* My brother took a leave from the set of *Space: 2099*† and flew in from LA. The rabbi who officiated over my grandmother's funeral had retired. The new rabbi was not much older than I was and appeared to be in something of a hurry. Some old friends and acquaintances showed up, a few Moonblatts and New-mans who were still around. Appreciative things were said. Then we all pitched our shovelful of dirt onto the casket with a sound like a gust of rain against a window. A first cousin of my grandfather's who lived out in Wynnewood provided her house for the post-funeral gathering. We knocked back shots of slivovitz and I heard sketchy and conflicting accounts of some of the foregoing incidents. I heard a few cute or clever things my brother or I had said as boys. Then my brother had to grab a plane back to L.A. After it was over my mother and I drove to the hotel near the airport where we were spending the night.

We were sharing a room with two queen beds. We went over some

---

* Uncle Ray died of heart failure in 1985, in Los Angeles, where he had found work as a "billiards consultant" for movies and television. Despite his monocular vision he won the occasional tournament and still hustled games from time to time on the side. I was living in Paris at the time of his death and missed the funeral.

† The series, alas, was never picked up.

of the things we had seen or heard in the course of the day and then my mother put out the light. I had sensed some kind of agitation in her all day that I attributed to grief or tension. As we lay in the dark I could feel it gathering. She rolled one way and then the other. Her arms made sounds like harsh whispers across the sheets of her bed. She couldn't sleep, so I couldn't sleep.

"Mike, are you awake?"

"Yeah."

"I wanted to ask you about something."

"Okay." I knew what she wanted to ask me, or at any rate when she came out with it, I was not surprised. I had been turning it over and brooding over it since that day.

"Last week," she said, "I walked in on you and Dad, and he was telling you not to tell me something."

"Yeah."

"So, what was it you weren't supposed to tell?"

Her tone tried for insouciant but ended up closer to jittery. It sounded like she was steeling herself; it sounded like she had her suspicions.

Of course, at the time I didn't know anything about the story my grandmother had told Dr. Medved; my visit to Mantoloking in the wake of Hurricane Sandy was still fourteen years off. All I knew, that night at the Philadelphia Airport Marriott, was that my grandmother had given her doctor an account of herself, of her life in Europe during the war, that differed—in dramatic fashion, it seemed— from the account she had given my grandfather, or at least cast it in a new and disturbing light. Dr. Medved had seemed to think, at least, that when my grandfather heard the new story, he was going to be disturbed. Implicitly, my grandmother had lied to my grandfather, and to my mother, and that was what my grandfather hadn't wanted me to tell my mother. He worried that simply knowing my grandmother had lied, regardless of the nature of the lie, might undo all my mother's fragile work of forgiveness. That was all I knew.

Was it even possible to forgive the dead? Was forgiveness an emotion, or a transaction that required a partner? I had made a promise to someone who would never see it kept. I wanted to respect my grandfather's wish, and it would have been no trouble to evade my mother's question. Keeping secrets was the family business. But it was a business, it seemed to me, that none of us had ever profited from.

"It was something she told the psychiatrist at Greystone about herself," I said. "But he didn't know what."

I told her the story of Dr. Medved as my grandfather had told it to me. She laughed when I got to the part where my grandfather decided that he didn't want to know. In the darkness of the motel room, her laughter had a forlorn sound.

"She was always making things up when I was little," my mother said after I was done. "I used to catch her out all the time. She called them 'stories.' *'Oh!'*" She put on her mother's accent, the rasp and pitch of her voice. "*'You're right, I told a story.'*"

In the dark she sounded so much like my grandmother that the hair rose along my forearms.

"She just used to tell me plain old stories," I said. "When I used to stay with them in Riverdale."

Outside the door of our motel room, the ice machine appeared to be in some kind of distress. It took me a while to hear the sound of my mother snuffling softly in the dark.

"Do you think they were ever happy?"

"Definitely," I said.

"*Definitely?*"

"For sure."

"She went crazy. His business failed. They couldn't have children of their own. He went to prison. HRT gave her cancer. I shot his brother in the eye and then married a man who cost him his business. When were they happy?"

"In the cracks?" I said.

"In the cracks."

"Yeah."

The next morning we had to get up early to catch our respective planes. My mother set her alarm to give herself fifteen minutes longer than I felt I would need to be ready, but when my own alarm went off she was still in her nightgown, sitting on the edge of her bed. She had the piece of LAV One my grandfather had brought to California, the first piece, the moon garden. She was holding it up to her eye and looking in at the OO-scale versions of us, among the tiny hydroponic roses and carrots.

"Why'd you bring that?"

"I did this crazy thing where I packed a bag with his stuff, the book, the pictures. Like he was just going home to Fontana Village after a nice long visit."

I got up and she passed me the spray-painted disk. I peered in through the uptilted flap of the hatch at the little people my grandfather had hoped and failed and succeeded to shelter and keep safe. The three-quarter-inch grandparents on their gravity couch, the three-quarter-inch mother in a G-chair with her half-inch preteen son in the chair beside her and her pea of a second-grader perched on her lap. Everyone wearing comfortable but practical blue coveralls and grip slippers. The lush tops of the carrots, the lipstick-kiss roses. The detail was rudimentary at that scale, so my grandfather had painted the faces with skin tones and left it at that. At first the blankness of our faces always used to seem weird if not symbolic in some way I didn't care to contemplate, but now I was used to it. You could imagine smiles into those blanks. You could write any kind of story across them that you pleased.

◑   ◑   ◑

My grandfather stopped talking a day before he died. In the course of what turned out to be our last real conversation, I happened to ask if he had ever again crossed paths with von Braun after the time in Cocoa Beach. My grandfather shook his head. It hurt to shake his head. He tried to push himself up into a sitting position with a grunt of impatience. I helped him adjust the bed so that the back was more vertical, but he said that was worse. So I lowered the back to a more oblique angle than the original one. He said that was double worse. I raised the bed, fluffed the pillows, slid a pillow under his knees. That put too much pressure on his heels. The pain medication, he said, was making him feel like he wanted to crawl out of his skin. And it wasn't like it made the pain go away; it just helped you swim across it without sinking. We gave up trying to make him more comfortable.

"Nah, I never saw von Braun again," he said. "He died a couple years later. I forget what the cause was, something painful. I heard he was in a hell of a lot of pain."

I waited, thinking he might be about to append something along the lines of *All of which he richly deserved* or *So maybe there is a God after all.*

He didn't say anything. He lay there with his eyes closed for a long time after that, sculling along the surface of the sea of pain a little nearer toward his story's end or maybe, if that great eschatologist Wernher Magnus Maximilian Freiherr von Braun turned out to be right, toward the story on the opposite shore that was waiting to begin.

ACKNOWLEDGMENTS

Walter Gates Gill (collection manager for the Health branch of the New Jersey State Archives, Trenton), Judy Fosca and Evan Alkabetz (respectively research librarians at the John F. Kennedy Space Center Library, Cape Canaveral and the CIA Library, Langley), Esther Stecher (née Mangel), Jessica Sichel, Barry Kahn, and Lorraine Medved-Engel, if they existed, would have been instrumental to the completion of this work. Ian Faloona and Justine Frischmann most decidedly do exist, and their kindness and hospitality repeatedly saved this book's life. The MacDowell Colony in Peterborough, New Hampshire, would seem in its unstinting perfection to be impossible and yet it, too, miraculously exists, as do Phil Pavel and all the staff at the highly unlikely Chateau Marmont, Hollywood.

Not long before he died, my mother's maternal uncle, Stanley Werbow (1922–2005), a professor of medieval German at the University of Texas and a former staff sergeant operating in the field with the 849th Signal Intelligence Service at the Battle of Monte Cassino, was persuaded by one of his daughters to dictate some memories of growing up Jewish in Philadelphia and Washington in the early part of the twentieth century. Though fragmentary and rambling, that narrative, as vivid, intelligent, and wry as Stan Werbow himself, provided the spark that kindled this one, along with some crucial bits of atmosphere. Uncle Stan—who stirred the pot that served up *The Yiddish Policemen's Union*, too—was among my most supportive and most exacting readers. I hope that he would have been pleased with this monstrous stepchild of those artless reminiscences; I know that, if not, he would never have hesitated to tell me.

Neither Stanley Lovell's *Of Spies and Stratagems*, Michael Neufeld's *Von Braun: Dreamer of Space, Engineer of War*, Annie Jacobsen's *Operation Paperclip*, Bob Ward's *Doctor Space*, Dennis Piszkiewicz's *The Nazi Rocketeers*, Murray Dubin's *South Philadelphia*, nor Gilbert Sanders's *Jewish Baltimore: A Family Album* is to blame for this pack of lies. Keith Jarrett's *The Köln Concerts*, Windy and Carl's *Depths* and A Winged Victory for the Sullen's self-titled first album reliably screened out the voices whenever they stirred in their corners. And when I was looking for a path of escape, Alejandro Jodorowsky's charming introduction to his *The Way of Tarot* made a Fool of me.

I am grateful for the help of Steven Barclay, Jennifer Barth, Jonathan Burnham, Sonya Cheuse, Amy Cray, Mary Evans, Simon Frankel, Madalyn Garcia, Courtney Hodell, Adalis Martinez, Maddie Mau, Howie Sanders, E. Beth Thomas, Lydia Weaver, Matt Weiner, and Emily Werbow, and for the inspiration, understanding, and blessed distraction provided by Sophie, Zeke, Rose, and Abe Chabon.

Finally, as at the beginning and at every step along the way: eternal gratitude for the support, encouragement, love, protection, and, above all, for the existence, however improbable, of Ayelet Waldman.

ABOUT THE AUTHOR

Michael Chabon is the bestselling and Pulitzer Prize–winning author of the novels *The Mysteries of Pittsburgh, Wonder Boys, The Amazing Adventures of Kavalier & Clay, Summerland, The Final Solution, The Yiddish Policemen's Union, Gentlemen of the Road,* and *Telegraph Avenue;* the short story collections *A Model World* and *Werewolves in Their Youth;* and the essay collections *Maps and Legends* and *Manhood for Amateurs.* He lives in Berkeley, California, with his wife, the novelist Ayelet Waldman, and their children.